WHISPERS

OF

THE

WATER

WHISPERS

OF
THE

WATER

The Broken Fae Trilogy
SYLVER MICHAELA

WHISPERS
OF
THE
WATER

Cover Design: Emily Wittig Designs
Editing: Ad Astra Editorial
Formatting: Enchanted Ink Publishing

ISBN: 979-8-218-18889-4

To the **Bria's** of the world

May you see that you are beautiful, strong, and **loved**

Trigger Warnings

This book contains explicit sexual content, mention of off-page death, and on-page/off-page abuse (mental, emotional, physical) of a minor.

CHAPTER

ONE

I THINK I'M GONNA PUKE."

I cradled my head in my hands and worked to take deep breaths. The jet jostled as we hit some turbulence, and the queasiness in my stomach clenched tightly. While the rough plane ride didn't help with my nausea, it wasn't anxiety from the flight that had me wanting to throw up my breakfast. I wished that were the worst of my worries—vomiting in front of everyone.

Strong fingers gripped my hand and pulled it away from my face. Amber eyes met mine. My heart instantly warmed, and I was reminded of how much I'd come to love this man whose brow creased with worry.

Rune squeezed my hand and rubbed soothing circles into my skin. "You're going to do great. Don't stress. You've studied almost two months for this. We're *ready*."

He was right. I'd worked hard in preparation for this trip to his hometown as his pretend girlfriend. For nearly two months, I'd worked endlessly to learn about Rune, his past, and his world.

The world of Fae.

When I'd agreed to be his fake girlfriend, it was solely with the intent of getting one step closer to my dream of studying abroad and becoming a professional painter. I'd never anticipated that he wasn't human. Because this was the real world where things of myths and fairytales didn't exist. At least, so I'd thought. He and his friends were Land Fae, magical creatures who took on the forms of different animals. If that wasn't weird enough, they each had special abilities to go with the shape-shifting, and while it was hard to fathom at first, there was no denying who they were.

Or who I was.

"You're right," I said, taking another deep breath. "I just don't want to screw this up for all of our sakes."

"You won't screw anything up, Bria-chan," Akira chimed in. His bright smile set against his soft complexion and dark eyes always calmed me to my core. Hearing the Japanese nickname he'd given me helped settle my nerves slightly, too. It was familiar and inspired good memories, which I needed right now.

Akira sat across from Rune and me, and the table separating us was a stark reminder that this private jet was no joke. It housed tables with seating, a lounger, and a bar in the back. That was harder to process than all the Fae stuff at this point. Money truly was no object for my rich "boyfriend."

Avana smiled brightly from where she sat next to Akira, sipping her cup of hot tea. She flipped a stray black and gold braid behind her bare brown shoulder as she met my eyes. "He's right. Things are going to go splendidly. Between my Fox Fae illusion that you'll be wearing and all the work you've put into learning about everything, no one should figure out you're human."

Right.

Human.

I swallowed hard and fought the panic rising up my throat yet again. I had believed I was human my whole life because what else could I be? I was as unexciting as a slice of bread. Long blonde hair. Blue eyes. Thick thighs and pudgy middle. Introvert. Unremarkable really.

Until that night I dared to fight Jonah, the Bat Fae who'd been trying to kill me. Something had awoken within me when he'd tried to drown me during our match, and that's when I learned what I really was. Water Fae. And not just any Water Fae. I was the Water Fae *Princess*.

The enemy of everyone on this plane and those whom I was about to meet.

"You know," Bassel started. His large, tan frame was pressed back against the lounger across the aisle from our table. He scratched his chin thoughtfully. "It's weird. Ever since the other night, the magical aura surrounding you has gotten stronger."

"I noticed that, too," Marlow added from where he sat next to Bassel, tugging on one of his red curls.

Rune shrugged, and his honey gaze drank me in. "Maybe it's from all the stress. Maybe it amplified what little magical essence she has."

It's not so little, but you don't know that.

From the get-go, they'd all believed I had a Fae somewhere in my distant ancestry, which gave me a faint magical aura. In actuality, my aura had been faint because I hadn't awakened as who I truly was yet. Despite knowing this now, I was going to let Rune and the others believe I had diluted Fae in me. That was better than them knowing the truth. It, however, was *not* good for my stomach currently.

Smirking, I said, "Or maybe it's from hanging out with all of you day in and day out. Your freakiness must be rubbing off on me."

3

Bassel laughed and pointed a large finger at me. "Hey now. Don't be hatin'. You know you love our freakiness. Isn't that right, Rune?"

Rune glared at his friend, and my cheeks heated. It was no secret to the others what Rune and I were slowly becoming. I'd gone from wanting to strangle him every time I saw him to craving his time, his touch, his *everything*. It took time to peel back his layers and see him for who he really was, but that time was worth it. Underneath the hard exterior, he was thoughtful, supportive, and caring. He had quickly become one of my best friends, and I hoped we could be even more now that we had both opened up about our feelings for the other.

My chest tightened, because while the idea of becoming a real couple was something I longed for now, it also felt harder than ever before. How could we start a relationship when he didn't realize the truth about me?

Turning back to me, Rune's scowl softened. "Want to grab some water?"

Smiling, I nodded. "That sounds great."

He stood, and I followed him into the aisle. There was a hallway in the back of the jet, which housed a small bar with drinks and snacks. We stood in the alcove, our bodies inches from pressing together.

The sight of Rune never failed to turn my legs into jelly. Tall and built like an ancient god, he towered over my small frame. Stray pieces of his long white hair fell into his eyes, which sat above high cheekbones and lush lips that I swore were made for kissing. His toned arms flexed as he reached for a bottle of water.

I gratefully accepted the drink and instantly downed half the bottle. Water had always been my safe place, something that managed to calm me down even in my most frenzied state. My obsession with water should've been an indicator that something was off about me, yet I never pieced it together.

Meeting his eyes, I grinned. "Thanks. I know I shouldn't be this stressed. We've worked hard for this. I obviously knew this trip was coming, but the fact that it's actually *here*, we're actually *going*, is a surreal feeling. It's also nerve-wracking since, you know, my life could be in danger if we're caught lying."

"They won't figure it out if we're careful and follow the plan."

"Right. The plan. Can we go over that one last time?"

Rune nodded. "The plan is to convince my mother that you're the right partner for me, showing her that you're just as good, if not better, than whomever she has picked out for me."

"Because you absolutely want to avoid a real marriage and procreating," I finished.

He smirked. "Hey, the baby-making process I'm down for. It's everything that comes *after* that I'd like to avoid."

I rolled my eyes and took another swig of water. "And how do I convince her I'm the right candidate? Remind me what she'll be looking for."

"Just hold your head high. When you walk into a room, pretend that you command it and everyone inside. You don't have to be overly affectionate toward me. In fact, that would give the opposite impression of what we want since my mother knows I'm not like that. My mother cares about power, strength, and intelligence. As long as we can show her you have those things, which you do, we can convince her that my mate should be you."

The pressure on my shoulders to be this jaw-dropping potential partner for Rune was a lot, but it wasn't anything surprising. I knew I'd be faced with this challenging task, but that didn't make carrying it out any easier. The normal drive to impress a lover's parents was tripled in this case, because if I were deemed unworthy and found out to be Water Fae, not only would Rune's entire world change, but my life could be at stake. From all I knew about Myra, Rune's mother, she didn't seem like a forgiving woman, and I didn't think she'd take too kindly to being tricked.

5

Especially not by a Water Fae like me.

Twirling the plastic bottle in my hands, I leveled my curious eyes on Rune once more. "What happens if I fail? What if she still demands you marry her pick? Can't you say no?"

Rune's eyes darkened a fraction, and his jaw hardened. "If that happens, I don't think I'll have much of a choice. I'll have to do as she says."

Absolutely baffled at Rune's sudden lack of fight, I furrowed my brow and asked, "Why? I didn't think there were too many people who could *make* you do anything."

He closed his eyes briefly before whispering, "She has my brothers. That's always been her leverage against me." He looked away from me, his brow furrowing with the burden of his words. "If I don't give her what she wants, they suffer for it. It's why I've stayed away from them for so long. My being there means putting them in danger, because one step out of line on my part results in something severe for them, especially Newt. That's part of the reason why we have to be careful this week. If we get too defiant or deviate from what Myra wants, the twins will pay the consequences."

I inhaled sharply, remembering the photo of the two smiling boys that Rune had given me. They were just little kids, and for Myra to use them as a sort of bargaining chip made me sick. It also made my need to do well even more profound, because I didn't want these boys enduring any hardship over something I did or didn't do to Myra's liking.

"I didn't think it was possible, but the more I hear about this woman, the more I dislike her," I grumbled.

"Yeah, she's definitely not the mother she used to be."

Rune's shoulders stiffened, and his gaze took on a distant note. Despite his looking away from me, there was no missing the forlorn expression taking over his features.

"What is it?" I asked softly, taking his hand in mine. "What's wrong?"

He swallowed hard and closed his eyes as he shook his head. "She used to be … different. I just—I want—" His head fell back, and he seemed to struggle to find the words. "I know it's dumb, but I really hope that seeing me this week, seeing me happy and us together, will somehow remind her—"

The words died on his tongue, and he hung his head. Clearly, things were complicated between him and his mother, but this was the first time he'd expressed something more vulnerable about their relationship with me. Typically, he kept his feelings locked up tightly, and it was only recently that he'd started letting me have a glimpse behind the curtain that shielded those emotions. It was still hard for him, but with time, I hoped he'd open up fully to me.

And I wanted to do the same with him.

Just not right now. We had enough on our plates without the added stress of who and what I was.

I squeezed his hand. "I'm here for you, you know."

That caused some of the trouble clouding his features to retreat, giving way to a soft smile. "I know. Thank you. For everything. And I want you to remember as we go through this week that you aren't alone. We're going to be with you every step of the way."

They were words we'd shared just last night and this morning. Rune had taken me out for an afternoon full of normalcy, and while we'd picnicked, we'd laid ourselves bare to one another emotionally. Rune was hesitant to expose such feelings then as well, but I'd worked hard to reassure him that opening himself up was not only worth it, but necessary.

Now we were in this weird place where we knew how much the other cared, but it was still unclear what that made us. That lingering question had been plaguing me and would continue to do so if I didn't get a clear answer.

Not needing any distractions like that during this trip where my very life was on the line, I finally decided to broach the subject. "There's something else I've been wanting to talk to you about. Um, it has to do with last night."

His eyes turned down at the corners once more, and he rubbed at the back of his neck. "Me too."

Curiosity piqued, I said, "Okay. You first."

His gaze searched mine, and the longer it did, the deeper his frown grew. "I've thought about what you said yesterday. How I should let myself feel the emotions I've tried so hard to cut out. How I should let myself openly care about you and others again."

I swallowed hard. We were both thinking the same thing, but judging by the pain written in his eyes, I had a sinking feeling that we weren't in agreement with where this should go.

"After going over it a dozen times in my head, I realized—" He closed his mouth and seemed to fight for the words before he finished, "I can't."

The floor fell out from beneath my feet, and my throat tightened under the grip of disappointment. Working to swallow past the ache in my chest, I started, "Rune, you—"

He closed his eyes and shook his head. "I know what kind of monster I become when I lose those I care about. I know what I turn into and what I do after the fact. I don't want to become that again. I don't want to feel that much *hate* again."

I reached for him, cupping his face in my free hand. He inhaled sharply and seemed to, ever so slightly, lean into my touch, as though he were afraid doing so may sear his skin. I held his gaze with confidence, imploring him to listen. "You won't have to feel that way again. You are *not* going to lose me."

He gripped my wrist and gently pulled my hand away. His large hand slipped into my own until we held each other, fingers intertwined. He had to understand. I knew he was afraid of losing me in any sense of the word. He had experienced great loss after his father died, but I wasn't going anywhere. I was here to stay, and my eyes pleaded with his to make him understand that.

"I will lose you, though," he said. "I'm bound to make you hate me again. If it's not that, it will be the difference in our lifespans. Something is bound to take you from me, and I can't go through that. I can't feed into these feelings any more than I already have."

"But—" I stopped.

The words begged to leave my tongue, and I nearly let them. I wanted to tell him that our lifespans would be relatively the same now. As Fae, I'd live centuries, just like him. We'd be together without worry of my impending death. But the reassurance died with my next swallow. I couldn't tell him who I was, which meant as long as he thought I was human, destined to die in what would feel like a blink of an eye to him, there would be no convincing him.

My frustration with the situation warred with my hope for a future with him. Rune and I had finally moved one step forward after talking in the field, but now it was like we were moving ten steps back. A void started to slowly stretch inside me, threatening to consume me, and the bottle of water I held began to vibrate. The water inside was starting to jostle within the plastic prison.

Taking a deep, calming breath, I waited until my water bottle stilled before meeting his eyes. "So what now? What does that mean for us?"

He rubbed the back of his neck. "Honestly? I'm not sure. I'm still trying to figure that out."

There was no denying the hurt that washed over me like a tidal wave. It didn't matter what I said. It didn't matter what reassurances I gave him—or, rather, *didn't* give him since I *couldn't* provide him reassurances given my current secret identity. He was too afraid. The possibility of feeling agony was too consuming for him to even give this a chance.

Rune had once said to me that fear could bring even the strongest of men crashing to their knees. How right he'd been.

He was one of the most powerful men I'd ever met, and here he was, freezing up under the paralyzing weight of dismay.

And there was a part of me, that pessimistic side of my brain, that briefly wondered if he was right. Maybe us being together was wrong, because he was Land Fae, and I was Water Fae. We were enemies after all. Perhaps letting things end here peacefully before either of us got hurt was for the best. Yet as soon as the idea crossed my mind, I immediately squashed it. Rune and I were not a mistake. I refused to believe otherwise.

Crooking his finger under my chin, he tilted my head up to meet his eyes. My heart constricted at his touch, but I had to ignore that feeling. He was giving me no choice but to fight against my pull toward him.

And just when I had thought I'd finally be able to give in to my desires.

"You helped me more than you will ever know, Bria. I was in an awful place when you came into my life. You experienced firsthand a small taste of how ugly I can be when I fall into that spiral. You pulled me out of that dark place, and I don't want to go back. I don't want to treat people, to treat *you*, like that ever again."

"I understand that, but pushing me away isn't going to help you. It's going to hurt you *and* me."

He frowned when I mentioned myself. He knew the hurt he was causing. He knew how much he meant to me, yet he was still turning me away. He was denying himself the chance of exploring this, and he was preventing me from loving him openly and honestly.

"Maybe it will. Even so, I'm just not ready to be anything more than friends."

The news broke me, but I refused to let on exactly how much his words stung. Nodding, I excused myself and went into the bathroom. As soon as the door locked behind me, I gripped the sink and let the sliver in my heart crack wide open. This wasn't how I'd envisioned this trip starting out. I thought we'd show up, and instead of me merely pretending to be Rune's girlfriend, it would become real.

Emotion clogged my throat, and as my internal war heightened, water suddenly burst from the sink faucet. Gasping, I quickly went to turn off the handles, but I realized the sink wasn't turned on, which left only one culprit.

Me.

Frantic and unsure of how to control the water, I held my hands toward the sink and ordered, "Stop!"

The water continued its relentless pursuit, and I let out a frustrated groan. Trying to put a bit more thought into the command, I flung out my hands at the sink, but the water shot from the spout toward me, engulfing my hands in gloves made of liquid.

"Shit, shit, shit," I hissed, trying to shake the water off.

Completely aggravated at my lack of control, I realized I was letting my emotions get the better of me. The water seemed to respond to my strong emotions, so I closed my eyes and willed my mind to be still. I let go of my heartache, my frustration, and my annoyance with my lack of skill. I focused on breathing and the water until I felt the trickling stream calm alongside me. It pulsed as if in sync with my heart, and as I felt our energies beat in tandem, I pictured the water ceasing its descent and releasing its hold on me. Deafening silence suddenly filled the room, and my eyes slowly fluttered open. The sink no longer spewed or overflowed, and water dripped from my hands, creating a puddle beneath them.

Letting out a proud sigh, I slumped against the wall. I smiled to myself, excited that I'd managed to control the stream of water all on my own. It felt like a small victory in understanding my new self.

If only I could understand Rune, too.

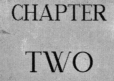

CHAPTER

TWO

I RETURNED FROM THE BATHROOM to find Rune back in his seat, looking sickly as he stared at the floor. He didn't even look up at me when I took my place next to him. Guilt weighed down his shoulders and brow, and oddly enough, I was glad. Maybe that guilt would knock some sense into him since my words hadn't. He was about to put us both through hell. He said we could stay friends, but how did he expect us to not fall harder when we had to portray lovers in front of his family?

He was practically setting us up to fail.

And if I were being honest, I hoped we would. I hoped this backfired on him. I wanted the pretending to get to his head. I wanted it to show him that being friends wasn't what either of us wanted, and hopefully, the desire to be together would outweigh his reservations.

It was probably foolish of me to hope for that outcome. He'd made his intentions clear, and if I didn't accept them, I was bound to get hurt. So why did I bother hoping for something more?

Deep down, I knew why.

It was because of the way my heart sang when I caught him staring my way when he thought I wasn't looking. It was because of the gentle way he would reach for my hand, making my entire body light with sparks like an exposed wire. It was because of those rare, fleeting moments when he would let his built-up wall crumble, allowing me a peek inside at the caring man hidden there.

It was because I loved him. More than I had ever loved anyone.

The jet descended and slowed as it drove across the small runway. Akira yawned and shifted in his seat. "Thank God we've landed. My butt is numb. I feel sorry for you flightless creatures. Flying myself is *way* better than being in a plane."

I laughed softly, but it didn't quite sound right to my ears. My nerves exploded in a swarm of frantic jitters that danced across my skin. The moment was finally here. I was going to meet Rune's family, including his nightmare of a mother. Part of me desperately wanted to impress her due to that gut reaction everyone experienced when meeting their partner's parents, but the other half wanted to give her the middle finger. She was a monster who emotionally abused her son, Newt, all because he had a disability. And I wouldn't be surprised if that was the least of her crimes. She wasn't worth impressing, but I still needed to do my part to win her over. Failing to do so would only give her ammunition to force Rune into marriage with another, as well as put his brothers at risk.

It wasn't just the idea of meeting Rune's family that had my stomach twisted in knots, though. It was the risk to my life that suddenly had me panicking. Even before I'd realized I was Water Fae, there had been a risk that Myra could take out her anger on me for tricking them. As human, I knew my friends would have had my back and made sure nothing happened to me should worse come to worst.

Things had changed, though. My human self was dead, and filling that space was a Water Fae. My ability to control my powers was pretty much nonexistent, which meant I was going to have to be extremely careful. If anyone discovered I was Water Fae—their enemy—I wasn't so sure they'd have my back like when they'd thought I was human. Instead, they may have my *head*.

I had at least one person here who would protect me at all costs if needed. It was a secret from everyone on this plane that Dallas, my best friend and guard, had traveled here as well for my safety. I wasn't sure where she was currently, but I knew she'd be close by and ready to intervene if necessary.

"We should probably get into Fae form now," Rune said to the group.

"Now?" I asked. A fresh wave of nerves spiraled inside me.

"Good idea," Avana said. She looked at me as she explained, "We're driving straight to Myra's home where we'll all be expected to arrive in Fae form, as it's natural for us to be that way when around other Fae in private settings. This plane has more room for me to work with than if I were to try to put the illusion on in a car while both you and Rune are sitting."

Everyone nodded in agreement.

Rune glanced at me and added, "This town is mainly human just like yours. We'll be in the limo with tinted windows the entire ride to my mother's house, so no one should see us as we drive through town."

Bassel stood, and he stretched his long arms and legs. "Well, let's get this show on the road."

As he lowered his arms back to his sides, he began his transformation. His fingernails sharpened into claws as his teeth elongated into fangs. Yellow striped fur inched its way across the tops of his hands and up his arms. Two pointy striped ears sprung out from beneath his long black hair, and he adjusted the secret hole in his pants for his long tail. His Liger Fae form was just as fascinating to look at now as it had been the first time I saw him this way.

Marlow followed suit. His eyes became glassy, and his arms broke out in gold and brown patches of moist skin. His Salamander Fae form was always eerie at first, but I quickly became used to seeing it.

"Alright, Bria," Avana chimed, clapping her hands animatedly. "Let's get you transformed for the big day."

Rune stood with me in the aisle, and together, we faced Avana. The Chameleon Fae and her ability to change a person's outward appearance were the key to ensuring I looked the part during this trip.

Next to me, Rune straightened. A small orange flame erupted from his hand and slowly circled up his body. My breath hitched in my throat as I watched in awe. As the flickering flame passed over him, a fluffy, white-tipped black tail slipped through the back of his pants. His fingers turned into deadly claws, while his canines elongated into sharp fangs. Two pointy ears stood erect on top of his head as the flame disappeared above him. The ears were white like his hair at the base, but they gradually turned black the higher they went.

He glanced sideways at me, and my chest tightened. It was the first time we'd *really* looked at each other since he'd rejected me. I knew I should look away, but my eyes were locked onto his with steadfast confidence. I wanted him to see. I *needed* him to see the hurt written there but also the love. I loved him, even this Fox Fae side. He was stunning in this form, and I wanted him to understand that nothing would change how I felt.

Not even our differences.

Or his denial.

"*Ajabu!*" Avana observed, her Malagasy accent ringing thick.

I faced her fully, breaking the connection with Rune. Avana quieted as she studied Rune, walking around him in a slow circle. She took in every detail of the fox features to replicate them onto me. We'd practiced this once before, but since this was the real deal, we all wanted it to look perfect.

Finally, she came to stand in front of me. Avana was a good head taller than me, so I had to look up slightly to hold her warm, dark gaze. Slowly, I felt the tingle of her magic reach out to me. The tips of my fingers, the top of my head, the gums in my mouth, and the top of my rear all itched as her illusion got to work. I had to bite the inside of my cheek to keep from flailing about in an effort to alleviate the incessant itching.

The concentration faded from Avana's face before she beamed at me once more. "All done, my dear."

"Wow," Akira said as his now fully black eyes trailed my body. He had transformed into his Raven Fae form while Avana worked on me, giving himself onyx eyes and large black feathered wings, which were tucked to his back due to the small space of the jet. "You look stunning!"

Bassel gave a low whistle as his gaze took me in. "Looks even better than when you guys practiced."

"Thank you." My mouth felt full with the sudden invasion of fangs. I knew from the previous practice that it would take me a few minutes to adjust to the feeling.

Everyone gathered their belongings and made their way to the door. Rune grabbed my arm, halting my move to follow. He waited until everyone was gone before facing me.

His eyes drank in my body, and he walked a slow, deliberate circle around me. My skin came alive everywhere that gaze of his dipped, and the air in my lungs became stifled as his fingertips barely brushed along my waist. I was flushed, throbbing low, and hungry for more by the time he finally came to stand in front of me again. There was a fire churning in his eyes, and he bit his lip as he stepped in close to me. There was an unmistakable thirst in his touch, and his gaze told me I was the only drink that could quench it.

Clearing his throat, his voice came out husky when he said, "You look absolutely beautiful. Truly. I've never seen a more stunning Fox."

Swallowing hard, my breath came out fast. "Thank you. That means a lot since I'm supposed to be your *chosen partner*."

Smirking, he slipped his hand along my hip, trailing it against my lower back. Suddenly, his eyes lost some of their spark, and he quickly pulled back his hand. "I wanted to see if you were okay before we went out there."

"In what regard?"

"Any, I guess? Are you okay doing this? Are you okay after the transformation? Are you okay with things between us? Just, are you okay?"

Taking a deep, painful breath, I decided to answer honestly. "No. But I will be. Are you okay?"

A short laugh burst from his lips, but the ache in his dim amber eyes told me he found nothing funny about this. "Nope."

Smirking, I tipped my chin up a notch and walked past him. "Good."

I heard him sigh, but I didn't turn back to acknowledge him. I kept my head held high as I walked down the stairs of the jet and into the autumn sun. The cool Massachusetts air greeted me, and I welcomed the slight chill amid the sunshine.

The small, private runway faced a line of trees decorated in red, orange, and yellow leaves. A few fluttered to the ground with a promise of fall, and I found it to be a breathtaking sight, one that made the waiting black limo seem like a brewing storm cloud in their midst. A man in a traditional black butler's suit stood by the limo, watching us as we gathered around our belongings.

Rune came up beside me and slipped his hand into mine, our fingers intertwining. Swallowing down the mix of hurt and euphoria that his touch inspired, I worked to meet his smile with one of my own. Only one stranger watched us, but it was showtime nonetheless.

"Ready?" Rune asked, his voice low enough for only my ears to pick up.

I squeezed his hand and nodded. "As long as you're with me."

The response left my lips before I had time to think it through, and because I said it for him alone, it was clear I meant it. His brow pinched tight as he forced his smile through the ache so clearly embedded in his eyes.

Forcing myself to turn away from his obvious discomfort and my own, we followed the rest of the group toward the limo and its waiting driver.

As we got closer, the man bowed slightly. He remained stoic as he straightened to greet us. His green eyes lingered on me for a moment before traveling down to where my hand intertwined with Rune's. When he looked back up, he gave Rune his attention. "Welcome home, Master Rune." He looked at the rest of us and greeted, "Master Rune's friends."

"It's been awhile, Edgar," Rune said.

"Indeed, sir. Your mother and the others are awaiting your arrival. Although, I must inform you that they were not expecting six of you." His eyes found me as he finished his sentence, and I swallowed hard at the scrutiny in his stare.

Rune released his hold on my hand to wrap his arm around my waist instead. Cheeks tinting pink at the intimate act, I looked up at him as he pulled me closer to his side. He smiled at Edgar and said, "This is my girlfriend, Bria."

I looked at Edgar and gave a small wave. "Hi. It's nice to meet you."

Edgar raised his eyebrows in surprise before becoming completely impassive once more. He cleared his throat and said, "Yes, well, I do think it is best for us to be on our way now. We mustn't keep everyone waiting."

Edgar moved to open the door of the limo as Rune's butler-turned-assistant, Charles, loaded all of our bags into the trunk. Rune stood to the side and held my hand as I got in first. There were three black leather benches—one at the rear of the limo, one facing the rear seat, and a middle connecting piece that ran along the length of the vehicle. I slid across the rows of seating, taking special care to hold my fox tail so as not to crush it, and I finally opted for a window space.

Rune slid into the space next to me. Marlow and Avana took the middle connecting piece, and Bassel and Akira sat across from Rune and me. A small bar with treats and drinks was situated across from Marlow and Avana's seat with a television mounted where a window would normally be.

With the slam of the door, Edgar and Charles made their way to the front of the limo, and finally, we were off. The passing trees were like an ominous sign. There was no turning back now, no option but to see this through and be the best Fox Fae I could be.

Across from me, Akira and Bassel fought to situate Akira's large, black wings in the seat. Avana laughed at their struggle, and she too now sported her Chameleon Fae form. Her dark skin had an almost iridescent shimmer to it, and depending on where you looked and for how long, her skin glimmered in different shades of green and blue. She also had a long, curled green tail, which was draped on the seat next to her. Marlow hummed to himself as his gold-and-brown patched hands dug around in a jar of candy from the bar.

It was then, while looking at all of my friends, that I really stopped and wondered. Could I do this? I wasn't like them. I wasn't Land Fae or Fox Fae. I wasn't a part of their world, despite knowing I was Water Fae now. I'd lived as a human, which meant I still had human values and experiences, no matter what coursed through my veins. There was an undeniable gap between us. We would never be the same.

They were of the Land.

I was technically of the Water.

With such vast differences, could I really pull off this charade?

I stared down at the illusion of my clawed fingers with a frown. In a low voice, I asked, "Do you think I can really do this? Do you think they'll actually believe I'm Fox Fae?"

The cabin fell quiet as they each regarded my question. I knew it was a worry we'd all shared at one point, and maybe some of them still had doubts just like me.

A tap came at my left shoulder. I slowly turned my head to look at Marlow, who had leaned forward with his arm still stretched out toward me. He smiled warmly as his skin shimmered under the layer of moisture gathered there.

He nodded and said, "I believe in you, Bria. You can do anything you put your mind to. You're strong. Stronger than any of us. You've proven that by putting up with everything that's happened these past few months. You're incredible and amazing in every way, and I know that you can do this."

My eyes watered. I had never heard Marlow say so much or something as kind as that. Usually, he mumbled incoherent words that made no sense to anyone except him. When I looked at the faces of everyone else, they mirrored my shock.

A smile slowly lit up my face, and a lone tear trailed down my cheek. With it, my insecurity vanished. "Thank you, Marlow. That means a lot to me."

He grinned even wider at me before leaning back against his seat. His glassy eyes turned to stare out the window, and he started talking about how he really liked it when it rained. The sun blazed high in the sky with no hint of rain, which meant he was back in his own world again. Seeing him rocking his head side to side as he mumbled to himself calmed me with a sense of fondness. It no longer unnerved me when he got that way. I found comfort in hearing his strange stories and watching his unpredictable personality.

I realized that I had found comfort in each of them and their differences. Despite our short time together, being with them felt like being home. I had a place with this group unlike any other, even my adoptive family. The Ashmoores and I always remained cordial, so much so that it oftentimes felt rehearsed and forced. Being with Rune and the others felt effortless. It was like finally being able to take in a real breath of air after choking for so long.

The people here, surrounding me. They were my family.

And family cared for you despite your sins, your faults, your secrets, right?

I swallowed hard, and I knew I'd have to tell them soon—likely not on this trip given everything that would be happening—but *soon*. I'd have to find a way to be honest and tell them I was Water Fae. They wouldn't reject me, at least not forever. At first, it would be hard to grasp, for both them and me. I'd most likely have to earn back their trust, and I'd have to prove that I wasn't their enemy. We'd have to learn how to navigate our new dynamic, which was bound to be difficult. But I knew it would be okay in the end given all we'd been through. They'd entrusted me with the knowledge of their world, allowed me into their home, faced down numerous people who wanted to do me harm, and created a bond unlike any other I'd ever had. So I knew it would be okay, because my home was here with them. And, no matter what, you could always count on coming home.

CHAPTER THREE

T HE LIMO CAREENED DOWN A long, secluded driveway. A forested, private property that practically oozed wealth surrounded us. Glancing out the window, I swallowed hard as my prediction was confirmed. The home was freaking *giant*.

An expansive white mansion stretched out before us. It appeared to be three stories tall with large windowpanes spanning the front of it. Large stone steps led up to the doors, which were made of a dark, fine wood.

The car pulled around the large, circular drive and stopped in front of the stairs. Edgar opened the limo's door for us while Charles unloaded our belongings. The sheer magnitude of the estate forced me to take in measured, deep breaths. If the home itself was this intimidating, I wasn't sure if I was truly ready to meet the woman who commanded it.

Rune slid his hand into mine. I turned to

him as he smiled and gave me a reassuring squeeze. "Everything will be fine."

I wasn't so sure.

The group filed up the steps, shuffling close together. Despite their stoic expressions, I could practically feel the nerves rolling off of everyone. No one was looking forward to this, which didn't necessarily help the sinking pit forming in my stomach.

Stopping in front of the massive double doors, I took note of the intricate design decorating them. There were foxes chasing small prey carved into the wood, as well as Fox Fae holding fire in open palms. Land Fae were depicted, slaying what looked like people surrounded by water. Water Fae, no doubt.

I swallowed hard at the reminder of what was at stake once I crossed this threshold. Glancing at Rune, I deadpanned, "Lovely doors."

He grimaced. "My mother has rather poor taste in design and, well, everything else."

"No kidding," Akira mumbled behind me, and I noted the way he glowered at the scene of Land Fae slaughtering Water Fae. His distaste for the war between Land and Water Fae was a sentiment we shared.

"She keeps the more alarming pieces in her private quarters, so you shouldn't have to see anything too horrific while here," Rune added, and my blood ran cold.

Before I could ask Rune to clarify, Edgar came around us to open the double doors, and my breath was stolen as I walked through the entrance with Rune. A large foyer greeted us, if you could even call it that. The Ashmoores' whole house could fit in this entryway alone. A grand marble staircase was set in the middle of the room, leading up to the second floor. On either side of it were hallways that led deeper into the house. A door to my right was open, showcasing a massive dining room with a dark, wooden table that could seat at least twenty people. On the opposite side of that room was a door that appeared to lead into a formal sitting room.

Akira came up on the other side of me and frowned as he looked around. He nodded matter-of-factly and said, "I like our small house much better."

In agreement, we shared a smile.

No one had time to make it more than a few steps past the door before a loud squeal sounded from near the stairs. I turned toward the sound just as a stunning girl rounded the banister. Her long black hair matched her fox ears perfectly, and it whipped behind her as she raced toward us. She wore a short, red dress that revealed far too much, and her chest bounced as she ran.

"Aidan?" Rune said, a frown instantly forming.

I swallowed hard and felt my stomach twist up in knots as she flung herself against him. She wrapped her arms around his neck and smiled up at him as her black-and-white fox tail swished behind her. My eyes widened when she leaned in with puckered lips, but before she could kiss him, Rune used his free hand to pry her off him and hold her back.

My blood boiled with an emotion I wasn't familiar with, but it burned like an inferno.

Pushing her lush bottom lip out in a pout, she batted her brown doe eyes at him. "What's wrong? You don't want my welcome home kiss?" That's when she seemed to notice me. Her eyes traced Rune's hand, still joined with mine. She then trailed her gaze up my arm and over my face until we stared at each other. Narrowing her eyes, she curled her lip in a snarl. "Who are you?"

"Aidan," Rune said, keeping his voice surprisingly calm. Meanwhile, I was buzzing with unspent anger. "This is my girl-friend, Bria."

I tilted my head up with pride at the introduction.

She looked from him to me and back. "Girlfriend? Since when do you date?" She took me in from head to toe, her brow plunging in revulsion. She scoffed as she met my eyes again. "She isn't even pretty. Why would you want to date garbage like that?"

"You did *not* just say that," Akira said aghast.

Utterly speechless, I inhaled sharply. Never had I been so insulted, so embarrassed, so *pissed*. Who the hell did this girl think she was, speaking about me like that? I mean, my God, could she be any ruder?

I opened my mouth to say as much, but Rune beat me to it. "The only garbage I see is the person standing in front of me. Someone really ought to take out the trash around here."

Rune gripped my hand tighter as he shoved past her. Her jaw fell open, and she stared after him. Akira laughed and skipped along next to me, and Marlow stuck his tongue out at her. She huffed in rage and glared at me again. Absolutely satisfied with the rejection she'd received, I smiled from ear to ear as she stalked down one of the halls near the stairs, her hands clenched in tight fists.

Rune looked at me apologetically. "Sorry about that. That was Aidan. She—"

"Is still obsessed with you," Bassel finished. He patted Rune on the shoulder, as though to comfort him. "I thought you were going to make sure she knew you weren't interested in meeting up again after the last time you two—" Bassel stopped and met my eyes. Clearing his throat, he rubbed at the back of his neck and looked away. "Never mind."

Rune let out a deep sigh and glanced at Bassel. "I did make it clear. She knows it's never happening."

Avana scoffed. "Try telling that to your mother. It's clear she's the one who picked Aidan as your potential mate."

Potential mate.

He and Aidan.

God, I'm gonna be sick for real this time.

My chest constricted under the viselike grip of jealousy. So Aidan was one of Rune's previous partners just as I'd suspected. I knew Myra was going to have her pick of partner in mind, but I didn't know that said person would actually be *here* where I'd have to meet her face to face.

The history between Aidan and Rune was clear. I hated it. I hated that he'd shared a bed with such a gorgeous woman. I hated that she knew him in ways I didn't. But, most of all, I hated how jealous it made me. This burn in my chest, the sinking feeling in my gut. I hated feeling this way.

We all trudged further into the room like sloths crawling through molasses.

Rune nudged me gently with his elbow. He leaned in close, his brow furrowed. "Hey, I just want—"

"Rune!"

We all looked up as a little boy ran down the steps toward us, and my heart instantly grew warm. Recognition sparked the memory of Rune gifting me with a family photo of him and his little brothers. This twin looked a bit different now than when the picture had been taken. His black hair was longer, and he had it up in a small ponytail. His ears seemed a tad bigger, too, standing taller on top of his head. He wore purple rimmed glasses and a pair of black dress pants with a white button-up shirt.

Rune's entire body immediately brightened as he knelt down and held his arms open wide. The little boy squealed in delight as he wrapped his arms around Rune's neck and hugged him tightly. His tail swished excitedly from side to side.

"How have you been, Newt?" Rune said, pulling back to look at his younger half-brother.

"I've been g-g-good. G-Greshim is still cleaning his half of th-the room, but I g-g-got d-done early to come see you! D-d-do you like my new g-glasses?"

Seeing Newt in the flesh was like basking in sunlight. He was a pure and sweet soul with a special kind of glow to him. Recalling the stories I'd been told of how their mother treated him made my heart break. I'd never understand how someone could treat anyone so badly, simply for being different.

Rune laughed and adjusted the crooked purple frames on Newt's face. "I love them. They look wonderful on you."

I looked up as Greshim came barreling down the steps. His hair was a bit shorter than Newt's, barely touching his shoulders, much like his older brother. His mouth was open in a toothy grin, exposing his small canines. Despite their size, the teeth still looked like they could cause some damage. His tail seemed longer and fuller than Newt's as he flung himself into Rune's outstretched arms.

"Rune! We've missed you! We would've come out sooner, but mother made us clean our room."

Rune smiled and ruffled the top of Greshim's head. "It's okay. We just got here."

I looked from Rune to Greshim—who had started talking about the rabbit he'd caught the other day—before training my gaze on Newt. He stood back from the other two, and I realized that he was looking at me. Suddenly eager to make a good impression, I smiled at him and gave a small wave.

He crept closer and stopped when he stood directly in front of me, staring up at me with vivid eyes that matched his older brother's. "Who are you?"

"My name's Bria."

He tilted his head to the side as one of his fox ears twitched. "M-m-my name is Newt."

Be still, heart. Be still!

Somehow, I felt like Newt and Greshim were the real critics this week, and in a sense, their approval would be the one I needed, not Myra's. Her acceptance would just mean relief for Rune, but if the twins welcomed me in, *that* would mean something real to Rune. And to me.

Kneeling so we were on the same level, I extended my hand to Newt. As soon as he registered the movement toward him, he flinched and stared at my outstretched hand. Seeing his reaction made my heart squeeze painfully, and it took every bit of restraint I had to keep my face neutral. It was hard to ignore the blaring reason why he was so startled by the gesture. Clearly, the abuse wasn't just verbal or mental.

Finally, Newt slipped his small, warm grip in my own, and his lips tilted up at the sides.

I shook his hand and gave him a smile of my own. "It's very nice to meet you."

Suddenly, his eyes went wide, and his cheeks grew pink. He held firm even after we were done shaking, and he leaned in close as he said, "You are th-the prettiest g-g-girl I've ever seen, Bria."

Heart warming, I laughed. "Thank you, Newt."

"Are you a friend of our brother?" Greshim asked as he walked over to us. He slung his arm around his twin's shoulder and looked me over like he was searching for the answer on my person.

"Boys," Rune said, smirking at them. He walked over to me and gave me his hand as I straightened. He wrapped his arm around my waist, pulling me close to him. "This is Bria, my girlfriend. She came with me all this way to meet you guys. Make sure you help her feel welcome, okay?"

"Of course! Bria will be our new friend-d-d. Right, Bria?"

"That's right."

Greshim beamed at me and said, "I'm Greshim!"

"It's nice to meet you. I'm Bria."

"Do you like to play games?" Greshim asked, looking at me with large, expectant eyes.

"Want to g-g-go play with us in our room?" Newt asked, not allowing me any time to answer.

"Yeah!" Greshim shouted. He grabbed my hand and tugged on it in the direction of the stairs. "We can play like you're a princess, and Newt is an evil wizard who kidnaps you. I can be the prince that rescues you."

"Hey! I want to be th-th-the Prince!"

"Woah, woah!" Rune said. Each arm scooped up a boy and slung them over a shoulder, a feat that was only possible due to his Fae strength. The twins laughed and flailed around as Rune said, "She just got here. Let her settle in before you ambush her to play, all right? You don't want to scare her off now, do you?"

They shook their heads, which must've satisfied Rune, because he sat them back down on the ground. Their giggles didn't stop, however, even as Greshim helped Newt fix his glasses, which had gotten crooked during all the excitement. Unhindered joy bubbled inside my chest as I watched them. This was a family. A *real* family. Something that I had always longed for. The brothers cast a beautiful glow around the room.

Then all at once, the room changed. A dark, foreboding aura settled over the air and on everyone's shoulders. The laughter died on the next breath, and the twins suddenly became serious. They each ran, Newt hiding behind Rune's legs and Greshim standing tall and poised beside him. Rune straightened and stared blankly at the entrance of the hallway Aidan had disappeared down. The rest of the group gathered closely around me, and Rune took my hand in his. I swallowed hard, and my heart thundered with each breath I took.

My eyes followed theirs to the hallway, and my stomach rose into my throat. I recognized the woman before us as Rune's mother, Myra. She wore a black, Regency style gown, which added to the darkness around her. Her black fox ears stood out starkly in contrast to her silky, platinum hair, which traveled down the length of her body, nearly reaching the floor. Her hands were clasped in front of her, making her sharp, pointed claws stand out. If that wasn't enough to have my confidence quaking, I found her staring at me with cold, venomous gold eyes.

She was terrifyingly gorgeous.

"Hello, Mother," Rune said, his voice completely devoid of emotion.

She ignored him and kept her narrowed eyes on me, taking me in from head to toe. Goosebumps broke out along my skin, and the back of my neck prickled with a fresh wave of worry. *Oh no.* Something was wrong. Could she tell I was fake already? Maybe part of the illusion was askew or fading, making it obvious that I was a complete fraud. I held my breath, waiting for her to point out what she had discovered before setting me aflame with her fire.

Myra raised an eyebrow and said, "So, this is the young lady you've been seeing, Rune?"

"She is," Rune answered, holding his shoulders back. "Her name is—"

"Who are your parents?" Myra asked, cutting Rune off. She took slow, measured steps toward me, waiting for my answer.

"My parents were Blayze and Seraphina Bowen," I answered, reciting the names that Rune had prepared for me.

Myra narrowed her eyes. "Interesting. I was under the impression that their daughter died with them in their home those 100 or so years ago."

"Many people thought that. Luckily, I was not actually in the house when the Water Fae showed up. It wasn't until later when I went back to our home that I found them. After that, I ran. I've lived alone, not sharing with anyone who I was, until I met Rune."

Rune had told me everything to say, because he knew she would ask about my parents to see if I had potential for a good bloodline. He was right, and his story was a good one. I'd initially practiced the speech to sound like that of a grieving daughter, but Rune had been quick to correct me. I was to say it with no hint of pain or mourning, because those would be seen as a weakness in Myra's eyes. I hoped I'd pulled off the charade and said it as coldly as Myra preferred.

I held my breath and placed my shaking free hand behind my back. I didn't want her to see my trembling. Any shortcoming, any sign that I was lesser than what she'd want for Rune, could make all of this come tumbling down. I had to keep my wits about me and at least pretend I was calm, cool, and collected.

Myra studied me in silence again. Her eyes were harsh and cold as she took me in, and I began to wonder if she'd already figured out that I was a lie.

Aidan came up behind Rune's mother with her arms crossed. She sneered at me, showing me her vicious canines that she no doubt wanted to use to tear into my flesh.

The two terrifying women before me took no care to hide the contempt burning in their eyes. I felt like the world was going to fall out from under me as we all stood there, silent and motionless.

Aidan stepped closer to Myra. "See. I told you she isn't anything to look at. When did Rune even start dating?"

Rune raised his lip, baring his sharp canines at Aidan. "One more word, Aidan. One more word about Bria, and I'll personally see to it that it will be your last."

Myra raised her chin and stared Rune down, unperturbed by his threat to Aidan. "Why would you bring this thing here when you knew full well that I had already chosen you a proper, worthy mate?"

Rune's eyes narrowed into thin slits as he stepped toward his mother.

My heart rate spiked under the building tension in the air. There was no trace of fear or hesitation in Rune's eyes as he faced off with his mother. As I watched them, I realized Rune looked just as terrifying as she was, if not more.

"Do not start, Mother," Rune hissed. The sound of his voice brought chills to my skin. "Why would *you* bring someone here when you knew full well that I would decline? I'm with Bria, and nothing you have up your sleeves will change that."

I could sense a fire burning between the two fearsome Fae before me, and everyone else seemed to feel it, too. Akira and Bassel huddled closer together around me, and Newt and Greshim flanked each of my legs to clutch them tightly since Rune had advanced. Aidan's gaze darted between Myra and Rune, and her face paled as she backed away. My own legs buckled as I watched the rage between mother and son light the fires in their hands.

Before anything could transpire, a voice rang out from the top of the stairs. "Damn, it feels tense in here."

Everyone's attention turned to the stairwell where I immediately recognized a man from the photos I'd studied with Rune. It was his cousin, Ardley.

Ardley leaned against the top post of the stairs, a smirk on his handsome face. His toned arms were crossed over his wide chest. His wavy black locks were mussed in an attractive fashion, and his fox ears and tail matched the deep shade of onyx with a slight dusting of white on the tips of his fur.

Laughing, he pushed away from the post and began his descent. "How you doing, R? Miss me?"

Rune grinned and turned toward his cousin. "Hardly."

"Aww, come on. Don't be like that. I know you love me."

Myra sneered at Ardley. "You interrupted us."

Ardley rolled his eyes as he reached the rest of us. "I think what you mean is, I *saved* you all. No one wants to hear the two of you bitch at each other first thing. Now, why don't you and the unwanted guest," he said while pointing at Aidan, "go back to your study? You guys are irritating and depressing."

Aidan fumed as she glared at Ardley. She raised her fist as though she were going to swing at him. "I swear, you are such an a—"

"Aidan," Myra snapped, her voice demanding obedience. Aidan lowered her hand and looked at Myra with innocent eyes. A now expressionless Myra turned and said, "Ardley is right. I'm bored with this already. Let us go back."

"Yes ma'am."

Myra's emotionless eyes found Rune's, and she added, "I expect to see you in my office once you have your things settled in your room."

Rune's jaw worked, and his voice came out with an edge as he said, "Understood."

Eyes wide, I watched the two women finally retreat. I couldn't believe Myra had backed down like that. I was under the impression that no one could speak to her that way and get away with it. Perhaps it was because with Rune and Ardley together, she didn't stand a chance?

Rune had mentioned before that he was extremely close with his cousin, but seeing the bond between the two really made Rune's brief mention seem like an understatement. They clasped hands before leaning in to wrap their arms around each other in a tight squeeze. They seemed like an invincible duo, standing side by side, which only confirmed my suspicions. Myra had to play things smart with these two.

Ardley greeted Akira, Bassel, and Marlow with pats on the back. He leaned in close to Avana, giving her a quick peck on the cheek. They all shared a warm welcome before Ardley turned his large grin on me. Despite myself, my cheeks colored under the brightness of his smile and warm eyes.

He held out his large hand toward me. "Hi. I'm Ardley."

I shook it. "I'm Bria."

A teasing smirk crossed his mouth, and he bit the corner of his lip to hide it. "I know who you are. You may not recognize me from the previous times we met. I was a lot less fleshy and more furry then."

My heart stuttered as I processed his words. It was *him*. I was finally meeting my fox.

When I'd first met the Silver Fox in the woods behind my campus dorm, I never would've guessed he was actually a man, or rather, Fae. We'd immediately formed a bond, and ever since then, I'd been hoping to meet him. I couldn't believe the moment was finally here.

My fox.

In the flesh.

And it wasn't Rune.

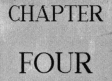

CHAPTER

FOUR

AKIRA SMILED AND SLUNG HIS arm around Ardley's
shoulder. "See Bria! He's the fox you've been dying
to meet in person!"

With crimson heating my cheeks, I ducked my
head under the intensity of Akira and Ardley's large grins. The
way Akira had worded that made my interest in the fox sound
like far more than what it was.

Yes, I'd been dying to meet him, but it was because I wanted
to thank him. He'd been there when I'd been struggling with
my failed relationship, lending an ear to my pain. It was something I was grateful for, and because of it, I'd hoped to
form a friendship with him.

Although, meeting him now, seeing that
the fox was Ardley, something deep inside me
twisted. It hurt in only the way disappointment
would.

In the back of my mind, I'd always secretly hoped that my fox was Rune.

Pushing away the acidic burn of disappointment, I grinned at Ardley. "It's good to see you again."

Beaming, he walked over to me. Rune narrowed his eyes at his cousin's back as Ardley slung his arm around my shoulders. Guiding me toward the steps, he said, "Why don't I take you to your room? We can get reacquainted while I help you unpack."

"We'll help!" Greshim yelled.

Newt followed close to him, trailing beside us as we turned toward the stairs. "M-m-me too. I can help you unpack, too!"

As we worked our way up the stairs, I glanced over my shoulder at Rune. He wore a grim frown as he followed us at a distance. He was quiet, and there was clearly something that had him upset. While I knew he was agitated, I wasn't sure if it was the confrontation with his mother or something else entirely. He could be feeling the weight of our earlier talk and his decision as he watched me walk away. Whatever the reason for his displeasure, it made me anxious. I wanted to understand his pain.

Newt and Greshim walked beside me, and they chatted the entire walk. Something told me they didn't get many play dates with friends or opportunities to talk openly, so I welcomed the conversation. They told me about their favorite games and how they couldn't wait for me to play with them. I laughed and responded at all the right times, even if I wasn't necessarily giving my one hundred percent authentic reaction. I wanted to, but I was still battling my own inner demons brought out by Aidan's insults and Myra's hostility.

We climbed stairs until we reached the third floor. Our group turned right and walked down the length of the intricate red-and-white patterned carpet until we reached a series of closed doors.

"All right," Ardley said. He dropped his arm from my shoulder as he opened the door. "This should be your room. Akira and Bassel are in the room next to yours."

Our group had decided beforehand that everyone would bunk in pairs for safety, though it was never made known to me who would be paired together. Akira and Bassel walked past us. They smiled at me and waved before going into their own room to unpack. Avana and Marlow took up residence right across from Akira and Bassel. We were all close, for which I was incredibly thankful. I'd need them close by in case I got any late-night visitors who sought to disembowel me simply for being here, a threat with which I was unfortunately all too familiar.

Jonah had made numerous nightly visits during the past few months—though they were more so ambushes than visits—which forced me to be prepared for attacks like this. I had packed my dagger, a gift from Rune after our training sessions, as a precaution, though I wasn't sure if I'd be strong enough to win against Myra if the need to use it arose. It was why I was glad to have the extra security blanket of having my friends nearby—both those here in the home *and* those like Dallas, who would be lurking nearby in secret.

I looked for Rune and found him at the other end of the hallway, digging through his pocket in front of a closed door. When he pulled out a key, he unlocked the door, then went inside without looking in my direction. He shut it behind him, and I heard the unmistakable sound of a lock clicking into place.

I wanted to go to him and see if he would confide in me about what was eating at him, but I also didn't want to leave Ardley and the twins, who were over the moon as they bounded into my room. After all, Rune had locked himself in for a reason. He'd tell me what was bothering him when he was ready.

Or rather, *if* he were ever ready.

I tried pushing Rune out of my head for now as I followed Ardley and the boys into my room. My jaw nearly hit the floor as I took in my quarters. A king-size bed sat against the wall with a downy green and white comforter. A dark, oak entertainment center with a flat-screen TV took up residency across from the bed. French doors faced us from across the room, leading to a balcony that looked out on the backyard and a lake. The room also had its own bathroom, which contained a shower that could easily fit at least five people.

Looking around in amazement, I asked, "This is my room?"

I gave a nervous laugh as I walked toward the bed where my luggage sat. I guessed that either Charles or Edgar had brought it up while everyone had been talking downstairs.

Ardley smiled and nodded. He stood at the foot of the bed, watching me with a twinkle in his eye. "Even though no one else was expecting you, I was. My parents and I arrived here a few days ago, so Myra gave me the task of picking rooms for Rune's guests. I picked this room for you since it's one of the nicer ones. It's also one of the few with a TV since Myra hates them so much."

Early in our trip planning, Rune had told Ardley the truth about me. He let his cousin in on the charade we were putting on, as well as the fact that I was human. At least, they believed I was. Ardley was the only one who hadn't arrived with our group who knew the truth about what was really happening and who I was.

Processing his words, I grinned. The knowledge that he was excited for my arrival made my earlier disappointment about him being the fox turn into guilt. Maybe he'd been looking forward to our meeting just as much as I had. His thoughtfulness in preparing a room for me was charming to say the least.

"Well, let's unpack your bags!" Greshim said, climbing onto the lavish bed. Newt followed close behind, crawling toward my belongings.

Ardley rolled his eyes and scooped the twins up off the bed. They groaned before breaking out into fits of laughter. "Don't be rude, you two. You can't go through someone else's things."

I reassured the boys that they were fine and grabbed my luggage to lay it on a small settee in the corner of the room. I didn't really feel comfortable unpacking all of my things in a house full of people who were against me. It felt odd, like opening my suitcase with items from my life would somehow open myself up, too. I wanted to keep my belongings guarded, just as I'd keep myself.

"Hey," Ardley said, setting the boys back on their feet. "Why don't you two go get Bria something to drink?"

"Okay," Greshim said with a quick nod. Grabbing Newt's hand, he pulled his brother toward the door. "We'll be right back, Bria."

As soon as they were gone, Ardley turned toward me. "Sorry about them. They're just really excited to have everyone here."

"They're fine. I've been excited to meet them, too, after the way Rune talked about them."

Grinning, Ardley slowly moved closer. "I hear they're not the only ones you've been excited to meet."

Cheeks heating, I fought for a less embarrassing way to phrase my desire.

His grin stretched from ear to ear as the distance between us grew smaller. "Am I everything you thought I'd be?"

I gave a nervous laugh as I quickly averted my eyes from his. My fingers fumbled with the zipper on my suitcase as I said, "To be determined. I haven't had time to get to know you as yourself yet."

"Well, you are most certainly everything that *I* remember," he said. I glanced up at him as he closed the rest of the space between us. His eyes roamed over my body, a hungry look in his eyes. "Absolutely gorgeous. Ever since that day we met, I've wanted to—"

"*Ardley.*"

The dark-haired boy stepped away from me, giving us both a view of the doorway. Rune stood there with his bags, a glare aimed directly at his cousin, and his canines exposed. The deep command in Rune's voice raised the hair on my arms, and oddly enough, it sent a jolt of want straight to my core.

Ardley laughed and held up his hands. "Calm down, R. I was only playing."

Rune rolled his eyes and walked further into the room. "Whatever. Just go."

Ardley saluted him. "Yes, sir." He broke out in a wide smile and patted Rune's shoulder on the way to the door. Ardley stopped at the threshold, grabbing the knob. He gave us a mischievous smile over his shoulder. "You two have fun."

As soon as the door was shut, Rune sighed and turned to me. "I'm sorry about him. Did he do anything to you?"

"No, not really."

He nodded and mumbled to himself as he lifted his suitcase onto the bed and began sorting through it as though he were looking for something.

My eyes widened as I realized who my roommate was. Mouth suddenly dry with a fresh wave of nerves and a hint of excitement, I worked to stay calm on the inside. This was fine. Totally fine. Sharing a room with Rune. I mean, I'd shared space with him before. Granted, there was only one bed in here, but really, how different would that be from sleeping on a couch near where he slept?

Very different, Bria. It's very different!

A devious part of me was almost glad to know that Rune and I would be rooming together, because it would present more opportunities to break down the new wall he'd placed between us. Though, it would also provide more chances for the guilt about keeping my secret from him to fester like an infected wound. Suddenly, I wasn't sure if this was as good of a situation as my initial gut reaction made it seem.

His eyes were unfocused as he riffled through his belong-

ings, and a somber frown painted his usually carefree face. Seeing the expression pulled me back to the present.

"Is everything okay?" I asked, sitting on the edge of the bed
next to where he stood.

He stopped fiddling with his things as his gaze met mine.
Seconds ticked by where we simply stared, and within those
gold depths, I saw the pain he was trying so hard to hide. Finally, he squeezed his eyes shut and shook his head.

"Yeah. I'm fine. Just—" he paused and looked out the French
doors. Swallowing hard, he finished, "Just a lot going on in my
head. Doesn't help that there are lots of memories here."

My heart seized as I realized what being back here probably meant for Rune. It meant pain, remorse, and heartache.
It meant the past haunted his mind. I knew things between
us were still rocky and unclear, but in that moment, it didn't
matter. Rune was hurting, and I refused to let him suffer alone.

I reached for his hand that rested on the bed, and I was
happy to see he let me. I gave it a squeeze and rubbed a soothing circle along the back of it with my thumb. Looking up at
him, I asked, "Memories of your dad?"

He offered a sad smile. "Yeah, of him. Of my mom when she
still had a heart. Memories of when we were a family." Clearing
his throat, he finally met my eyes again. "Sorry. I don't mean to
be so melancholy."

"Don't. Don't ever apologize for missing him or the way
things once were. It's okay to hurt. It's okay to grieve. Never be
sorry about that."

He released a shaky breath and sat next to me on the bed.
The mattress sank beneath his weight, and I moved closer to
wrap my arms around him. He leaned into my touch, and I took
some comfort in that. I knew it wasn't easy for Rune to open
up, so his trust in me was a gift I'd always welcome, regardless
of the circumstance.

It was also like a knife sinking deep into my gut, because here he was, trusting me, while I was actively withholding a huge part of myself from him. It wasn't fair to him, and the fact weighed heavily on my heart. Now just wasn't the time to tell him. He had enough burdens on his shoulders without my added issue.

"It's silly," Rune started softly. "But every time I see my mother, I see pieces of the old her scattered, and I can't help but think that maybe, just maybe, I can do something to collect all those pieces and put them back together again. This week, my birthday, was an excuse for her to bring me home to try to set me up with someone, but it's also, in a way, an excuse for me to try to fix her."

I rubbed my fingertips up and down his rigid back and shook my head. "That's not silly. If anything, I think it shows how lucky Myra is to have you for a son. For you to care so deeply about someone who doesn't deserve it."

He gave a humorless chuckle and hung his head. "I think the lucky one was me, because for a time, I had her and my dad when they were whole. That will be a time I'll always love. And miss."

We stayed like that for a while, sitting in the vulnerable moment. I knew from experience that he didn't need words of comfort right now. Those words would do nothing to bring back his dad or all he'd lost. Words were as flammable as paper in situations like this. Easily torched to ash under the flames of grief. All I could do was give him the support he needed in whatever form he needed. A shoulder to lean on. An ear to listen. A firm hand to remind him that he still had someone here who loved him. It was something I'd always provide, so long as he'd let me.

Eventually, two sets of small footsteps came pounding down the hall. Newt and Greshim burst through the door carrying bottles of water, juices, and a tray with a mug and teapot.

"We didn't know what you might want, so we brought everything," Greshim said. As soon as he saw Rune, his face lit up like a Christmas tree. "Brother!"

The life finally came back to Rune's eyes as he stood to catch Greshim, who'd set the tray down before flinging himself at Rune. I laughed, my heart full, as the three brothers immediately began playing. I cheered the twins on in their attempts to wrangle Rune, which in turn, made me Rune's target. Giggling, I ran around the room to avoid being caught, and the twins quickly came to my aid until Rune feigned defeat, pinned on the bed by Newt and Greshim.

It was an absolutely perfect moment after a very rough start to a hard day.

CHAPTER

FIVE

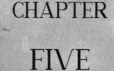

ow. I can't believe you grew up here. It's absolutely gorgeous."

We drove through the small, coastal town, and everywhere I looked, I became even more enraptured by the beauty of it all.

After everyone had gotten their stuff settled in their respective rooms, we'd decided to go on an outing around town. We had all returned to our human forms before we set out. It had been years since Bassel, Marlow, and Akira had been here, and Avana, a decade or so. They were eager to revisit their favorite haunts, and I was absolutely enamored of their hometown.

Quaint local shops lined the leaf-littered road, and families strolled the sidewalks with bright smiles. In the distance, the setting sun glittered on the rippling waves of the sea. Boats dotted the water, and I made a mental promise that I'd most definitely recreate some of these views with my paints when I got the chance to study abroad in Italy.

Even though we'd only be here for a week, I'd brought some sketchbooks with me, but it wasn't the same as when I wielded a paintbrush. I couldn't *not* paint for too long. Art was in my blood. Painting was the whole reason I was here in the first place.

I'd agreed to help Rune in exchange for the chance to study in Italy under my idol, Luca Romano. It was something that felt a bit distant now with everything that was happening in my life, but it was still a dream I intended to see through. I was determined to become a professional painter, even if I had to fight tooth and nail to get there.

We'd just finished perusing an indie bookstore, and now Rune drove our group near the coast as we looked for a place to have dinner since Myra was letting us have today to get settled. The thought still made my insides burn—Myra *letting* us go out. Apparently, when Rune met with her in her office like she'd requested, they'd agreed that our group could do as we pleased while here, as long as we joined Myra when she desired. As if she dictated our lives and what we did. It was infuriating, but she had cards stacked against Rune in more ways than one. There was little we could get away with during this week without Myra's say-so.

I initially thought her giving us some wiggle room to be on our own was her giving her adult son and his friends freedom during this week, but Rune was quick to tell me it was her setting us up. She wanted us to go out in hopes that we'd somehow act wrong or I'd be seen acting weak around town, which she could then use as a reason for why I wasn't right for Rune. Everything Myra did, she did for a reason.

"It's a great place to live," Bassel chimed in from the back of the SUV, bringing me back to the beautiful drive and my previous comment. "I miss it sometimes."

"It's especially nice during this time of year," Akira added from where he sat in the middle row with Avana.

"I bet the autumn festival will be happening while we're here. It's an annual event our town does every year with fall-themed foods, games, and activities," Rune said, briefly looking at me before turning his attention back to the road. "If it is, would you like to go one day this week?"

"I'd love to. That sounds like so much fun."

Beaming at me, he nodded. "It's a date."

I held my breath as my heart clung to those words and the brightness of his smile. I tried not to read into it, but how could I not? Everyone in this car knew our truth, knew the whole dating thing was a charade, so why lie around them? Rune seemed to realize his mistake, too, or rather his unfiltered confession, and he quickly turned stoic again before facing the road once more.

The car went quiet, and I was feeling claustrophobic under the amount of tension in the air. I was fighting for something, *anything*, to say when, from the back seat, Marlow whispered, "Awkwarddd."

"*Marlow*," Ardley hissed, wrapping his arm around the other Fae. He smiled at me in the rear-view mirror before leaning close to Marlow and whispering, "Just because we're all thinking it, doesn't mean you say it, buddy."

The rest of the car burst out into laughter, and I found myself joining them. Even Rune's mouth lifted up at the corners as he glanced at me. The old me would've cowered in embarrassment at a time like this, but that wasn't who I was anymore. These people had changed me. My chest and shoulders felt lighter when I was around them, and they had a way of making me feel comfortable, even in awkward situations like this.

We finally spotted a small restaurant on the ocean that everyone immediately demanded we go to. The blue and white building was situated by the shore, and it had a wrap around deck with outdoor seating. The breeze coming off the water below the eatery was cool, salty, and carried a hint of the fish living in its depths.

"This place has amazing crab," Rune said as he met me at the front of the car.

"And lobster," Akira threw in. "Never forget lobster."

I worked not to drool, and my stomach growled in demand for the food. Our group began to make our way inside with Rune and me taking up the rear. Our arms brushed as we walked, lighting up my insides like an explosion of fireworks. I swallowed hard and tried to suppress the growing desire—when ever so slightly—he wrapped one finger around mine before intertwining all of them.

I gave him a brief, questioning glance, and he smiled. "Small town. People talk. Don't want to look like just friends."

Of course. This was pretend. He wasn't having a change of heart where he suddenly wanted to be with me. Where there were strangers' eyes, there would be public displays of affection. It was all for the show we were putting on, and that fact cut into me like a warm knife through butter. A deep, clean cut right through my chest.

I swallowed past the burning in my throat and followed the group inside the restaurant. I knew what I was here to do. There was no sense in being hurt over the deal I'd made going into this.

We were strictly business.

Although, we both knew that was a lie with our shared feelings. Despite his desire, Rune had made it clear what he intended to do about those emotions. Nothing. Nothing except squash them. That meant I knew what I had to do about *my* feelings. Nothing. Nothing except do exactly what we'd agreed upon.

I was going to play his girlfriend, and in doing so, I'd shove in his face what he'd be walking out on. I'd show him what we *could* be if only he'd let us. He'd lived in fear of love for far too long. I understood he wasn't ready to feel the pain of loss again after having lost so much, but I refused to let someone I cared about live that way. With time, hopefully, we could build a real relationship like the one we were faking.

So, I leaned into his touch, walking with my cheek pressed into his shoulder and a smile plastered on my lips. My steps became lighter as though I were a girl waltzing through a seaside restaurant with the boy for whom I was head over heels. Which I guess wasn't too hard since it was true.

We were seated at a wooden table with a prime view of the large windows, which looked out past the outdoor deck and onto the ocean. The rushing blue water snagged my attention. It was faint, but I could hear it in the back of my mind. A whisper among the waves. It was muffled, almost like my head was underwater, but it was there.

Calling me.

Urging me to come closer.

Rune gently tugged on my arm, breaking the connection. The motion brought me back to the here and now.

"You okay?" he whispered, his brow pinched in concern.

"Hmm? Oh, yeah. Sorry. I-I thought I saw a dolphin."

He grinned, which made the lie burn on my tongue. Each fib I told was leaving a mark on my conscience, and I knew I couldn't put up with this much longer. I was going to have to come clean and tell him eventually, but I also knew how much the truth would hurt him. I wasn't ready to rip off that Band-Aid yet. Doing so could wait until we were back in Tennessee.

When we were seated, Rune kept a hold of my hand, which I tried not to read into. Though, it was harder not to read into the way his thumb brushed ever so slightly along my hand, tracing a soothing trail against my skin. Our hands weren't visible to others beneath the table, but I was sure he was just taking precautions. Instead of contemplating the intricacies of his actions, I focused on the menu and all of its mouthwatering seafood options.

Or rather, I *tried*.

"Well, well, well. Look what the fox dragged in."

I turned to the head of the table where a petite honey-skinned boy stood. He smiled warmly at everyone, and based on his black uniform and ordering pad, it was clear he was our waiter. The smile he wore said he was more than that, though.

"Carlos," Rune greeted, smiling at him. "When did you start working here?"

Carlos shrugged, glancing briefly at Bassel, who seemed very interested in the menu all of a sudden. Carlos turned back to Rune. "I haven't been here long. Bruno was short staffed here, and since it's busy season, I offered to help out."

"Ever so thoughtful," Avana said with a bright grin. "I hope you're enjoying your work here."

Carlos waved a dismissive hand, his handsome face lighting up once more. "I am actually. Speaking of work, what can I get everyone to drink tonight?"

Carlos took our drink orders and retreated with one final glance at Bassel. As soon as our waiter was gone, Bassel let out the breath he'd seemed to be holding the entire time.

Akira nudged him, a smirk on his face. "Carlos looked pretty good, didn't he?"

I gave Rune a questioning look, and he leaned in to whisper, "Carlos and Bassel dated for a bit when we lived here. They broke up, because they didn't want to do the long-distance thing, but we all know Bassel is still in love with him."

Giddy at the idea of Bassel in love, I watched everyone tease him relentlessly. It was light hearted jabs at him, which he swatted away, but no matter how he tried, he couldn't keep the color from his cheeks. The big, bad kitty had a soft spot for Carlos.

Ardley had just finished telling a story that had everyone in stitches when another unfamiliar voice called out to Rune.

I turned to find a beautiful brunette standing behind Rune's and my chairs. Her vibrant brown eyes held Rune's with a curious tilt. "Wow, you're really back in town. Aidan said you were coming in to finally form a bond with her." The brunette's gaze flicked over to me, and they sharpened as she assessed me. "Or maybe not. Who's this?"

"Talia," Rune said, his previously cheerful voice suddenly cold, "this is my girlfriend, Bria."

I mustered up the best smile I could under the scrutiny of her stare. Something searing hot filled the back of my throat, and it burned like rage. This complete stranger's open hostility toward me, paired with the reminder of Aidan, had my blood boiling inside.

It took everything in me to keep my voice even as I said, "It's nice to meet you."

She grinned, but the gesture didn't quite reach her eyes. She turned back to Rune. "What about Aidan?"

Rune let out a frustrated sigh as he turned in his chair to face her. "What about her, Talia? I'm trying to enjoy a nice dinner with my *girlfriend* and our friends. If you'll excuse us, I'd like to get back to that."

Her pretty features morphed into a grimace. "Whatever." She narrowed her eyes on me. "Enjoy Aidan's leftovers while you can. It won't last long, seeing as how he belongs to her."

I laughed, all humor removed from the sound. My patience had been snuffed out like a flame on a passing breeze. "Rune doesn't belong to anyone. Not me or Aidan. And you forget. I'm the one sitting at this table, not Aidan. I'll let that speak for itself."

"Ha!" Ardley boomed from the other end of the table. "Well said, Bria; well said. Hey, Talia, girl with the stick shoved up her ass. You've had your petty fun. Run along now before we have to make you."

Ardley's threat made Talia swallow hard, and after sparing one more moment to glare at me, she finally stormed off. I bit the inside of my lip and bunched up my dress in my hands beneath the table. My stomach was in knots from the intense conversation, and I had to work hard to breathe evenly. It was true that her words didn't hurt, but damn, they definitely had an effect on me. I was a tangled, swirling ball of frustration, embarrassment, and outrage.

I mean, really. Who the fuck did this girl think she was, confronting Rune and me when we were out for dinner with our friends? It was infuriating!

Feeling my emotions getting the better of me, I quickly excused myself and made my way outside. The wind coming off the ocean quickly soothed the furious heat in my cheeks. I closed my eyes and tilted my face into the breeze as I walked across the outdoor patio to the overhang above the water. There were only a few couples out here braving the autumn chill, so the space provided enough privacy for me to cool my head— something I really needed at that moment.

I folded my arms against the wooden deck railing. Closing my eyes, I took a deep breath and tried focusing on that.

Breathe. In and out. In and out.

Salty sea mist kissed my face, and I angled my head toward the cold spray.

I was beyond annoyed with the direction this easygoing dinner had gone. Aidan wasn't even with us, but I somehow couldn't escape the dark cloud that was her. It was a small town, so of course everyone knew each other and their business. Aidan and Rune clearly had a history that was being shoved in my face. It had my stomach curled into dozens of tight knots. I knew I said I didn't care what Talia or Aidan or anyone else thought of me, but damn it, I *did*. Talia's words stung like a fresh cut, and no matter how hard I tried to ignore the insult, I couldn't. It clung to the edges of my mind like glue.

Opening my eyes, I stared down into the water. The waves lapped against the legs supporting the deck, and I attempted to focus on that sound. The memory of Aidan rushing toward Rune and throwing her arms around his neck like they were long lost lovers surfaced in my mind. Jealousy coated my insides, and I clenched my fists tightly on the railing as the waves below began to rise higher before crashing back down in an angry rush.

How dare she? Rune was clearly there with me, yet she acted as though I were dirt beneath her shoes. And how messed up was that? I was Rune's girlfriend—at least, under the pretense of this charade—but Aidan didn't give two shits. What kind of person makes advances on someone who's spoken for and then goes on to belittle that person's partner?

A narcissistic bitch, that's who.

The water farther out began to roll higher, rushing toward the deck only to bleed out into the rest of the current before it could reach the patio.

I couldn't help but wonder as I watched the raging sea if it was wrong of me to be jealous of Aidan. Rune had blatantly rejected her, but hadn't he also said no to me? He and I weren't really dating. I had no claim on him. The thought made a crevice form down the middle of my heart. We'd been so close to giving into our mutual feelings.

So close to becoming a real couple.

So close to exploring what it meant to love each other.

My chest ached with the lingering fear that I'd never get the chance to really be with Rune.

The water below churned, and it smacked into the poles with a ferocity that shook the boards beneath my feet. The vibration brought me back to my senses, and I quickly focused on the chaotic movements of the sea.

Frantic to calm the sea that I'd clearly stirred up, I fought to take a deep breath. Panic blossomed in my chest, which only seemed to fuel the rampant waters below. My mind didn't stop racing, and before I knew it, a wave of water reached up toward me like a large arm stretching right out of the dark depths. I had to act quickly. Instead of wasting time trying to calm down, I decided to take action.

Keeping my arms close to me, I held my hands out toward the rising water and focused on the ripples. With the next breath I took, a buzz sparked in my hands. My heart suddenly beat in tandem with the push and pull of the waves. The water jerked as it fell under my control, and after it ceased its ascent and waited for my command, I took another steadying inhale.

"Lower and calm," I ordered in a firm whisper.

Within an instant, the water fell back to the ocean with a loud crack, and after tossing around for a moment, it returned to its normal movements once more. I let out a sigh of relief and slumped against the railing again. A smile lit my face as I felt a rush of triumph. I knew right then that the sensation of connecting to the water would never get old. It was exhilarating, like the first drop on a roller coaster.

It made me feel *powerful*.

I stood there for a few more moments, still giddy from the success I'd had. Ready to face everyone again, I turned to make my way back inside. The lingering power high I felt dissipated as I froze in my tracks. A beautiful, dark-skinned waitress watched me from the other side of the deck. She had her notebook and pencil poised to take the order of the two patrons sitting before her, but her narrowed eyes were locked on me, oblivious to their food request.

I swallowed hard. I knew the water had not risen high enough for anyone but me to see, so the most she could've witnessed was me holding out my hands. While that would look weird, there could be so many explanations for why I did that. There was no reason for her to think anything of it, yet with the way suspicion seemed to be growing behind her eyes, I knew it was best to leave.

Offering a polite smile, I quickly strode back inside, praying that my growing worry was for nothing.

CHAPTER

SIX

BY THE TIME WE MADE it back to Rune's family home, we were all stuffed full of the delicious crab-and-lobster dinner. We were thankful no one was in the foyer when we got back, because we'd had enough run-ins tonight. Our group made it safely to our rooms without bumping into any of the fearsome Foxes.

"Should we all get settled into our PJs then maybe hang out in mine and Bassel's room?" Akira asked as we congregated in the hallway outside our rooms. "Maybe we can watch some movies?"

"That sounds great," I said.

Avana nudged me and leaned in close to whisper, "Should I sneak downstairs and grab some wine? We can have girl talk."

I giggled, finding the idea so tempting right now. Akira bounced over to us and leaned in. "Whatever you two are cooking up over here, I'd better be involved."

Laughing, I looped my arm through his. "PJs. Wine. Gossip."

"Um, yes please. Meet up in thirty minutes?" Akira asked.

We agreed then parted ways for our respective bedrooms with Rune following me into ours. The door clicked shut behind him, and I turned as he made his way over to me. Tension polluted the air between us, but I wasn't sure of its source. Maybe it was the lingering sting of his rejection, maybe it was the frustration from our rude dinner guest, maybe it was suddenly being alone together in the same room. Or maybe it was all those things mixed into one.

"Are you okay?" Rune asked, his voice like sudden thunder in the silence.

I sank down on the edge of the bed and folded my hands in my lap. "I'm fine. Embarrassed. A little frustrated. But I'm fine. How about you?"

He ran a hand through his long, white hair and let out a sigh. "I'm pissed, to be completely honest. Aidan and her friends have always been prone to starting needless fights. I'm sorry about Talia and even Aidan. I knew my mother was going to play matchmaker, but I didn't expect her to have that potential partner stay here."

So many questions warred on the tip of my tongue. How long ago had he and Aidan last seen each other? How many times had they slept together? Each question was like a fresh sting against my skin, and they were all spurred by jealousy— something I didn't want to feel. I didn't want to play into that game and demand answers that I had no right to. I didn't want to let Aidan or her friends get under my skin more than they already had.

Meeting his eyes, I smirked. "Do you think Talia will let Aidan know what I said?"

Rune sighed and flopped down on the bed next to me.

"Probably. Talia loves drama. She's addicted to starting shit if you couldn't tell."

I leaned back on my hands and groaned. "Great. She sounds real nice."

"What Talia said was wrong, you know. Aidan isn't better than you."

I gave him a half-hearted smile. "I think that was regarding my abilities in the bedroom, not my character."

"Well, that comes with time. You'll learn and experience those things one day."

"Oh yeah?" I leaned in close, our lips mere inches apart. I glanced down at his mouth before meeting his now lust-filled eyes. "Are you going to be the one to teach me?"

He swallowed hard as the air between us became charged with desire. I'd only closed the gap between us and said that to tease him, but now that I was leaned in, our bodies close enough for his warmth to caress me, my mind clouded with want. Memories of his spellbinding kiss, the feel of his hands on my bare skin, the weight of him on top of me, elicited a sharp inhale. Need throbbed low in my core, and my fingers itched to reach for him.

"Rune," I whispered, my voice coming out on a strangled breath.

He tilted his head just enough for our lips to graze. It was a whisper of a kiss, a touch so light, I could've mistaken it for my imagination if not for the jolt of electricity it shot down my spine. As soon as the brush of his lips came, though, it was over, and he was pulling away.

Rune got to his feet, and he shot me a devious grin. "Don't tempt me. I don't have enough self-control to say no to you again."

I followed him, closing in until our bodies were almost pressed flush against each other. "What if I want to tempt you?

What if I don't want you to have self-control?" His eyes burned into mine as I finished, "What if I want you to teach me?"

He opened his mouth to respond, but the door to my room flung open. Newt and Greshim burst into the room, talking away about the different movies they carried. Heat climbed up my cheeks, and I quickly stepped away from Rune as the twins looked up at us.

"Big brother!" Greshim squealed, grabbing at Rune. "We didn't know you were in here, too."

"Ardley came and told us to join you for m-m-movies. We came to see what m-m-movie Bria wanted to watch," Newt explained, holding a stack of DVDs out to me.

Rune sighed and knelt down to look his brothers in the eye. "Guys. You can't barge into other people's rooms without knocking or asking permission. Bria could've been changing into her jammies."

Hearing Mr. Big-Bad-Alpha-Rune say the word "jammies" had a laugh bubbling up inside me, but I quickly pushed it back down.

"Oops," Greshim said, his face growing bright pink. He ducked his head in apology. "Sorry, Bria."

"Yeah. Sorry," Newt mimicked, frowning in a way that pierced my heart.

Rune nodded at the door. "Why don't you two try that again?"

The twins quickly turned on their heels and ran back out the door. As soon as it swung shut, two soft knocks came from the other side. I grinned at Rune as he stood up and nodded at me.

"Come in," I laughed.

The boys didn't hesitate to race back in.

Rune patted their heads. "Much better. Do that from now on, okay?"

After minutes of the twins showing me all the movie options, we finally decided on *Jurassic Park*. Rune wrangled the boys and took them next door so that I could change, telling me to take my time. It had been a long day, so I opted for a quick shower, too.

I stepped into the tiled, steam-filled room, and as soon as the first drops of water hit my skin, the tension in my shoulders seeped away. In its place was a calm caress, a quiet lullaby, a soothing promise. The water seemed to tell me that it was there for me should I need it. All I had to do was call out.

Rinsing away the stress of the day, I smiled at the memory of Rune scolding his brothers and then praising them when they corrected themselves. It made me wonder what he'd be like as a dad. He'd no doubt dote on his children, spoil them silly, and discipline them to be good people. Though children weren't something he had any interest in having, so the idea was a far-fetched one. Unless Myra got what she wanted, and he ended up with a fierce Fox Fae, not someone like me.

Water Fae and his sworn enemy. I was the very target he and his kind had been searching in vain for to annihilate.

The truth I was keeping from him sat heavy on my chest. I wanted to be honest at some point, but I was terrified of his reaction. He'd rejected me as a human. What would he say if he knew I was Water Fae, the thing he hated most in this world? The thing that stole his father from him.

He'd not only reject me.

He'd *loathe* me.

I shook the negative thought from my head since that was a worry outside of this week and turned off the shower before I accidentally made the bathroom into an indoor pool. God knew I'd had enough slip-ups with water today. It was while I got changed and wrapped my damp hair in a towel that I finally called Dallas.

"Gummy worm?" she shrieked as soon as she answered the phone.

Shaking my head, I groaned, "No. Not Gummy Worm."

"Well, I just wanted to be sure."

Gummy Worm was the code we'd agreed upon for this weeklong trip. It meant I was in imminent danger and needed help pronto. Dallas had no doubt been expecting me to call or text the signal all day, but she was mistaken. I was safe with my friends around. At least, I hoped so.

When I'd awoken as Water Fae, I'd sought out answers as to who and what I was from the only place I could: my best friend, Dallas, who also happened to be my personal guard—because I was the Water Fae Princess who'd been hidden away for my own protection. I was still trying to wrap my head around that one.

So naturally, when Dallas found out I was going on this weeklong trip with nothing but Land Fae around, she'd refused to let me go unless she came too. If all had gone according to plan, she'd have booked herself a room at an inn nearby and been keeping watch over me ever since we landed. I had a feeling she'd brought back up, too, which meant I'd have extra security watching me in public from the shadows. When I was in the house though, I was to have my phone on me at all times with Dallas on speed dial so that I could call in Gummy Worm if needed.

I leaned against the sink and let out a heavy sigh. "I wanted to hear your voice. It's been a long day."

"I heard. One of my guys said that some bitch harassed you at dinner."

I gave her the rundown on Aidan and Talia. "It's so frustrating that I feel like I'm having to compete with her."

"But you're not. Rune made it perfectly clear he's not interested in her, even with their history. He chose you, fake or not." She paused, then let out a groan. "I can't believe I'm defending a Land Fae. And a Fox, no less. What has the world come to?"

"Dallas," I warned.

"Yes, yes, yes." I could practically see her waving her hands dismissively. "You want us to get along with them, I know. This would be easier if I'd gotten to know them more than just that one time."

That time she referred to was the attempted robbery at the club those few months ago. It was what brought Rune and me together and allowed us to strike our deal—my help in exchange for his money for my art trip. This was also, of course, before I had realized Fae existed.

Rune and I had both changed so much in these few months, and it was crazy to think back on how we used to be. We'd gone from having instant chemistry to business partners who were constantly annoyed with the other to dear friends, and now ... Now I didn't know what the hell we were.

"Well," Dallas started. "I guess since you love him, I've got to learn to love him, too. Tell me about Fox boy."

A wide smile broke out across my mouth. She was putting their differences aside to give him a chance, because he was important to me. I loved her for it.

I tidied up the bathroom as I recounted the months with Rune and all the great moments. I gave her all the details about how I learned about Fae, my training sessions with Rune, and all the small things he did that meant the world to me. We laughed as Dallas reminded me how much she still hated his painting from our first date, which I'd hung proudly in our dorm room. She squealed over my dinner date on the deck of his boat—a date I never got to tell her about since that same night was the first night Jonah attacked me. It was also the night when Rune and I had first kissed. My favorite date of all though was only yesterday, the day before we'd left for the trip. He surprised me with a painting picnic, and I pretended that life was normal again after having just found out the truth about who I really was.

"Damn," Dallas sighed. "I'm gonna have to tell Rance to step up his dates."

I laughed before asking, "Do you have any updates on who hired Jonah?"

The true mastermind of my attempted assassination was still a mystery since Jonah was dead. Dallas and I had deduced that it must be someone in my close Water Fae circle since no one else knew who I was, but I'd yet to hear any news on her findings.

"None yet," Dallas sighed. "I passed that assignment to Dax since I'm focused on you right now. He's looking diligently into a couple of leads, but he doesn't have anything concrete yet."

Before I could answer, a knock came at the bedroom door. "Wait. Looks like I've gotta go. We're about to watch movies."

"No worries. We can talk later, and hopefully, I'll have more news for you then. Have fun. Take a shot for me. And Bria. Be safe. I love you so much."

"I love you, too, Dallas."

We hung up, and I opened the bedroom door to find Avana and Akira in their pajamas. Avana wore a gold silk sleep romper, and her dozens of braids were pulled back in a ponytail. Akira had on a traditional navy-blue yukata and some slippers.

"Sorry," I said as I shut the door behind me. "I was cleaning up the bathroom after my shower." I followed them to Akira's room, combing my fingers through my slightly damp hair.

Akira waved dismissively. "*Mondai nai.* The boys were downstairs making popcorn. Everyone just got in there."

Bassel and Akira's room was larger than mine. It had a formal sitting room that you entered into, and their bedroom connected to it. It was expansive with a couch and two love seats, as well as a separate seating area across the room in front of a fireplace. An entertainment center stood across from the couches, and the previews of the movie played on the flat screen.

Everyone sat about the couches in their human forms, including the twins, who wore matching dinosaur pajamas. I took my place at the end of one of the love seats. Newt crawled up next to me, and Greshim was by him, pulling Rune down on the other side. Rune and I shared a warm smile over the tops of the twins' heads before everyone else found their places, and the movie began.

If anyone was bored with the film, the boys definitely kept them entertained. They got so excited every time the T-Rex came on screen, and they hollered like the velociraptors at all the right moments. It was safe to say they'd seen this movie one too many times. The night was fun, and it made me crave more—more moments when we forgot a world outside of this one existed. It was times like this when I knew what it meant to have a family.

When the end credits started rolling, Ardley broke out a deck of cards. Another movie was put on, and Akira, Avana, and I took this as our cue to grab the bottle of pink Moscato and move to the chairs by the fireplace on the other side of the room. They also had me run to my room for my sketchbook, because they were eager to see my artistic skills in the flesh. Everyone else suited up for a game of slapjack.

"Thank God Myra had wine downstairs," Akira said as he plopped down in one of the plush chairs.

Avana knelt on the floor by the coffee table and uncorked the bottle. She filled three glasses and said, "Agreed. I think we all need it, especially you, Bria."

"Are all of Aidan's friends so pleasant?" I asked, sarcasm laced into my words. I opened my sketchbook to a new page and poised the pencil over the textured paper.

"Ha!" Akira laughed. "Undoubtedly."

"Part of it *is* in their nature," Avana explained as she sipped her wine. "Her friend group is made up of Foxes, who, as you know, are territorial and hot-headed, as well as Felines, who are sassy and always looking to start trouble."

"Hmm. I'm guessing Talia is a Feline?" I asked.

Akira winked at me and tilted his glass in praise. "Bingo."

I sighed and took a hearty sip of the bubbly, sweet wine. It went down easy, and I marveled at the taste. In the past, I never drank alcohol, but I'd slowly become accustomed to the taste of wine as Rune introduced me to different kinds. I rather liked the big girl drink now.

Slowly, I sketched rough, jagged lines of Akira and Avana as they sat in their respective places. A burst of contentment broke free in my chest as I moved my hand over the paper. It felt so good to finally be drawing something again. It didn't give me the same weightless warmth that painting did, but it was close enough for now.

"Can I say," Akira started, snickering from his perch. "I nearly *died* when you put Talia in her place. She's so immature. I just loved it."

The three of us laughed, and my cheeks heated at the reminder of the face-off. I still couldn't believe I'd had the courage to stand up to her, but gosh, it was so worth it. I refused to take that treatment from her or anyone else. Being bold felt good, something I'd only recently learned after Rune helped to instill a confidence and strength within me that hadn't previously existed.

"Bria?"

I turned from my place on the floor across from Avana to find Newt standing nervously at the edge of the ring of chairs. He fidgeted when we all looked at him, and his cheeks instantly reddened under the attention.

Smiling warmly at him, I said, "Hey Newt. Were you wanting to join us?"

He glanced at us from behind his crooked glasses. "Never m-m-mind. Sorry."

He started to turn away, but I quickly called out to him. "It's okay. You can sit with us. Right, guys?" I turned to Akira and Avana, who smiled just as brightly. They gave him reassurances that he was welcome, which made a spark of life erupt in his eyes.

I set my book and pencil aside to hold out my hand for him, and he took it with an eager grin. He sat beside me as our small group started talking again, planning things to do and things to see while we were in town—with Myra's permission, of course. Newt didn't talk much, but he seemed content to sit, smile, and listen to us.

Eventually, he opened up more as we talked about his favorite activities, and at one point, he ventured into my lap with his back to me. I beamed at the boy and ran my fingers through the long black tangles of his hair. He tilted his head back and fell quiet again while Akira informed me that Bassel and Carlos had secretly met for a minute before we left the restaurant.

"I hope they make up," Avana sighed. "They were both so happy together, and their energies match really well."

"Do you think they'll get together while we're here?" I asked as I started a braid in Newt's hair.

"Let's just say," Akira dropped his voice low. "I'm probably going to be waking up in the middle of the night to Bassel being gone."

We snickered and glanced over at Bassel, who'd just gotten slapped by Greshim as they fought to be the first to slap the jack. The boys whooped and hollered as Greshim giggled endlessly over the blow. Rune ruffled his brother's hair before looking across the room toward me. As soon as our eyes locked, the air between us became charged. His eyes were lit with a needy flame as he took me in, tracing my hands that combed through his brother's hair. I swallowed hard under the intensity of his gaze and quickly turned back to Newt's hair before I got swept away.

Finishing Newt's braid, I tied it off with a spare hair tie I had on my wrist. I gave him my phone so he could look at the finished product. "What do you think?"

His mouth broke into a wide grin. "I love it. Th-Thank you."

"Of course. I love playing with hair. It's relaxing."

He handed my phone back and turned around to look at me. Life shimmered in his eyes as he said, "M-My m-mother never plays with m-my hair. I've always wanted her t-to brush m-m-mine like she does G-Greshim's. Th-Thank you for doing it."

My heart fractured at the knowledge, but I kept my smile plastered on. Newt didn't want my sympathy. He only wanted to express how happy he was, and I refused to take that happiness away by reacting.

Swallowing the negative emotions, I squeezed him tighter. "Well, you can come to me anytime you want your hair played with or for anything else."

Newt skipped around the room to show off his hair. Akira, Avana, and I rejoined everyone for the next round of cards. Not even thirty minutes later, the games were over, and the twins were knocked out on my lap and Rune's.

Yawning, Bassel stood and stretched. "Well, I guess it's time to hit the sack. I'm spent."

"Mmhmm. I'm sure you're *so* ready for bed," Akira smirked.

Avana and I shared a knowing look and fought our smiles.

Everyone started to collect their things and move to their rooms. Rune stood gently with a sleeping Greshim tucked against him. He smiled down at me where Newt sat in my lap, his small head resting on my shoulder as he, hopefully, dreamed of nothing but wonderful adventures.

"Ardley," Rune whispered. "Will you carry Newt for me?"

Ardley knelt in front of me with a sleepy grin before carefully plucking the boy from my hold.

Rune readjusted his grip of Greshim as he turned back to me. "I'm gonna go put them to bed. I'll meet you in our room in a minute."

After saying goodnight to everyone, I made my way back to the room. The large space seemed to swallow me in silence after laughing and talking with everyone. I hugged my arms around myself, trying to ignore the overwhelming urge to flee. I didn't want to stay in this big room alone, so when I saw Rune's things still present, I sent up a silent thanks that he would be here with me.

At the same time, though, my nerves skyrocketed when I pictured Rune and me, under the same sheets, our skin pressed flush against each other, his body right next to mine. I swallowed hard as my mind played out different scenarios for what could happen if we really did share a bed.

Taking a deep breath, I steeled my resolve. If he were truly staying in here, I'd be bold like before and not hide away from what I wanted.

I looked down at my flannel pajamas, which weren't the sexiest thing in the world. Oh well. At least I'd showered earlier.

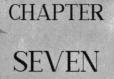

CHAPTER

SEVEN

I'D JUST FINISHED TURNING DOWN the bed when Rune walked into the room, locking the door behind him. My heart flared with excited nerves at the sound of the lock catching, and I gave Rune a questioning look.

Smirking, he said, "Despite my talk with them, I'm not confident that Newt and Greshim won't burst in here at the crack of dawn. I thought you'd appreciate some undisturbed rest."

Laughing, I plopped down on the edge of the bed. "They're fine. I'm glad they like me. I was worried about that."

"How could they not like you? You're amazing."

An uncontainable tug pulled up the corners of my lips, and a rush of warmth flooded my chest. Rune didn't give compliments freely, yet this one was so direct. The clear adoration in his voice sent my hopes soaring.

He moved closer until he stood right in front of me. "I want to thank you." There was a look glittering in his eyes and settled in the lines of his face. I realized as he spoke that it was respect.

I quirked a curious brow at him. "For what?"

"For being so good to Newt. Honestly, it means more than you'll ever know. I hate not being here for him. I hate leaving him with a monster of a mother. So, I'm really thankful for all the kindness you've already shown him."

"You don't have to thank me, Rune. I love spending time with him. I love spending time with both boys. It's like having two younger brothers, which is something I've always wanted."

Chuckling in that deep rumble of his, he made his way over to his suitcase. "Let's see if you still think that come tomorrow. I believe they're wanting to give you a personal tour of the home."

"Well, I look forward to it. I'm getting a VIP tour from two experts on the house. They'll most definitely know all the great hiding spots, which I'm sure I'll need eventually with your mother and Aidan lurking about."

Recalling the twins and the way Newt mentioned Myra's neglect, I nibbled on my lip and said, "Can I ask you something?"

"Of course."

"If Myra is so awful to the twins, why doesn't anyone do anything to get them away from her?"

Rune took a deep breath and ran a hand through his hair. "It's a tough situation. Fox Fae are brutal in the way they raise their young. A lot of Canine Fae are. So when Fae see strict, almost abusive upbringings, no one bats an eye. If anything, they encourage such parenting, because it will mold strong and powerful Fae for our kind."

My brow creased as I worked to understand why anyone, Fae or not, would appreciate parenting that belittled children or hurt them. I didn't care if it made them into badass Fae. It was still wrong. Newt and Greshim were just *kids*.

"Have *you* ever thought about taking them away and giving them a better life?" I asked.

"Absolutely, but I know if I were to take them, the three of us would have to spend our lives constantly on the run. Myra would hunt us down, because she is obsessed with power, and she sees Greshim as the next in line for our family, following me. I wouldn't want the boys always looking over their shoulders, afraid of the moment Myra shows up. It would be a death sentence for Newt and me. Since she has no use for Newt other than for manipulating others, she wouldn't hesitate to kill him and return with Greshim. It's safer for them to stay here. At least here, they're both alive and well for the most part.

"The only way they could be taken from Myra without issue would probably be if their father, Alvaro, did it. I'm not close with the man, but I do know his children are his world. If he wanted to take them away, he'd most likely be far more successful than anyone else. He hasn't made a move to do that, though, and I'm not sure if he plans to. He may not see an issue with the twins' upbringing."

My stomach bottomed out. It was so unfair. Newt and Greshim deserved better, but I also saw the risk that everyone would be taking if they tried to remove the boys. It was like having to pick between two evils—leave and never feel safe again while putting Newt's life on the line, or stay and accept the occasional abuse.

Heart heavy, I whispered, "They're really sweet boys."

Rune offered a bittersweet smile. "They are. I wish I was able to be here for them more."

"Maybe you can one day. Maybe Myra can change for the better, and you'll be able to be a family again."

Rune's lips quickly fell, and a sense of doubt seemed to weigh his shoulders down. "We'll see."

He shook off the gloom that had clouded the air between us and finally pulled a matching pajama set from his belongings. As he walked toward the bathroom, he yanked off the tags.

"Rune," I called.

He stopped and looked back at me.

Pointing at the garments, I asked, "Did you buy new pajamas for this trip?"

He glanced at them and gave me a sheepish grin. "Yeah. I don't own pajamas, so since we're sleeping in the same room, I bought some. I didn't want you to be uncomfortable."

I swallowed hard, heat pooling in my lower abdomen. "What do you normally sleep in?"

The innocent grin he wore suddenly changed with a playful and mischievous tilt. Without missing a beat, he held my eyes and answered, "Nothing."

His answer along with the memory of his bare skin made me want to see it again. I wanted to feel his body, run my hands along his broad shoulders, and press against his chiseled torso with my own. I'd made a promise to myself to go for what I wanted without fear or worry or embarrassment, and now was that moment.

"I don't want you to tiptoe around me. I'm fine. I want you to sleep how you normally would." My voice came out surprisingly confident and steady, despite the heavy thumping of my heart.

His golden eyes held mine, and the smile on his face slowly seeped away until he regarded me seriously. It was a dare from me, a challenge. I was throwing him the bait to give into what I wanted, and despite his denial, I was fairly confident he wanted it, too. The choice was his, and I held my breath as I waited for him to make it.

Without breaking my gaze, he tossed the new pajamas aside, where they fell somewhere to the floor. I was too busy watching him to track their final destination. He still wore the black button up shirt from earlier, and my breath hitched as he slowly unbuttoned each one. It was agonizingly delicious, watching his skin become exposed little by little until the dark garment fell away to the floor. The deep, sharp V of his abdomen disappeared beneath the waistband of his pants, and my mouth watered as he slowly pushed the trousers and his boxers to the floor.

His gaze never once left mine, even as he stood back up to his full height.

The brief glimpse I got of his naked skin before had nothing on seeing him fully exposed, and I unapologetically drank him in from head to toe. His broad shoulders gave way to a hard chest and sculpted stomach that was formed from centuries of combat. My heart tripped over itself when I reached his length, which had hardened under my visual caress, and I tried not to think about all the ways he could love me with that impressive shaft.

Ever so slowly, my eyes worked their way back up to his, where I found deep longing blazing in those amber depths. Face flushed, I forced out my words despite my strangled breath. "Good. As long as you're sleeping with me, I want you to do it how you always would."

Smirking past his obvious desire, he tilted his chin down. "Yes, ma'am."

I slid across the mattress so Rune could get in. My nerves were shot, and need pooled in between my legs. Rune climbed under the covers, the warmth from his naked skin radiating around me beneath the sheets. I was on my back, staring at the ceiling when he got settled. The yellow-tinted bedside lamp cast the room in a soft glow, and once he was firmly on his back, I rolled onto my side to face him.

"You never slept like this when I stayed over all last week," I said, referring to when I'd stayed at his house leading up to this trip. "Why? You're not shy."

The corner of his mouth tipped up as he tucked his well-formed arm behind his head. "Correct. I'm not shy. But, again, I didn't want you feeling uncomfortable coming into the living room if I were still sleeping."

My eyes trailed down the planes of his chest, down his stomach to where a trail of hair disappeared beneath the sheet draped over his waist. My cheeks heated, and I rolled onto my back once more as I fought to catch my breath. Liquid fire spread in my core, and I squeezed my legs against the sensation as I mumbled, "I'm uncomfortable."

He was still for only a moment. One minute he was lying next to me, and the next, he hovered over me. An unmistakable heat lit his eyes as his intense stare held me firmly in place against the bed. He sat back on his heels, taking the covers with him. The new position gave me a close-up view of the entirety of his nude body, which spurred the mounting inferno inside me. He gently grabbed behind my knees and pulled my legs up and apart until he was nestled in between them.

"What do *you* normally sleep in?" he asked. His voice came out deep and seductive, and he cocked his head to the side as he peered down at me. My eyes stayed locked on his as he lifted my butt effortlessly and guided my pants down my legs.

Swallowing hard, I forced out my words. "This. Normal pajama pants and a t-shirt."

"Hmm. You should try shedding some clothing. Maybe that will make you more … comfortable."

His knuckles grazed up my calves and thighs until he reached the waistband of my panties. My heart beat heavily against my chest, but I didn't stop him. My body craved this. My heart sang for him. My very being came alive under his caress.

I wanted more.

So much more.

He pulled the panties down my thighs, taking care to do so slowly, no doubt trying to make me even hungrier for him. It worked, too. His eyes finally left mine to look down at my legs spread before him, and while my first instinct was to cover myself, I didn't. Being looked at and touched in such an intimate way was new for me, but there was no one I would rather have doing it. This was the man I trusted. This was the man who held my heart in his hands. Because it was Rune, I kept my arms at my sides and let him look his fill.

And look his fill he did.

My skin ignited under his lustful eyes, and my center throbbed hot as he drank in the sight of me. The cold air hitting my parted legs made my already sensitive desire heighten, and I squirmed beneath him, desperate for the incessant ache to be satisfied.

Sensing my impatience, his gaze flicked back up to mine, and he leaned forward as his hands blazed a trail back up my legs and along my inner thighs where they came to rest, his thumb inching dangerously closer to my heated core.

He smirked, and his voice came out husky. "So wet."

His thumb struck, just grazing across my throbbing clit. The sensation produced a sharp exhale, one that came out before I could stop it. Pleasure seized me tight as he moved his thumb in a slow, tantalizing circle, and I gripped the sheets beneath me in tight fists. My hips started to rock against his finger of their own accord, and soft moans left my parted lips.

Rune leaned down, cupping my cheek with his free hand. "Shh, those sounds are mine. Don't let anyone else hear you," he purred.

A grin graced his mouth as he moved his hand from my jaw to trail a path along my bottom lip. He pressed his thumb along the seam of my mouth, and I bit down on his finger in an effort to keep my sounds at bay.

A greedy fire lit his eyes as he watched me sink into the pleasurable abyss that his one digit caused me. His own need was still very much present, and in the back of my mind, I wanted to know if I was able to make him feel the way he was making me as his thumb continued to graze teasingly along the edge of my clit.

"Do you really want me to teach you?" he questioned in a low voice.

He slipped his thumb free from my lips enough for my breathless response. "Yes. Please, yes."

"What do you want to learn?"

Another circle along my wet, throbbing core.

I moaned out my approval, and my eyes fluttered shut. "Everything."

Circle and a sharp gasp.

"I want to learn everything."

Circle and a strangled moan.

"I want to learn *you*."

He stopped.

My eyes snapped open and met his. I opened my mouth to protest the sudden absence of his touch when he leaned down. His lips merely skimmed mine in a sensual tease as he whispered, "Lesson number one."

He gripped my hips and moved his warm hands to my inner thighs. He parted my flesh, his breath against my sensitive core eliciting a shiver along my spine. I watched him as he looked up from between my legs. The intensity of his eyes held me in place as I felt the first flick of his tongue against my throbbing need.

A fire erupted in between my legs, sweeping every part of me in pure ecstasy. My head fell back, and I groaned against the pure pleasure swarming my entire body. His tongue was relentless in its pursuit, and my legs quaked from the building pressure at my core. With every up and down flick of his masterful tongue, my breath hitched, and electricity zipped across my middle, making me tingle and ache in the best way possible—in a way I never *knew* was possible. I tightened, curled, throbbed, and then erupted as my climax forced breathless gasps from me.

Pleasure still gripped me tightly as Rune sat up. His eyes were glazed in pure want. He gripped his large shaft, which glistened with drops of desire, and I watched him in utter awe as he pumped himself over top of me. His breath became labored as he neared the edge of a cliff, and in moments, he fell into the waves of bliss, grunting as cum spilled from him and onto my bare stomach where my shirt had ridden up.

He collapsed next to me, both of us still fighting for air. Never in my life had I felt pleasure like that, and my heart was hyper aware of the fact that Rune and I had just crossed a line neither of us could come back from.

And I didn't want to.

Rune already had my heart, even if he wasn't ready to give into that or put a label on what we were. There was no regret to be found. Just the opposite. I was *happy*. My head resided in the clouds, and my body warmed from the inside out, all because of him. I couldn't possibly contain the bliss that filled me to the very brim after sharing something so intimate with him.

Rune took a deep breath and sat up on his elbow to peer down at me. Admiration clouded his eyes as he looked at me, and his mouth curved in a lazy grin. "Wait right here."

My eyes were glued to his well-rounded ass as he retreated into the bathroom. The shower clicked on, and after a few minutes, Rune reappeared, hair dripping wet, rivulets of water dripping down his chest toward the towel wrapped around his waist.

He sat down on the bed with a warm, damp washcloth, and my heart leapt into my throat as he began to clean me off. His movements were slow and gentle, and he took care to be thorough. I didn't know someone could touch me with so much tenderness, and when I searched his face for some sort of hint as to what he was thinking, all I found was devotion in those amber eyes.

If there had been any doubt in my mind before on whether or not Rune felt the same way as me, there was none left now. I could see his feelings in his gaze, feel it in the way he touched me, and hear it in his voice. I didn't need the declaration of love from his lips. Because, really, what were words in the grand scheme of things when actions so clearly spoke another language? His actions showed me all I needed to know, and I was beyond content with that for now.

Smiling with my head still stuck in the clouds, I said, "If that was lesson number one, I'm going to need to prepare myself for lesson number two."

Laughing, he used the towel around his waist to dry me off. "Good thing we have plenty of time for you to get ready."

I let his words wrap around my heart in a sweet cocoon. I didn't argue that he had denied us of such a thing earlier. Instead, I let both of us finish riding out this wave of pleasure and satiated longing we'd been harboring. When we woke up tomorrow, he may realize what he'd said and try to brush it away, but I wouldn't. I'd tucked this moment away in my heart, and I wouldn't regret it, even if he did.

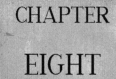

CHAPTER

EIGHT

A SINGLE THREAD OF LIGHT filtered through the curtains on the French doors. The warmth from the covers urged me to fall back under sleep's spell, but when I rolled over, I snapped out of my stupor. Beside me, Rune's cheek was turned into the pillow, his arms tucked beneath it. His lips were parted slightly as he dreamed of unknown tales. He'd shifted at some point during his sleep into his Fae form, so I got a clear view of his two sharp canines and black-and-white fox ears.

Last night came rushing back in a dizzying blur, and I bit my lip to keep my smile contained. Heat pooled in between my legs as I recalled the way he'd touched me, tasted me, *devoured* me. It was a perfect moment, and I was pleased that I felt no shame or regret this morning. I was still just as sure of my decision to trust him as I'd been last night.

Wanting to let Rune sleep, I carefully got

out from beneath the blankets and tiptoed across the carpet to the bathroom. After relieving myself, brushing my teeth and hair and throwing clothes on, I crept out into the hall. Akira and Bassel's door was cracked, and I could hear the soft sound of some show on the TV.

I knocked quietly on the door before Akira said, "Come in."

He lounged on the couch in his Raven Fae form as he watched a cooking show, and his black eyes brightened as soon as he saw me come in. "Well, good morning, Bria-chan."

Grinning, I flopped down beside him as he tucked his wings close to his back to make room for me. "Good morning to you, too. Is everyone still asleep?"

"Ardley is downstairs making a pot of coffee, but other than him, yes. Bassel will probably be knocked out for a while. He had a rather late night."

"Oh, really?"

We shared a knowing smile. Akira's instincts had been right. I loved that Bassel was going after what he wanted. He deserved to be happy, and Carlos seemed like a really sweet guy. I hoped things worked out between the two of them.

"Speaking of late nights," Akira said with a curious tilt to his head. "How did sharing a bed with Rune go? Anything juicy happen?"

Crimson heat crept up the side of my neck and onto my cheeks. Clearing my throat, I played with a strand of my hair. "It went fine."

Akira bounced on the couch, nearly taking me out with his feathered wings as he spun to face me fully. He grabbed my hands, and his eyes glittered with excitement. "I know that look. Tell me everything. Don't leave a single thing out."

Laughing, I tried thinking of a way to explain what had happened without getting too graphic, but the door opened. Ardley walked in with a tray of coffee cups and a pot of coffee.

His face lit up when he saw me, a dimple appearing on his cheek, and his fluffy fox tail swished excitedly behind him. "Look who's up. Morning, gorgeous."

Akira let out a frustrated groan, and he picked up a throw pillow, launching it at Ardley. "*Kuso*! You couldn't wait five more minutes before coming in?"

Ardley ducked, narrowly missing a pillow to the face. "Woah! What gives? Hot pot of coffee over here."

Akira rolled his eyes and leaned closer to me to whisper, "We'll save this conversation for later."

Ardley set the tray on the coffee table and flopped down next to me, his fox tail nearly landing in my lap. "How'd you sleep?"

"Good," I said. "You?"

He shrugged and smirked mischievously at me. "I would've slept better if I had some company. Maybe we can—"

"Ardley," Rune snapped.

We all turned to find Rune, still in Fae form, standing in the doorway, and his eyes narrowed on his cousin. Any trace of amusement was nonexistent as he stalked toward the couch, his clawed hands flexing at his sides.

Chuckling, Ardley held up his own hands. "Sorry, sorry. I can't help myself. She's a beautiful, single girl. Can you blame me for trying?"

"She's not si—" Rune stopped, and anger pulled his shoulders taut.

My heart and mind got hung up on the last part of his sentence. We all knew what he'd started to say, and every fiber of my being sparked to life with that near declaration. It was happening. He was stumbling over his decision to stay friends, and that knowledge made my heart dance wildly in my chest.

Rune took a deep breath and met Ardley's eyes. "Just knock it off."

Ardley slapped his legs and stood. "Well, I guess I should move then."

"You'd be guessing correctly."

Ardley clapped Rune on the shoulder as he walked by and whispered something in his ear. Rune's brow furrowed at whatever Ardley said, and conflict warred in his eyes. Ardley pulled back to nudge Rune one last time before flopping down on the love seat.

Curiosity gripped me tight. All thoughts about the shared secret disappeared as soon as Rune's eyes finally met mine. The internal battle that was previously apparent disappeared. A weightless light filled his eyes and brought a smile to his lips. Those intimate moments we'd shared came rushing back. Heat crept up my cheeks, and I offered a smile so that I wasn't just staring at him awkwardly. The jitters in my stomach only heightened when he moved toward me.

"Good morning," Rune greeted as he came to stand near me.

"Morning." My voice came out far smaller than I meant it to, and I mentally chided myself. I was confident in my decision, and I didn't want my tone to suggest otherwise.

He poured a cup of coffee and handed me the steaming mug, which I happily accepted. After filling his own, he sank down on the cushion next to me. The parts of my body closest to him electrified with awareness, and I found myself leaning in closer to his side.

The four of us sat around and discussed our plans for the day—mine and Rune's consisted of tea with his family at eleven, followed by a tour of the house with the twins—as the rest of our group slowly trickled in with sleep still clouding their features.

"Thank Zanahary there's coffee," Avana said with a large yawn. The iridescent shine of her Chameleon Fae skin rippled blue and green as she reached for a mug.

Marlow followed closely behind her, stretching his arms wide. The two of them got coffee and sat around the other love seats. Bassel finally joined our party almost thirty minutes later, but it was only because Marlow sneaked into his room and scared him.

"Looks like Sleeping Beauty finally decided to grace us with his presence," Akira laughed.

"Hardy-har-har," Bassel mocked, dropping heavily onto the seat by Ardley. His thin liger's tail landed in Ardley's lap.

"Late night?" Rune asked, smiling from behind his mug.

Ardley plucked Bassel's tail from his lap and draped it over the liger's firm thigh, though Bassel hardly seemed to notice. Bassel laid his head back, and his eyes drifted shut. "You have no idea. Can someone pour me some coffee so I can drown myself in caffeine?"

While Akira poured the last of the brew for Bassel, Rune nudged me. I turned to him as he said, "You and I are expected downstairs for morning tea soon. We should probably get ready."

Unease seeped into my veins, but I tried to ignore the foreboding sensation. Instead, I nodded and followed him to the door. Akira's and Avana's smirks were not lost on me either as I left the room with Rune. As soon as we were alone in our room, my body became charged with his presence. It was the first time we'd been alone and conscious since last night, and I couldn't help but feel a little nervous. I wasn't sure what I was supposed to say or do, but even more than that, I wasn't sure what *he* was going to say or do. Part of me was afraid he was going to brush off what happened and reiterate that we were simply friends, while the other part of me was drowning in hope that it would send us in a new direction for him. Though, if it did succeed in spurring us into a more real relationship, that created a countdown for my telling him the truth about being Water Fae, which I still wasn't prepared to do.

Rune turned to me, his eyes glittering as his gaze traveled from my feet to my eyes. He squared his shoulders as if preparing for a physical blow when he asked, "Are you okay?"

"I'm great. Are you okay?"

Laughing, he rubbed the back of his neck. "I'm good, yeah."

Pursing my lips, I crossed the space between us until I stood directly in front of him. Holding his worried eyes with confidence, I gave him a reassuring smile. "If what you're really trying to ask is do I regret what happened, the answer is no. I don't regret it, Rune."

Relief instantly seeped into the lines of his face and the hunch of his shoulders.

Taking that as a positive sign, I asked, "Do *you* regret it?"

"Hell no," he said with a wide smile. He wrapped his arms around my waist and pulled me tight against him.

A tingling warmth cocooned my heart. I'd never get used to being in his arms. Our bodies molded together like we were two puzzle pieces finally conjoining, and my body hummed a contented tune while he held it. This was the place I loved to be.

Wrapping my arms around his neck, I said, "Then stop fretting. I'm great. You're great."

His mouth suddenly morphed into a frown, and his features turned serious. "I'm not great. In fact, I'm really struggling right now."

Concern clouded over my previously high-spirited mood. I searched his face for any signs of what had suddenly changed. "Why? What's wrong?"

He sighed and pressed his forehead to mine. "We now have less than thirty minutes alone, but I need way more than that for all the things I want to do to you."

Sickly sweet flames lapped at my core, and I bit my lip as I pressed further into him. "Maybe later."

"Definitely later."

He placed a kiss on my neck, which sent a delicious shiver down my spine. I wanted to pull him back into my hold, lock the door, and spend all day lost in each other. But I also knew doing so was not smart. We had people as cuddly as cactuses waiting on us.

We parted to get ready for the day, with Rune taking the bedroom and me the bathroom. I wanted to take a shower, but I wasn't sure how smart that was with Rune right in the other room. It would be just my luck to have something go wrong and Rune walk in to find me in a water suit instead of my birthday suit. Until I found the right time and way to tell Rune the truth, I didn't need any slip-ups with water. What I *did* need was guidance. My ability to confidently harness my powers was nonexistent. It was still so new and confusing. I needed help figuring out how it worked, as well as better ways to control it.

As I finished getting ready, a thought occurred to me. Formulating a plan, I quickly shot Dallas a text before meeting Rune back in the bedroom.

He wore dark jeans with a black button-up. The fit of the material left little to the imagination, and I second guessed my decision to not lock ourselves in the room.

Bad Bria. No fornicating right now.

Clearing my throat, I said, "I guess we should run next door to have Avana get me ready."

We quickly met back up with the others in Akira's room where Rune stood tall in his Fae form, and Avana did her magic. Tingles erupted along my skin in the targeted places, and within seconds, I too looked like a Fox Fae. Two fox ears were erect on either side of my high ponytail, and a fluffy black-and-white tail flicked behind me against my knee-high black dress.

Ardley gave a low whistle from the couch. "Damn. You really do look fine as hell as a Fox."

Rune opened his mouth, no doubt to rip his cousin a new one, when Akira quickly interrupted to say, "It's 10:55. You should probably head to your doom and gloom family meeting. Wouldn't want to be late."

Anxiety climbed up my throat. The idea of sitting down with Rune's family had always been nerve-wracking, but having that time finally be here amplified that emotion to new levels. I knew Rune would be right there next to me, but having a room full of fearsome Fox Fae staring me down and judging me was becoming harder to stomach. The closer Rune and I drew to the sitting room, the more I floundered on the inside. What if my Fox Fae illusion didn't hold up? What if I said the wrong thing? What if my emotions got the better of me, and I accidentally made someone's tea jump right out of their mug?

"Ready?"

I looked up at Rune to find him watching me with a steady confidence. We were outside the closed oak doors that led to the sitting room, and I knew that right on the other side was a whole group of people eager to assess me. They were ready to find any flaw they could, yet as Rune looked at me with nothing but respect and trust, I found my anxiety dwindling.

Rune believed in me, and it was time I did, too. I had trained for this. I'd worked tirelessly to learn what it meant to belong in his world, and I *did* belong here. I was Fae, damn it. I was a *Princess*. And I was worthy, Fox Fae or not.

Holding my head high, I nodded. "I'm ready."

Rune opened the door, and I strode inside the expansive sitting room with the grace and prowess of a Princess. All eyes found me, but instead of crumbling beneath their immediate scrutiny, I smiled and continued to stand tall.

"Good morning," I greeted, and I was pleased with how boldly my voice came out.

Myra sat in a high-backed chair by an empty fireplace, and her golden eyes followed me over the rim of her teacup as Rune and I took the open spaces on a couch. Across from us was a couple I recognized from photos Rune had shown me—

Sinopa and Crevan, Rune's aunt and uncle and Ardley's parents. Aidan sat on a chair between ours and Sinopa's and Crevan's couch. Aidan's hostile gaze tracked my movements and Rune's.

"I'm glad you could join us," Myra said. She waved her hand at the tea and array of sandwiches and treats on the coffee table in front of us. "Help yourselves."

"Where's Ardley?" Sinopa asked. Her glossy black hair was piled in an updo around her erect onyx fox ears. She narrowed her brown eyes at Rune and said, "Did he not come down with you?"

Rune leaned back against the cushion of the couch with a look of ease. "He didn't. I think he decided to skip out on this little get-together."

Crevan sneered, his sharp canines glistening. "That boy."

Sinopa shook her head and let out an exasperated sigh. "I can never make him listen anymore. Really, Myra. You must tell me your secret on how you manage to get Rune to obey at this age."

Myra grinned coyly, and her eyes left Rune to find a picture on the mantle of Rune and the twins. "Oh, a mother has her ways."

I gritted my teeth to keep from lashing out at Myra. For her to sit there and be proud of how she manipulated Rune at the expense of her other children was repulsive.

"Where are Grandmother and Grandfather?" Rune asked, and I noticed that despite the evenness in his voice, his shoulders had grown tighter. It seemed he hadn't missed his mother's message, either.

"They'll be getting in later today, as will Alvaro," Myra answered as she set her teacup on the table beside her. She folded her clawed, manicured hands over the skirt of her dress, and her eyes found me once more. "So, Bria. I'm afraid we know very little of you."

"Yes, why is that?" Sinopa asked skeptically.

"Because she isn't an accomplished Fox, clearly," Aidan said snidely. She tipped her chin higher and scanned me over in the same way someone might look at a pile of week-old trash.

Forcing a polite smile, I ignored Aidan and addressed Sinopa. "I've not been involved in Fae affairs for some time. After my parents, Blayze and Seraphina Bowen, were killed, I spent much time in hiding for my safety. The Water Fae who killed them, as well as other Fae, believed I had died with them, and I had to keep it that way."

"So you were a coward," Aidan said as she studied a scone that she'd taken from the tray in front of her. "Instead of tracking the Water Fae down and annihilating them, you hid like a spineless weakling." Her eyes snapped to mine as the scone in her hand erupted in flames before falling to the floor as mere ash.

Rune went rigid next to me, and he leaned forward with a growl building in his throat. He was about to explode and come to my defense, but I quickly placed a clawed hand on his thigh to keep him in place.

This was my fight.

Holding Aidan's bitter gaze with my surprisingly calm one, I said, "You say it's cowardly; however, the cowardly thing to do would've been the *easy* thing. Sure, I could've gone after them. It would've been the natural thing to do. Give chase, slaughter, and keep being angry. I made a choice to do the opposite. Instead of doing what others would've expected, what my very nature begged of me, I chose to walk a different path, one that led me to where I am today. I chose forgiveness, and *that* takes far more courage than giving in to anger and what it would ask of me."

Aidan's brow furrowed as she seemed to weigh my words, but she quickly shook away the idea and said, "That's not very Fox of you."

"Isn't it, though?" Rune asked, placing his hand over mine. I turned to find him watching me, and my heart quickened when I saw the awe warming his eyes. "Foxes are the embodiment of strength. What's more powerful than compassion and grace? I think we've focused on one meaning of strength for so long that we've forgotten all the forms it can come in, and it's Bria's strength—her heart, her kindness—that drew me to her. It's what made me realize she was the perfect and only Fox Fae for me."

A fresh wave of emotion stole my breath. Hearing Rune say something that felt so genuine while looking directly into my eyes left me feeling like the moon and all the stars had just been gifted to me. Yet at the same time, I felt robbed of air, because right now, it was Rune and his Fox Fae girlfriend sitting here, not Rune and *Bria*. We were putting on a show, but his words felt so *real*. They confused the hell out of me as I searched his eyes for whether they were true or not.

I swallowed hard and remembered that we were still being watched. Rune had said his mother would be overly skeptical if we were too affectionate, so I glanced at Myra to see if we'd gone too far with our speeches, hand holding, and intimate eye contact. My entire body froze when I saw the look marring her features.

Grief.

That was the first word that came to mind when I saw the subtle yet poignant crease to her brow. Her typically alert gaze was glazed over with a faraway look as she stared at mine and Rune's clasped hands. Everyone else was so busy staring at Rune and me in disbelief that no one seemed to notice the anguish seeping into the lines of Myra's face, but *I* saw it. It wasn't my imagination.

As I sat there wondering what had evoked this surprising reaction from Myra, Sinopa finally snapped out of her shocked stupor and said, "The kind of Fox you describe doesn't sound very powerful, Rune."

Sinopa's words seemed to bring Myra back from wherever she'd gone, and both she and Rune turned to Sinopa.

Rune's jaw hardened, and his hand tightened around mine. "On the contrary, the kind of Fox I describe is not only fitting for Bria, but it's the same kind of power held by another Fox we all knew and respected. A Fox Fae we were all lucky enough to have in our lives while we did. Would you call *him* weak?"

The question seemed to silence the entire room. No one dared to move or speak. No one but Myra.

She shot to her feet, and her previously sorrowful eyes suddenly blazed like a fire that had been fed gasoline as she narrowed that look at Rune. Her eyes flicked to me with unhindered loathing before the look abruptly vanished all-together. Her features smoothed over as quickly as they'd hardened, and she held her chin high as she strode to the door. "That's enough visiting. I have work to do."

Aidan quickly got up to follow Myra from the room like a persistent puppy following its master. Sinopa and Crevan stared at the doorway where the two women had left, but before they could make a move to do the same, Rune leaned forward to rest his elbows on his knees, leveling irate eyes on his aunt. "You didn't answer me, Sinopa. Would you call Balgair weak?"

The hairs on my arms stood at the cold animosity in Rune's voice. Even more chilling was the realization that Rune had been referring to his father, and he'd been comparing the kind of Fae I was to the kind his dad had been.

Myra's reaction made much more sense now as she seemed displeased with the idea of my being like Balgair. I wondered if it was because she knew someone like Balgair was better suited for Rune, meaning she'd been wrong in choosing Aidan. Or maybe it was because any reminder of Balgair hurt her. I briefly thought back to how she'd seemed consumed by sorrow when watching Rune and me together. Perhaps Myra had truly loved Balgair, and now, any reminder of him and that lost love sent her to a dark place she wanted to avoid at all costs. Memories of him made Myra *feel* again, and the woman had grown so accustomed to *not* feeling that now she was afraid to do so.

Just like Rune.

Silence blanketed the room, and Rune let out a low growl as he hissed, "Sinopa. Was. Balgair. Weak?"

Sinopa swallowed hard, and fear seemed to actually flash across her brown eyes. In a small, quiet voice, she answered, "No. He was not."

Rune nodded. "Then I suggest you refrain from referring to Bria as such."

Rune stood and offered me his hand. I gladly accepted it, and together, we left the sitting room just as confident and strong as when we'd entered it.

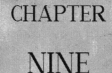

CHAPTER

NINE

WHAT A FUCKING MORNING," ARDLEY said with a low whistle. "Now I kinda wish I'd gone to witness this myself."

Rune and I had just finished telling everyone how tea had gone. We were back in Bassel and Akira's room, and everyone sat around in amazement.

"I'm glad that shut them up," Akira said, wrapping a proud arm around my shoulders.

"For now," I added.

I knew the scrutiny was far from over, though everyone seemed placated for now. Comparing me to Balgair did seem to make me untouchable in a certain sense since questioning my level of Foxness would essentially question his, and I was sure the only one who would dare do so now would be Myra.

"You two are doing the tour with the twins now, aren't you?" Bassel asked.

"We're supposed to," Rune said as he glanced at the clock on the wall, which read 12:35. "They were supposed to meet us in here at noon."

"Maybe they lost track of time," Avana offered.

Rune and I shared a worried look. I didn't think either of us crossed a line during the family gathering, but it wasn't sitting right with me that the twins were running late right after the tense interaction.

"Maybe we should—"

My words were cut off as a knock came at the door. Rune nearly leapt for the door with me right behind him. Newt and Greshim stood there, and it looked like they'd been in the middle of whispering something between each other when the door opened.

As soon as they saw us stepping out into the hall, Greshim offered an apologetic smile. "Sorry for being late. Mother wanted us for some training practice."

Newt kept his attention on Greshim as he spoke, leaving his head turned so that we couldn't see the left side.

Stomach plummeting, I gently said, "Newt?"

He glanced at me, and when he did, his head turned just enough that I caught a flash of red on his cheek.

Inhaling sharply, I asked, "What happened to your cheek?"

Rune knelt down and gently grabbed Newt's chin to turn his head. A fresh cut like that from a clean swipe of a blade ran from the corner of Newt's nose toward his ear. Newt quickly pulled free from his older brother's hold to look away from us.

"It's fine," Newt grumbled.

Rune's face contorted with barely contained fury. "It's not fine. What happened?"

"It was an accident," Greshim said quietly. His eyes were trained on the floor with his shoulders hunched. "I tried to go easy on him, but Mother kept pushing me to fight like I meant it."

Newt grabbed Greshim's arm and tried to make his twin look at him, but Greshim refused to tear his eyes away from the floor. "I'm fine, G-G-Greshim. It's alm-most healed. I know you didn't m-m-mean it."

Rune's jaw worked as he no doubt tried to reign in his anger. We'd both assumed Myra had been behind the wound, which she was in a way. Instead of physically hurting Newt herself, she'd forced Greshim to do it. The cheerful, carefree boy from yesterday had all but disappeared, and I wanted nothing more than to wrap him in my arms where he would be safe and loved.

Rune reached forward to place a hand on Greshim's shoulder. The little boy glanced up as Rune said, "It's not your fault. We all know how Mother can be when it comes to training. I know you both hold back as much as you can. Don't let her break you or the bond you have. You're stronger than that. I know you are." Rune paused a fraction of a second before asking, "Are both of you okay?"

The twins nodded.

Rune studied both of them for another moment before finally taking a deep breath and standing. "Then let's have some fun, just the four of us. You wanted to give Bria a tour, right?"

This seemed to bring some life back to the boys' eyes, even Greshim's. Newt grabbed my hand and pulled me after him while Greshim walked alongside Rune, who lovingly ruffled his little brother's black locks. Greshim swatted Rune's hand away with a small laugh as he tried to fix his hair, and Rune chuckled at his efforts.

It seemed Greshim and Newt had all but forgotten about their troubles, for which I was grateful. I was glad Rune and I could provide that distraction.

We started on the third floor, and the twins explained that this was the guest wing. Across the long stretch of hallway—in the east wing of this floor—was Rune's old room. Curiosity reared its head, and I desperately wanted to explore that wing. That clearly wasn't part of the itinerary though, because we by-passed that wing in favor of heading downstairs to the second floor.

Rune and I listened as the twins animatedly told me about themselves and all their memories with their older brother. My personal favorite was the time the twins were bored inside the house during a thunderstorm. Rune had gathered both boys, dragged them outside in the pouring rain, and started a game of wet, muddy tag. They'd played for hours, and when they were done, Rune made them hot chocolate and huddled them by the fireplace to close out the day with s'mores and movies.

We reached the second floor and had started for the twins' room when two Fox Fae came up the set of steps at the other end of the hall. Greshim and Newt immediately went quiet. They stood straighter and moved in closer to me and Rune. I froze and held my breath as the newcomers strolled in our direction. Recognition sparked the closer they got, and I recalled their faces from the images Rune had me study back when first preparing for this charade. It was Lilith and Devoss, Rune's grandparents. Which was weird since they looked like they would be in their mid-to-late forties.

My God, Fae aged beautifully.

At least that was one thing I had to look forward to.

Lilith's long, black gown trailed behind her, and her gait was tall and proper. Devoss strode next to her in a dark suit with his head held high. Each of them met my stare with narrowed eyes, their curiosity evident on their pinched faces.

"And who are you?" Lilith demanded. She remained poised with her clawed hands folded in front of her and an unrelenting scowl on her face, which displayed her canines in all their sharp glory.

I plastered on a polite smile and said, "Hi. I'm Bria."

"She's my girlfriend," Rune added.

Devoss gave a slight chuckle as Lilith raised an eyebrow at me. I swallowed hard, feeling Greshim and Newt lean further into my legs. Rune snaked his arm around my waist, which provided the reminder that he was there. I wasn't alone. Even so, I had no idea what to do or say. All I could remember was that, when it came to his grandparents, I was not supposed to speak unless spoken to first.

"Grandmother, Grandfather," Rune started to fill the sudden silence. "You're both looking well."

"Hmph," Lilith grumbled. "As are you. I have to admit, though, I don't understand. You've chosen someone of such poor taste when your mother has a fine Fox picked out for you. What are you thinking?"

I fought to keep my face stoic despite the deep cut her words inflicted. It was hard being so blatantly criticized and insulted. Especially since they were comparing me to Aidan. They didn't know me, yet they were already passing judgment on who I was. I couldn't put my finger on what I'd done wrong in the short minute we'd been standing here, but I guessed just my presence upset them. I was an unwelcome guest in their world of perfection.

Rune's face turned hard, and his shoulders went rigid. "Bria is from a well-respected bloodline. You'll do well not to insult her, especially not in front of me."

Lilith scoffed at Rune's effort to defend me, and she brushed past me without a second glance. "We shall see about that. Something's off. I can feel it. There's something wrong about her."

Chills crept along my back. Could she tell that I was a fake? I suddenly worried that something was wrong with my illusion. Maybe something wasn't placed right, or perhaps part of it was fading. I tried to calm my racing heart as my eyes followed her into the room to where she'd been heading. She left the door cracked, no doubt waiting for her husband to join her.

I turned back to Devoss, who now stood directly in front of me. He searched my eyes, then said, "I'm not quite sure what everyone is making a fuss over. Obviously, there's something good about you, otherwise Rune would never have given you a chance. It may not be obvious what that is, but there has to be *something*. Keep your chin up, and show everyone that you are worthy to be in our presence."

He moved past me to join his wife. I stood frozen, staring at the place where he'd just been. My mind worked to process what had happened, and his authoritative voice continued to bounce around in my head. I had a weird suspicion that was Devoss's passive-aggressive way of being nice.

When the door to Lilith and Devoss's room shut, Newt and Greshim stepped back and looked up at me. Greshim crossed his arms over his chest and tilted his chin up in the air, distaste written in his features. "You should've told them off, Bria. There's nothing wrong with you."

I smiled down at him. "You think so?"

"Of course!" he exclaimed, throwing his hands up into the air.

"Now let's keep g-g-going," Newt said, linking his hand in mine once more.

Rune gripped my other hand. "Hey." He dropped his voice low enough so only I could hear him as the twins chattered. "Don't let what my grandparents said get to you. They're just old bats who wouldn't know anything good, even if it hit them in the face."

His words were a small comfort in the stinging wake of their rejection. Normally, having two strangers dislike me wouldn't affect me so much; however, it was the degree to which I'd already been so flagrantly dismissed and disrespected by everyone that made this hard to swallow. I'd known I'd be starting off in a negative place since I wasn't Myra's pick, but I hadn't realized how far back from the starting line that meant. The reality versus what I'd conjured in my head was far harsher, which made it feel like I was swallowing needles when around Rune's family.

I wasn't going to let their dislike of me win, though. I was prepared to do exactly as Devoss said. I'd keep my head held high, and I'd prove myself worthy of being by Rune's side. Because I *was* worthy, just as he was worthy to be by mine.

Squeezing Rune's hand, I said, "I'm fine. You think two elder Fox Fae scare me? I've faced *you* and come out alive. I can face anything."

He chuckled, and his eyes glittered with a fresh wave of need. He glanced at the boys, who had drifted ahead of us. He leaned in close, and his warm breath against my ear elicited a fire within me as he whispered, "I want to taste you on my tongue so badly right now."

My face instantly pinkened, and I bit my lip as his words brought last night rushing back. His tongue coasting up the seam of my pussy. The tip dancing just shy of my clit then barely flicking over the sensitive bud. Need gripped me tightly, and I wobbled on my feet.

"Hey," Greshim shouted.

I quickly stepped away from Rune to clear the sensual fog from my head, and I found Greshim glaring at his older brother with his arms crossed.

"No telling secrets," Greshim pouted.

Laughing, Rune ruffled Greshim's hair. "Sorry, sorry. I won't tell any more secrets."

We continued with the tour, which helped to clear my thoughts of intimate moments with Rune. The second floor consisted of the families' rooms and lodging for their guests. The twins' room was on this floor as well, but we skipped it for now. They wanted to save it for last. Because according to them, it was the best room in the house.

The first floor housed the formal sitting rooms, the dining room, a library, the kitchen, and Myra's private wing. We bypassed that section of the home, but the rest was stunning. Everything looked right out of a Jane Austen story—ornate cornices along the ceiling, pristine sconces lining the walls, and columns at certain entryways—with a few modern touches that Rune explained were his doing, including the TVs on our floor.

I thought with the end of the first floor, the tour was over, but I was surprised to find there was a whole other level to the home. In the basement, we explored a large room that looked much like the training facility Rune and I had used when he taught me self-defense and combat. Blue mats littered the floor, and weapons hung on the far wall, ranging from daggers to bows to … *was that a* scythe? I swore some of the weapons even had dried blood still caked in spots.

"This is where we all come to train," Greshim explained, slapping the mats with his foot. "Mother said we have to be strong and ready for an attack at all times. We've gotten really good at fighting."

"Some better th-than others," Newt mumbled as he glanced at his twin.

My stomach tightened with unease. Newt and Greshim were only ten years old, yet they were already being taught to fight and kill. And I had a pretty good hunch that their target was Water Fae. What kind of things had they been told? What had they been through as they worked to understand what it meant to kill Water Fae? I found Newt's perfectly healed cheek as I realized I'd seen first-hand some of what they went through. My heart squeezed as I wondered what these two sweet boys would think of me if they knew the truth. Would they hate me as they'd no doubt been taught to?

The lingering thought gave way to another that had been plaguing me.

Rune.

We'd come far in our relationship, and he'd grown a lot in how he viewed Water Fae. He'd admitted once before that while he still didn't trust them and wanted payback for the death of his father, he also had hesitations about killing them now.

When faced with Dax, my Water Fae ex, Rune hadn't taken the chance to kill him, and instead, had helped me since I'd just been attacked by Jonah. Before us, he wouldn't have allowed Dax another breath. More than that, when Rune had been suspicious of whether or not I was Water Fae, he'd blatantly admitted that he couldn't hurt me, let alone take my life. I only hoped when I finally told him the truth, he'd still choose me over his hate.

"It's a really nice training space," I said in an effort to not be swept up by my worries.

"Isn't it?"

My blood ran cold at the newcomer's voice. We all turned to find Myra striding out of a room behind us. She'd traded in her gown from earlier for form-fitting trousers and a tunic. Her long hair had been braided, and it swayed behind her with her tail as she approached the mats.

"This room has seen the evolution of many Fox Fae, the newest addition being Greshim," Myra said as she stopped by her son.

Greshim stood tall and stared up at his mother in the way a soldier might stand at attention for their commanding officer.

"You fought well earlier," Myra said to Greshim. Her amber eyes flicked to Newt, who hovered a few feet away with his hands twitching at his sides. Myra's eyes narrowed on him. "You're still weak and need to work harder."

Red hot anger sizzled in my chest, and it took everything in me to remain expressionless.

Newt's back straightened. "Yes."

"Yes what?" Myra hissed.

"Mother," Greshim started. "You know he can't say his—"

"Silence!" Myra snapped at Greshim, who jumped at the boom of her voice. She turned her fiery gaze back on Newt. "Yes *what*?"

Newt swallowed hard, and his lips trembled. "Yes, M-M-Mother."

"Say it properly," Myra hissed as she stalked toward Newt.

My eyes widened.

This evil woman!

The unease coating my skin was morphing into rage with every passing second. Newt had a stutter! He couldn't help that, and to demand he fix it on the spot was cruel. My clawed fingers dug into my palms, creating burning pin pricks in my skin. I couldn't stand by and watch as she closed in menacingly on the trembling boy, but before I could make a move to intervene, Rune stepped forward, getting in between Newt and Myra.

He leveled his bitter eyes at his mother, and his voice came out eerily quiet as he said, "That's enough."

Myra smirked and tipped her chin up. Her eyes never left Rune's as she said, "You won't always have your brothers to protect you, Newt. Remember that."

"He's still young, Mother," Rune said. "He won't see real battle for a while, so he has time to grow. You don't need to be so harsh with him."

"That's how I teach," Myra said. "It's how I ensure our bloodline remains powerful and fierce."

Rune's eyes narrowed in challenge. "It wasn't always how you taught."

Myra's mischievous smirk melted away, replaced with a cold, venomous sneer.

Rune's words were another reminder of the past, of *Myra's* past, and how she used to be. I couldn't be certain, but his words implied that Myra used to teach and train in a much different way, most likely when Balgair was still alive. The suggestion of this distant history triggered a fresh wave of simmering rage in Myra, and that's when my suspicions were confirmed.

Myra's weakness was Balgair.

I tucked that information away in case I needed it later.

As mother and son faced off in a silent battle, Myra's features slowly smoothed until she wore a blank mask once more. Without a word, she turned and slowly approached the wall of various weapons.

"Bria," Myra said cooly with her back to me.

My heart dove into my stomach as I took a deep breath. Being Myra's target after she'd just been set off surely didn't spell good news for me. "Yes?"

"I'm sure you've seen your share of battles, yes? Despite hiding?"

I glanced at Rune, whose attention was on Myra's back.

"I have," I finally said.

She turned back around with a long sword now in hand, and my nerves skyrocketed as light caught on the silver blade. "What is your preferred fighting method?"

Fuck. Me.

She was about to challenge me.

I knew she was.

And that definitely *wasn't* good news.

I couldn't fight Myra. She had centuries of battle experience, and that was something I couldn't fake, even with the little combat training Rune had shown me. I felt sick to my stomach as Myra gave a test swipe of her sword, and the mental image of me being on the other end of that lethal weapon nearly brought me to my knees.

If I were really about to fight Myra, I needed to choose a fighting option that excluded weapons and fire, because I obviously couldn't conjure that up, either.

Squaring my shoulders to mask my dread, I answered, "Hand to hand combat."

Myra smirked as she stalked back across the mats until she stood directly in front of me. Rune let out a low growl and stepped in our direction, but before he could close the distance, Myra lifted the sword and pressed the point at Rune's chest. I inhaled sharply as Rune froze. Myra never looked away from me as she smiled and said, "Let's see your skillset in action. You'll battle Rune."

My panicked eyes locked with Rune.

That had not been what I was expecting. I'd assumed Myra would want the pleasure of attacking me, but instead, she wanted to watch from the sidelines as she pitted lovers against each other.

Just like how she put Greshim and Newt against one another.

Rune bared his teeth at Myra. "Mother, we're not—"

"Would you rather watch your brothers fight?" Myra asked as she finally slid her gaze to Rune. Her devious smirk made my blood boil. "I'm sure they would love to spar again for their big brother."

"Rune and I will battle," I said quickly. I bit the inside of my cheek to keep from following that sentence with, "You fucking bitch."

Myra grinned and lowered her sword. "Excellent. You can change in that room behind you," Myra nodded toward the room she had appeared from. "I look forward to seeing your abilities firsthand."

CHAPTER

TEN

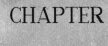

I EMERGED FROM THE CHANGING room after Myra *kindly* let me switch out of my dress and into breeches and a tunic.

Kind my ass. That word and Myra don't belong in the same sentence.

The twins stood at the side of the room with their mother, while Rune waited barefoot in the center of the mats. His face was impressively blank, and I could only hope that I seemed as unbothered as he did as I finished tightening the ponytail in between my fox ears.

I squared off with Rune, and he closed the space between us. He dropped his head until his cheek pressed into mine, and his lips brushed over the shell of my ear as he whispered, "You're going to have to fight me. She will know we're faking if you don't give it your all. You won't hurt me, so don't hold back."

I swallowed hard and nodded.

Rune pulled back to look into my eyes, and for a split second, his mask of ease cracked, showing me the angry, worried mess he really was right now. I knew my own gaze mirrored the emotions swarming his, because I didn't know how far Myra was prepared to take this. Was she going to threaten Newt to spur us into fighting to the point where one of us was bloody and broken on the floor? I couldn't be sure, and I choked on the uncertainty.

"Enough stalling," Myra said from where she watched impassively next to the twins.

Rune and I took measured steps back, and as I watched him get in his defensive pose, my heart clenched painfully. Seeing him like that took me back to a happier, simpler time when Rune and I trained. We'd spent countless hours practicing combat techniques and self-defense skills, as well as how to kill a Fae. That space had been *ours*, and it was always a safe, warm place.

Now that same experience was being used as a way to hurt and manipulate.

"What are you waiting for?" Myra asked, raising an impatient brow at me.

Taking a deep breath, I moved, lunging at Rune with a quick swipe of my arm. He leaned back, narrowly avoiding being clocked in the cheek. He retaliated with a swing of his own, one that I recognized from our training sessions. I maneuvered around him, avoiding the blow to my abdomen, and with the next string of Rune's quick jabs and movements, I realized what he was doing. He was using the exact steps and motions that he'd used when we trained so that I knew how to avoid being hit. It was the same movements we'd practiced over and over, so as we continued to punch and kick at the other, we kept meeting each other's blows with calculated blocks.

My breath came out fast and hard as sweat lined my brow. Rune had thwarted another of my kicks to his side when Myra huffed and said, "You're holding back. This looks like child's play. I said *fight*."

She swung her sword as though to punctuate her words, and the tip barely grazed Newt's ankle. He hissed and bit his lip as tears welled up in his eyes, but he kept his shoulders back and head held high next to his mother. Greshim glanced warily from his twin to his mother to us. The warning was clear. If Myra didn't see real fighting soon, there would be consequences.

Rune gritted his teeth and turned to me again, and I nearly wobbled when I saw his eyes clouding in desperation. We were being backed into a corner, and our options to get free unscathed were growing slim. His expression seemed to plead with mine, reminding me of his earlier instructions.

You're going to have to fight me. You won't hurt me, so don't hold back.

Biting the inside of my lip with my fox canines, I steeled myself for my next move. Darting forward, I faked an attack from the left side, and while Rune raised an arm to block it, I delivered a blow on the right, my claws slashing four gashes into his neck. Blood seeped from the razor thin marks, and I bit back a whimper. Hurting Rune, seeing him injured and bleeding, caused me physical pain, and it was that shock to my system that made me miss Rune's fist coming at me.

His knuckles slammed into my midsection, making me double over as the wind was knocked right out of me. Rune's eyes flashed in alarm, because he no doubt expected me to avoid his attack, but he also couldn't stop to check on me. Not with Myra still watching and Newt right there for her to use against us. Rune's leg swung toward me, aimed to smash into my face from where I was doubled over, but thankfully, he moved just slow enough for me to anticipate it. I rolled to the side, avoiding the blow, and I pushed past the throbbing in my stomach to stand.

At the same time, I caught movement out of the corner of my eye. My stomach pitched forward as I saw Myra slowly lifting her sword, the tip inches away from Newt. His tear-filled eyes followed the blade as it moved from his feet, up toward his chest. Myra still wasn't satisfied, and she was ready to push for more.

Desperate to satisfy her somehow, I swung my fist at Rune's face, but he caught it in one hand as the other snapped out to grip me by the throat. The air moving through my lungs froze, and my wide eyes locked on Rune's frantic gaze. A thousand emotions flashed across them, the next more potent than the last—alarm, hopelessness, anguish. Myra knew he couldn't refuse this battle or turn against her with the immediate threat to his brothers still present. He was at a loss as his mother forced him to choose—his brother or me. His arm trembled, and I fought for air and a way out of this for the both of us.

Thinking on my feet, I gripped Rune's shirt with fumbling fingers and yanked him forward, until his mouth pressed to mine. His body went rigid at my abrupt kiss, but his grip on my neck loosened enough for air to snake its way back into my lungs. Rune groaned as I deepened the kiss, and with his sudden lapse in attention, I quickly pulled away and dropped down, swinging my leg out as I did. Rune's legs went out from under him, and he smacked onto the mats with a grunt. Before he could recover, I climbed on top of him and slammed my fist into his chest over his heart and gave a twist.

It was the move we'd practiced for so long when training together, the one that would be a deadly strike to an opponent had I been wielding a dagger. This fact wouldn't be lost on Myra, which meant this battle was over. Recognition flared in Rune's eyes as his chest rose and fell heavily beneath my hand.

Giving him a faint smile, I found myself repeating the same words from those happier moments long ago. "You shouldn't get distracted when in a fight. Isn't that Basic Fighting 101?"

Rune's eyes closed, and the deep rumble of his laugh made my heart sing. Much like before, he suddenly grabbed my arms and rolled to pin me beneath him. He swallowed hard as he stared down at me, and an ache that was almost tangible seemed to grip his features as he leaned down to press his forehead to mine. "Are you okay?" he whispered.

I nodded slowly, focusing on the warmth and weight of his body pressing to mine. It was a reminder that we were both still here. We were both okay. Rattled, but okay.

I glanced at Myra from between Rune's hair, which mostly shielded our faces from view. I found her sword hanging limply by her side as she stared at us with much the same look she had worn back in the sitting room. Whatever she saw in Rune and me right now made her leave the present for some distant memory, and she became a wilted flower.

"Is it a draw?" Greshim asked, as he subtly grabbed Newt's hand and pulled him closer to his side.

Myra seemed to snap out of whatever head space she'd been in as Rune got to his feet. He offered me his hand, which I took.

"It wasn't a draw," Rune answered. "Bria won, though she cheated to do it." He smirked and nudged me in the side.

Laughing, I placed my hands on my hips and raised a brow. "Sounds like something a sore loser would say."

We came to stand in front of Myra, whose face had been stripped of all emotion. Her seemingly lifeless eyes glanced between the two of us.

"I think that's enough sparring for today," Rune said evenly as he addressed Myra. "Don't you?"

Myra's eyes narrowed a fraction. "For now."

She returned the sword to its place on the wall, and our group watched as she retreated up the stairs the way we'd come. As soon as she disappeared, I bent down to look at Newt's ankle where Myra had cut him. The cut had already healed, which made the tightness in my chest ease a fraction. That meant the wound hadn't been severe.

"Thank you, Bria," Greshim said.

I looked at him in surprise. "For what?"

"For fighting so that we didn't have to."

Offering him a warm smile, I placed a reassuring hand on his shoulder and squeezed. "Of course. I just wish there was more I could do."

"We're fine," Greshim said with a wave of his hand. "Mother can be loud and expects a lot at times, but she's teaching us to be strong warriors. It's rare for her to hand out physical punishments."

"Yeah," Newt said as he rubbed at his healed ankle. "She's only extra strict and m-m-mean when big broth-ther or fath-ther are around. Oth-therwise, she m-m-mostly ignores m-me."

Rune's face fell as though he'd been gutted. "I'm sorry."

"Don't be," Greshim said quickly, reaching up to grab Rune's hand. "We love it when you come into town."

"We really m-m-miss you when you aren't here," Newt said as he leaned in to hug his older brother.

Rune's eyes squeezed shut as he got down on his knees to pull both boys into his arms. "I miss you guys, too. More than you know."

Wanting to give the brothers privacy for this intimate moment, I quietly slipped away and into the changing room. I sank down onto a bench by my clothes, and the gravity of everything I'd just seen, heard, and did hit me with the force of a freight train. My fight with Rune had been a tense and strenuous one, far more so than any practice session we'd had, and the blow to my gut had been just as excruciating as when Jonah had nailed me there in one of his previous attacks.

I tugged off the tunic and looked down at my throbbing stomach. Thankfully, there were no bruises surfacing on my skin, because I was sure if Rune saw evidence of his punch, it would devastate him all over again. God knew I didn't want to see the marks I'd left on him.

I stood, inhaling sharply at the protest in my limbs, and carefully stepped out of the slacks. As I reached for my dress, the door opened and shut behind me. I quickly went to cover myself, until I realized it was only Rune.

Sighing in relief, I let my body relax. "You startled me. I thought the twins were coming in."

He shook his head and slowly started for me. "They're waiting on the mats."

I nodded and quickly slipped on the black dress, pulling my fox tail through the opening in the back of the garment. Thankfully, Avana and I had prepared one in almost all my clothes for the trip. "Are they okay?"

"They're fine. They're tough, far more than most kids their age. But then again, that is the way of Fae." Rune's fingers curled around my chin and forced my eyes to meet his. His usually deep, confident voice broke as he asked, "How badly did I hurt you?"

I shook my head and placed my hands on his chest. "You didn't hur—"

"Don't lie to me," he growled, a mix of anger and agony pinching his brow. "I didn't mean—"

"Exactly," I said. "You didn't mean to. Everything that just happened was Myra. We were put in the middle of her sick game, and I don't blame you for any of it. I'm *fine*."

His eyes searched mine. For what? I couldn't say. Perhaps he was trying to decide if I was lying, and if that was the case, he'd come up empty. I was truly okay, because he and the boys were all safe. We'd narrowly avoided Myra's wicked trap, and because we had, all was fine. I just hoped we'd be as lucky the next time our paths crossed.

Rune took a deep breath and finally released me. "If you're sure, we'd better get back out there. The twins are eager to forget this whole shit show happened and continue the tour."

I blew out a tired breath. "I think that's a splendid idea."

"You know, your hits packed a decent punch today. Have you been secretly working out?" Rune chuckled.

He was teasing me, yet the joke made a fine layer of sweat break out on my brow. My Fae strength must've slipped through in some of my jabs.

I forced a smile and nonchalantly flipped my hair over my shoulder. "Better watch out. I'm becoming a secret badass, Rune Beckett."

"I look forward to it," he answered, holding the door open for me.

We rejoined the boys, who were happy to resume our interrupted tour. Greshim pointed at all the different doors here in the training facility, explaining what was behind each.

Newt tugged on my hand, pointing down a hallway. "Th-There's m-m-more. Th-This way."

Happy to finally be leaving the training room, I followed Newt down the short hallway. There was a closed door at the end of it, and the closer we got, the more a soft hum started up in the back of my head. It was like melodic voices whispering amid the soft trickle of water, urging me forward.

As soon as Newt opened the door, I realized why the whispers had started. Bright, fluorescent lights reflected off an indoor pool's surface, and the strong smell of chlorine invaded my nose. My eyes locked onto the large pool, and the water immediately began to slap against the concrete's edge as if someone had jumped in.

"Woah," Newt whispered, watching the churning of the water.

I wanted to groan, because I knew I'd done something to unsettle the water, but I had no idea what. Maybe it was because of the stress induced by the Myra confrontation, or maybe it was something else entirely. Trying to think quickly with Rune and Greshim coming down the hall and Newt inching closer to the pool, I focused on the water until I felt that familiar warmth spread throughout my limbs, ending in the tingling of my fingertips. Recognizing that I was now in control, I silently commanded the water to calm. In mere seconds, the water stilled, becoming a lazy, peaceful pool once more.

"Are you two okay?" Rune asked as he came up behind me. His worried eyes flicked between Newt and I.

Clearing my throat of any trace of nerves, I said, "Yeah. I think we opened the door too hard. Either that or your house is haunted."

"Cool!" Greshim cheered. "I wouldn't mind living in a haunted house!"

"I would," Newt said as the color drained from his face.

Laughing, Rune hoisted his younger brother into his arms. "Don't worry. If it's haunted, I'll get rid of all the ghosts for you."

Greshim crossed his arms and glared at Rune. "Party pooper."

I glanced back at the water as the boys began to bicker. It remained steady like a pool should be, but I couldn't help but feel on edge. That was a large pool. One wrong move, one burst of emotion, and I could accidentally do something crazy—and considering my already rattled state, the idea wasn't improbable. Part of me was being ushered in its direction with a need to dive right in, while the other half of me wanted to book it out of there. It wasn't a good idea to be here; not without knowing how to manage my powers.

"Earth to Bria," Rune said, his warm breath kissing the back of my neck as he came up behind me. He wrapped me in his arms, hugging my back to his chest, and he leaned into my ear to whisper, "You all right? You zoned out there."

Smiling, I sank into his hold. His touch seemed to physically ground me, and it evaporated almost all worries and thoughts of water. The storm of fears, anxieties, and what-ifs quieted inside of me. In its place, strength, confidence, and bliss blossomed.

Glancing over my shoulder at him, I said, "I'm fine. I was just thinking about how cool it must be to have an indoor pool. I love swimming."

A playful smirk lifted his lips, and I saw mischief brewing in his fox eyes. His arms tightened around me, and he cocked a brow. "Oh really?"

Sensing what he was about to do, my smile dropped. "Don't you dare."

In the next instant, Rune swooped me up into his arms, my feet leaving the safety of the ground. His deep laugh filled the space between us as I tried to wiggle my way free from his hold. Even with my increased strength, it proved to be no match for his. He swung me back then tossed, my body flying through the air before sinking into the depths of the water.

The cool kiss of the water swept around me, and I felt a surge of power rush through my limbs. The bubbles from my splash clung to my skin, and the humming returned tenfold. The whispers of the water were now words, clamoring around my head in order to be heard.

Use me.

Control me.

Princess.

I squeezed my eyes shut against the onslaught of voices, and it was hard to find my own amidst them all. Just as I was about to surface, I found my inner voice and urged the whispers to be silent. The incessant chatter stopped at the same moment I reemerged. My breathing came out labored as I treaded the water and tried to fight to stay calm. My mind was running all over the place, but I couldn't let those thoughts overwhelm me. I had to keep a level head, especially since I was now floating in my current greatest weakness.

And greatest strength.

Rune stood by the pool edge, clutching his midsection as he laughed. He fought to catch his breath, and I immediately began plotting ways to get revenge. The twins beat me to it. They rushed him from behind and slammed into the back of his legs, sending all three of them into the water.

As soon as they resurfaced, we all looked at each other before breaking out into fits of laughter. Our clothes were soaked, Newt's glasses were somewhere at the bottom of the pool, my limbs throbbed from my match with Rune, and my powers were still an ever-present worry.

But none of that mattered in this moment.

What did was how much fun we had, splashing each other, twirling about the water, and diving deep before resurfacing. The water, thankfully, didn't react anymore. Maybe it was because it could sense I wasn't in danger, or perhaps it still obeyed my earlier command to be silent. Either way, I momentarily let go of all my troubles—even if only for an afternoon.

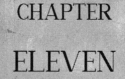

CHAPTER

ELEVEN

"WELL, THAT WAS FUN," RUNE said, shutting the door to our bedroom.

Grinning at him over my shoulder, I finished digging through my suitcase for a change of clothes. We were still soaked to the bones, no doubt leaving a trail of water through the halls despite our attempts to towel off. The smell of chlorine clung to my dress, hair, and fur, so I decided a shower was in order.

"I'm glad Avana's illusion didn't wash away," I said, touching the damp fox ears that were still firmly in place on my head.

"It's like she explained before. The illusion can last roughly twelve hours. It doesn't wash away like paint. Unless she removes it, you should be fine."

"That's definitely a handy-dandy ability."

Turning to face him, I was suddenly aware that we were alone since Newt and Greshim had gone to their own room to get cleaned up. My heart quickened from an onslaught of nerves and anticipation. This was the first time we'd been alone all day without someone waiting on us or standing nearby, and the sudden privacy for just the two of us swept me up in thoughts of golden skin, electrifying kisses, and husky whispers.

Rune stalked over to where I stood. His warm eyes held mine as he wrapped his strong arms around me, pulling me close. "I know I said this before, but I want to say it again because I don't think you understand how much it means to me. Thank you. Thank you for treating my brothers with so much kindness. Even though I can't be here for them the way I should, they're everything to me. So to see the way you make them light up and forget—" he paused, swallowing hard. A surge of raw affection bled onto his features as he held my gaze and finished, "Thank you, Bria."

I smiled and ran my hands along his broad shoulders. "They're really good kids."

"They are. Even with a mother like Myra. I think it's because they have each other."

"Or maybe it's because they have a brother like you to look up to."

The room seemed to melt away as we held each other's gazes. The deafening silence was almost overwhelming. I wasn't sure if I wanted to break it or have it go on forever so that we could stay here, locked on each other. His hand skimmed up my hip, along my side, over my breast, and onto my neck. The cold, wet dress warmed everywhere his palm caressed me, and I held my breath as his thumb brushed my bottom lip.

He inhaled deeply and leaned down to press our foreheads together. "You're ruining me."

I tilted my face toward his so that our lips were only a breath away. "Am I ruining you or ruining the promise you made with yourself to keep me out?"

He pulled back enough to look down at me. Frustration. Longing. Pain. Adoration. Fear. All those emotions flickered through his gaze as his eyes searched mine for an answer as to what to do. An answer he already knew.

My voice was barely a whisper. "Just give in, Rune."

The hesitation left him. He crushed his mouth to mine, and the air in my lungs stilled. His kiss was rough and full of need like he was trying to brand me with his lips. I wanted this heat, this fire, this passion. I parted my lips, giving him entrance, and his tongue swept across mine. I met his kiss with the same intensity, and his groan sent a shot of desire straight to my already wet pussy. His canines scraped teasingly along my bottom lip, and I nearly came undone from that alone. My own elongated canines nicked my tongue and his, creating the subtle taste of copper, yet even that couldn't stop our hunger for each other.

He cupped me beneath my butt and lifted me in one fluid motion. Our wet bodies pressed firmly together, and I wrapped my legs around his waist, not leaving his mouth for one second as I looped my arms around his neck. There was no coming up for air, not when that meant this kiss had to end. My bones had turned to jelly, and my heart nearly beat out of my chest. He was pulling a deep-seated need from me, and I wanted to give it all to him.

We moved, and I was vaguely aware that we were heading to the bathroom. Once there, he set me on the edge of the sink, and our kiss finally broke enough for him to reach down and pull my dress off over my head. The wet material smacked on the tiled floor somewhere, but I barely noticed. I was too focused on the way his ravenous eyes traced every curve of my body, every inch of exposed flesh—and fur, since my illusion tail was draped next to me on the countertop and my ears stood erect atop my head. He had me throbbing for his touch as his fingers made feather light touches along my bra straps.

His heated eyes met mine. "You are so gorgeous. Every part of you. Absolutely stunning."

116

I was breathless and slick with desire. I wanted to pull him back to me and keep kissing that wicked mouth, but he was rooted firmly in between my legs, watching me as he pulled off my bra. I didn't hide away from his blatant attention. In fact, I soaked it in. The way he looked at me was as if he were taking in the most stunning piece of art he'd ever seen. He made me feel beautiful and confident, despite my insecurities. His gaze empowered me, so I let him take in his fill before he reached for me again, kissing me breathless once more.

Butterflies danced around my stomach as his hands drifted up my inner thighs, and a shiver traveled along my spine from his touch. I leaned further into him, and he responded with a brush of his finger over the heat in between my legs. I gasped against his lips, wanting to feel his skin actually on mine, not through the fabric of my panties.

Want.

"Rune," I moaned against his mouth, pushing my hands into his damp hair. "I want—"

Him.

"What?" He nipped my lip playfully and slid his finger across the middle of my soaked underwear. "What do you want?"

Need.

His lips closed over mine, and I gasped against his mouth as overwhelming desire clouded my brain. The warm pads of his hands coasted up my hips, over my stomach, and finally cupped each breast. My thoughts scattered as he trailed his mouth from my lips to my jaw and along my neck. I leaned back on my hands, reveling in his touch and the sensations it elicited, when my hand hit the spigot of the sink, and I realized it was dripping.

The sudden feel of water had me glancing over my shoulder, and my stomach dropped. The sink was off, but a steady, silent stream of water slipped from the faucet. The water was crawling up the sink bowl and along the counter, headed right for us.

Heart racing with dread, I gripped Rune's shoulder as his tongue caressed the budded peak of my nipple. My toes curled from the pleasure in my core, momentarily distracting my focus on the water creeping toward us.

Glancing at the water, which now climbed up my back in a cold trail despite my sitting up, I forced my mind to reach out to the water. Easier said than done, because *God*, Rune's tongue was skilled. As soon as I felt the tingle along my skin—the magical kind, not sexual … well, maybe sexual, too—I silently urged the water back into the sink and down the drain.

Another flick of Rune's tongue had me gasping, and I lost what little hold I had on the water. Instead of going down the drain, the water swelled and rushed across my bare back and down my arms. It was creeping close to my hands, which were still clutched tightly to Rune's shoulders.

I panicked. Any second now, Rune would look up and see the water starting to coat my skin like puzzle pieces linking together, and my secret would be out. I couldn't let that happen. I wasn't ready to reveal what I was, because I wasn't ready to lose him, which meant I had to act fast. A pit formed in my stomach at my only option left.

I focused on the water again as the buzz erupted along my fingertips. I held onto that connection and pictured the water rolling away and down the drain as I commanded with a firm voice, "Stop."

The water instantly halted and receded down the drain, but with my command to the water, also came Rune's rigid pause. His breath froze against my skin, and his caress stopped. Slowly, he pulled back until his eyes found mine.

My heart pinched tight when I saw the confusion distorting his features and the worry clouding his previously euphoric eyes. The belief that he'd done something wrong was written all over his face.

Forcing a smile to ease his concern, I ran my fingers through his hair. "Sorry. It's just that I realized the twins could finish cleaning up and come here to hang out any minute. We wouldn't want them walking in on us like this."

My attempted grin faltered at the hurt that flashed briefly across his face. The lie burned on my tongue and festered like an open wound in my chest.

The bedroom door was locked. He knew it. I knew it. We both knew there was only one way he could read my words. As an excuse. A rejection. The idea pained me, but I had to let him believe it or risk accidentally summoning the water again but in a greater magnitude, which would get me caught. Telling the truth was an option, but as soon as I started to form the words, they got lodged in my throat under the weight of fear. I couldn't bring myself to say them out loud.

Not yet.

Rune quickly recovered from the blow, and he smiled, although the expression didn't even come close to reaching his eyes. "Right. You're right. I'll leave you alone to get ready. I'll be in Akira and Bassel's room when you're done."

I couldn't find my voice to respond, so I nodded and covered my bare chest. My heart squeezed as I watched Rune walk away. I so badly wanted to call out to him and take back what I'd said, but I couldn't. I couldn't afford to give him the truth yet. So instead, I watched in agonized silence as he moved to leave.

When he got to the threshold of the bathroom, he kept his back to me. His voice came out low and rough as he said, "I'm sorry."

I opened my mouth to tell him he had nothing to be sorry for, but before I could, he was gone. My head fell into my hands. What had I done? He'd finally let down some of his walls and given into what we both desperately wanted, and I'd rejected him. At least, that's how he was probably perceiving it, because I had done nothing to correct him. I'd promised him I wasn't going anywhere and that he could trust me. I'd reassured him that if he gave me the chance, I'd prove opening himself up to his feelings would be worth it. Yet when he'd made progress in allowing those feelings to take root, I'd grabbed hold of the roots and yanked with the little effort it took to say, "Stop."

I'd hurt him.

Anger gripped my heart tightly as I leapt off the counter and turned toward the sink. "Why did you do that?" I shouted at the last few drops of water in the bowl. "Nothing was wrong! Why did you react? I don't understand!"

I collapsed to my knees and rested my head against the cabinets. I was frustrated, confused, and so *angry*.

Angry at the water.

Angry at my secrets and lies.

Angry at *myself*.

I hated that I found it so hard to be open. Here I was, trying to convince Rune to be honest with himself, yet I couldn't do the same.

I was Water Fae.

I was the Princess.

No amount of avoiding water or lying about it would change who I was. I had to let go of the human version of myself, because that girl didn't exist anymore. She never had. If I wanted Rune to open up and come to love me the way we both wanted, I had to be honest with him and myself. If he were going to love me, he would have to love me as the Water Fae Princess.

As painful and dangerous as it may be to come clean, I couldn't hide anymore.

I had to tell him the truth.

Tonight.

Freshly showered and clothed, I stood outside Akira and Bassel's room. My new found resolve to come clean acted like armor against the doubts, fears, and worries trying to pierce through me. I could do this. I was a damn Princess for fuck's sake. Granted, I had no idea what that truly meant or how to be one, but that was another problem for another day. Right now, I had to focus on taming the heart of my fox, which started with the truth.

Taking a deep breath, I poised my fist to knock when the voices on the other side of the door made me pause. Leaning against the wooden frame, I listened to what I recognized as Rune and Akira.

"Here's some water," Akira said. "Can you please tell me what's wrong now? You're as pale as a ghost."

There was a pause before Rune said, "I'm such an asshole."

"Did something happen?"

"I pressured Bria. That's what happened. She wasn't ready, and I made her uncomfortable. I'm so fucking pissed at myself! How could I do that to her? After all she's been through? God, I can't even face her. I'm such a bastard."

I covered my mouth with my hand to stifle a gasp. Rune thought he had forced me into moving too quickly? My God, that couldn't be further from the truth. I wanted him. I was the one who'd initiated our physical direction. Sure, I thought he could've taken what happened as a rejection, but I didn't consider that he might perceive it as his *forcing* me. Hearing how much he loathed himself right now over something he wasn't guilty of shattered my very soul.

I moved to go into the room and explain everything to him when two sets of pounding feet came barreling down the hall. Newt and Greshim nearly crashed into my legs when they stopped running, and their smiles were nearly contagious as they looked up at me.

"Bria!" Greshim said. "We're glad we found you. Do you want to come play with us and see our room now?"

I glanced back over my shoulder at Akira's room. I couldn't hear their conversation anymore, and I wasn't sure that I wanted to, either.

Rune had said he couldn't face me right now, so maybe leaving him to Akira's reassurances would be best. Plus, I couldn't deny the twins' need to play.

Turning back to the boys, I nodded. "I'm ready. Lead the way."

I followed behind them, their fluffy fox tails wagging happily as they went. We bounced down the stairs, and as soon as we reached their bedroom floor, a monster of a man approached from the other end.

As soon as the boys saw him, their faces lit up, and they ran toward him.

"*Papá!*" Newt shouted.

"You're home!" Greshim cheered.

The man I now recognized as Rune's step-father, Alvaro, knelt with a bright smile and flung his arms open wide as the twins crashed into them. Laughing, he picked one up in each arm and kissed their heads.

"I'm home, *mis amores.*"

His rich brown eyes were full of so much love as he looked down at his sons, and it bewildered me how a man who clearly adored both of his children could stand to be with a woman who was so cold to them.

Setting the boys back on their feet, he grabbed their hands and made his way over to where I stood. His expression was unreadable as he regarded me. "So, you must be Rune's partner. What was your name? Brianna?"

Smiling politely, I corrected, "Bria. It's nice to meet you."

"Ah, Bria. Forgive me. I'm horrible with names." He smiled, but unease settled in my stomach as the expression didn't quite reach his eyes. "*Mis hijos*, why don't you two go to your room? I'd like a moment alone with Bria."

"Okay," Greshim nodded and turned to look at me. "We'll be right in there when you're done." He pointed toward their room before grabbing his brother's hand and walking away. Alvaro fiddled with some flowers in a vase nearby until the twins' door shut, leaving the two of us out in the hall.

Swallowing hard, I faced the beast of a man and waited. His physique did little to settle my nerves. Wide shoulders, a broad chest, arms the size of my thighs, and those eyes. Those chocolate brown eyes seemed to see right through me and into my very soul. They commanded attention, respect, and obedience. They also brewed a dark emotion within me, one that coated my insides in a grimy layer of fear.

Alvaro plucked a single red rose from the vase and twirled the stem, thorns and all, in his fingers. "Now that we're alone," he started, his deep voice paralyzing me. "I'll be frank. I don't know you, and therefore, I don't trust you. What game are you playing?"

"Game? I'm not playing any game, sir. I'm here because—"

"Because you're Rune's chosen partner, yes. So I've heard. To be honest, I don't care about your relationship. I don't care who Rune ends up with, whether it's some stranger like you or someone of standing my wife has picked out. What I do care about are my sons. They love their brother, and what happens to him affects them. So watch yourself, girl. If you do anything to hurt Rune that in turn affects my children, you'll be answering to me, and trust me when I say, it will be long and painful."

The red rose suddenly burst into flames, and when the blazing heat cleared, only the charred skeleton of a lifeless, colorless flower remained.

Alvaro leaned in close, his hot breath on my ear as he growled, "I'd be mindful while you're here. You have many enemies in this house."

With the final warning, he tucked the scorched rose into my hair and walked past me. I was rooted to the spot, my stomach in knots. The man who had first appeared so kind and gentle was anything but when it came to things that threatened what he cherished. I wasn't sure why I was surprised considering that was how all Foxes were. Even so, being the target of that kind of hostility was bone-chilling and not a warning I'd take lightly.

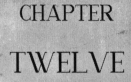

CHAPTER

TWELVE

FTER THE UNNERVING RUN-IN WITH Alvaro, I hoped for some light-hearted fun with Newt and Greshim. Standing outside their bedroom, I knocked and waited.

"Come in," Newt yelled from the other side.

As soon as I entered, the floor fell out from beneath my feet, and pain pierced my heart. Their room was a large space with two *very* different looks.

On one half of the room was a small, white bed with a wooden table next to it that was barely big enough to house the lamp it supported. A desk sat against the wall, piled with books and papers. Next to it stood a bookshelf, full of books of all different genres and reading levels.

On the other half of the room was a full-size bed with a vibrant royal blue comforter. It had an impressive black nightstand beside it, piled with toys, a lamp, and notepads. At the foot of the bed was a trunk that appeared to be overflowing with toys.

I looked back and forth from the two different sides, and my heart sank as I realized what it meant. As if Myra's favoritism of Greshim wasn't obvious enough, she wanted it clearly laid out for them in their belongings. The distinction was meant to hurt Newt, to make him think he was somehow lesser than his twin.

I couldn't understand how a mother could do that, and for Alvaro to be as protective as he was, how could he allow this obvious mistreatment?

Greshim noticed where my attention had gone, and he said, "I hate it, too. I don't like that Mother gives me so much while ignoring Newt."

Newt turned to his twin. "You share your th-th-things, so it's fine."

Greshim's brown eyes traced the monotone half of the room. "When I'm bigger and stronger, I'm going to give Newt everything Mother hasn't."

"G-G-Greshim," Next snapped, his brow suddenly furrowing in annoyance. "Stop it. I d-d-don't want your help. I can d-d-do those th-things m-myself."

Newt spent every day being told he wasn't good enough, wasn't strong enough, wasn't *Fox* enough. The one comfort and friend he had in all of that was Greshim, so to have Greshim insinuate those same ideas, even if they were coming from a good place, no doubt added another laceration to Newt's self-worth—probably even more painful than when Myra berated him, *because* it came from Greshim.

"Hey, hey," I said, kneeling down to place a hand on both boys' shoulders. I passed a look between the two, each of whom kept his narrowed eyes on the other. "Newt, I don't think your brother meant anything but love in saying that. And Greshim, I know you want to look out for your brother, but have faith in him, too. He's strong. You *both* are." I paused and smiled at the boys. "And you're very lucky to have each other. A brother who loves you so much."

Newt nibbled the corner of his mouth and swayed his shoulders as he begrudgingly said, "I g-guess I'm pretty lucky."

Greshim looked up at me. "Do you have any brothers, Bria?"

I shook my head. "I don't. But I've always wanted one. A brother to look out for me," I said, giving Newt a pointed look. "One that would believe in me, even when I didn't believe in myself." I added while looking at Greshim. "What you guys have is special. Don't lose that, okay?"

Greshim smiled and took Newt's hand. "From now on, I'll ask if you want my help. I know you don't always need it, but if you ever do, I'll always be here to give it."

Newt's face brightened, and he nodded. "Th-thanks, G-G-Greshim."

With the air feeling lighter, I clapped my hands and looked eagerly between the twins. "Now, who's ready to play?"

Their hands immediately shot into the air as they cried in unison, "Me!"

We spent the rest of the afternoon playing cops and robbers, princess and princes, and Land Fae versus Water Fae—a rather awkward one to say the least.

When it was time to eat dinner, the three of us headed for the kitchen. We found all the guys and Avana at the bottom of the main staircase, and my nerves spiked when my eyes connected with Rune's. There was a silent pain buried in his eyes as he tried to smile at me.

"Hey Bria," Ardley said when I reached the group. "I think we're all going to eat in Akira and Bassel's room since there's no more family fun time for the day. You're gonna eat in there with us, right?"

I looked at everyone's expectant faces. Rune watched me with his troubled eyes, waiting for my answer. For his sake, I didn't want to be near him until I could explain myself since my presence troubled him. It would be far easier on him to eat and relax without me nearby, and God knew that I would be a distracted, nervous wreck if I had to sit in the same room as Rune without being able to address what happened. The guilt was already overwhelming. It hurt to breathe around him, so I knew being near him was not an option until I found time alone for us to talk.

I smiled softly at Ardley and shook my head. "I'm not very hungry. I just came down with Greshim and Newt while they grabbed food from the kitchen."

Ardley frowned. "Oh. Okay. Well, if you change your mind, you know where to find me. I mean, us. *Us.*"

I ignored Ardley's wink and moved past everyone in the direction that Newt and Greshim had gone. Before I could reach the doorway to the kitchen, they came scampering out again, each with a plate of various fruits and meats.

"We're all set! Let's go watch a movie in our room now." Greshim said, inclining his head for me to follow them.

"Sounds fun," I said.

I glanced over at my friends as we passed them on their way to the kitchen. Rune lingered in the back of the group, and his eyes followed me as I trailed up the stairs after the twins. With each step I took, the cloudier his bright eyes became. I wanted to wipe that look off his face and replace it with one of his smiles. Seeing him distraught was like a punch to the gut.

He needed the truth.

As soon as we were alone later, he'd get it.

When we reached the top of the stairs, the twins giddily charged into their room with their plates of food. They sat down on their soft, plush carpet, facing the TV that hung on the same wall as the door. Newt patted the space between them, gesturing for me to sit with them. Greshim set his plate aside to put in a movie before coming to settle back down next to me, his fox tail bumping mine as they draped behind us.

Gosh, I still can't get used to having a tail. Even if it is fake.

Scenes from *Peter Pan* played out on the TV, and the boys slowly ate their food as they watched the film. My heart warmed, seeing how engrossed they were in the movie, and I was pretty enraptured, too, since it had been awhile since I'd seen it. When Peter, Wendy, and her brothers took flight, the twins' faces lit up. They got so excited, and they began shouting that they wished they could fly, too. I was definitely in agreement with them. Who *wouldn't* love the ability to fly?

Lucky Akira. Getting to do this every day.

They got on Greshim's bed and started jumping up and down. Their laughter was contagious as they waved me over. I got up and approached the bed. As soon as I was close enough, Greshim leapt toward me, spreading his legs and arms out as if he were trying to take flight. Fearing he would fall, my reflexes took over under the weight of panic, and I quickly jumped to catch him.

He giggled as soon as he landed in my arms and exclaimed, "Help me fly, Bria! Help me fly!"

I let out the panicked breath I'd been holding as the corners of my mouth rose. Laughing, I said, "Okay. Here we go!"

I held him out and above me as if he were a baby, careful to avoid grabbing him with my claws. He was surprisingly light for a ten-year-old, but I realized that was most likely due to my new strength. I twirled him around as he giggled harder. Newt bounced up and down on the bed, exclaiming that it was his turn. I bent my knees slightly before jumping up and tossing Greshim onto his bed. He landed on the soft mattress, laughing hysterically. I did the same thing with Newt, and we repeated this process until my arms became noodles and I could no longer lift them.

I collapsed onto Greshim's bed, falling in between them. My breath came out hard from the amount of energy that it took to play with them, and their giggles started to die down. The three of us lay there side by side, and after what seemed like mere seconds, Newt and Greshim were sound asleep.

My heart swelled at the sight. Since I never had any siblings, I never got to experience seeing my little brothers sleep soundly after hours of playing together. Moments like this were a dream to me.

I slowly stood up, trying not to make a sound. I gently picked up Newt and held him close to me as I tugged down the covers of Greshim's bed. I wasn't about to put Newt in his horribly small and sad bed, so I placed him next to his sleeping brother and guided the covers up to their chins. Pulling Newt's glasses from his round face, I placed them on the nightstand. I offered them one final look before I clicked off the light and quietly shut their door.

As soon as the door shut, I turned to finally make my way to my room, but as soon as I did, I stopped dead in my tracks. Myra stood at the end of the hall, blocking the stairs to the third floor. Every limb in my body locked up, and my blood ran ice cold. Her face was blank, but her posture spoke volumes. Straight back, head held high, hands clasped in front of her, and eyes scarily empty. She was calculating, cold, powerful.

And she was waiting for me.

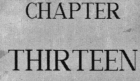

CHAPTER

THIRTEEN

MYRA," I SAID AND HOPED my voice didn't give away how unsettled I felt to run into her again. I subtly placed my clawed fingers behind my back to feel for my tail, which was still firmly in place. I was sure we were approaching the twelve-hour mark, which was when my guise would fade. "Good evening."

"I'd like to speak with you in my office now that you're done being a child. Follow me."

There was no room to argue. It was a demand, and when Myra ordered something, I knew it was best to do whatever she said. Even if she was a bitch for calling me a child. I hadn't realized being there for *her* sons was childish.

I followed after her, and each step we took toward her study on the first floor made my feet feel like they were being weighed down with cinder blocks. I was walking straight into the Fox's den, all on my own. My friends didn't even know I was going somewhere with

Myra, so should she decide to rip my heart out of my chest with her claws, Rune and the others wouldn't even be able to reach me before my screams went silent under the hand of death.

Way to think positive, Bria.

Myra's study was the first room on the left in her private wing. The room sat cold with an unlit and barren fireplace. Two couches faced each other, but they looked stiff and far from comfy. No personal touches decorated the space, and the colors were all dark and uninviting.

I glanced behind me, and that's when I noticed what decorated the wall facing Myra's desk. Bile rose up my throat.

Heads.

Dozens of dismembered, frozen heads mounted on the wall. Men, women, children. Each face wore a different, more horrific expression than the last. A woman forever frozen in a petrified scream. A man's face contorted in what looked to be a final gasp for air, his eyes long glazed over in death. A little girl, her no-doubt once pink cheeks now pale and littered with gashes, her tongue sagging out of her parted lips.

My stomach churned, and I bit the inside of my cheek to hide any sign of revulsion.

Don't puke. Don't puke. Don't puke.

I recalled Rune's earlier statement about how Myra kept her more grotesque decor in her private wing, and I realized this was what he'd meant.

"Do you like my art?" Myra asked. I glanced over my shoulder at her. She gestured to the wall and flashed me a sadistic smile. "They're some of my favorite Water Fae kills. I had a friend of mine, a Polar Bear Fae, freeze them so that I could always have their dead faces to stare at when I felt the urge to do so."

Oh God, please don't let me puke.

Trying to take a breath without giving away that I was struggling, I nodded. At least, I thought I was nodding. I was so unnerved and sick I couldn't be sure I was actually moving.

Art. She called this—*dead fucking people*—art. Up until that very moment, I hadn't realized exactly what kind of heartless monster I was dealing with. A shitty mother and person in general? Sure. But *this*? She was an unfeeling, malevolent husk of what should've been a person.

And I *despised* her.

"Well then," Myra started as she sank down gracefully onto one of the couches—the one that let her view the wall of heads. She gestured to the couch across from her and commanded, "Sit."

My feet moved on autopilot, guiding me to the couch where I slowly sat less gracefully than Myra, despite my effort. My heart beat erratically within my chest, and I prayed Myra couldn't hear it. Any sign of weakness around her would be like a drop of blood being spilled in a frenzy of sharks.

Deadly.

I was grateful that I at least didn't have to sit where I'd see those empty eyes of long-lost souls staring at me.

"So you intend to be with my son, yes?" Myra started. Her cunning gold eyes pierced into mine with an intensity that only the sun could match.

Somehow finding my voice, I said, "Yes, ma'am. Rune and I are serious about one another and plan on getting married eventually."

"And you believe you're fit to breed with our family line? How many Water Fae have you killed?"

This was a question Rune had anticipated his mother would ask at some point. His family had been key figures in the war with Water Fae, so having a partner who had ruthlessly killed hundreds was high on Myra's list of requirements—though

Rune had failed to mention her wall of trophies. Having to pretend that I'd killed loads of Water Fae had always been stomach-churning, but now knowing I was one made it even more gut-wrenching.

Despite my unease, I responded with that answer Rune and I had rehearsed. "I've lost count of the exact number. Their faces blur together after a while since their lives are of little importance. I stopped counting at 181, but I've since killed plenty more. I'd guess I'm up to 300-something now."

"1,086."

"Pardon?"

"1,086," she repeated. Her clawed fingers reached for a teacup that sat on the table between us, and she sipped on the steaming mug with a calm that disturbed me. We weren't friends having a fucking tea party, yet her entire demeanor was so calm it was *unnatural*. She met my eyes over the rim of the china and continued, "That's how many Water Fae I've killed. I can remember each and every one. Every face, every last word, every expression they had when they died at my hands. I was expecting the same of Rune's partner. Someone who revels in the kill. Someone who is likely to create strong and powerful offspring that can continue the Beckett line. I don't believe that individual is you, so tell me. Why are you here?"

My skin prickled with disgust. The sheer magnitude of what this woman had done. How many mothers, fathers, sisters, and brothers she'd stolen from the world, including the ones behind me.

The *Water Fae* behind me.

My people.

Lifeless eyes bore into my back, and knowing that they were my people made the room seem to spin. Imaginary wails seemed to fill my mind like the dismembered heads were crying out to me for not being there. I'd failed them, letting this woman steal their lives in what I could only imagine was a myriad of gruesome ways. The worst part was she'd *enjoyed* it. She didn't remember each face out of guilt or remorse. She *wanted* to remember them, because she reveled in the kill. It made me sick.

Forcing myself to focus on Myra's question and not how much I abhorred her, I considered how to answer her. Why was I here? That was easy. I was here because of Rune. I was here *for* Rune. He needed me, so even though I'd initially agreed to come solely for the sake of our deal, it was now my choice to be here, because I loved Rune and refused to let him do this alone.

Rune had given me a chance to back out. He gave me the money I needed for Italy and told me I no longer had to come. But I couldn't just quit, not when Myra was putting him between a rock and a hard place. While Rune didn't want to settle down, refusing Myra of what she wanted would result in her hurting the twins to force Rune's hand. He had to convince her that he was ready for marriage and kids, but it was to be with me, or at least, Myra had to believe that. The alternative was Rune being sacrificed to a life he loathed, and after seeing the type of Fae she expected him to be and create in offspring, my resolve to pull this charade off had only intensified. I refused to let his psycho mom force him into a marriage where he had to "breed" Water Fae killing machines.

"I'm here," I started, my voice coming out surprisingly even, "because I love Rune and plan on spending my life with him."

Myra flashed me a cynical grin. "And you believe that somehow makes you fit to be with him?"

My brow furrowed before I could stop myself. "He and I are happy together. Don't you want him to be happy?"

Myra's features smoothed out once more until she stared at me blankly. "Happy? Do you think Alvaro and I are together because we're happy with one another or because we love each other? No. We're together because we are strong, powerful Fae who stand to create offspring just as capable. We had one failure, sure, but Greshim is on his way to becoming a tenacious Fox as planned."

My throat closed from the grip of rage, and suddenly, I was seeing red. Failure? She thought Newt was a *failure*? Greshim was a great kid, but Newt was just as wonderful. So he had a stutter, but what the hell did that matter? He was healthy, kind, warm, funny, and a *good* kid. The only failure was Myra for being a shitty and unworthy mother.

"So no," Myra continued. "I don't care about Rune's happiness. What he feels means nothing. He's a Fox Fae with a duty to his kind. He's expected to create powerful Fox Fae to continue our path toward annihilating every Water Fae, and if he's unable to do that, he is useless to me and our kind. How he feels is of little importance."

Utterly baffled, I slowly said, "But … he's your son."

"You say that as if it's supposed to mean something."

I did, and I wasn't exactly sure why. I should've known better, especially after seeing this horror show of a room. This woman didn't feel anything for anyone. She was numb. Hollow. Bitter. And I couldn't help but find that sad, even more so since I knew Rune hoped to restore her to the way she'd once been. Even that was hard to picture at this point. She was far too gone and unable to care about anything. What could make a person, a *mother*, end up this way?

"You are not the Fae for my son," Myra continued after my silence. "For your own sake, I'd back away now and find yourself a different mate, one more fitting for your place in life."

She stood, and I took that as my cue to follow suit. I got to my feet, and without another word, I made my way to the door, taking care not to look at the wall as I did. I had no idea if Myra thought I was actually giving up like she'd ordered, but I didn't care at this point. I needed out of that suffocating room and away from that evil woman. I needed to get away from all of those unseeing eyes.

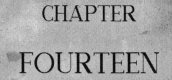

CHAPTER

FOURTEEN

M Y BLOOD BOILED AS I hurried down the halls and stairs for my room.

I was angry at Myra for treating me like I wasn't worthy of her son. I was angry that Newt had to grow up in a home with a mother who hated him. I was angry that the one parent Rune had left was one who'd never love him the way his dad had, despite his wishes and futile attempts to restore her.

Needing to find Rune quickly before I imploded, I barreled into my room. I expected to find Rune waiting for me, but the room was empty. Confused, I checked the bathroom and balcony, but he wasn't there, either. That was when I noticed a note on his side of the bed, and my stomach sank.

I'm sorry for earlier. I was stupid and rushed things.
I'll sleep in another room. Sleep well and sweet dreams.

Rune

My heart clenched painfully, and the anger in my veins turned its energy from Myra to myself. One stupid secret had caused this. I had to clear up this mess, but I also knew snooping through the rooms in this house to find him wasn't smart. Like Alvaro said earlier, I had a lot of enemies in this house, even more so now after Myra's clear warning that I needed to leave.

While I hated to let this misunderstanding go on longer, I knew this sleeping arrangement worked in my favor for at least part of my plans tonight. I wouldn't be able to talk to Rune until the morning, but I'd get to follow through with the outing I'd planned with Dallas earlier in the day.

Pulling my phone out, I called Dallas, who answered on the first ring. "Gummy worm?"

I rolled my eyes. "No. Everything's fine. Well, mostly."

Except for all the dead Water Fae hanging on Myra's fucking wall.

"Just wanted to be sure. So, are you ready?"

That morning, I'd texted Dallas to see if she'd be open to training me after everyone was asleep. For me to be completely confident in my decision to come clean to Rune about who I was, I first needed to *be* confident in who that was. Right now, with my extreme lack of knowledge and skill, I didn't feel that way. I hoped Dallas could help fix that.

Plus, it would be nice to see her again, especially after all the stuff that happened today with Rune and Myra.

"I'm ready," I answered as I checked the time. It was nearly ten, and the rooms next door were quiet. I hoped that meant I could make a discreet exit. The last thing I needed right now was another run-in with someone.

"Okay," Dallas said. "Me and a few others scouted the area on the far side of the lake, outside of their estate and away from any public eyes. It's a pretty far walk for you, but it's all clear and perfect for training."

"Give me a few to get out of the house. I'll be there soon."

After hanging up with her, I changed into leggings and a sweatshirt, noting how difficult it was to pull on the tight leggings with clawed fingers. I had to pull my tail out of the waistband of the pants, which made the furry extremity feel constricted. I had to give Avana credit, though. Her illusion was *solid*, though it probably had less than an hour left before it faded.

As I got ready, I was surprisingly calm for someone who was about to be sneaking around. It was when I finally stepped out into the dark hallway that my nerves got the best of me. The manor was huge, and if not for the twins' tour, I'd most definitely have gotten lost trying to navigate the halls.

I hugged all the corners as I waited and listened for the sound of anyone roaming about. Though, if caught, I could always explain that I was on my way to the kitchen for a drink.

Tension curled around my shoulders by the time I made it down the flights of stairs and to the back door. I crept outside and made sure to hug the house as I looked up at all the windows. There wasn't a single light on in any of the windows out back, and my heart danced with hope that luck was on my side. It seemed everyone was settled in bed after the long day.

Myra had an expansive backyard with a massive lake sat a short walk from the back door. It would be around the water's edge and through the dense trees that Dallas waited for me, hidden beneath the blanket of nightfall. Not knowing how far she was from the house, I started the long trek in search of her.

When I was shrouded under the canopy of trees and safely hidden from view of the house, I pulled out my phone.

"Gumm—"

"Not Gummy Worm," I laughed. "I'm in the woods along the lake's edge. Where are you?"

"I'm glad you asked. Here's your first lesson. Find me."

I stopped walking, my brow furrowed in confusion. Turning to scan the endless dark trees and silent water, I mumbled, "Find you? This lake is massive. How am I supposed to find you with absolutely no direction?"

I could practically hear the smile in her voice as she answered, "You have thirty minutes. Find me, or you fail and I'm leaving."

Without another word, she hung up. Baffled and utterly lost as to how I was supposed to locate her among the acres of wilderness, I started walking again. It became very clear very quickly that my efforts were futile. I'd gotten so turned around and confused that I didn't even know where *I* was, let alone where Dallas was, and I'd spent so much time searching in vain that even my Fox Fae illusion fizzled away.

Glancing at my phone, I saw I only had a handful of minutes left. Groaning, I picked up a rock and chucked it at the water. The stone cracked against the dark waves before sinking to the bottom of the lake. I didn't understand what Dallas wanted. We were supposed to be working on honing my abilities and learning how to control them. How was playing hide and seek going to do that?

Sighing, I knelt by the water's edge and skimmed my hand across the surface. The tension in my shoulders immediately seeped away. The frustration cleared from my mind, and with the loss of the negative voice came a new one. A soft hum. A whisper.

Bria.

Use me.

Here.

Call out.

My attention was now focused solely on the lapping water at my feet.

Is this how I find Dallas? The water will show me?

With nothing to lose, I stood up straight and took a deep breath. Closing my eyes, I tuned out the gentle wind whistling through the trees, the faint flutter of leaves falling to the ground, and the crickets hard at work. Soon, all I could hear was the nearly silent slap of the water against the rock and dirt at my feet. The heaving of the water began to mix with the voices in the waves. Honing in on those sounds, I felt the buzz of the connection.

"Where's Dallas?" I mumbled to the water.

When I opened my eyes, three drops of water, no bigger than my thumb nail, hovered in front of me. Surprised, I jumped back with a gasp. This triggered the water at my feet to lurch forward as though to shield me from whatever startled me.

The lake water started to rise up from the ground in front of me, so I quickly shook my head. "No, no. I'm fine. Go–Go back to how you were."

The water did as it was told, and it went back to wading calmly in its place. Turning my attention back to the three drops of water, which were still suspended in front of me, I asked, "Can you help me find Dallas?"

The drops bounced.

This way.

The orbs floated past me, and I quickly followed behind them. I was afraid I'd lose sight of them in the dark, but they seemed to glow white from the inside, almost like moonlight reflected off the water's surface. The way they floated through the air was so graceful and magical, which made sense since it *was* magical. I was thankful that they kept a fairly even pace.

After making a few turns and hopping over some fallen trees, I came to a small stream farther back in the woods that most likely connected to the lake somewhere, though even the lake had disappeared behind me. The three drops of water exploded and fizzled back down into the brook. I glanced around for Dallas, but I came up with nothing. Thinking that maybe I'd done something wrong, I pulled out my phone to call her when, across the stream, Dallas leapt out from behind a tree.

I nearly jumped out of my skin with a scream at her sudden appearance, which sent her into a fit of laughter.

"Oops. Sorry. I didn't mean to scare you."

"Sure you didn't," I said, finally joining in with her laughter once my heart was done reassembling itself.

Relief and a warm rush of euphoria washed over me at her presence. It had only been a few days since I'd seen her, but oh, how I'd missed her and the sound of her laugh.

Dallas had her fiery red waves piled up in a messy bun. She wore a pair of joggers and a t-shirt, which all hugged her fit and muscled body. She'd always had toned arms and legs, a firm stomach, and a butt many envied. I'd assumed it was from a love of fitness—one of the few things we didn't share—but now I knew it was from all the years of training she'd gone through. As my personal guard, she had to be in excellent physical condition.

Dallas's full, pink lips broke out into a wide smile, and she ran toward me, leaping over the stream like it was nothing. Suspecting her intentions, I ran forward and met her open arms with my own. We hugged each other tightly, and I inhaled her familiar scent—lavender with a hint of honey.

"I'm so proud of you," Dallas cheered and pulled back to look at me with vibrant green eyes. "I knew you'd figure it out. You used the water! All on your own!"

Grinning, I said, "Well, I figured what was the harm in trying. Stumbling around in the dark with no guidance wasn't working."

"What else have you managed to do with your awakened abilities?"

I told her about all the other incidents where I'd accidentally tapped into water, ending with my most recent episode when Rune and I were in the bathroom.

She held up a finger for me to pause there. "Okay, first of all, what the hell? You've been leaving out *major*, steamy news. We will definitely come back to that, and you'd better not leave out any juicy, naked detail. Second, I guess you've noticed by now that your abilities are tied to your emotions."

I sighed. "Sadly, yes. It's frustrating to say the least."

She smirked and mumbled, "Oh, I'm sure you're frustrated."

I smacked her arm, and she laughed at my flaming cheeks. Leave it to Dallas to tease me about my unfulfilled sexual desires.

"Well," she started once she'd finished laughing. "You'll be happy to know that your power will stop responding like that eventually. It's only responding to every heightened emotion right now because it's still very new. The water is getting a feel for your bond and vice versa. Once you've gotten used to your powers and established a solid relationship, the water will only react when called forth or in circumstances when it senses *real* distress."

"How do I control it until then?"

"You'll have to get a better grip on your emotions. It's hard, I know, but until that bond and trust is established, the only way to control it is to not let your emotions get the better of you. At least, not while you're around any water."

I groaned. "Easier said than done."

Laughing, she tugged on my hand and pulled me over to the stream. "That's why we're doing this. Thankfully, since it's still new, you have to be right next to water for it to react, but as you hone your abilities, you'll be able to tap into water at greater distances. It just takes time, but you'll get the hang of it, I promise. You were born to be a powerful Fae. It's literally in your blood."

"Why? Because I'm a Princess?"

She shrugged. "Sort of. More so because you were bred to be a badass."

I frowned, not liking that word. *Bred*. "You make it sound like I was a science experiment."

She scrunched her nose at that. "No, definitely not. I guess it does sound weird since you don't know our history. Your advisor will teach you everything you'd possibly need to know once we go back to the Water Fae Kingdom, but for now, I'll tell you a piece of your own story."

Excitement flooded my senses, making me shift impatiently on my feet. I'd spent so many endless years wondering who I really was. There were nights when I'd lie awake, glaring up into the star-sprinkled sky, and I'd wait for a shooting star to streak against the midnight void so that I could make a wish for my real parents to find me. I wanted to know who I belonged to, what my mother smelled like, what my father did for fun. To suddenly have all of those truths at my fingertips felt like being suspended in midair.

Exciting yet terrifying.

"When I say you were made to be a powerful badass, I mean it," Dallas started. "For centuries, our Kingdom had focused on ensuring the most powerful of Water Fae led our kind, and they did so by producing an heir even more powerful than the last. Your father, King Khal, was born to the previous rulers and was an incredibly gifted Fae. When he came of marrying age, all of the most powerful women in the Kingdom were called together to compete to prove who was the strongest. It didn't take long for everyone to realize that person was your mother. Alesta.

"She came from a powerful family line, but her abilities were still uncharted. We'd never seen someone so strong. They were immediately married, and after a few centuries, they finally had you. You were born from two of the most powerful Water Fae to ever exist, which means you are capable of things that others have only ever dreamed of."

My smile faltered as I processed her words. I was conceived for the purpose of creating someone powerful. Was that it? I was a byproduct of a power-hungry arranged marriage? The notion briefly took me back to Myra's office and all the talk of breeding powerful Land Fae. The mere thought that my parents shared even an ounce of Myra's mentality made me want to collapse like a house of cards in a passing breeze.

Dallas turned toward the stream. She raised her arm out in front of her, and the water rose up with the motion. It raced forward and circled up and around her body as though trying to wrap her in its hold before coming to rest in the palm of her hand.

Wanting to busy myself with something while talking about all of this, I decided to give what she'd just done a shot. We were supposed to be practicing, after all. I focused on the water in the stream until warmth spread through my limbs. I lifted my hand and silently urged the water to follow. Without hesitation, it barreled toward me, but instead of stopping at my outstretched hand, it smacked into my chest, throwing me onto my back.

"Holy shit!" Dallas yelled, rushing to my side.

Groaning from the impact, I sat up. The water was gone, either having returned to the stream or soaked into the ground beneath me. At least, I wasn't drenched. Somehow.

Turning to Dallas, I said, "I don't think I did that right."

She threw her head back as she burst into a fit of laughter. "Not quite. The water was clearly too excited to have you calling on it."

"Excited? You make it sound like it's a person."

Her laughter died down until she smiled warmly at me. She held her hand back out to the stream, and the water danced through the air toward us. It twirled and bounced until it floated above her hands in an orb no bigger than a basketball.

Meeting my eyes again, she explained, "Water isn't a person, but it has real emotions. It feels like we do. It has a voice. It's *alive* in a way."

Watching the water push and pull in a gentle sway within the ball, I thought about what she'd said. The water was indeed talkative, whispering things to me whenever I was near. It also responded to me like it wanted to protect me and be by my side. Then there were the times we'd connected, and somewhere within the current, I'd felt a faint heartbeat like my own.

I started to understand what Dallas was saying, and with that in mind, I held my hands out for the water. It darted across the space toward me, but this time, I was ready. I caught it in my arms, and the orb melted across my skin until I was encased in water from head to toe. My eyes slipped closed, and I focused on the cool touch. In the back of my mind, I figured this was almost like the water's way of hugging me.

After a few moments, the water pooled back down my head and arms, up from my legs and torso, until it gathered back into an orb above my hands. It hovered there, now waiting for my command.

"What should I do now?" I asked Dallas.

"Let's try something easy. Try to make the water into different shapes. A square. A star. A unicorn. You know, small shapes or figures. Picture it in your mind, and guide the water as necessary. It will understand what you want and need."

I did just that. I focused on the water and started out small, morphing the sphere into a square, then the square into a star, and so on. Once my mind was busy, and I felt I had a hang of it, I glanced at Dallas and finally voiced the question that had been strangling me since she'd said the word *bred*. "Did they love each other?"

Dallas frowned. "Your mom and dad?"

I nodded, suddenly afraid of the answer. I wanted the truth, but I was no longer sure if I was ready to know it yet. The reality of who I was may be ugly, and the fantasies I'd dreamt up of my faceless parents could be much darker than what I'd always envisioned.

Dallas sighed. "To be completely honest with you, no. They didn't love each other."

My stomach plummeted, and I was forced to look away.

"At least, they didn't at first."

Hope blossomed in my chest, and I found her gaze again with eager eyes.

"At first," Dallas began, "your mother loathed your father. According to the rumors, she wanted no part in being Queen, and she found him insufferable. He wanted to impress her, which often came off cocky and conceited. It supposedly took a long time for them to finally open up to one another, hence the reason it took centuries for you to be born. They loved each other in the end from what I've heard."

I took comfort in knowing that my parents came to love each other. I hoped they shared that love for me, too, not just for being a potentially powerful offspring, but because they wanted *me*. My chest squeezed with the ache that came from missing someone with your whole being. Did it make sense for me to miss them? I mean, I didn't know them, but God, how I longed to.

Another question teased my tongue. It was something that had been plaguing me since I first learned about who and what we were.

Sensing my burning question, Dallas snickered. "Spit it out. What are you dying to ask?"

"How old are you? You're clearly not nineteen like I thought since you speak as though you were alive to witness all this."

"I'm 219."

Eyes wide, I nearly fell over. The news was like a punch to the gut. I knew there was plenty Dallas had kept secret over the years for my safety, but every time I learned something new, it was like a fresh cut on my heart. A nagging voice in my head kept asking if I really knew her, if she really thought of me as a friend, or if our whole friendship had been a lie, too.

"Wow," I said, forcing the negative thoughts from my head. She'd reassured me that our friendship was very real when I'd first discovered who she was, and I believed her. "You're old."

Dallas's mouth fell open, and she shoved me, nearly causing me to drop my water, which I'd just shaped into a basic flower. "*Excuse you.* I am not old. Do I look wrinkly and saggy to you?"

Laughing, I asked, "Okay, what's old to you guys?"

"Late 800s, 900s. Some have lived into their thousands, which is crazy."

"I can't even imagine living that long." I held my hands wide, watching as the water stretched to form a stegosaurus. I was having way too much fun with this. "How did I never notice that you weren't aging?"

She groaned. "God, that part was awful. I had to wrap my boobs back in high school and gradually lessen it so it looked like I grew into my assets. Plus, I kept doing haircuts that made me look younger until it was okay for me to look the way I do now."

Narrowing my eyes, I joked, "Deceptive. Very deceptive of you."

Well, I was kind of joking.

"Deceptive, sure. But it was necessary. I'd rather have a few lies sprinkled into our friendship than not have had you as a friend at all. Those lies let me grow up with you. They gave me the best years, the best *memories*, of my life."

Her words pushed away the last bit of doubt, the lingering voice of worry. Grinning with a full heart, I whispered, "Me too."

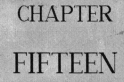

CHAPTER

FIFTEEN

MY LIMBS WERE HEAVY AS I stumbled back through the woods toward the house. After almost two hours of training and catching Dallas up on all the less graphic details about Rune and me, I was spent. I wanted to crawl into my bed and sleep.

Emerging from the trees lining the lake, I noted the dark house in the distance. All was still and quiet, which meant the time to sneak back in would be now.

I raced across the yard and crept inside through the back door. As soon as I was across the threshold, I waited and listened. The hallway was dark, and the house was eerily silent. The still darkness made a wave of goosebumps break out along my arms, but I ignored the unsettled feeling and tip-toed through the halls and up the stairs.

As I reached the third-floor landing, soft voices drifted to me from down the hall. My heart rate spiked when I realized it was Rune and Aidan. I crept along the wall and peeked around the corner.

They stood outside the room Rune had disappeared into on our first day here, and if not for the faint light coming from the cracked door, they would've been two voices lost in the darkness.

And I wished that were the case.

Rune leaned against the wall in sweats and a t-shirt while Aidan stood in front of him in thin, black lingerie that left little to the imagination, even from this distance.

As soon as I saw them, I quickly retreated around the corner and pressed my back firmly against the wall. My heart thundered, and I held my breath as I listened.

"Is she in there?" Aidan's soft, sultry voice wrapped around my mind like a swarm of bees. I wanted to claw my ears at the mere sound. Bitter emotions I couldn't even name rushed through my veins.

"She is," Rune answered, and I realized that they were most likely talking about me. "Is there a reason you're knocking on my door at midnight?"

"What do you think?" Her voice dropped with a seductive lilt. "I've been thinking about you nonstop and fucking myself to the memory of you. Let's go have some fun in my room. She'll never know. Come see how wet I am for you."

Her invitation sank into my gut like a hot knife, and my stomach coiled around the blade. I held my breath as I waited for what felt like endless minutes for Rune's response. Would it be a scoff? Would he snap at her? I wanted to hear his answer with every fiber of my being but also run away screaming from this nightmare.

Rune's response came with little hesitation. "Do you want to have sex?"

My hand flew to cover my mouth on instinct as my body trembled. All the air had been punched out of my lungs like I'd been slammed into with a sledgehammer. My fight or flight kicked into overdrive, with flight winning. I raced back the way I'd come, taking the steps two at a time. Tears brimmed my eyes, and I choked on my attempt to keep my cries from escaping. As soon as I made it outside, I didn't stop. I picked up my pace and ran. I ran and ran and ran until I reached the place where Dallas and I had been training, and as soon as I made it, my legs finally gave out. I crumbled by the creek's edge and screamed. Tears rolled down my cheeks as I clutched my stomach and rocked back and forth to the sound of my agonized wails.

Rune was kissing Aidan.

Rune was sleeping with Aidan.

Another cry slipped through my lips, and I struggled to catch my breath. Of course he was having sex with Aidan. I'd rejected him this morning, and it wasn't like he and I were actually a couple. He technically had no ties to me, no reason not to take Aidan up on her offer. I had no right to be upset, yet that didn't stop the crevice from opening wide within my chest.

It was then I realized that the water from the stream coated my entire body. I hadn't even noticed the water move or climb over my skin, but now that I was paying attention, its whispers invaded my mind and urged me to calm down.

Images of Rune and what he may be doing this very second tried to cloud my head, but the water forced all thoughts out of my mind. For once, I didn't resist the pull. I didn't fight against the voices. I wanted to be *numb*. I wanted to fade away with the steady, gentle current.

One second, I was crying and aching in every bone of my body, and the next, everything went dark. I was floating, drifting, moving. I was calm, peaceful, and light. I was …

I …

MY EYES SHOT OPEN, AND I let out a sharp gasp. I quickly sat up from where I'd been sprawled out in the grass and looked around me with panicked eyes. I was still by the creek, the moon high in the onyx sky.

"What the hell?" I mumbled as I rubbed at my eyes.

I had no idea what had happened, but I was pretty sure I'd blacked out. I didn't know if I'd hyperventilated or what exactly made me lose consciousness, but when I checked my phone, I saw it was nearly 1 a.m. It had been nearly an hour, and my stomach clenched all over again.

An hour since Rune and Aidan ...

I took a deep breath and clung to the calm still flowing through my bloodstream. The water was no longer coating my skin, but it was like it had embedded a dose of peace within me. That was the only thing keeping me from breaking down all over again, because while Rune and I weren't dating, I had thought we were moving in that direction. Him being with Aidan *hurt*.

I quickly swallowed the lump in my throat before I lost my mind to the claws of agony all over again. It was late. I was exhausted, even more so now after crying and passing out, so while I had some energy left in me, I got to my feet and headed back to the house. As I trekked across the backyard, I prayed to God that Rune and Aidan were done, because if I heard them, I'd be sick. I didn't know how I was going to make it through the rest of this God-awful trip after knowing what they'd done.

But I'd already accepted Rune's end of the bargain—the money for Italy—so I had to keep up my end. Plus, if I backed out, I wasn't sure if Myra would take that as a blunder on Rune's part and punish the twins to hurt him. I couldn't live with myself if that happened. So even though the thought of sharing a bed with Rune after he'd just shared one with Aidan made me physically ill, I had to push on. I had to see this week through.

The closer I got to the house, the more I realized I most likely wouldn't make it.

Fuck.

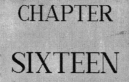

CHAPTER

SIXTEEN

A s soon as I reached the back door, it swung open from inside. My stomach dropped as I came face to face with a woman. Surprise flickered briefly in her rich, brown eyes before being replaced by open hostility.

"Wasn't expecting to find you," the newcomer said. "What are you doing wandering around so late on your own? I thought you were with Rune."

"I'm not sure how that's any of your business," I told the stranger.

Only, as I looked at her, I realized she wasn't a total stranger. I'd seen her before. *Somewhere.* That flawless dark brown skin, that tall frame, that stunning curly afro, and those large, suspicious eyes. It finally clicked. She was the waitress from the seafood restaurant who'd watched me on the deck.

She narrowed her eyes at me and took a step in my direction. "Oh, but I think it is. You're in the way of the person I love. You're a nuisance. You shouldn't be here."

Groaning, I said, "So what? You're another ex-lover of Rune's?"

Just saying his name sent a sharp pang to my heart.

She gave a humorless laugh. "Try Aidan."

Relief seeped into my gut with this news. I wasn't sure what I'd do if faced with yet another gorgeous ex-partner of Rune's.

"If you're in love with Aidan, why are you treating me like an enemy? Rune and I are together, which means Aidan is free for you to be with. We want the same thing, you and I."

"Wrong," she snapped. "I want Aidan to be happy, which means I want her with Rune. *You* are in the way of that."

Frowning, I asked, "What about your happiness?"

"Don't you dare," she growled, an orange flame erupting around her tall frame. It traveled the length of her body, and when it disappeared, orange fox ears sat in the mess of her dark curls. She sneered at me, exposing her canines, and a burnt orange tail with a white tip trailed behind her.

She was a Red Fox Fae.

"Don't talk as if you know me—know *us*. You're an outsider who has no business being here."

Anger churned low in my chest, and I took a moment to stamp those growing flames. The lake was behind me, and I didn't need this Fox Fae—who clearly already loathed me—to have any more reason to come after me.

"I have every right to be here," I said, holding my head high. "This is Rune's home. I'm his lover."

A growl rumbled low in her throat, and I noticed her clawed fingers curling. Apprehension settled in my core. I could sense an attack coming any second, and while I didn't want to expose who I was, I also refused to stand idly by should she advance. I'd fight back without hesitation. I *would* protect myself.

Before she or I could make any move, though, the French doors opened again. Rune's large body filled the space, and my heart fractured a little more. I wasn't ready to see him yet. His eyes widened in surprise when he noticed me, but he quickly turned his attention to Aidan's visitor.

"Yasmine," Rune said. "What are you doing here?"

Yasmine turned her ruthless glare on Rune and crossed her arms. "Consoling *your* mate."

"Aidan's not my mate, Yasmine."

"Right, right. This complete outsider is." Yasmine turned her scowl back on me. She glanced out toward the woods where I'd been, then back at me. Her voice dropped dangerously low as she said, "Something's not right about you. I don't know what it is yet, but I'm going to find out."

Yasmine spared one final moment to glare at Rune before making her way across the yard for the front of the house. With her absence, the silence between Rune and me became deafening, and I looked away from him. It was past one in the morning, so he no doubt wondered what the hell I was doing out here on my own. It had to be pretty weird to find your pretend girlfriend wandering around your property when everyone was supposed to be asleep. Even worse, I couldn't bring myself to say what I'd overheard in the hall earlier. The confession sat poised on my tongue but refused to break past my trembling lips.

"Are you okay?"

I nearly leapt out of my skin at the sound of Rune's voice. Heart dancing wildly in my chest, I found his eyes watching me carefully. I searched his gaze, which was turned down ever so slightly at the edges. I looked for any sign that gave away what he'd been up to, but all I saw was worry etched into his mouth and forehead. What was the root of that pain? Was it my being challenged by Yasmine? Was it fear that I'd somehow know what he'd done? Or was it still the guilt he'd been harboring since the bathroom incident? I had a suspicion it was probably all of it, but the lingering self-loathing was still definitely present in his eyes.

"I'm great," I answered, forcing a smile.

He glanced around at the dark yard. "Should I be concerned as to why you're wandering around outside at 1 a.m.?"

"Nope. I was out for a walk. Getting some fresh air. What are *you* still doing up?"

I loved torturing myself, apparently. Knowing what he was doing clearly wasn't enough. I wanted him to say it, too. Rub some salt in the open, bleeding wound.

He shrugged and stepped out of the doorway to the house. He held the door open and gestured for me to go in first. I did, trying not to pay any mind to the slight brush of my shoulder against his chest as I walked past. The warm graze of contact made me want to shatter all over again.

"I couldn't sleep," he answered, following close behind me through the darkened halls.

"Oh, I'm sure you couldn't," I said and cringed at how harshly those words came out. The hurt, anger, and betrayal I'd been feeling poured out with each word. I sucked in a sharp breath as tears threatened to spill over again.

"What?" Rune asked as he fell in step beside me, and the confusion in his voice made me see red. How fucking dare he act like he didn't know what he'd done?

I couldn't even look him in the eye. I kept my gaze trained dead ahead and picked up my pace, heading straight for my room where I planned to lock myself in and shut the world out.

"Bria," Rune called as I barreled up the steps leading to the third floor.

I refused to look left where Aidan and Rune had been before. Instead, I darted into my room, and my stomach pitched forward when I realized Rune was right on my heels.

As soon as we stepped inside, Rune shut the door behind

him. His voice sounded perplexed as he asked, "Bria, what's wrong? What did you mean by—"

"I saw you, Rune," I snapped as I whipped around to face him. "I was in the hall when you and Aidan …"

I couldn't even bring myself to say the words, but I didn't need to. Realization flickered across his eyes, followed by a heavy dose of alarm. For some reason, seeing his shock made me want to bury my head in the sand to hide my shame. Quickly wanting to fill the awful silence, I rambled, "Which I know I have no reason to get upset about. I mean, you're single. You're allowed to do whatever you want. We're not actually together, so—"

Rune stepped toward me with wide eyes. "Wait, do you think that she and I …?"

"I don't think, Rune. I know. I heard you ask her to have sex."

He shook his head slowly. "That's not what I said. I asked her if she wanted to have sex, not if she wanted to go have sex with me."

Annoyed, I furrowed my brow at him and crossed my arms. "I'm sorry. I don't see what the difference is."

"So, I take it you didn't hear what I said after that, either?"

"No. I'm afraid after hearing the guy I'm into ask another girl to have sex with him, I made my swift exit. I didn't really *want* to stick around to hear more."

His jaw worked as he slowly said, "I asked her if she wanted to have sex in a general sense. When she said yes, like I knew she would, I told her if she wanted to have sex, she could go hit up Ardley, because he's always down to have sex. Then she got mad and clearly called Yasmine over to gripe about how I'd turned her down. Again."

The air moving through my lungs stilled, and all thoughts vanished from my head until I was left staring at Rune like a deer in the headlights. "You … You didn't …?"

"No, I didn't sleep with Aidan. I didn't do anything with her."

Relief hit me so hard that I was forced to sit on the bed. All the grotesque emotions and images that had clouded my heart were for nothing, and while their absence was a massive weight off my chest, embarrassment took their place.

"Did you really think I'd sleep with someone else when you and I are—" Rune stopped, his features strained. I latched onto what he'd started to say and waited with eager ears. He looked at the ceiling and took a deep breath. "You and I are still fake dating. Did you really think I'd get involved with someone else?"

Fake dating. Right. I knew that's what our relationship was, but it still felt like a slap to the face to hear him say it. Even more hurtful was how guilty I felt. I had assumed the worst about Rune, even though I knew he wasn't like that. Rune enjoyed fooling around, but I'd never known him to cheat. I'd gotten hung up on his words, which definitely sounded bad without the rest of the context, and I hated that I'd gotten so worked up over it to the point where I'd snapped at him.

I wasn't a stranger to being cheated on. My ex, Dax, cheated on me daily. Yet it had never hurt the way Rune's possible infidelity did. It just went to show how much I loved this man.

Which only made me feel worse for doubting him.

"I'm sorry," I whispered, my voice coming out thick. "I know you aren't like that. It's just everyone keeps saying I'm not good enough, and this gorgeous girl that you have a history with keeps getting thrown in my face as the one you *should* be with. So, after what happened between us this morning, when I heard you ask her if she wanted to have sex, I assumed the worst."

"I get it," Rune said as he leaned against the wall across from me. "If I had heard that without the rest of the story, I would've assumed the same thing, so I don't blame you for getting upset at all. I want you to know that I'm not sleeping with or seeing

WHISPERS OF THE WATER

anyone else. I haven't slept with anyone since ... well, since you came into the picture."

My breath caught in my throat as I asked, "Why?"

"Because at first, I was too busy. We were hanging out every day, so there was never time. When we started getting serious about the fake dating plan, it felt wrong. Then when we started getting physical—" Rune stopped, and tension seeped back into his shoulders as he turned away from me. "I'm sorry about earlier."

He fidgeted as though preparing to flee at a moment's notice. He was suddenly on edge with me, and I knew it was because his mind was now back to what happened in the bathroom.

"Rune." His name came out as an intimate whisper, which I hadn't intended.

Rune's eyes found mine, and a desperate, hungry emotion blazed to life as he watched me stand and walk closer. Longing seared in his gaze like a match to paper. It was heated and all-consuming, but something was trying to hold it back like a dam keeping the flood of emotion in check. His uncertainty and self-hate from what happened earlier, no doubt, prevented him from giving in.

Our bodies were only inches away now, and if I took a deep enough breath, our chests would touch. When I inhaled, his musky, cedar scent filled my senses, and it made my toes curl in the best way possible. It took everything in me not to lean into his intoxicating scent, his warmth, his touch.

Biting my lip against all the indecent thoughts now swarming my mind, I stared up at him. "Rune, about earlier—"

"I know. I'm sorry. I shouldn't have—"

"No, no," I quickly stopped him, pressing the tips of my fingers to his lips. The contact made my heart sing, and I felt his breathing still. His burning eyes never wavered from mine.

"Don't you dare apologize. You did nothing wrong. Do you hear me? *Nothing*."

He glanced down at my fingers. I slowly slid them down his chin, along his throat, and onto his chest. His heart thumped wildly against my palm, and feeling how hard it raced over *me* was like an intoxicating drug that I didn't mind being addicted to.

Finding my eyes again, he asked, "I didn't pressure you or make you feel rushed into anything?"

Laughing at the ridiculous idea, I said, "Not even a little. I wanted to. I *want* to. I was the one who asked you to do those things because I wanted it. And not because I felt like I had to or because you were pressuring me. You aren't pressuring or rushing me. Frankly, that's impossible."

He searched my imploring gaze for a few endless moments. When he saw the truth of my words there, he finally let out the breath he'd been holding, and it was like a weight instantly lifted from his shoulders. His head fell into the crook of my neck, and his strong arms wrapped me into a tight embrace.

"Thank God," he laughed into my throat. "I've been a mess all day thinking that I'd forced you or pushed you into moving too quickly. I was so ashamed, I couldn't even face you. It made me sick thinking I'd made you uncomfortable or made unwanted passes at you like some people have in the past."

I knew which person he was referring to. Dax. On one occasion, Dax had grabbed me forcefully and tried to claim ownership of me, and on another, he'd kissed me while I was battered and broken. It had made me so angry then, and thinking back on those times, I just wanted to erase those bad memories.

I realized then that nothing Rune did ever made me feel that way. All I felt when he touched me was love, security, and happiness.

Pulling back to look at him, I cupped his cheeks. "Not even close. Being with you is a very real desire that's coming from *me*, not pressure from you."

"Promise me you'll tell me if I ever make you uncomfortable."

"I promise."

"Promise me you'll tell me if you're ever not ready for something."

A smile lifted the corners of my lips. I leaned in and placed a gentle kiss on his mouth. "I'm ready for everything as long as it's with you."

The floodgates opened, and the desire he'd been holding back finally rushed forward in a large wave. He reached for me, pulling me flush against him. The heat of his body permeated through my clothes and sank deep within my bones. He gripped the back of my neck with one hand and tilted my head, angling his mouth mere inches away from mine. His burning eyes met mine as he whispered against my lips, "Can I?"

The question took me back in time to our first kiss. He'd pulled me onto his lap and held me close, and he'd posed the same question then. It sent a sweet heat down my body and straight to my core, just as it had the first time.

Grinning, I held his searching gaze. "Always."

He didn't hesitate. His kiss was like pure ecstasy, and it made shivers erupt along my spine. His grip on the back of my head slid down my shoulder, along my back, and over my rear until he cupped me there and hoisted me up. I wrapped my legs around his waist, never breaking our heated kiss. His tongue parted my lips, and the minty taste of it grazing my own elicited a breathy moan from me. Need coursed through my veins, settling deep in between my thighs. I wanted more, craved more.

More kissing.

More touching.

More of his skin on mine.

My fingers tugged at his shirt in a silent plea to have him bare before me. He grinned against my mouth and walked us over to the expansive bed where he deposited me on the edge. My hungry eyes were glued to him as he stood in between my legs. He made quick work of removing his shirt, and while he did that, I gripped the waistband of his sweatpants and slid them down his toned thighs.

I wasn't shy about looking over his deliciously naked body. I didn't think I'd ever get tired of his tan, sculpted stomach, his broad, toned shoulders and biceps, or the deep V of his abdomen. He was seduction given physical form.

My mouth watered as my gaze roamed his hard length. He was long and thick and need made me want to open my mouth wide to taste him. And what was stopping me? If I made him burn with desire like he did me, he no doubt would be hungry for my touch.

My hands glided back up his muscular thighs and came to rest on either side of his swollen shaft. Looking from beneath my lashes, I met his lust-filled gaze. I leaned forward until my mouth hovered centimeters away from his cock, and I didn't miss the twitch of longing there as my warm breath hit the head.

"I want to do what you did for me. Can I?" I asked.

"Hmm." He bit his lips as he pretended to mull it over.

As I waited for his reply, he grabbed the hem of my sweatshirt and pulled it up and over my head. His golden eyes traced my bare skin, lingering on the swells of my breasts, which were still shielded by my bra. His finger trailed a fire along my collarbone, down my cleavage, along the fabric, and back up to my shoulder. My breath hitched in my throat as he reached around my back and unclasped the garment with one skilled hand. It slipped down my arms with his guidance and fell to the floor.

I sat, exposed and breathless, staring up at the stunning man to whom I'd gladly give my all. He looked back at me like I was a work of art that he was lucky enough to admire, and under the power of that amber gaze, that's exactly how I felt.

Bold.

Beautiful.

A masterpiece.

Meeting my eyes again, he finally answered, "Always."

Grinning, I leaned forward. Nerves spiraled around my stomach. I had absolutely no idea what I was doing, but I wanted to learn. I wanted him to guide me so that I could make him feel as good as he made me. Right now, worry tumbled around my thundering heart. What if I made a fool of myself by doing something wrong? Something more powerful than that fear burned brighter inside me, which pushed those anxieties down. *Excitement.* I desperately wanted to see the look on his face when I satisfied him the way he did me.

Without hesitating over uncertainty any longer, I slid my hands along his thighs again until I gripped his hard cock. I grazed my tongue over the tip of his swollen head, and his body jerked under my caress.

He groaned, and I glanced up to find him watching me with hooded eyes. "If you tease me like that, I'm not going to last very long."

Smirking, I took the head and shaft into my mouth. His breathy sigh was enough to make my core throb with desire, and the sound urged me to keep going. I sucked, rubbed the slit of his head with my tongue, and stroked the base of his length with my hand. Spit dripped out of the corners of my lips as he pumped into my mouth, and it took effort to keep my fast pace. My mouth was full, *too* full, and just as my jaw began to ache and the need to take a break became too much, his head fell back, and he let out a deep groan. His hot, salty cum spilled into my throat, and I drank it in all-too-happy swallows.

I'd done that.

I'd brought him to the edge of a dizzying cliff, and he'd tumbled over it, falling into a sea of heated pleasure.

All because of me.

My skin was alive with what I'd done, and my heart hummed with love and pride as I looked up at him. He didn't bother catching his breath. He cupped my cheeks gently, despite the need and urgency I felt beneath his surface, and his lips crushed against mine in a spellbinding kiss. His tongue parted my lips, seeking entrance, which I granted.

He guided me onto my back, trailing kisses along my jaw and neck before traveling lower. My skin electrified everywhere his lips pressed. Wet desire coated my core, and it only intensified when he gripped my leggings and panties, pulling both off together. My legs still dangled off the edge of the bed, and I watched in pure wonder as he got on his knees, spread my legs apart, and leaned his face in for the kill.

My back arched at the first swipe of his tongue over my sensitive clit, and a gasp rushed up from my lungs. He was relentless. Licking, coaxing, tasting me with unhindered fervor. My body was on fire, ignited by so much want. I fisted his hair, moving my hips against that deliciously wicked tongue of his. The tension built and built, turning from a simple flame into an all-out explosion as my orgasm climaxed. My legs shook on either side of his head, and I couldn't hold back my moan under the blinding pleasure I felt in every fiber of my being.

Rune climbed back up my body until he had a hand on either side of my head. He licked his shining lips before smiling down at me. "Delicious."

Breathless and still in a daze, I laughed and closed my eyes as Rune moved to clean us both with a rag. The exhaustion I'd felt after training came rushing back. A content, tired buzz weighed down my limbs, and within seconds, it blanketed my mind. Sleep pulled me under, enticing me with images of sweet kisses, warm arms, and a glittering crown.

CHAPTER

SEVENTEEN

WELL, *FUCK.*

As soon as I opened my eyes and saw early morning light streaming in through the closed curtains, I realized my mistake. I'd fallen asleep right after Rune and I pleasured each other, and I'd slept through the night.

It was now Rune's birthday.

While this wouldn't normally be a cause for alarm, it put another hold on the talk I needed to have with him. I'd meant to tell Rune the truth about who I was last night when we'd gotten back to our room, but with the turn of events, I'd completely failed. His touch, his tongue, his body had all been very distracting.

Today was a day to celebrate him. Dropping the news on him that I was his enemy, the thing he loathed most in the world, wouldn't be the best of birthday presents.

It was fine, though.

What was one more day?

Resolute with my decision, I took a moment to digest my surroundings. I was on my side of the bed, beneath the covers, in an oversized t-shirt. It hit me then that I most definitely had not been in this state when I'd fallen asleep, which could only mean one thing. Warmth blossomed in my chest like a flower basking in the sun's rays. The small, meaningful things he did never failed to amaze me.

He had me wrapped in his warm, strong hold with my rear against his morning erection. The even breathing whispering against my neck told me he was still sleeping, but that didn't last much longer. I wiggled, my butt pressing against his hard length. He groaned, the sound low and deep under sleep's hand. Giggling at his unfiltered response, I moved my hips again, and his arm tightened around me.

"Fuck," he grumbled behind me. He leaned in, pressing his forehead into the crook of my neck. "You're going to be the death of me."

Laughing, I rolled over in his arms. I found his eyes, and my smile grew. "Happy birthday, Rune."

He held my stare as the corners of his lips slowly lifted until his face was completely lit up. He leaned in and pressed a small kiss to my forehead. "Thank you," he said against my skin.

We stayed like that, simply holding each other. I basked in his warmth, and he soaked up my affection. I knew I could spend the entirety of the day like this. That, of course, couldn't happen, though. We had far too much to do, starting with a secret celebration among our friends and ending the day with a dreaded family dinner.

"We should probably get ready before someone comes look-ing for us," I said against his chest.

His chuckle vibrated against my ear. "You're probably right."

We got out of bed, and I took that time to appreciate the

full glory of Rune's naked assets. Statues depicting ancient gods and warriors of old would be jealous of the Silver Fox Fae. From his long white hair to those golden eyes that promised deep pleasure to the toned, hard muscles of his arms, torso, and legs. He was almost too beautiful to look at. Then there was his impressive—

"Do you want the shower first?"

My attention snapped up to meet his eyes, and I didn't miss the smirk he wore. I'd definitely been caught eye fucking him.

Smiling through the rising heat in my cheeks, I practically ran for the bathroom. "Sure. Thanks."

After washing away my embarrassment under the nice, hot stream of the water, I moved to the mirror to blow-dry my hair. As I raked my fingers through the strands, a flash of color caught my attention.

"What the—" I mumbled, grabbing a strand of my hair that typically stayed tucked under the rest. Pulling it into my view, I cocked a confused brow. The tip of my hair was a faint, almost sky blue.

"Well, that's new," I whispered. I pinched the color between my fingers and tried to wipe it off, but it was like the tip had been dyed.

Wariness gripped me tightly as I checked the rest of my head for any other signs of color. Thankfully, I didn't find any, but that did little to settle my nerves. I could only guess that this had something to do with being Water Fae, because my hair turning blue on its own accord wasn't normal. I wasn't sure why this was happening *now*, but I knew it didn't spell good news for keeping my identity a secret.

Checking my toiletry bag, I dug out my fingernail clippers. It wasn't ideal, but it was all I had on hand. As I snipped the strands and watched the blue hair fall down the sink drain, I waited with bated breath to see if it would regrow or suddenly make my whole head blue. Seconds ticked by, but nothing happened. I let out a relieved sigh and tucked the chopped hair back beneath the rest.

Great. Just great.

As if I didn't have enough worries, now I had to worry about my hair turning blue for some damn reason. Dallas didn't have blue hair. Neither did Dax or Rance, so why the hell was mine trying to change?

I sent up a silent, desperate plea to the universe not to let my hair turn blue in front of everyone.

At least, not until I was safely back in Tennessee.

After throwing on my jeans and sweater, I double-checked my hair one last time before letting Rune have his turn in the bathroom. I paced the bedroom and waited not so patiently for Rune to finish getting ready.

The click of Rune shutting off the hair dryer sounded from beyond the door. My heart leapt, and I stood up straighter next to the bed. I wasn't sure what Rune would think of the gifts I held behind my back, but I really hoped he'd like them.

He came out of the bathroom, hair dry, Fox Fae features on full display, and clothes in place. His honeyed eyes shone with affection as they met mine before traveling down to the red gift bag now in front of me. I glanced at the bag with a small, nervous smile. Meeting his eyes again, my grin grew wider and warm as I held the bag out toward him.

"Happy birthday again."

Surprise lit up his eyes, and a tender smile kissed his lips. "You got me something? You didn't have to do that. I told you my family doesn't actually care about that kind of stuff. No one would look at you funny if you didn't get me something."

I shrugged. "I know. This isn't for the charade or anything. I wanted to do something nice for you, even if it's something small like this. Plus, it's your birthday. How can I not get my 'boyfriend' something for his birthday?"

He smirked at my emphasis on boyfriend, and I returned the look. We still hadn't talked about what exactly our relationship was; although, I felt positive we were more than friends, especially after Rune confessed that he wasn't fooling around with anyone. I just wasn't entirely sure if I could say we were a couple. Until that became clear, the charade and jokes about us dating were going to remain just that. Jokes.

Rune took the bag from my hands, and he sat on the edge of the bed with it. I sank down next to him, resting on my knees. I couldn't help but fiddle my thumbs as I waited eagerly for him to open it.

Ripping the tape off the bag's top, he revealed its contents. I swallowed hard as he pulled out the movie, flipping it over to look at the cover. His lips lifted at the corners, and he looked at me with an excited gleam to his eyes.

"You know me so well," he laughed, looking back down at the horror movie.

Sitting up straighter, I leaned closer to him. "You like it? I wasn't sure which movie to get since I don't watch scary films."

My mind went back to the day I'd bought the movie. I had felt so many emotions at that time. Blake, the guy who'd sold me the movie, was a bystander during the few human attacks against me. He'd gotten tied up with the wrong group of people, so he'd been a monster in my head up until that day when he'd revealed that he was Water Fae. I didn't forgive him for his part in what happened, but it did become a bit easier to see him as less of a monster and more human. Or rather, Fae. It was a surreal feeling, thinking about it now. Compared to back then, I was a completely new person in an entirely different world.

Coming back to the present, I took in Rune's bright eyes as he said, "I love it. I can't wait to watch it together."

He set the DVD to the side and gazed back down into the packaging. Holding my breath, I waited. I'd been unsure of what he'd think of the movie, but I was terribly nervous about what he'd think of the last gift. It was the coffee mug I'd made specifically for him during one of my art classes. It was supposed to represent him with the blue background and fox head carved into the surface. But what if he didn't see it that way? What if he thought it was silly? The anticipation was driving me absolutely crazy.

Finally, he pulled out the mug. I forced myself to look at his face, searching for his thoughts in the tilt of his eyes and mouth. I had seen Rune smile before. It was something he did more often these days, but even all the times he'd given me a warm grin couldn't hope to compare to the look he wore now.

He swallowed and looked sideways at me, the hint of some strong, blazing emotion touching the corners of his eyes. "Did you make this?"

I nodded slowly.

His eyes went back to the mug, and he carefully turned it over to take in its entirety. Pink splotches tinted his cheeks, and his mouth was tense as he tried to keep from revealing his smile. Despite him trying to contain his grin, his entire body gave away his joy. From the glow on his cheeks to the glimmer in his eye, the elation nearly bursted out of him.

"Do you like it?" I asked, watching him continue to turn it over in his hands.

The dam trying to hold back his emotion finally snapped down the middle, and the wave of glee rushed to the surface. He leaned toward me, resting his forehead against mine. My skin warmed, and I closed my eyes.

"I love it," he whispered. A tender heat was laced into each word. "I absolutely love it."

Tilting my head closer, I melted into him. The taste and feel of his mouth sent an excited shiver along my spine. My skin grew hot with desire, and my lips begged for more of him. He let the mug sink down on the mattress next to me before plunging his hands into my hair. The sensation of him drawing me closer, pulling my body roughly against him, drove my heart mad. I responded by climbing slowly onto his lap and wrapping my arms around his neck.

My heart pounded against his chest, and my body was ablaze with an intense need for him. Everywhere his hands touched electrified my skin. As his tongue reached for mine, he grabbed at my hips and pulled me down with him, falling back onto the mattress. I rested on top of him, not once breaking our kiss.

Hot, vivid memories from the night before flooded my head, and my stomach twirled with excited flurries. I could hardly contain my eagerness to feel his naked skin on mine. I ran my hands up underneath his shirt, letting the feel of his abdomen and broad chest send my heart soaring.

Just as I started to undo his hard work at dressing, a knock came at the door.

I gasped, breaking our kiss and rolling off him. He sat up next to me, glaring at the door as if it had just murdered his dog. "Someone better be dying out there. What is it?"

Akira's melodic laugh came from the other side. "The only thing dying is whatever you two were doing in there. Come out! We all have something for you, birthday boy."

I flashed Rune a smile, which he reluctantly returned. He leaned in to press a kiss to my cheek and lingered at my ear to whisper, "We'll pick this back up later."

I bit my lip at the promise. Later couldn't come soon enough.

CHAPTER

EIGHTEEN

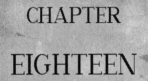

RUNE AND I FINISHED READJUSTING our clothes and made our way to the room next door. Rune went first after my insistence, and as soon as he opened the door to Akira and Bassel's room, our entire group shot colored streamers at him and yelled, "Happy birthday!"

Everyone, including Ardley and the twins, was gathered around the living space. They wore pointed party hats and had hung up balloons and streamers all over the room. A large breakfast of eggs, bacon, biscuits, fruit, coffee, and orange juice covered every inch of the coffee table.

Akira skipped over to us and handed me a party hat. Grinning, he asked, "Well, what do you think, birthday boy?"

Rune laughed as he begrudgingly let Akira put a hat on him. "You guys didn't have to do all of this. It's practically just another day."

Akira shrugged. "We know, but Bria wanted your day to be special. And, to be honest, I forgot how fun it can be to put together a birthday party."

Rune raised a surprised brow as he looked at me. "This was your idea?"

I gave him a sheepish grin. "I hope it wasn't too much."

Before we'd left for Massachusetts, I'd secretly sat down with Avana and the guys to plan what we'd do for Rune's birthday. They'd told me that Fae didn't really celebrate birthdays after the age of twenty-one since that was the age where Fae fully matured in their abilities, and their aging slowed drastically. Every other birthday became unimportant and uncelebrated.

While I understood that Fae lived far longer than I could comprehend, I didn't want today to just be another day for Rune. This was the day he'd come into the world, the day when he'd taken his first breath, the day that had brought him another day closer to meeting me. It deserved celebrating. *He* deserved celebrating. So if Myra was using his birthday as an excuse to get him here, I could use it as one too to have this small celebration of him.

He wrapped an arm around me and pulled me in for a tight hug. "It's perfect. Thank you."

Our small group moved to sit around the coffee table. We spent the morning eating the breakfast that everyone had whipped up downstairs, much to Myra's dismay. She'd apparently requested that everyone join the family for breakfast, but Ardley had declined on behalf of the group. Normally I'd be worried about refusing her, but seeing as how the twins were here, safe and sound with us, I figured this one time was fine. The *real* get-together for today was the required dinner, so declining breakfast wasn't that big of a deal. So, we stayed tucked away in our own little world full of paper party hats, rainbow confetti, good friends, and booming laughter.

Everyone had a story about Rune to share, most of which were embarrassing. Ardley reminisced about the time when they were little, and Balgair, Rune's father, was trying to teach them how to master their ability to control fire. Rune had gotten overly confident and actually set their house on fire. Then there was the time Rune had been teaching the twins how to sled, and as he'd been barreling down a hill outside their home, his sled hit a rock, which sent him rolling down the embankment. According to the twins, he'd looked like a snow monster by the time he was done tumbling down the slope.

There wasn't a dry eye in the room by the time everyone shared, and my stomach hurt from laughing so hard. Rune punched Ardley in the arm for starting the endless cycle of embarrassing tales, to which Ardley laughed and ruffled Rune's hair.

"So, what else should we do today?" Avana asked, popping a strawberry in her mouth. "It's your day, Rune. What would you like to do?"

"Definitely something outside of this house," Rune replied. He draped an arm over the back of the couch, and my body became hyper aware of his touch against my shoulders. "I know my mother will find an excuse to get us involved with them downstairs, so it's best to leave."

"The weather is nice today," Ardley said. "How about something outdoors?"

"The beach?" Rune offered, looking at everyone. "We could picnic out there, play some beach volleyball, soak up some sun."

"Yes, please!" Akira practically squealed.

"Is that good with you?" Rune asked, meeting my eyes.

Was it good with me? Not really. It meant being surrounded by water—currently a concern of mine—but I was struggling to come up with a reason to say no to the beach. Rune knew I loved being near the water. I'd just have to be extra careful that my emotions didn't get the better of me.

Finally, I said, "It sounds perfect."

With our plan made, we finished up breakfast and spread

out to divide and conquer tasks. Avana and I packed a lunch down in the kitchen while the boys cleaned up breakfast and organized the beach bags. With everything set, we headed off for a day of fun in the sun.

When we got there, the crowd was small, most likely because the autumn weather didn't make the water very inviting. Still, there were a few families out enjoying the warmth of the day.

"Last one to the beach has to carry all the stuff," Ardley yelled as he flung open the car door and raced toward the lapping waves.

Laughing, the twins were quick to jump out with Marlow, and the trio chased after Ardley.

Avana punched Bassel's arm and said, "How about it, Liger? I bet I could beat you there."

Bassel smirked. "Oh, you're on."

They quickly fumbled out of the SUV and set off at high speeds toward the water.

"Well," Akira said, sticking his head in between the driver and passenger-side seats. He passed a bright expression between Rune and me. "Should the three of us carry everything down together?"

"How did the birthday boy get stuck with the manual labor?" Rune grumbled, but I saw him fight a smirk as he climbed out.

Together, we loaded our arms with baskets, bags, and folded chairs. The hike down the embankment was short, and our group was already in play mode, chasing each other up and down the shoreline.

"Who do you think won?" I asked Akira and Rune.

They followed my gaze to where Bassel and Avana were huddled by the water, bent at the knees, laughing. Rune and Akira shared a knowing look and said at the same time, "Definitely Bassel."

We laid the large blankets out on the sand, and the gentle breeze stirred the waves of my hair. I tilted my face into the wind and inhaled the salty, fresh scent of the ocean. Within the push and pull of the waves were the whispers that always followed.

I closed my eyes and honed in on the whispers until they were all I heard.

Bria.

Princess.

Home.

Here.

Smiling at the water's greeting, I silently said hello and focused on the peace that settled within my bones. I hoped that, by showing the water I was calm and well, no mishaps would occur while we were here.

Opening my eyes, I turned my attention to the sunny horizon. As I basked in the beauty of it all, strong arms went around my waist and hoisted me up. I squealed as Rune settled me into a princess hold, and he took off for the water, whooping and hollering.

"You look like you need a swim," Rune chuckled as the water reached his bare toes.

I wrapped my arm tightly around his neck in an effort to anchor myself to him. "Don't you dare! I didn't bring a change of clothes!"

Mischief brewed in his eyes. "You can go naked. I definitely don't mind."

"Oh really? You're fine with everyone here seeing me naked?"

He frowned as if just remembering there were other people around. He glanced at the few strangers and our friends. "Damn. We should ditch them."

Throwing my head back, I laughed. "You're ridiculous, Fox Boy."

He rubbed his nose along my neck and jaw, whispering against my skin, "What can I say? I'm possessive over what I cherish. Comes with the territory."

Cherish.

My heart clung to the word as though it were the only shred of light in a tunnel of darkness. His admission was something I needed, now more than ever. It meant he cared for me, and those feelings gave me hope. When I told him the truth tomorrow, I hoped those feelings would be enough to overcome the anger, hurt, and distrust he'd no doubt feel. I hoped he'd choose me over his hate for Water Fae. I couldn't lose him.

He was *home* to me.

Despite how happy his words made me, there was also a major question mark over them. He'd said before that he couldn't let me in any further, but since then, we'd shared numerous vulnerable moments. Maybe he'd finally realized that giving in and opening himself up would be better for the both of us.

Swallowing hard, I wiggled in his arms until he set me on my feet. The sand burrowed in between my toes, and the cold water moved about my ankles. As soon as our gazes collided, the corners of his eyes softened, and the look made my heart beat wildly.

Placing my hands on his shoulders, I asked, "Cherish as a good friend or something more?"

A flicker of emotion crossed his features, but it was gone too quickly for me to read. "I think you know the answer to that."

"I want to hear you say it."

His heated gaze traced my own. He opened his mouth to say something when, all of a sudden, we were hit with a cold splash of water.

Gasping, we spun to find Ardley doubled over, laughing. "You two looked like you needed a nice cold shower."

Rune growled and stalked toward his cousin. "You're such an ass."

The two began fighting in an all-out splash war, so I quickly retreated to the safety of the blanket where Akira sat back on his hands. While it sucked not hearing Rune's answer, I knew we could finish our conversation later where we'd have far more privacy.

"Those two are such a handful," Akira said as he watched the cousins try to knock each other into the rolling waves.

"An unstoppable duo," I agreed. I reached into the beach bag to pull out my sketchbook and pencil, eager to draw the scene before me. The sand, the rolling waves, the smiling faces of my family. Nothing could be more perfect.

"Here comes another unstoppable duo."

I followed Akira's attention a little way down the beach. Carlos raced across the sand toward Bassel, who met him half-way. Bassel caught the lean boy in his strong arms and twirled him in the air before claiming Carols' mouth with his own. It seemed the two were doing great now, and I wasn't sure if I'd ever seen Bassel smile that brightly.

"I'm happy they made up," I said, matching the reunited couple's warm expressions.

I turned back to Akira, and my grin faltered. Akira stared at the two, but he had a far-off, wistful look, as though he wasn't really *seeing* them. As seconds ticked by, his smile grew fainter, and pain began to creep its way into the corners of his eyes. Just as I'd never seen Bassel smile so fully, never had I seen Akira look so ... lost. He always wore a smile and looked at the bright side. To see him so distraught made my heart twist with concern.

"Hey," I said, leaning toward him, my art forgotten. "Are you okay?"

He took a deep breath before turning his brown eyes on me. A smile was plastered back on, but now I saw it for what it was.

A mask.

"I'm fine."

"Don't," I said firmly. "Don't pretend around me. You can talk to me. About anything."

He held my unwavering stare, and I knew what he'd find as he searched my gaze. A promise. My words were a promise that I'd always be there for him, good or bad, just as I would any of our friends. They were my family now, and each of them occupied a place within my heart. If they hurt, I hurt. If they were happy, I was happy. If they needed to talk, I'd be there to listen. Always.

Which made my secret hanging between us even more gut-wrenching.

Finally, he ducked his head. "I was remembering things of old. Things that shouldn't matter anymore."

Going out on a limb, I asked, "Is it about the guy? The Water Fae you told me about before?"

The night I'd first been attacked by Jonah, I'd discovered the truth about who Dax and Dallas were. At the time, I'd heard nothing but bad things about Water Fae, so when I realized that Dallas, one of the most important people in my life, was Water Fae, it felt like my world had imploded on itself. Akira had opened up to me briefly about his views on that kind of Fae, and in doing so, he'd mentioned that someone incredibly special to him was Water Fae. I hadn't pried then as it wasn't a good time, but I'd always thought the person he'd referenced must have been his lover.

Akira gave a silent, humorless chuckle and faced the sea. "Jesiah. Yeah. Jesiah is the Water Fae I told you about before. He's who I was thinking about, even though I shouldn't be."

"Why shouldn't you? You've made it clear that you being Land Fae and him being Water Fae mean nothing to you."

"It doesn't. At least, not anymore." Akira gave me a half-hearted smile. "Jesiah and I were together for decades. He was—" he paused, searching the waves for words. Finally, he looked up at the clouds and smiled. "He was my sky. My wind.

What made me soar. Water Fae and Land Fae were on good terms back when we found each other, so it wasn't an issue for us to be together. But when talk of war began and our kinds started feuding, we'd started disagreeing. He was advisor to the King and Queen. He sided with his people, and out of anger, I sided with mine. When war broke out, we parted ways. Stupidly."

I swallowed hard. I couldn't even begin to imagine what that felt like—to have other people's issues keep you from being with the person you loved most. I glanced over to where Rune was now on his knees, head thrown back in a laugh as he buried Newt in the sand.

Well, maybe I did know what that felt like, in my own way.

Looking at Akira again, I asked, "So what happened then? Did you reach out to him once you realized that letting the war keep you apart was stupid?"

He closed his eyes and hung his head. "I haven't been able to find him. I—" His voice caught, and he had to swallow down the emotion before he finished, "I don't even know if he's still alive."

"Do you have any evidence to suggest that he isn't?"

"No more than I do to suggest he still is."

"Then don't think that way. You have to hope. Hope that he's still out there somewhere, missing you just as much as you miss him."

Akira met my eyes. After a few moments, he nodded. "You're right. I shouldn't think so negatively. I guess it got so much harder to picture where he was over time that I eventually assumed the worst. I was in a really dark place back then. I lost sight of who I was, what I wanted, and I even forgot what it felt like to laugh."

My eyes widened, and it took me a moment to recover from my shock. "*You?*"

Akira chuckled and nodded. "Crazy, right? It's true, though. I was so broken and alone. I never smiled anymore. Didn't like to talk or be around people." His attention suddenly turned to Rune across the sand, and the corners of his mouth lifted as warmth flooded his eyes. "Not until I met Rune."

Pulling my knees close, I waited with eager ears. "How did you guys meet? What happened?"

Akira tilted his head as he watched Rune decorate his little brother's buried torso with sea shells. "I came to the human realm in search of Jesiah. When I couldn't find him, despite years of searching, I fell into a downward spiral. One day, I went out to drown myself in alcohol, as one does. While I was sulking alone at the bar, Rune walked in. It wasn't long before a woman came up and slapped him right across the cheek. He didn't even look fazed as she left, almost like that was a normal, daily oc-currence. He sat down next to me and said, 'You look like you've seen better days.' I'd obviously just watched him get smacked, so I told him so had he. And you know what he said?"

I shook my head. "Not a clue. What?"

"He paused a minute, looked at the door where the woman had left, and said, 'No, today's actually a pretty good day.'" Akira laughed at the distant memory. "Don't ask me why, because I really don't know, but when he said that, I lost it. I laughed until my sides hurt. For the first time in years, I *laughed*. He made me remember what it felt like to feel alive and happy again."

Grinning, I asked, "Was that the start of your friendship?"

"It was. From that day on, we were always together, and he never failed to make me smile. He was there for me in my darkest moments, helping me to see the light that I'd forgotten existed at the end of the tunnel. Not long after that, it was my turn to be there for him."

My chest tightened. I knew what Akira was remembering. Akira had to comfort Rune when his father died. When I tried to picture Rune back then and what he must've been like during that time, my heart bled with agony. Losing his dad had to be one of the hardest things he'd been through, and the pain, grief, anger, and loathing he'd surely felt as a result had shaped him and his beliefs. Beliefs that all Water Fae were evil and undeserving of life. Beliefs that allowing people into his heart would only destroy him. It hadn't been easy, but slowly, he seemed to be realizing that maybe he'd been wrong about those things.

Grief was a fearsome opponent, but so was support from those who loved you. Hate could leave you blind to truths, but forgiveness could heal that hurt and allow you to see again.

Hopefully, his view of Water Fae as monsters was also shattering. He had to know there were good Water Fae out there after realizing I was best friends with one, and he'd even said that if faced with a reality where I was Water Fae, he wasn't sure he could bring himself to hurt me. That notion gave me hope for the conversation we'd have tomorrow. It didn't quell all my fears, though, because while I knew he wouldn't hurt me, there was still a chance he could reject me and I'd potentially lose him forever.

Turning back to Akira, I grabbed his hand and squeezed. "Thank you for telling me that. All of it. I'm sure it's never easy to talk about Jesiah."

Grinning at me in his usual way, he said, "Thanks for listening. I don't talk about him often with the guys, even though I know they'd let me. Despite him being Water Fae, they'd still listen, because they love me. Still, I don't want to bring up stuff that triggers bad memories for them. It was nice talking about him and getting it off my chest."

Swallowing hard, I turned my attention to our blanket. I picked at the edge, needing something to do with my hands. Akira had been so open and honest with me. He'd done that because he trusted me. He knew there would be no judgment, no shame, no ill will in talking to me, because we were friends. I knew the same to be true of him. No matter what was burdening my soul, Akira would listen without issue because that was what friends did. It was what *family* did.

Taking a deep breath, I sought out his ever-patient and loving smile. "Hey, Akira?"

"Yes, Bria-chan?" He looked at me, giving me the exact comfort I needed.

"I want to tell you something. Something really important." I glanced nervously around us, afraid the wind would pick up my whisper and carry it to nearby ears.

Sensing my worry, Akira stood from the blanket, wiping a few particles of sand from his legs.

"Rune!" Akira called.

Rune looked up at us from the mountain of sand he was now molding into a castle with his brothers.

"Bria and I are gonna run to grab something from the store. We'll be back."

I leapt to my feet and started after Akira, but before I could make it far, a warm and firm hand slipped into mine. I was yanked back and spun around until my chest was pressed against Rune's torso. Affection made its home in his gaze as he looked down at me, making my breath catch in my throat. Still in a blissful head spin from being pressed against him, I didn't realize what he was doing until his mouth was pressed to mine. His lips were soft like velvet, and they urged my own apart for his tongue to ever so slightly graze against mine. This kiss was soft—so unlike our heated kisses—yet this one felt much more intimate. It was slow and over as soon as it started, which made each second his lips were on mine all the more precious.

Rune pulled back and looked into my eyes. His voice was for my ears alone as he said, "Hurry back. Be safe."

"I will be."

I meant those words. Sure, I was about to reveal my secret to a Land Fae, but that Fae was Akira. I'd trust the Raven Fae with my life. Despite knowing that I was safe with him, my anxiety still fired off in my bloodstream, because as soon as I left here, as soon as I said the words, *everything* would be different. There was no turning back.

CHAPTER

NINETEEN

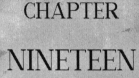

WHATEVER YOU'RE ABOUT TO TELL me, just know that I love you."

Akira's words took root in my heart, and I clung to the warmth of that feeling as I smiled at him across the patio table. We'd driven a small way down the beach to a nearly empty coffee shop.

The waitress brought us our lattes, and I gripped the hot, steaming mug on either side. The faint burn seeped into my palms, and I focused on that instead of my next words. I decided the best way to do this would be to just get it over with, like ripping off a Band-Aid.

Meeting his brown eyes, I took a deep breath. "I'm Water Fae."

His brow furrowed, and confusion seeped into the tilt of his eyes. "Come again?"

I shook my head and pressed my palms harder around the mug. "I know. It's a lot, but it's true. I'm Water Fae."

"How can that be? We did that test on the boat, and when you were attacked, you didn't heal right away."

"That's because my abilities were still suppressed during that time. I hadn't awakened yet."

I could practically see the gears turning in his head as he fought to make sense of what I was saying. After taking a large sip of my latte, I dove into my story. I explained what happened that night I fought Jonah, as well as the explanation Dallas had given me.

Akira's eyes nearly bulged out of his head, and he leaned toward me. "You're the Water Fae Princess? *Uwa! Sugoi!* You're a Princess, Bria!"

Laughing at his excitement, I nodded. "Apparently so. I don't feel like one, though."

He looked up at the moving clouds and gave a short chuckle. "Princess. Ha. No wonder Land Fae couldn't find the prince. There was no prince."

Downing the last of my coffee, I stared into the now empty mug. I'd finally laid everything out for Akira. While, on one hand, it felt like an immense weight had been taken off my shoulders, a new pressure settled on my chest. He'd listened to my entire recounting and explanation, and his face had remained blank for the most part. I had no idea what was going through his head right now or what he now thought of me. Not knowing was making me sick.

His small hand slid across the table until it rested on top of mine. My eyes immediately lifted to his, and the world seemed to still.

He was smiling at me as he said, "This changes nothing between me and you. You're still one of my best friends, and I still love you. Human, Land Fae, Water Fae. None of that matters. You're still Bria, and I love you."

Tears crept into my eyes as relief began to grow in my chest and stomach.

Akira moved from across the table and wrapped me tightly in his arms. I hugged him hard, holding onto this moment where I finally felt momentarily free and weightless of the burden I'd been carrying. This revelation could've gone so differently. He could've turned me away, shunned me, or given up on me. But instead, he loved me, regardless of whether I was Water Fae or not.

"Thank you for telling me," Akira said. "I know that couldn't have been easy. Does anyone else know?"

Pulling back, I wiped my eyes. "No. I've only told you so far. I finally decided to come clean to Rune, but I haven't yet. To be honest, I'm completely terrified about telling him the truth."

Akira studied me before gripping both of my hands in his. "I know you're scared, but I think you'll be surprised by how he takes it."

The air in my lungs stopped, and I choked out, "Surprised good or surprised bad?"

"I've known Rune for a long time. I've seen him at his best and his worst. When Rune lost his dad, he also lost his mom, in a way. Believe it or not, Myra wasn't always so cruel and twisted. She changed after Balgair died. Then, when their family was starting to rebuild and he was given two brothers, Myra became even more wicked. Rune was forced to leave when he realized that Myra would hurt the twins as a way to hurt Rune. To keep them safe, he left, which meant losing them.

"With each loss, pain chipped away at his spirit more and more until there was nothing left but a big, empty void. He put up so many walls and defenses, and in doing so, he lost his ability to love or really feel anything except hurt and rage. You got a hint of that when you first met him."

The memory of Rune at the start of our journey was crazy to recall. In the beginning, he'd always been standoffish. He never smiled, at least not really. He avoided deep conversations, and it was easy to trigger his anger. He'd changed so much since then.

We both had.

"But then you came along." My attention snapped back to Akira as he continued. "For the first time in so long, I finally saw my best friend laugh and smile again. I watched as that void inside him started to get filled slowly but surely, all by you. So have faith. I don't think he'll respond the way you think he will."

THIS CAKE LOOKS FREAKING DELICIOUS," I said as I climbed out of the car with the large dessert in my hands.

After Akira promised that he wouldn't tell anyone my secret, we'd ditched the coffee shop. We swung by a local bakery to pick up a birthday cake since we needed to bring something back as our excuse.

"Isn't all cake delicious?" Akira asked as he rounded the front of the car.

"Absolutely not," Carlos answered as he jogged up the embankment from the beach and headed right for us. Smiling wide, he placed his hands on his hips. "Red velvet cake is *no bueno.*"

Akira's jaw dropped, and he spewed off something in Japanese that I was sure translated to him being offended.

Carlos ignored it and turned to me. "I was coming to see if you needed help carrying anything. Plus, I wanted to introduce myself properly since we haven't met yet."

"That's kind of you," I said warmly. "I think I've got everything. But it's really nice to meet you finally. I'm Bria."

"Carlos," he said brightly as he fell in step with Akira and me.

"She knows." Akira snickered, clearly having moved on from the cake slander. "We told her about your and Bassel's love story."

Carlos' tan cheeks pinkened. "Well, that's embarrassing."

Laughing, I gave him a reassuring look. "Don't worry. I got a very brief version. I'm happy you two reconnected. Bassel seems absolutely smitten."

Carlos ducked his head to hide the flush climbing up his neck and ears.

"Thank God. They didn't die," Ardley announced as our trio walked across the sand.

The twins saw us with the cake, and they immediately began jumping up and down in celebration. Everyone gathered around the blanket and, despite Rune begging us not to, linked arms and sang happy birthday at the top of our lungs. Rune tried to blame the crimson of his cheeks on the sun as the cake was cut and passed around.

"Bria."

"Hmm?" I turned to Ardley, and as soon as I looked at him, he swiped his finger on my cheek, smearing frosting on me.

He threw his head back, laughing at my shock. "I'm sorry. I couldn't help myself."

"What did you do to her?" Rune asked. He crooked his finger under my chin, turning my head to face him. A mischievous glimmer touched his eyes as soon as he saw the white frosting trailing from my cheek to the corner of my mouth.

"He truly is your cousin," I mumbled.

This moment reminded me of when Rune took me on our first "date" to a painting class, and at one point in the night, Rune had gotten my attention in much the same way, all so he could smear paint on my face. The jokes clearly ran in the family.

Grinning, Rune kept his hold of my chin and leaned forward. My stomach coiled tightly with anticipation as his tongue made quick work of the frosting. He licked away the icing with two flicks, and I couldn't help the slight hitching in my throat that came with what the motion called to mind.

"Yum," he whispered in my ear, lust making the word strained.

I swallowed hard as he pulled back enough for his eyes to lock on mine. So many emotions rushed to the surface in his gaze, each one coming and going so fast that I couldn't decipher them all. The ones I did, though, made me want to lean in and claim his mouth in a soul binding kiss.

Someone cleared their throat, and I suddenly remembered we had an audience, two of whom were only ten. Cheeks flaming, I glanced over at the twins. Marlow had each pinned to his sides, shielding their eyes with his arms. The knowledge did nothing to extinguish the heat of embarrassment in my face.

Rune leaned back to reach around me and punched Ardley in the shoulder. "No jokes, dick."

Ardley chuckled. "I can do what I want. She was my friend first, remember?" The way he drew out the last of his sentence made Rune narrow his eyes. His cousin merely laughed and winked at me.

Pursing my lips, I commented, "Your fox version seemed to have a much different attitude. Less …" I paused, searching for the right word.

Ardley snickered. "Spirited? Fun? Joyful?"

Rune tensed next to me, so I glanced at him. He was focused on his cake, shoving fork fuls into his mouth. Maybe he'd almost choked? I patted his back, just in case.

Facing Ardley again, I said, "I wouldn't have used those words. You just seemed … different."

Their characters were too dissimilar. One could argue it was because communication as a fox was limited for him, so I couldn't gauge his personality accurately when he was in that form. My gut said that wasn't right, though. My fox had been calm, calculating, receptive, and curious. Ardley was the exact opposite. It felt like, as a fox, Ardley would be active, hyper, quick to nip as a joke, and far less reserved. It was *too* different, even for a lack of communication.

Ardley's black curls spilled over his forehead as the wind blew. His brown eyes held mine as he shrugged. "I was probably just at a loss. It's not every day you stumble upon a gorgeous girl by the river."

"Ardley," Rune snapped.

The cousins grumbled at each other, but I missed the exchange. I was too busy studying Ardley. He'd said river, but we'd met at a stream. Sure, the guy could've called it a river since the stream technically branched off from the river near campus. Still, I found that choice of word odd. That wasn't the only weird thing I'd noticed about Ardley being my fox, either.

I decided to test him with something he couldn't confuse.

Cocking a brow at him, I nonchalantly scooped a bite of cake onto my fork. "I was wondering. Do you still have that ring I gave you that day we met? I was just curious if you held onto it or not." I chewed on my cake, waiting to see if he'd slip up or not.

He grinned. "I sure do. It's not on me, though. It's back at the house. Didn't want to risk losing it here at the beach."

I tried not to choke on my swallow. Forcing a smile, I nodded. "Good thinking."

Wrong.

He hadn't corrected me.

When we met, I'd given the fox a *necklace*, not a ring. There was no way he could confuse those two, so either the exchange didn't mean as much to him as it did to me, or he wasn't my fox. My gut told me it was the latter.

I glanced at Rune. He stared at Ardley, jaw tense and eyes focused. He noticed me looking at him, and his gaze flicked briefly to mine. The tension around his mouth evaporated. He gave me the smallest of smiles before looking away altogether. That sealed my suspicions, and the list of things for Rune and I to talk about later had just gotten longer.

Everyone finished up the last of the cake. With some time left before we had to return to Myra's for Rune's birthday dinner, we played around the beach. I helped the twins find seashells, and Rune and I competed in a sand sculpting contest to see who could create the best castle. It was artist versus architect, and after being judged by the esteemed panel of judges—Marlow, Avana, and Carlos—I won. Rune was a sore loser, and he tackled me into my castle, destroying the structure beneath our weight. It was worth it, though, because as soon as our friends turned their backs, his mouth was on mine in a slow, tantalizing kiss.

I wanted the day to go on forever, but sadly, it was time for us to head back to Rune's for the dinner everyone was dreading. None more so than me.

CHAPTER

TWENTY

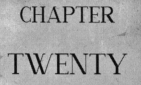

I QUICKLY SHOWERED AND CHANGED into my floor-length
blue dress. Rune waited in the hall, and I found him leaned
against the wall across from my bedroom door. A dark
button-up hugged his arms and chest, leaving little to the
imagination, and the black dress pants hinted at the muscles in
his legs.

God, I loved it when he wore all black.

As soon as he saw me, his eyes softened. "You look exqui-
site."

Cheeks warming, I ducked my head. "Thank you."

"Come on. Let's finish getting you ready."

We turned to head into Akira and Bassel's room
where Avana waited to put her illusion on me. Our
friends gathered in the space, all wearing somber
frowns.

I looked around and asked, "Where's
Carlos?"

"He went home," Bassel said. "I told him he didn't want to be here for this shitty dinner."

"Speaking of dinner," Rune started. "It's probably ready, so go ahead and get downstairs."

"Oh?" Akira said, looking out the door warily. "You mean, we're actually doing it? Eating downstairs? With your family? In the same room? At the same table?"

Rune hung his head and rubbed at his eyes. "Unfortunately."

Akira straightened his shoulders. "Well, then, let's get this over with."

He gathered the twins, taking one of their hands in each of his. Everyone slowly followed him out until only me, Rune, and Avana remained. She made quick work of adding the fox features to me, and I noticed she did it with more ease every time we put it on. I was even getting used to the pinprick sensation that came with the transformation.

Something I wasn't used to and probably never would be was the way Rune looked at me when I wore my fox features. A sweltering heat seemed to enter his gaze when I turned toward him, and the air between us became charged with an electric, pulsing desire. I knew, for him, seeing me looking like one of his kind must be reeling in the best way possible. I was sure it made him wonder, *what if?*

What if I were actually a Fox Fae?

What if I were an actual potential mate?

What if I were someone from a good, strong Fox Fae bloodline?

Would things be different?

They were interesting questions, ones that gave me plenty to think about, but there was no point dwelling on them. Because I wasn't Fox Fae. I wasn't even Land Fae. I couldn't change who I was, and I didn't want to. So the *what ifs* were pointless.

"Ready?" Rune asked.

His eyes searched mine, and I knew if I said no, he'd do everything in his power to keep us away. No wasn't an option, though. This was the moment for which we'd worked so hard. We were finally going to be sitting down with his whole family with nowhere to run, and hopefully, our studying and plans paid off.

Squaring my shoulders, I nodded. "I'm ready. Let's do this."

Our group gathered outside of the dining hall. The carefree smiles and laughs from earlier in the day had been traded for straight faces, stiff shoulders, and nervous fidgeting. Everyone was clearly on edge, especially Marlow. His whole body shook, and he was dripping actual puddles of sweat onto the floor.

Or maybe that was water.

"One dinner, that's all," Rune said to the group. "The sooner we go in, the sooner we can go back to our rooms."

Everyone nodded in agreement before we made our way into the dining room. It was an expansive space with windows that rose high to the vaulted ceiling. Gold curtains hung over the glass panes. A large, dark oak table sat in the center of the room with a deep red rug laced with gold and cream patterns beneath it. There were twenty-two chairs seated around the table—ten chairs on each side and then one at either end.

Myra was already seated at the head of the table, facing the entryway, and I didn't miss the way her features tightened when she saw me. I guessed she'd really thought I'd tuck my tail and run after our talk. I made sure to hold my head a bit higher so that the message was clear.

I wasn't going anywhere.

Sinopa, Rune's aunt, sat to Myra's right with her husband, Crevan, on her own right. Aidan was seated next to him. On Myra's left was Lilith, with Devoss on her left. Alvaro sat at the foot of the table, and he turned in his chair to look our way. They all watched us as we filed into the silent room.

I tried keeping an air of confidence about me as I followed closely behind Rune. Newt and Greshim entered with shoulders back and chins up, like soldiers marching. Alvaro didn't give them nearly the same welcome as he had the day I met him. I wondered if that had something to do with Myra's presence.

Ardley smiled brightly, not seeming the least bit phased by the tense atmosphere. He slid into the chair next to Aidan, winking at her as he sat down. She grimaced and quickly turned to face the other way.

Rune took the seat next to Devoss, and he gestured for me to sit next to him. I sat down, flanked on my left by Newt. Greshim took the seat next to his, and Marlow sat next to him. Akira plopped down next to Ardley, while Bassel sat next to Akira, and Avana flanked him.

Once everyone was seated, I felt the room's silence deep within my bones. No one uttered a word, and everyone sat so still that if a stranger walked in right now, they'd probably confuse everyone here with statues. A veil of awkwardness settled as all of Rune's party began to glance between each other. None of us wanted to be here, and frankly, I didn't think Rune's family really wanted us here, either.

"So," Alvaro started.

The sudden boom of his voice nearly made me jump out of my skin. I turned and found him looking in my direction.

Alvaro placed his fingers on his chin as he propped his elbow on the arm of the chair. "Bridgett. How was it you and Rune met? We've never seen you at Fox gatherings, so we're curious."

Forcing a polite smile, I said, "It's Bria." *Asshole.* "We actually met when we were both out one night with friends."

"She won me over with her dancing," Rune added. He smirked as he threaded our fingers together on top of the table.

The feel of Rune's warmth grounded me, and the nerves

started to subside. His touch was a reminder that I wasn't alone in this stifling room with people who didn't want me here.

I glanced at Aidan and found her narrowed eyes locked on my fingers laced with Rune's. I wanted to smile, finding some satisfaction in her anger. It felt good to be openly chosen, especially after Aidan had tried seducing Rune the other night.

"So you met at a club," Myra said, her tone matter-of-fact.

"How esteemed," Lilith mumbled dryly.

"It's how a lot of people meet these days," Rune said, and I didn't miss the edge creeping into his voice.

"Perhaps people with no class," Sinopa commented without even looking in our direction.

Before anyone could respond, Myra asked, "How many children do you plan to have?"

Ardley spluttered on the water he'd just drunk. All eyes zeroed in on him as he choked, for which I was thankful, because I was pretty sure I resembled a tomato at the moment. I knew kids were a big part of why I was even here—to show Myra that Rune was ready to settle down and make lots of Fox babies. Still, being blatantly asked the question in front of *everyone* made me feel like I was sitting there naked with a single spotlight on me.

"Drink slower, son," Crevan said with an unconcerned shake of his head.

"How about we don't discuss babies and reproduction at the dinner table?" Ardley asked, giving an incredulous chuckle. "How does talking about our days like a normal fucking family sound? I'll start. Today, we went to the beach."

Ardley went through the events of the day, and he seemed overly happy about not letting anyone—specifically Aidan and Myra's group—get in a word. Rune squeezed my hand and traced a small circle along my skin with his thumb. I gave him a faint smile, grateful that he was there. I was even more grateful that Ardley didn't stop talking until the food arrived.

Men and women, including Charles and Edgar, came out a set of doors off the dining room. They carried trays covered with silver lids and placed them in a neat arrangement in the center of the table, easy for everyone to access.

When they removed the lids, my stomach dropped into a pit of unease. This dinner was about to get a lot harder.

CHAPTER
TWENTY-ONE

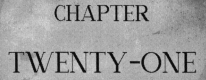

RAW MEAT. THERE WERE MULTIPLE trays with nothing but uncooked—and, in some cases, bloody—meat. One dish had slices of raw fish with the head of the creature placed in the middle of the pieces, and the round glassy eyes, devoid of all life, seemed to practically stare at me with a promise that I was next.

I also noticed something small and narrow on the fish platter. Anger simmered low in my blood, extinguishing my previously unsettled nerves. Near the fish head was a dead, preserved salamander, and it didn't escape my attention that they seemed to have placed that plate directly in front of Marlow.

He began to squirm in his seat as he started mumbling, "Good salamander. Be a good salamander or that will be you. Good salamander. Be a good salamander. Don't let them eat you, too."

I frowned, wanting more than anything to reach out and hug him. I glanced at Myra to see if she was enjoying his reaction like the sick woman she was, but she wasn't paying any mind to him. Instead she, like those near her, was taking different foods from the dishes set closest to her.

I glanced back at all the food, and my nerves seemed to come barreling back. Only one platter held fruits instead of meat, but it did little to reassure me. The Fae around me ate raw meat, but I wasn't sure if it was safe for me to do so. Sure, I was Water Fae, but did that mean raw steak and chicken were safe?

I wasn't confident, and even if it was safe, the very idea of trying to bite into chewy, bleeding beef made me gag. The fruit was the safest route, but I worried that eating fruit alone would make me suspicious.

I glanced warily at Rune as he pulled an array of foods onto his plate. When he finished, he grabbed my plate and started piling it with the different fruits that were set out before him.

When he handed me my plate back, I looked sideways at him as though silently asking, *Is this okay?*

He gave me a subtle nod and set my plate down in front of me. I looked down at the colorful rainbow of fruits. Red strawberries and raspberries, green kiwi, and dark blackberries. They glistened in vibrant hues, looking fresh and delicious. My stomach instantly growled, and my mouth watered.

I looked up to see if anyone else was eating the fruit yet. I wanted to see how they ate it, so I would know what to do. Normally, I would use my hands for fruit, but I wasn't sure if that was proper etiquette, which I knew Myra valued. I'd be damned if I got rejected yet again just because I didn't eat some berries properly.

Sinopa plucked a strawberry from her plate with her fork.

I let out a relieved sigh as I picked up my own fork.

Just as I started to eat, Myra called, "Bria."

I looked up at her, a viselike grip seizing my throat.

She cocked a curious brow as she questioned, "Why aren't you having any of the meats? We have some of the finest meats in the country here."

"Bria doesn't eat a lot of meat," Rune said, looking over at his mother. "She likes fruit more. Everyone has their preferences."

"Is her tongue broken?" Myra asked calmly. "If not, I'd prefer Bria speak for herself."

"Agreed," Lilith started. "Plus, your mother went to all this trouble to prepare this food. It's rude for her not to have *any* meat."

Rune opened his mouth to respond, but I gently laid my hand on his arm. He looked at me, and I flashed him what I hoped was a reassuring smile. "It's okay. Lilith is right. It's rude of me not to eat what they prepared."

I slowly looked over all my options. Right now, it wasn't about putting on a good show for the sake of the relationship. It was about ensuring they didn't suspect I was something other than Fox Fae. If they discovered I was anything else, they'd be furious, and I was pretty sure I'd end up exactly like that fish. I could eat some raw shit to live another day.

Unless it poisoned me.

Then it was a lose-lose situation.

Since I wasn't sure if my being Water Fae protected me from food poisoning, I decided to look at it as if I were still human. I knew to stay away from the raw chicken, since that could seriously hurt me. I was pretty sure that I could eat the steak and be okay, but I wasn't confident in my ability to keep a poker face upon tasting it. Bile rose into my throat at the thought of blood seeping out of the flesh with every chew, slowly filling my mouth.

I turned to the fish. I enjoyed sushi, so maybe it wouldn't be so bad? I'd pretend it was nigiri while I ate it.

I had Marlow pass me some slices, and I stared at the milky white meat that sat next to all of my mouth-watering fruit.

Man. I really wish I could just eat the berries.

Rune watched me with a mask of ease, and I had to admit, I envied his ability to appear indifferent. I hoped that I could replicate it as I ate the fish. I swallowed hard, feeling everyone's eyes on me.

Plucking the fish from my plate, I brought it up to my lips. A waft of the fish's aroma hit me as I lifted it to my mouth, and I had to bite the inside of my cheek to keep from gagging. My elongated fingernails bit into my flesh as I tightened my hand into a fist under the table, hoping the sting would help me keep my composure. If the smell did this, I was horrified to see what I would do upon tasting it.

I readied myself to keep a straight face no matter the taste and opened my mouth. Suddenly, Rune grabbed my wrist. He pulled my hand toward him, angling the food in his direction. Before I could protest, he leaned forward and ate the fish off my fork.

My mouth hung open. I furrowed my brow at him as he gave me a mischievous grin. I yanked back my hand, picking up another piece of fish. I held my breath again, trying to conjure the same confidence I had before. The fork was nearly to my mouth again when Rune leaned over and ate the meat off of my fork once more.

Irritation pricked at my insides, and I couldn't hold back my glare. "Rune," I forced out between clenched teeth.

How was I going to prove anything to his family if he kept eating my proof? Everyone else looked between one another with raised eyebrows and, some, with frowns.

Ardley laughed and leaned across the table. He stole the remaining bit of fish off my plate before eating it himself. My stare was fixed on his amused grin while he chewed, and my anger became directed at both of them.

"Ardley!" Sinopa huffed. "Don't steal other people's food."

"Sorry, Mother," Ardley said with a devious glint in his eye. He passed that look between me and Rune before giving his mom a cheeky grin. "What can I say? I really love the fish."

Myra glared at Rune and Ardley. Her voice was cold as she said, "Stop acting like children. If it isn't a problem, which it shouldn't be, you will let the girl eat her food."

"Agreed," I huffed, giving both boys a pointed look. "You should really let me eat my food."

"Why don't you get more, girl?" Lilith said, nodding at the platter. "Eat those last two pieces since we've all had some."

Annoyed that I was still the center of attention, I forced my voice out evenly as I asked Marlow to pass me the last pieces. I really wanted to get this over with and eat it. The attention they were all drawing toward us was becoming stifling. Rune's face remained stoic as he watched Marlow nervously put the two remaining slices on my plate, but I could feel how tense he was sitting next to me.

My dish hovered in front of the twins as Marlow passed it back to me. They glanced at the plate, then at their older brother. I grabbed my dish, but before I could pull it back, Newt and Greshim reached out, snatching the two slices. They quickly shoved them in their mouths, and my eyes went wide.

"Newt! Greshim!" Myra growled.

Greshim swallowed his piece and warily glanced at his mother. "Sorry. We really wanted more."

Myra's eyes darkened as she stared at her two youngest sons. Fear made my stomach curl tightly, and I couldn't help but wonder what she'd do to them for that.

Not only were the twins in a precarious situation, but this also put me in a predicament. All that was left now was the beef and chicken. My throat closed up in protest when I pictured eating either option, especially the chicken. Clearly, the boys didn't understand that they'd eaten my only safe choice.

Rune and the rest of my friends shared a conspiratorial look. They all immediately snatched any food within their reach. Myra and the others watched in disgust as everyone devoured the food in mere seconds. No meat. No fruit. It was all gone.

I stared at the empty serving dishes with my mouth agape. As I passed a look between everyone while they worked to swallow the food, I was surprised to find that my anger had dissipated. In its place was the warm, light flutter of thanks. I understood what they were doing now.

They were watching out for me, even Ardley and the twins whom I had just met this week. I couldn't eat the food if there was no food.

"Rune," Myra said, her voice surprisingly calm despite the rage burning brightly in her eyes. "What kind of stunt are you trying to pull?"

Rune's mask of ease snapped, and he glared at his mother. "You want to know what stunt I'm pulling? Well, then, let me spell it out in clear terms for you. Bria is my chosen partner, and guess what? She's a vegetarian, just like your good friend, Lui. You know, the powerful Fox who's bested hundreds of Water Fae? Bria chose a lifestyle like him, but I knew you and everyone else would use it against her, claiming she's not Fox enough because of it. You'll find whatever reason you can to belittle her and determine that she isn't good enough, despite her being the person *I* chose. You wanted me to find someone, a mate to breed with and live beside. Well, I have. Bria is my lover, and no matter what you say or think, *Mother*, she's not going anywhere. Because she is Fox enough."

Myra narrowed her eyes on Rune, and chills ran along my spine. He, on the other hand, didn't look fazed one bit. In fact, he suddenly smiled as he turned to look at Ardley, and the two of them broke into conversation, talking about what they'd each been doing for the past three years. Akira, Bassel, Avana, and Marlow jumped in, erupting in pleasant conversation. It was like that blow-up—the declaration from Rune—never happened. The bubble of tension we'd been in popped and fizzled away into nothing.

Slowly, Rune's family started eating what little food was left on their own plates. Rune's words had been firm, leaving no room for debate.

My being vegetarian wasn't a part of our initial plan—nor was it true—but I was glad he'd thought to use that. Not only did it explain everyone's drive to defend me, but it also made it look like I was so invested in Rune and being good enough for his family that I'd been willing to eat meat. Maybe it would score me some brownie points, although knowing his family, they probably wouldn't care.

Something else about Rune's words really struck a chord within me, and I couldn't seem to shake the heavy weight of disdain.

He'd said I was Fox enough for him, and with the amount of conviction in his voice, it felt genuine. That was a hard pill to swallow. His words were yet another reminder of the vast difference between us, as well as the untold truth. Guilt seeped into my bones, digging sharp teeth into my very soul. I couldn't wait for tomorrow to get here so that I could finally rip off this Band-Aid, and hopefully, Akira would be right. Maybe Rune would react better than how I imagined.

I was a bit shocked to see Myra give up the argument so easily, but I also wasn't sure if I'd call her silence 'giving up.' Her methodical gaze stayed trained on me throughout dinner like a ghost of a touch, pulling at the hairs on the back of my neck or making my fox ears twitch. Even when I wasn't looking her way, I felt her stare, and I knew deep in my bones, she was far from done with this.

She was waiting.

Biding her time.

Looking for an opening to trip me and claim her kill.

CHAPTER
TWENTY-TWO

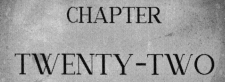

INNER ENDED AFTER WHAT SEEMED like hours, and we all returned to Akira's room. Silence hung over the group like a storm cloud, but once the door was shut, that cloud evaporated. Newt and Greshim rushed toward Rune with frightened eyes.

"Big brother!" they cried in unison and hugged one of his legs.

"Rune," Greshim sniffled. "Are we going to get in trouble with Mother?"

"I d-don't want M-Mother to hurt m-me again," Newt cried.

Grief pinched Rune's brow as he knelt down in front of them. He hugged them close, and his jaw worked as he fought to keep his voice gentle and calm. "Don't worry. I'm here, so nothing will happen."

My heart fractured as I watched the two small boys tremble in fear as they thought of what their mother would do to them. It made me sick. While the twins stayed with us, they would be protected but never truly safe. But who would protect them when we were gone?

"That was awesome," Ardley said as he collapsed on the love seat. "Did you see the looks on those clowns' faces? It was price-less! I wish I could've gotten a picture."

"We hardly ever have *that* much raw meat for dinner," Rune said, as he turned his attention to me while still holding the boys close. "We only eat it on really special occasions, and as we said, birthdays aren't special for us. So, it's obvious she did that to test you."

I shook my head as I let out a heavy sigh. "This is crazy. I thought we did well planning everything, but it's like she saw through it from the beginning."

"Why does she want to test Bria so much?" Greshim asked, looking up at Rune.

Rune smiled at him and patted his head. "It's nothing, guys. Why don't you two go get cleaned up and get ready for bed. I bet Marlow and Avana will let you sleep with them in their room."

Marlow's glossy eyes passed between Rune and the twins as he grinned. "I like having friends over. I do, I do."

Newt leapt toward Marlow and asked, "Can we m-m-make a water slid-de like last time?"

Marlow nodded with eager eyes. The twins quickly left the room, saying goodnight to everyone as they raced to get ready for bed with Marlow in tow. With them gone, we all sat down and tried to figure out our next move. Myra would definitely have something else up her sleeve, but we had no idea what it would be. I found my resolve getting weaker and my anxiety growing stronger the more we talked about it.

We finally dropped it when the air in the room had gotten so heavy that it was hard to breathe. The stress from dinner eventually caught up to everyone, so we parted ways for our respective rooms. I think everyone was eager to decompress.

"Are you okay?" Rune asked once we were alone in our room.

I sank onto the edge of the bed and pulled my fox tail around me to run my hands through the soft fur. "Just tired from that dinner. Who knew sitting in silence with a bunch of strangers who won't stop staring at you could be so exhausting."

He nodded in understanding as he came to stand in front of me. Tucking some hair behind my ear, he asked, "Is there anything I can do to help you unwind?"

I bit my lip as my mind immediately went to very dirty, hot, and naked places. There were most definitely some things we could do to unwind, but first, I really felt like getting some fresh air.

"I'm gonna take a walk outside real quick. But after that, yes, please."

The corner of his mouth tilted up. "You take your walk. I'll make some popcorn and drinks. We can watch that movie you got me."

I beamed at him. "That sounds great."

We weaved through the halls together and made sure to keep our voices low. We didn't want to draw any unwanted attention by alerting people to our presence. When we reached the first floor, we parted ways.

As I traveled down the carpeted hall, I took note of the walls on either side of me. They were barren. No photos. No art. Nothing to showcase any sense of family, something I'd noticed the day the twins gave me a tour. In actuality, there were hardly any personal touches throughout the house at all. I found it pretty sad. The home felt like an empty shell, a husk of what could've been.

When I had nearly reached the French doors, I saw what looked to be a sunroom to my right. It was one of Myra's offices, which had been closed the day of the tour. Inside, straight across from the door, sat a fireplace, and hung proudly above the mantel was a picture.

The painting was of Myra, but she wasn't alone. Standing next to her was a man with long, platinum hair, pulled back in a ponytail with a single red ribbon. He wore a white suit with a blood-red rose in the left-hand breast pocket. Myra's hair—shorter than what it was now but still long and lush—cascaded down her back. She wore a long, A-line gown that matched the same shade of white as the man's attire, and both were in Fox Fae form.

They were captured in a warm embrace. Myra's hands were wrapped around his neck, and dangling from her slender fingers was a bouquet of red roses. The two individuals smiled brightly at one another, their sharp Fox Fae canines glistening. I could practically feel the love radiating between them just from looking at the piece.

Wanting to see the image up-close, I turned to step into the room when I felt a sudden presence behind me. I quickly spun, gasping slightly. Myra stood there with a blank expression. She had her clawed hands folded neatly in front of her, and she stood poised and proper as always. She glanced from me to the picture. When she met my eyes again, I swallowed hard. This was it. She was surely going to snap at me for snooping, especially since she'd made it obvious that I wasn't wanted here.

"My previous husband and I," she said, her voice devoid of emotion.

She glided past me and walked into the sunroom. I looked after her, unsure if I was supposed to follow or not. She approached the painting until she stood directly in front of it, staring up at the wonderful event it depicted. She turned back to me again.

"I look much different, do I not?" she said with a bitter smile.

I let out a silent, nervous breath and dared to take small steps into the room. "Y–You are still just as beautiful. I envy how stunning you are, both then and now."

Her attention turned back to the picture. "Flattery will get you nowhere with me."

I ceased walking and held my breath again. Complimenting her was obviously the wrong move. While I worked to recover from my blunder, I noticed her eyes growing softer as she continued to gaze at the man in the picture.

"Still, I feel like that is something Balgair would have said, too." She glanced at me, then added, "Balgair was my husband before Alvaro. He's Rune's father. He was taken from me—from all of us—by Water Fae. I'm sure Rune has told you that already."

"He did," I answered softly.

I was reeling. It felt like I'd stepped into an alternate universe, because Myra was *talking* to me. About *personal* things. Maybe she was feeling ill.

As if sensing my thoughts, she spun around to look directly at me. Her face became blank and unreadable once more. "Fox Fae only fall in love once. Loving someone is extremely difficult. The mere idea is sickening. Fox Fae think of ourselves first and foremost. To care about someone more than ourselves is extremely rare. Most simply come together for the purpose of breeding and creating powerful offspring. I was one of the few who learned to love another person more than I loved anything else. Then he was stolen from me, and with the end of his life, was the end of mine.

"Rune hates the idea of love, relationships, or even caring about someone. He has never shown interest in anyone, just like every other Fox Fae. So, I'm sure you understand why it is so easy for me to see that this relationship between the two of you is nothing more than a farce. A game. That being said, I am a master of games, and I always come out victorious. You should back down now for your own sake and for Rune's."

She gave me a wicked smile as she started to make an exit. When her shoulder met mine, she stopped. I stared straight ahead, my body paralyzed under the weight of fear as she laughed darkly, whispering, "Of course, I do not know why I'm giving you a history lesson in our kind since you are one of us, too. Silly me."

She resumed her exit until I was the only one left in the room. My stomach was in my throat, and all the air seemed to have left with her. She knew. She knew that Rune and I weren't really together, and she knew I wasn't Fox Fae. The room spun around me in dizzying twirls. I had to do something. I had to convince her that she was wrong, if not about my being Fox Fae, about her idea of my relationship with Rune. Anything to salvage our hard work for this trip. There was too much on the line—Rune's future, the twins' well-being, my safety—for it to end like this, for Myra to figure it all out. There had to be something I could do or say to turn this around.

I raced after her. She had just reached the main entryway by the time I caught up to her, and she was starting to take a step up the staircase when she saw me. My clawed hands shook as I crinkled my dress in my nervous grasp. I swallowed hard, preparing myself for what I was about to say.

"I know I'm not who you picked out for Rune. I'm probably nothing like what you want for him. I mean, when you compare me to someone like Aidan, whom you did deem worthy of him, I obviously don't compare. She must be from a good family line and is just as frighteningly confident and headstrong as you."

I looked down at my feet and let out another breath. Squeezing my eyes shut, I barreled onward. "But I love Rune. Your son means more to me than I could even put into words. I've grown to love and accept his snarky, prideful, sarcastic side, as well as the part of him that's caring, sympathetic, and human. I love the man he is inside, and that won't change."

Releasing my dress, I stood up straighter and took a deep breath. With my head raised to stare straight into Myra's cold eyes, I said, "I love Rune, Myra. You can all throw insults at me, you can try to make me doubt everything, but it won't work. He and I are together, whether you want to accept it or not. We *are* dating, and we'll continue to do so, with or without your approval."

I tried calming my thundering heart as her narrowed eyes never wavered from mine. If not for her slitted eyes, I would've thought she hadn't heard me from how still she stood. It was like she was waiting for me to speak again or make some sort of motion. The silence filling the grand hall tightened my stomach until I thought I might heave.

Not able to take any more of this awkward air of stillness surrounding us, I opened my mouth to speak as she slowly turned away from me. Her attention went to the top of the steps, and I could practically hear the cynical smile in her voice as she said, "Well? What did you think about that?"

Confused as to who the hell she was talking to, my eyes followed her line of sight. As soon as I saw him, all the color drained from my face.

Rune stood at the top of the steps, and he stared down at me with his mouth hanging slightly open. His eyes were wide in surprise, and he started to take a small step down the stairs.

My heart tripped over itself, and I subconsciously stumbled back.

Holy shit, holy shit, holy shit, holy shit! Rune heard me!

What I said was true. Every word. But I'd never said anything so honest about my feelings to Rune's face. Sure, I'd said I loved him before, but never like *that*.

I needed out.

I needed water.

Whether it was suspicious or not, I couldn't stand here with Rune looking at me like I'd stolen all the air from his lungs and Myra bearing witness to my first *real*, lengthy confession to him.

Swallowing hard, I squared my shoulders and addressed Myra. "Since Rune's here, you can take up any issues, concerns, or suspicions with him. I don't answer to you."

Without another word, I turned on my heel and yanked open the front door.

Myra's laugh followed me outside as she cooed, "Lovely talking with you, Bria."

CHAPTER

TWENTY-THREE

CRAP ON A FREAKING CRACKER! I roared.

The water whipped up and out of the stream. It raced toward me until it wrapped around me like a second skin. Once I was encased in the cool current, my frustration and embarrassment slowly dissipated. I closed my eyes and focused on that sense of calm. There was no sense in getting worked up over what had already been done. Rune knew how I felt now, which meant the ball was in his court. He'd have to figure out what to do about that confession.

I took a final deep breath beneath the water's current, and when I released it, the water moved away from my skin until it hovered in front of me as an ever-shifting, shapeless form.

After racing out the front door, I'd retreated to the woods where Dallas and I had trained briefly. I needed the peace and quiet to sort through the situation, and plus, I could feel the buzz of my powers vibrating softly in my fingertips the closer I got to the lake. I knew that I was bound to have an accidental, magical outburst, so I thought it would be best to retreat to the privacy of this stream.

The shapeless water still hovered in front of me as if waiting for further command. Smiling, I said, "Thank you for calming me down. I'm okay now."

With my reassurance, the water bounced. It flipped backward, splashing into its place in the stream.

As I made my way back through the woods, the gravity of how I'd spoken to Myra really hit me. I'd been a mess of emotions at the time, and my anger had won. Part of me began to drown in worry. I'd wanted to impress her and the rest of Rune's family for the sake of the charade, but I was starting to gather that may be impossible. I'd definitely not be accepted once they knew the truth about who—or rather, *what*—I was.

Lights lit the back of the house from various windows, and I focused on that glow to guide me the remaining distance. From here, the expansive home looked inviting and warm, flooded with signs of family life.

Oh, how looks could be deceiving.

Family had your back at all times, and their faith in you was unwavering. Family loved you, despite your faults and mistakes. Family supported you and believed in you, despite obstacles that got in your way. Myra wasn't Rune's family. They shared blood, but that was the extent of it. His real family were the people right beside him, the people who'd flown all the way here to have his back. So, I'd forget about Myra. I'd stop worrying over what she genuinely thought of me. I'd stop caring what Rune's grandparents, aunt, and uncle thought when they looked at me. Because their opinion didn't matter. Rune's real family had already given me their approval.

As I drew closer to the mansion, I glanced up at the back of the house and realized Rune was sitting on the railing of our balcony. He gazed out a long way across the water, far into the distance. He didn't seem to notice me below. Even in the dark, I could see that there was so much pain and anguish written into the lines of his face, which made my stomach lurch.

I was still embarrassed about what happened back in the hall, but I wouldn't avoid him or our impending discussion. We had to come to an agreement as to where we stood, and I had questions for him regarding my suspicions from the beach—suspicions about my fox.

It felt like I was moving through quicksand as I walked through the rear French doors. I tried ignoring the fact that Rune had heard my passionate confession as I made my way to our room. The further I got away from the calm sensation of the water, though, the more panicked I felt about talking to him.

This conversation could change everything.

It could change *us* if that was what he decided.

It was too late, though, because I was already in our room, walking toward our balcony.

Rune sat on the stone railing, leaning against the corner post. His arms were crossed over his chest, and he stared out toward the lake that stretched beneath the night sky. The wind caught strands of his blond hair and tossed them gently around his face. His eyes shone even more brightly than usual with the moonlight reflecting off them.

When I stepped onto the patio, he looked at me. I forced a smile and asked, "Can I join you?"

Giving me a half-hearted smile, he shrugged. "Sure, if you enjoy shitty company."

Rolling my eyes, I leaned against the doorframe and hugged my arms around myself. "You're not shitty company."

I ducked my head and scratched at the fox ears atop my head, preparing to launch into a more intimate and real moment with him where I officially laid out my feelings in a clear and honest way, but he beat me to it.

"That reminds me," he started with his attention turned to the lake once again. "I've wanted to tell you how blind you are ever since we first met."

Arching a confused brow, I said, "Come again?"

"It was crazy to me. I didn't understand why someone with such a good heart would be with someone so terrible. How could someone like you fall for someone as blatantly heartless as Dax? I never understood that or why you ran off to shed tears over someone as worthless as him. But then again, I haven't been any better, have I? So my point still stands. You're blind when it comes to picking good men."

I frowned and narrowed my eyes at him, momentarily setting aside his diss of my taste in men. My gaze was drawn from his eyes down the planes of his face and to his neck. That silver chain that he occasionally wore hidden beneath his shirt, paired with his words, made my heart start racing. Fresh nerves broke out in my stomach, and my footsteps were measured as I walked over to his side. His eyes had turned down at the corners as countless emotions flickered across them before they seemed to settle on misery. I reached out my hand to pull the chain from underneath his shirt, exposing the pendant.

Time stood still, freezing my heart mid-beat. My breath caught in my throat when I saw the small, blue gem.

It was my necklace.

The one I'd given to the fox.

My hunch had been correct.

Shock battled with elation in a fierce tug-of-war with awe winning out in the end.

He gave me a small smile as he whispered, "I told you that you'd find him here."

I swallowed hard. "It's you. It's been you this whole time."

"It has. I wasn't planning on telling you yet, at least not like this, but Ardley fucked it up at the beach. I mean, I told him it was a necklace. How could the idiot confuse a necklace with a ring?"

Utterly baffled, I asked, "Why didn't you tell me the fox was you? Why'd you have Ardley pretend it was him?"

He closed his eyes and hung his head. After a moment of silence, he finally answered, "I was afraid."

"Afraid? Afraid of what?"

He took a deep breath and got to his feet. When he stood, I had to tilt my head back to look into his eyes. His features were stricken with some sort of internal burden. I desperately wanted to reach out and smooth away his frown and troubled eyes. I held back, though, waiting for him to speak.

"I've done a lot I'm not proud of. How I treated you in the beginning is something I regret."

Eyes going wide at the admission, I reached toward him, wanting to reject the idea, but he held up a hand.

"I was horrible to you." His voice broke, and the pain buried within the depths of his eyes came crashing forward like a tidal wave. "I treated you badly in an effort to keep distance between us, and in doing so, I hurt you. I said so many things that I wish daily I could take back, and the way I acted was unforgivable."

He squeezed his eyes shut against the memories that were no doubt resurfacing.

It was true. The start of our friendship had been unconventional, and his attitude back then was, at times, hurtful. He had been fueled by rage, grief, and fear, but that changed. *He* changed. I came to understand his motives and the reasons behind his words and actions. I didn't want his apology over *back then*, because it led us here to the point where I'd fallen in love with him. We'd both changed for the better because of our time together, which included the rocky start.

"Every time you brought up the fox, your face would light up," he said, his gaze searching mine. "You'd get this undeniable excitement in your eyes at the idea of getting to meet him. After all I'd done, I couldn't help but wonder if you'd still feel that way after finding out that fox was actually an asshole like me."

"Rune—"

"I didn't want to disappoint you. I wanted the fox to stay the way you imagined. Kind. Trustworthy. So, I asked Ardley to pretend to be him."

"So that time when we were all sitting around, finalizing plans, and Bassel made the comment that I'd met Ardley before …"

Rune shook his head. "A lie. He said it to make you believe Ardley was the fox."

This news was a lot. After Ardley's slip-ups, I'd suspected my fox was someone else, but having Rune confirm it was like finding out a print of a painting was actually *the* painting. I was over the moon. Rune and my fox being one in the same was enough to make any anger I felt over the lie dissipate on the passing wind.

Stepping closer to Rune, I fought against the excitement trying to lift the corners of my mouth. "You're right. If I had known the fox was you, it wouldn't have been the same."

He inhaled sharply as hurt flared behind his eyes.

Wrapping my arms around his neck, I finally let my smile break wide open, exposing my Fox Fae canines. "Knowing that the fox is you makes him even more special. He means more to me now. How could he not? He's actually the guy I'm in love with."

His eyes softened, and a swell of affection flooded them. "I don't deserve your love."

I shook my head and pulled him closer, pressing our foreheads together. "*We* deserve *each other*."

His arms went around me, and he pulled me all the way against him. The warmth of his body seeped through my clothes and into my very bones, bringing forth a sense of calm. This was where I loved to be. In his arms, pressed flush against him, our breaths intertwining, his heartbeat pounding in sync with my own. This was my safe place. This felt like home. We didn't need words. We just needed each other.

He gave a humorless chuckle, and the sound vibrated against my chest. "I was an idiot if I thought I could actually do this."

"Do what?"

"Pretend. Pretend I was fine only being friends. I was an idiot if I thought I could deny you. I can't do it anymore. I don't want to be just friends."

My heart started beating erratically. I held my breath and waited.

"I have a lot of flaws," he started.

I shook my head. "Not to me."

"I'm hot-headed."

"I don't mind."

"I'm naturally possessive and territorial."

"I know."

"I'm not good at expressing my feelings."

"Debatable."

He was quiet for a moment. "Even knowing all that, you still want me?"

I pulled back and grinned. "Always."

Looking completely at a loss, he shook his head. "Why?"

"You say you have flaws."

"Many," he said with a firm nod.

"I say you have quirks, just like anyone else."

"Quirks?" He cocked a brow at me, as though trying to weigh whether or not to be offended.

I nodded. "You're hot-headed, but you're passionate. You only lose your head when it's over something you genuinely believe in and care about."

He tilted his head side to side as he thought about it. "I guess that's one way to look at it."

"You're possessive and territorial, but it comes from a place of love. You're protective, loyal, and thoughtful."

"I don't like people messing with what's mine."

"And sure, you're not always the best at expressing how you really feel *verbally*, but I can still tell. It's in your eyes." I slowly traced a finger over his brow. "It's in the tilt of your lips." My finger trailed down his cheek and grazed lightly over his bottom lip. "It's in the *way* you say things. So, even when you can't say something, I still know."

His gaze changed then. All of the doubt disappeared, and instead, a warmth blossomed within his golden eyes. A smile slowly lit his face as he squeezed me against him. "Do you know then?"

"Know what?"

He cupped my cheeks and tilted my face up toward his. His words were a whisper against my lips. "That I love you."

My heart swelled with euphoria like a match suddenly catching fire. Hearing the words leave his lips was like finally stepping out into the sun after months of complete darkness. Warm, blinding, and exhilarating. Four words had never managed to steal the air from my lungs like those. Four words had never been so powerful.

An uncontrollable grin spread wide on my face. My eyes slipped closed, and I leaned in to his touch. "I love you, too."

His mouth crushed mine, and his hands moved from my cheek and into my hair. With the admission of his feelings, it was like any restraint he used to have disappeared. He was done holding back, which was evident in the way his lips claimed mine, the way his tongue slid along the seam of my mouth, and the way his hands grabbed at my body. He was hungry for me, and a needy shiver traced along my spine as I thought about what was to come from his unhindered fervor.

"I want you," he bit out against my mouth.

His tongue flicked against mine, and I gasped into his parted lips. "Then have me."

As soon as the words left my mouth, he didn't hesitate. His lips were back on mine, and he pressed his weight into me, pushing me backward. I worried about tripping or falling over the balcony threshold, but Rune's guidance kept me upright as I walked backward into the room. One of Rune's hands stayed buried in my hair while the other slammed the patio door closed behind him. He grabbed at my dress, pulling the material up and over my head.

His eyes traced my skin for only a moment before his lips reclaimed my own. The tips of his fingers drew a dizzying trail of fire up my waist, over my stomach, and across the fabric of my bra. Need pooled in my middle, and I grabbed at his shirt, yanking off the annoyance. His bare chest stole my breath, looking just as magnificent as it had the first time I saw his firm torso. His maker had been good to him.

"I want you naked underneath me," Rune growled against my throat. His lips trailed my neck, and I let out a gasp as he bit down on my earlobe. He made quick work of removing my bra as I twitched under the throbbing between my legs.

I fought to catch my breath before pulling his mouth back to mine. He ran his hands down my wide hips, and as he passed lower, his fingers slipped into the band of my underwear. Once beneath the fabric, he sank to his knees and took the clothing with him until the panties were pooled at my ankles with him staring up at my naked body.

I bit my lip under the intensity of his stare, and liquid heat slicked its way across my middle. I stood before him while still wearing my Fox Fae illusion, exposed and breathless, and he knelt there, worshiping me with his gaze. His eyes glimmered in awe as he beheld me, as if *I* were the most beautiful person he'd ever seen. If the fire in his gaze didn't tell me all I needed to know, the hard mass needing to be freed from his pants certainly did.

"You are perfect," Rune said once his gaze found mine.

"So are you."

His fingertips skimmed across my bare skin, starting at my ankle and moving up my leg. The pad of his finger slipped in between my thighs and swiped slowly across my sensitive clit. I gasped at the jolt of pleasure that shot down my spine, and my legs shook as I fought to keep standing. Rune's eyes never wavered from my face, and his chest rose with a sharp inhale as he watched my reaction.

"Tell me what you want," Rune commanded, his voice husky and deep.

What I wanted was *him*. All of him. We'd finally confessed how we felt. I wanted to experience him fully, with no boundaries left between us, but I knew I couldn't ask for that yet. He'd been honest with me tonight, but I was still hiding a huge part of myself. Until I came clean with that news tomorrow, I didn't want to cross this line. It felt like doing so would be a betrayal or almost like I was taking advantage of him. It was still his birthday, and I refused to ruin or complicate it with my truth.

Since this was a day all about him, I said, "I want you to teach me what you like. I want you to show me what you enjoy."

A devious and wicked smile, one promising unimaginable pleasure, graced his lips. "There's so much I'd enjoy doing to you. But *something* does come to mind. If you want to do it."

"I want to."

With a new kind of fire settling in his eyes, he got to his feet. My heart thundered in my chest as he placed his hands on my hips. I thought he was going to guide me to the bed, but instead, he pushed me toward the cushioned chairs in the small seating area. I swallowed hard under the intensity of his glowing eyes, and his hungry gaze followed me as I sat on the edge of the plush chair. He sank to his knees in front of me once more, putting us at eye level, and I thought I might come undone right there with how heated I got under his arousing gaze.

He bit the corner of his lip and leaned in until there was not even a breath between us. When he spoke, his lips grazed mine. "So many things I'd like to do to you. So many things I'd like *you* to do to *me*."

My eyes slipped down of their own accord to his luscious mouth, which still only skimmed mine in a teasing touch. "I can. *We* can. Every day now."

The sound of his chuckle rumbled deep within his chest. His large hands coasted up from my ankles, over my calves, around to my knees, and up to my inner thighs. My breath hitched in my throat as he parted my legs as wide as the arms of the chair would allow, and the cold air kissed my wet middle. The sudden touch of chill to my center tightened my core with a fresh wave of need and awareness, one that made me grip the arms of the chair and sit up straighter.

He pulled back enough so that his lust-filled expression could meet mine. "If you don't like this, tell me. We can stop anytime if you want."

The offer was one that had me curious about what was to come—no pun intended. All of the dirty possibilities that ran through my mind left me breathless, even before Rune moved.

He grabbed one of my hands and guided it from the arm rest to in between my legs. I inhaled sharply as butterflies took flight in the pit of my stomach. My eyes locked on Rune's as he settled my hand against my throbbing core and began to move our fingers together over the tight bud of nerves. Pleasure rocked through me at the press of our combined touch, and I couldn't contain my gasps, which only served to ignite the fire within his eyes.

"Touch yourself," he commanded in a whisper against my parted lips. "Touch yourself and think of me."

I let out a breathy moan as I did. His eyes glazed over with pure desire, and seeing the way he watched me while I worked and built toward my orgasm made the rush of satisfaction break through even quicker. My eyes slipped closed, and my head fell back. My entire body shook as the waves of my climax coursed through my body.

I was breathless, hot, and slightly embarrassed at having done something like that in front of him. But I didn't focus on any of those things. I'd been thoroughly satiated, but Rune was still rock hard within the confines of his sweatpants.

Biting my lip with my canines, I said, "Your turn."

Our faces were still mere inches apart as he pushed the band of his pants down and gripped his large shaft. He pumped himself fast, and I caught his groan on a kiss. My tongue brushed past his lips, and I wrapped my hands into his long hair to hold him in place. I could tell when he was close because his body went rigid beneath my hands. Moments later, he gasped into my mouth as his hot seed spilled over his cock, splattering across my stomach.

Our heavy breathing was the only sound that filled the space as our gazes locked once more. We were hot, sticky with cum, and unable to fight back our large smiles. It was the perfect ending to his birthday.

CHAPTER

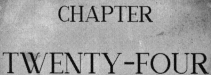

TWENTY-FOUR

L OOK HOW GORGEOUS!" I BEAMED, working to take in
the full view of my surroundings.

Our group of friends had just parked at the local
fall festival, in a spacious farm field by the edge of
town. There was a corn maze cut into the stalks at the back
of the property where families were already lined up to test
their maze-solving abilities. A tractor pulled a wagon of people
sitting on hay bales to the other end of the property where a
pumpkin patch was set up. Dozens of stands, carts, and ven-
dors lined the property to create makeshift walkways, and they
advertised food, games, clothes, art, *everything*. The yellow,
red, brown, and orange colors littering the décor and
grounds screamed autumn, and my fall-loving
spirit demanded we get started so that I could
see everything the event had to offer.

"Welcome to our little town's fall festival,"
Rune said as he rounded the front of his car.
His hand slid into mine, and our fingers wove

together. He looked down at me and nodded toward the entrance. "Are you excited?"

"Is pumpkin a fruit?" I fired back.

He quirked a brow. "Yes?"

"All right then!" I squealed, squeezing his hand tighter and pulling him toward the entrance.

When we'd gotten up this morning, I'd had every intention of finally telling Rune the truth about who I was. The twins however had other ideas. As soon as we'd gotten ready for the day—for the second time, since we'd ended up undoing each other's hard work from the first time—the twins had knocked on the door and wanted us to help them decide what to wear to the festival.

"Can we do the corn maze?" Greshim asked from where he held Rune's other hand.

Rune grinned. "Sure thing."

"What about th-th-the pumpkin patch?" Newt asked, looking up at me. He squeezed my hand, which he held onto.

"Whatever you guys want," Rune answered.

"Aw, what a good, doting big brother," Ardley teased, walking behind our chain of locked hands.

"Would you like me to be your big brother, too?" Rune smirked, glancing over his shoulder.

"Ha!" Ardley laughed, then dead panned, "No."

"We should make sure we do everything so that Bria gets the full fall festival experience," Avana chimed in as she and the rest of our group caught up with us.

"Definitely try the cider, Bria," Carlos said while walking hand-in-hand with Bassel. "The cider here is amazing."

"I couldn't agree more," Rune said as he glanced sideways at me with a spark in his eye.

The way he looked at me, the glimmer of something raw and warm in those amber eyes brought the memory of last night rushing back, and heat gripped me in its horny clutches. While

Rune and I had explored each other in a much more physical way, last night had also been about trust, openness, and honesty. Not only in our actions but in our words, too. For the first time, we'd both been completely vulnerable with how we felt. We'd finally said those words out loud.

I love you.

I didn't know what our confessions meant for us. I didn't know if they made us a couple officially, or if Rune's meant he was just ready to give us a shot. But that was okay. We would have time to figure that out together.

Hopefully.

Because today was the day my truth would come out.

Things were going to change, for better or worse. I just hoped how far we'd come and all we'd shared would be enough to convince him not to hate me.

Our group finally made it past the entrance, and excitement erupted inside me. The smell of pumpkin, cinnamon apple, fresh-fallen leaves, and fried foods wafted on the passing breeze. Kids giggled as they traversed the grounds, tugging their parents along. Up ahead, we joined the line to buy tickets and passes for all the activities.

After getting wrist-bands for unlimited games, we meandered through the long lane of stalls.

"Seeing as it's your first time," Rune started, squeezing my hand. "Why don't you pick what we do?"

I scanned the bustle of the festival. It was nearly impossible to choose, so I decided it made the most sense to start at one end of the festival and work our way to the other.

"How about the corn maze?" I said. "We can work up an appetite for some of that food."

The corners of his lips lifted. "Corn maze it is."

The ten of us ventured over to the corn maze. Greshim bounced beside Rune as he awaited our turn to enter.

"I'm excited. I've never done a corn maze before," I said.

"Really?" Greshim exclaimed. His wide eyes suddenly narrowed with mischief as he pondered something. "Should we have a little competition then?"

"A competition?" I laughed.

"Yeah! To see who can complete the maze the quickest."

"I like that idea," Rune said with a devious smirk. "Are we on teams?"

"Of course," Greshim said, with a confident tilt to his chin. He crossed his arms and continued, "Me and Newt versus you and Bria."

"I want in on this, too," Ardley said, raising his hand.

"Count me out," Marlow said with a quick shake of his head. "Mazes give me anxiety."

"I'm with you, buddy," Carlos said. "I get too overwhelmed too quickly."

"*Babe*," Bassel grumbled as Carlos left Bassel's side to link arms with Marlow.

Carlos just laughed at Bassel's disappointment and blew him a kiss.

"That makes it even then," Ardley said. "The teams can be Rune and Bria, Newt and Greshim, Akira and Bassel, and me and Avana."

"We'll wait by the exit," Marlow said with a sudden twinkle in his eye. "We can keep track of who wins and where everyone places."

"This is going to be so fun!" Greshim cheered.

After a short wait, we entered the maze and were greeted by a large opening in the corn with six different paths to choose from.

"Alright, here's the starting point," Ardley said as everyone huddled close. "I'll count down from three, and we'll all go."

Rune leaned in close to me and whispered, "You're in charge. Pick a path when he says go."

My heart rate spiked as everyone prepared to run. I wasn't expecting Rune to leave the decisions up to me since this was my first time doing this, and I suddenly felt a great sense of responsibility to solve the maze. I held my breath with my gaze darting between the different options.

"Three."

Left or right?

"Two."

The middle?

"One."

I held Rune's hand tightly as everyone darted for different pathways. Rune and I barreled into one of the paths on my right. Akira's voice carried over from the path next to ours before the maze carried us away from everyone. When only the sight of golden corn stalks surrounded us, I finally stopped running and surveyed our path.

Turning to Rune, I asked, "Do you think I chose an okay trail?"

Amusement glittered in his gaze. "Maybe. Maybe not."

I narrowed my eyes at him. "You're going to be frustrating with this, aren't you?"

"I'm going to have *fun* with this is what you mean."

Shaking my head, I turned back to the path. There were absolutely no hints or guidance on which way was best. I was sure there was a method to solve the maze quickly, but it was foreign to me. I'd have to rely on luck.

We came to the first fork in the road, and both options looked exactly the same—endless rows of tall corn stalks. I glanced over my shoulder to see which way Rune may be looking, but his eyes were focused on me, specifically on my rear. When he noticed my looking at him, he met my eyes and gave me a wide, shameless grin.

"Are you focusing?" I asked with my arms crossed.

He chuckled and stepped closer. "I'm definitely focusing."

Trying to ignore the heat wrapping around my core, I smirked. "I meant focusing on the maze."

"That's not nearly as fun."

"Well, what would make this more fun for you?" I asked, my voice catching at the end as I realized that asking him was going to open a door that couldn't be closed again.

And I wasn't sure I'd want it to.

Something seductively wicked landed in his eyes as he closed the remaining distance between us. I swallowed hard as the heat in his gaze promised something deliciously naughty.

I bit the corner of my lip as he grabbed the belt loops of my jeans to pull me against him. My hands pressed into his chest, and I hoped the proximity didn't allow him to feel how hard my heart thundered.

"How about we play our own little game?"

Curious, I raised an eyebrow. "What game would that be?"

"A game of chase, if you will. Predator and prey. Fox and rabbit. I'll give you a five-minute head start to try to lose me."

I swallowed hard. "And if you catch me?"

His lips curved, and he leaned into me. His mouth grazed the sensitive skin below my ear as he whispered, "I get to feast."

A needy shiver ran down my spine, sending a pang of desire straight to my core. Warmth flooded my limbs, and my breath seemed to leave me. His game sounded far more amusing than the original one.

Rune pulled back to look at me, and I saw the hunger now embedded in his eyes.

"Three," he said.

I took a step back.

"Two."

Another step back.

"Run."

I whipped around and raced down the left path, trying route after route. Five minutes. Surely I could lose him in five minutes. Hell, maybe I'd actually find the exit by then and win. Although part of me did want to know what it meant to fall prey to his predator.

I turned down another stretch of corn and came face to face with the third dead end since we'd separated.

"Shit," I hissed.

I turned to go back the way I'd come when the sound of approaching footsteps headed toward me. My heart skyrocketed, and I looked around frantically for somewhere to go. There was nothing but rows of corn. I had no idea if the approaching person was Rune, but if so, I'd be caught.

Thinking on my feet, I faced the dead end once more and quickly pushed my way into the corn. Was it cheating? Probably, but technically, he'd never said I couldn't hide in the corn. I crouched low and weaved my way as far into the tall stalks as I could before turning around to peer past the vegetation.

Voices drifted closer until I was able to make out Akira's voice.

"Another dead end. Great. I think I should lead now," he huffed.

"No. I've got this, I've got this," Bassel said calmly. "I was getting us a little lost on purpose to give everyone else a head start since I'm nice like that. We want to give everyone a fair chance of winning."

Grinning at Akira and Bassel's exchange, I prepared to leave the cover of the thick corn when a large hand covered my mouth from behind and pulled me firmly against a hard chest.

"Got you," Rune whispered against my ear.

Goosebumps broke out along my spine at the feel of his chest against my back, his hand stifling my sounds, and his arm wrapped around my waist. The position made me hyper aware of him, as well as the hard mass in his pants, which pressed against my butt where I knelt on my knees on the ground. Hot need pulsed through my core like a steady heartbeat.

I pulled away from Rune's hand and looked over my shoulder at him to whisper, "How the hell did you find me? And how did I not hear you moving through the corn?"

"I'm a predator, Bria. It's what I do."

I swallowed hard at the stipulation his words recalled. He'd caught me, his prey, which meant he'd get his reward. To feast. He'd never elaborated on what that meant, so my mind was left to fill in the blanks.

At least for a split second.

His arm shifted. He ran his palm across my stomach, dipping beneath the fabric of my sweater. My heart lurched when his hand drifted further down until it stopped on the button of my jeans. He flicked the button out of the hole and slowly unzipped the front, passing his fingers into the opening it created.

I quickly gripped his roaming hand and hissed as quietly as I could, "What are you doing?"

Something primal, unrestrained, and dangerously sexy flashed in his eyes as he pushed past my hold and settled his fingers beneath my panties. His digit slicked in between the crease of my folds, and I had to bite my lip against the urge to gasp from the electric jolt of pleasure.

"I'm feasting," Rune answered in a low voice against my cheek.

Rune's other hand reclaimed my mouth, covering it as his finger slid back and forth against my now-aching core. I was thankful for his muting me because, without it, my uncontainable moan would've been broadcast to anyone passing in nearby paths.

I knew this was a bad idea. We were in public, barely hidden amongst the corn at a very popular event. Anyone could come to this dead end, hear us or spot a peek of clothing amongst the stalks, and we'd be shamefully caught.

But as his digit circled, rubbed, and flicked against my clit, I found myself not caring. My head fell back against his shoulder, and my eyes slipped shut. He buried his face in my neck where his tongue traveled across my skin. A moan slipped past my lips, only to be caught by his palm, all while he worked my heated desire higher and higher.

Voices drifted near as people came closer to the dead end. My eyes shot open in alarm, and I quickly grabbed Rune's wicked hand to make him stop. This only fueled him though, and I shivered in his arms, gasping against his hand just as a couple headed in our direction.

"Shh," Rune whispered into my ear. He moved his hand down my lips and over my jaw, until he gripped my neck. "We have company. You don't want them to hear you, do you?"

"Rune," I hissed in a harsh whisper.

The people were close enough that I could make out one person's camo cargo pants and another with blue jeans. Rune still didn't stop. His finger beckoned me in exactly the right spot, and I bit my lip, fighting to hold in my cry, which only served to make the fire in between my legs hotter.

"Another dead end," a female voice said beyond the stalks.

Rune's finger made another quick swipe of my clit. My hips jerked on impulse as my body demanded more.

"Shit," the male voice groaned. "Let's turn back. I swear this maze gets harder every year."

My hips bucked, pressing Rune's finger more firmly against me, needing to feel more. He bit into my neck, and the sudden pain amidst the pleasure made me throw my head back and hold my breath against the threat of another gasp. His lips sucked on and kissed the spot while his finger pulled me closer to the edge of ecstasy.

"Should we cut through the corn here?" the female suggested. "We can just cheat."

My heart thundered at her words. They were going to come in here? The threat made me grip onto Rune's arms again, but my hips and his hand didn't listen. It felt too good. I was so damn hot. So damn close.

I whimpered softly, both out of frustration at not being able to let out my voice and because I was so hungry to reach that climax. Oddly enough, the threat of these strangers stumbling into our haven almost seemed to make me hungrier. It was exciting in the most bizarre way, and it had me rocking back and forth against Rune's finger even more, trying to stoke that flame and turn it into fireworks.

"That's right," Rune whispered into my throat. "Fuck my hand. Ride my finger like you want to ride me."

So close. I was *so close*.

"No! We're not cheating. We're doing this right. Come on," the male answered.

My half-shuttered eyes watched the jeans and camo retreat until silence surrounded us again.

"Good girl," Rune growled into my ear. "For doing so well and keeping quiet, I'll reward you."

There were no more teasing circles or half-hearted movements about his finger now. He rubbed against my throbbing wet need, pulling on that tight tether of my ache until, finally, it snapped. I came undone, shaking in his arms and letting out a harsh groan into the maze. His digit slowed until I finished gasping for air. He withdrew his hand from my underwear, and I looked over my shoulder to watch him lick the shining orgasm from his fingers with a satisfied grin.

CHAPTER

TWENTY-FIVE

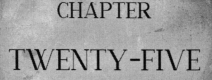

BETTER LUCK NEXT TIME, BRIA," Greshim said, reaching up to pat my back.

"Yeah," Ardley nodded from next to me. "Last place. That's gotta suck."

Rune wrapped his arm around my waist and pulled me closer. He glanced down at me with a ghost of a smile. "I don't mind last place."

Cheeks heated, I said, "Me neither."

Akira and Bassel had apparently made it out only a minute or two before us, so that was nice. I hoped no one suspected anything. The twins had won, and as a prize, they got to choose what we did after taking a small snack and restroom break, for which I was thankful. I was definitely in need of a trip to the bathroom so I could tidy myself up.

"I'll be right back," I said to the group as I headed for the restroom. There were a few stalls, and thankfully, one was open. After freshening up *downstairs*, I went to the row of sinks across from the stalls. As I washed my hands, a woman came up next to me at the neighboring sink and cleared her throat.

I glanced over, first seeing the blue ball cap, but as soon as she looked up, my heart danced with joy.

"Dallas!" I squealed, flinging my arms around her neck.

She laughed and squeezed me back. "Finally, I get a moment to see you."

Pulling back, I beamed at her. "What are you doing here?"

She raised a slender brow at me. "Shouldn't you know the answer to that?"

"I mean, yes. I just meant are you here at the festival and, you know, enjoying yourself?"

She bobbed her head side to side and mulled my question. "I suppose. Though, not nearly as much fun as what you're having from what I heard."

The air in my lungs stilled, and despite my attempts to keep my face devoid of signs of admission, I felt color rise to my cheeks. "What? How—"

Another stall opened then, and out walked a beautiful, dark-skinned woman. She had a shaved head and large doe eyes. Even beneath her black turtleneck and pants, I could see her body was toned and well formed. She looked like a stunning warrior goddess.

"Bria," Dallas started, with amusement laced into her voice. "This is Imani. Imani, you, of course, know Bria, but now you can officially meet."

Imani's face lit up, and she bowed. "It's so nice to officially meet you, Your Highness."

I immediately went to question the whole bowing thing, but Dallas spoke first. "Imani here just did the corn maze, too."

My voice got hung in my throat, and I quickly met Imani's eyes. She chuckled and rubbed the back of her head nervously.

Her grin was apologetic, and I immediately knew that she had been a witness to what happened.

"Oh my God," I groaned, hiding behind my hands.

"Don't worry," Imani said as she patted my shoulder. "I didn't see anything. Just, you know, heard some stuff. I was in the next trail over from you."

Heat climbed my neck and ears until I felt painted completely red. What a great first impression, catching me being salacious at a public family event.

"I can't believe you heard that," I mumbled.

"Me neither," Dallas huffed, glaring at me. "You've totally been holding out on me. If you did that here, in a corn maze of all places, I know you've done more. You'd better give me all the details later."

I glanced at her finger, which was currently pointing in my face, then met her green eyes. "Details later. Promise."

Her lips tilted up again, satisfied with my answer. A toilet flushed from one of the stalls farther down, and Imani and Dallas took that as their cue to leave. Dallas pulled her ball cap down closer to her face while Imani glanced out to be sure Rune and the others weren't looking this way. With one final quick hug, Dallas and Imani ducked out of the restroom.

I turned back to the sink and mirror again to finish washing my hands when the stall door at the end unlatched. I kept my head down with my eyes trained on the soap slipping from my hands down the drain as I fought off the heavy hand of embarrassment. The stranger had no way of knowing what exactly Imani, Dallas, and I were actually talking about or that I was the one who had been heard in the maze, but it still left me flustered.

As I washed away the last of the suds, I noticed the stranger's footsteps moving in my direction until they turned on the sink directly next to mine, bypassing all the other open ones.

Despite my better judgment, I glanced over at the stranger. My heart fell through my stomach when my eyes met hers.

It wasn't a stranger.

"Well," Yasmine said as she held my eyes through the mirror. "I didn't realize you had friends out here in Massachusetts."

I swallowed hard as I stared at Aidan's companion. "I don't. They're friends from my school. We're on fall break."

She raised a brow. "Interesting. Convenient how they're out here, too."

My nerves started to get the best of me. "Why? Is Massachusetts a members-only place? Loads of people come here, especially during fall."

Yasmine gave me a humorless smile. "Of course." She paused, then added, "*Your Highness.*"

I worked to keep my face blank. I bit the inside of my cheek and gripped the faucet to turn off the water. I was starting to panic, and I didn't need the call of the water to make the situation even worse. She'd overheard Imani call me "Your Highness," and my mind grappled for an explanation.

Thinking on my feet, I turned my back on Yasmine to get a paper towel to dry my hands. "It's an inside joke between my friend and me. She must've shared the story with Imani, and Imani was playing along."

I threw my paper towel away and turned back to Yasmine. I nearly jumped out of my skin when I found her standing directly in front of me, glaring down into my eyes. I held my breath as she reached her arm past my shoulder, leaning in closer to me as she did.

Her face was inches from mine as she whispered, "I don't believe you."

She swiped at the paper towel, and the sudden snap of the material ripping made me jump. Yasmine held my eyes as she finished drying her hands, and once done, she left without another word.

My feet were rooted to the spot, and my heart pounded fast in my chest. Things were getting risky here. I'd come closer to being caught just now than I had so far. I had to be more careful. Being found out by anyone outside of my friend group would mean a death sentence. At least, I hoped that ending wouldn't be my fate where my friends were concerned, but until I actually came clean, that was all I had.

Hope.

As soon as I stepped out into the fall air, my fears heightened. Rune and the rest of our group were across the walkway, but my stomach soured when I saw they weren't alone. The very gorgeous Aidan leaned against the counter as she talked to Rune, who looked as amused as a person fighting off a fly. To make matters worse, Yasmine had just joined them.

I quickly raced to reach them, jogging up to Rune.

As soon as his eyes found mine, they brightened. He reached out his hand for me, and I took it for him to pull me close to his side. I tried to smile at him, but my worries got the better of me. I glanced at Aidan and Yasmine.

Yasmine's gaze tracked me, and her blatant mistrust and loathing came rushing up to the surface like a shark after blood. "Where'd your friends go, Bria?"

Unease gripped my throat. "My friends are right here." I gestured to our group who'd quieted since Yasmine and I had arrived. They watched our exchange with nervous glances, but I knew none of them were as nervous as me. Yasmine was trying to dig a hole for me that I wouldn't be able to climb out of again.

"No, no," she said, waving her hand around. "The two girls from the bathroom. The ones from your school."

"You have friends here?" Rune asked, raising a surprised brow. "Did you want them to join us?"

The lies gathering on my shoulders weighed down my heart. Rune's genuine offer didn't help. As soon as he saw Dallas, he'd recognize her, and since he knew she was Water Fae, there would be no predicting what would happen.

I shook my head. "No, that's okay. I'm sure they're doing their own thing."

"Oh, come on," Yasmine laughed. "You should have them join. I mean, it sounds like you guys are really close."

Don't say it.

Her lips curved. "Your High—"

"Woah!" Akira shrieked.

He tripped over some unseen obstacle in the grass and fell into Aidan with his hot cup of what smelled like apple cider. The beverage splashed down the front of her golden maxi dress, and she gasped and leapt back.

"Ouch!" she roared, grabbing the front of her dress to pull it away from her skin. Her fuming eyes latched onto Akira, who nibbled nervously on his lip. "You fucking moron!"

Akira straightened and made a play of bonking his head with his fist. "Whoops. That's me, I guess. Sorry about that."

Yasmine glared at Akira and the rest of us before placing her hand on Aidan's back. "Come on. Let's get you cleaned up."

The two of them shoved past all of us.

I met Akira's eyes over Rune's shoulder and gave him a thankful smile.

He returned the look and silently mouthed, "I've got you."

Rune turned to Akira and patted his back. "Are you okay?"

"I'm totally fine," Akira waved his hand dismissively. "That cider was too sweet anyway."

Rune turned back to me. He gripped both of my hands and pulled me close until there was no room between us. His voice lowered so that only he and I could hear it. "What was that all about?"

Not wanting to talk about this here, I shook my head. "Nothing. We can talk about it later."

My dismissal of it left a sting on my heart, like the lie was now a brand I wore for all to see. I fidgeted on my feet in an attempt to do *something* about the nerves darting about inside me. The truth of who I was would be a hard one for him to accept. I didn't know how long he'd actually loved me, but it was only a handful of weeks at the most. He'd loathed Water Fae for a *century*.

I swallowed hard as my gaze traced the smooth planes of his face, his hard jawline, the way wisps of his white hair fell across his lashes, and how those golden eyes of his flickered with boundless love. I locked onto those eyes and etched the emotion I saw into my memory. Because this could be the last time I saw him look at me that way should our conversation not go the way I hoped.

CHAPTER

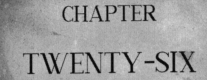

TWENTY-SIX

A S SOON AS WE ENTERED Myra's home, my anxiety intensified. While the rest of the gang joked and laughed about our day of fun at the festival, I was lost inside myself, trying to rehearse how I'd explain everything to Rune.

Should I come right out and say it like I did with Akira?

Should I start with, "You know I love you, right?" God, no. That will only have him freaking out about what's going to leave my lips.

"Hey," Rune said, bumping his shoulder into mine. "Is everything okay? You seem ... troubled."

I forced a smile. "I'm fine. This pumpkin is just heavy."

I hoisted the large pumpkin I'd gotten from the festival higher in my grip to feign being burdened with its weight. In reality, I could almost forget I was holding anything due to my new Fae strength.

Rune chuckled and gripped its stem. "I think I can help with that." He took it from me and shifted his own until he held both of our pumpkins in the crook of each arm.

We headed for the stairs, but I stopped at the bottom. "Rune?"

He looked back at me.

"Can we talk? Um, I thought maybe we could go for a walk outside, just the two of us."

Concern immediately clouded his features. "Are you okay?"

"Oh, yeah, no. Everything's fine. I'm fine. I just–I just need to talk to you about something."

The worry didn't leave the slant of his brow, but he slowly nodded. "Okay. Let me run all of our stuff up to the room. I'll meet you outside in a second."

I nodded and watched him take the stairs. I took a deep breath and tried to tell myself I was doing the right thing. This conversation *had* to happen. He deserved the truth, and I really did want to tell him. But I was still unsure and afraid, though I doubted there was any real way to truly prepare myself for this moment. I just had to do it, terrified or not.

I turned to head down the hallway to the backdoors, but as soon as I rounded the corner, I came face to face with Aidan in her Fae form. She no longer wore her apple cider dress, but instead sported jeans and a low-neck sweater. Myra stood behind her, and the elder Fox Fae's golden eyes hinted at some brewing plan as she watched me over Aidan's shoulder.

"I see you guys made it back," Aidan said, crossing her arms.

"I see you changed," I said calmly, despite my mounting disdain.

She scoffed. "No thanks to your dumbass friend."

Anger sank its claws into me. "Don't call him that."

"Or what?" She laughed, curling her lip at me to flash her sharp canines. "From what I've seen, you're all bark and no bite."

"I haven't had a reason to bite, but if you talk down my friends or any of the people I love, that will quickly change."

"Is that so?" She raised a brow and smirked. "Let's see it then. I challenge you to a game."

A game.

I glanced at Myra and realized this was what had her eyes glittering. She was setting me up with another test, and this time, she wanted my opponent to be Aidan, her choice of mate for Rune.

Rune had warned me about being challenged to a game before. The night we'd first kissed, he'd been explaining that if anyone challenged me, I was to ignore them and walk away, because it wouldn't be a game for me. He never elaborated on what that meant or what the game consisted of, but he'd also said it while believing I was human. Maybe it was because as a human, I wouldn't have the strength or the heightened senses to win. That wasn't the case now. I was Water Fae, which meant I had strength on my side.

Aidan clearly read my hesitation as fear because she laughed and said, "Are you not Fox enough?"

I should've ignored the obvious taunt and spiteful attitude. I should've walked away and waited outside for Rune. But I'd had enough of Aidan. She'd been nothing but a bitch, blatantly trying to get Rune to cheat and choose her. Logic was out the window, and seated in its spot was a need to put Aidan in her place once and for all. I'd had enough of her and her friends harassing me and my family.

Not only that, but with Myra standing there watching, I felt like I didn't have a choice. Myra probably expected me to cave under the threat and run away with my metaphorical tail tucked, but that wasn't happening. I *was* strong. I *was* worthy. And I was tired of being treated like I wasn't.

"Let's play," I forced past my bitter smile.

Aidan and I moved to the backyard where we stood ten feet away from each other. Aidan stood closest to the house, and her straight back and raised chin exuded nothing but confidence.

Myra's dark presence hung back to watch the unfolding scene. A sly grin graced her lips, and the obvious amusement in her gaze made chills run down my spine. Suddenly, the weight of my choice hit me, and I realized too late that this was probably a mistake.

"The game is simple," Aidan sang in the sweet tune that I pictured a demon would use when coaxing its prey into its hands. "Don't die. Easy, right?"

I swallowed hard. Before I could form a response, Aidan reared back her hand and launched a ball of flames straight toward me. I gasped and ducked, barely missing the orb of fire. My heart quickened as dread nearly swallowed me whole.

Fuck, of course *this game involves fire. Why didn't I think about that? Stupid, stupid, stupid!*

Before I could gather my bearings, she let out a roar as she threw another in my direction. I rolled to my left and quickly got to my feet, but she'd already thrown another right at me, which I narrowly avoided.

"Stop this, Aidan!" Bassel yelled as he raced from the back door with Carlos on his heels, both back in their Fae forms.

Hope blossomed at his sudden presence, but I soon realized hope was futile. Myra held out her arm to block him, and the narrowed slits of her eyes promised anguish should he intervene.

Aidan sneered at Bassel and hissed, "Stay out of this, stupid cat."

Realizing I was on my own, I turned and ran toward the lake in an attempt to distance myself from her until I was able to come up with a game plan. Her laughter followed my retreat. I glanced over my shoulder to see another flame heading in my direction. I tried ducking, but I was too slow this time. The flame brushed across my shoulder, and I cried out from the pulsing burn. My hand went to clutch the wound on instinct, and it shook as I slowly pulled it away from my shoulder with gritted teeth. My shirt was charcoaled and torn open, and the skin beneath it was red and blistered. Tears welled in the corners of my eyes, but I fought to keep them at bay.

The cool caress of the water greeted me as I blindly splashed into the lake until I was calf-deep. While I'd intended to get closer to the lake for safety, I hadn't meant to go *into* the water. The adrenaline coursing through my body was tapping into instincts tied to my Fae side, so on impulse, I'd gone into the waves.

"What's the matter, Bria?" Aidan taunted as she walked haughtily in my direction. "Why aren't you fighting back? Send some flames in my direction!"

Knots formed in my stomach as I tried to gain control over my erratic breathing. My shoulder throbbed, and the amount of turbulent fear flooding my system started an all-too-familiar buzz in my palms. That was something that couldn't happen right now, so I focused on the water and ordered it to stay calm, despite Aidan's inability to shut up. Calling upon and using the water would only serve to put me in *more* danger, because it would out who I was to everyone. I'd become target number one, and this lake would become my grave.

The back doors suddenly flew open again. Rune, looking fearsome in his Fox Fae form, dashed out of the house with everyone else following behind him. Lilith and Devoss stood close by Myra, taking in the scene. My friends joined Bassel before running a bit closer in my direction, most likely feeling better about intervening since they had numbers now. Rune stopped his sprint halfway as shock seemed to stun him. His eyes went wide as he traced my trembling body from head to toe.

His features turned dark and sinister as he snarled at Aidan, "What the hell have you done?"

Aidan glared back. "She agreed. We're playing a game, so don't interfere."

"You want to play?" Rune growled, low and animalistic.

One moment Rune was a few feet away and the next he was gripping Aidan's throat, dangling her thin, struggling frame above the ground.

I sucked in a sharp breath, watching as Rune prepared to deal a final, irreversible blow. While I wasn't Aidan's biggest fan, I didn't want her to *die*. Especially not by Rune. He'd taken enough lives, and I knew that each one stained him in its own way. I didn't want to see him resort to that, to turn back into the murderous Fox he used to be.

"Rune!" Ardley shouted. He raced over to his cousin, and after getting help from Bassel, managed to pry Rune away from Aidan, who fell to the ground with a loud gasp.

Rune's entire body shook with rage as his hands erupted in wild flames. Baring his fangs at Aidan, he growled, "Touch her again, come near her again, and I'll fucking kill you."

Even from this distance, I could see the seething hate and venom in his eyes. I'd only ever seen him so angry when talking about Water Fae. Now that animosity was directed right at Aidan.

Aidan slowly regained control of her breathing. She stared wide-eyed at Rune from where she knelt in the grass and finally nodded in understanding. Rune's glare followed her as she retreated to Myra's side, and once he was satisfied with the distance, he turned his cold stare on his mother, who had been watching the entire event, completely unfazed. She hadn't even stepped in to help Aidan when Rune had been ready to kill her.

Rune's stare lasted only a moment longer before he raced in my direction.

My limbs couldn't seem to stop shaking as I took a small step to meet him. I wanted to run to him and feel the warm protection that I knew I would find in his arms, but it felt like my feet had weights holding them down. Terror gripped me tightly from the reality of what had just transpired with Aidan. Rune had been right. It wasn't a game. She hadn't been playing.

She'd had every intention of killing me, and that knowledge kept me immobile.

As Rune neared the water's edge, my eyes caught motion over his shoulder. Myra's mask of nonchalance snapped, and suddenly, her fuming eyes were fixed to Rune's back. She raised her hand next to her face as orange flames hovered above her pointed fingertips. Without hesitating, she flicked her hand, casting the ball in Rune's direction.

My world seemed to stutter until everything around me moved in slow motion. Her flame was coming much quicker than Aidan's, but this time, the target was Rune.

She was going to kill him.

Instinct took over, and every thought in my head ceased except the urge to protect him.

"Rune!" My voice had a desperate catch to it as he reached the water's edge.

Something in my cry must've alerted him, because he quickly glanced over his shoulder just as the flame came inches away from searing right through his chest. I flung out my arm toward him in an effort to do *something*, and in the same instant, the tether on my magic snapped.

A cold jolt rushed from my core and through my limbs, and the sudden intensity of it brought me to my knees. As I crashed to the water at my calves, the lake rose up in a wall only large enough to block Rune and me. Myra's bright orange flame barreled into the rushing wall before exploding back in a gust of steam and smoke.

Rune was safe.

I'd stopped the fire just in time.

Oh shit.

I'd stopped the fire!

My heart turned into lead. The wall of moving water glistened in the sun as it streamed upward, shielding us from any more attacks and the view of everyone gathered. Rune slowly turned from the barricade until his wide eyes fixed on me. They flickered to my outstretched arm, which I quickly lowered back to my side. Only after I did that, the water followed, crashing back down to the lake. Rune's eyes never left me, and I watched in horror as his gaze slowly darkened and his mouth tightened into a grim line.

The air left my lungs, and my heart fractured. This wasn't how I wanted Rune to find out. I was so close to coming clean, to laying myself completely bare for him. Now it would look like I'd been hiding it with no intention of telling him the truth. That would break him.

Water dripped from my hair and face while I remained on all fours in the lake. I glanced behind Rune, remembering that he wasn't the only concern. Everyone stood motionless and stared in my direction. Akira's hands covered his mouth as unease marred his features. Bassel, Avana, and Ardley stood still, darting worried glances between me and Rune. Devoss, Lilith, and Aidan watched me with furrowed brows, but as seconds ticked by, realization slowly sank into their gazes. Myra was the only one who watched me with a completely blank stare, her posture and face devoid of anything. Her lack of a reaction unnerved me more than everyone else's shock.

"What was that?" Lilith shouted with anger seeping into her voice. "What the hell was that? Did she just control the water? Is she—"

"Sorry about that, everyone."

Heads snapped in Marlow's direction as he slowly stepped out from behind Akira and the rest of them. His glassy eyes darted to me before focusing on Myra and Rune's family. "I probably shouldn't have interfered, but I couldn't watch what was happening to my friends. I was worried that you were trying to hurt them, so I had no choice but to stop your fire."

I swallowed hard and stared at Marlow, the shy, overly-scared guy who rarely spoke. Yet, here he was, standing in front of all these people—all these *Fox Fae*—taking blame for what had happened. As a Salamander Fae, he had the ability to control a very small amount of water, something for which fellow Land Fae often gave his kind hate, because it blurred the lines between Land Fae and Water Fae. The ability to harness water was one we shared.

He and I both knew it wasn't him who'd controlled that water, which should've immediately made me enemy number one for him. Emotion clogged my throat as he stood there, shoulders back and steel faced, protecting me.

Suspicion still coated the air as everyone's gazes moved between Marlow and me. I wasn't sure if they bought his lie, but hope blossomed a fraction as acceptance and annoyance slowly morphed the spectator's faces.

My attention turned back to Rune, who still stared down at me. His hands were balled into fists, and my stomach rose into my throat as I recognized that look blazing bright in his eyes. Anger. Frustration. Disappointment. It had been so long since he'd looked at me that way, and I felt all the progress we'd made slip by on the passing wind.

"Rune?" I said in a shaky whisper. I honestly wasn't even sure if my voice came out or not.

It didn't matter, because Rune slowly walked toward me. He reached down, gripping my upper arm, and as he pulled me to my feet, I focused on the softness of that grip. He was practically boiling over with barely contained rage, yet he still handled me with restraint and gentleness. I appreciated that for numerous reasons, the most pressing being because my arm felt like it was on *fire* from the burn. If his controlled touch was all I had to hold onto for hope, I would, because damn it, I was quickly becoming a wreck on the inside.

Rune turned to Myra and the others, though I refused to look in their direction. I was too focused on him.

His voice dripped with menace as he said, "You took this too far. Don't come near her again. If anyone threatens her or even so much as breathes in her direction, I will personally see to your slow and painful end. Do I make myself clear?"

Rune pulled me in the direction of our fidgeting group. My heart pounded furiously in my chest as I struggled to follow his quick strides. Rune was rigid, and I so badly wanted to go somewhere private where we could talk. Because we *really* needed to talk.

When we were within earshot of our group, Rune's voice came out flat as he ordered, "Marlow, stay here with Newt and Greshim."

We hurried past everyone, and I glanced over my shoulder as every worry I'd had pumped through me. I didn't know where we were going, but Avana and the guys followed. The confusion and concern marring their features didn't help my anxiety.

I turned back to Rune and whispered, "Where are we going?"

Silence was my only response.

I swallowed hard. Rune was fuming, and *I'd* done that to him. Why hadn't I just come clean sooner? I could've controlled the situation more and not let him get to the point where he was so pissed for being blindsided. He knew now. He knew I was his enemy, the thing he hated most in this world. Nausea slicked up my throat as I fought to stay calm.

We walked along the lake's edge until we went down a hill a good distance from the house. The rolling green field blocked our view of the mansion until all we saw was the lake on one side and hills on the others. As soon as we were out of sight of the house, Rune let me go and took several steps away from me. Each felt like a knife sinking into my chest.

He paced back and forth, running his hands through his white hair. His frame shook from what I could only assume was rage, and I backed away to give him a second. That was the least I could do. Akira, Avana, Ardley, Bassel, and Carlos appeared at the top of the hill and slowly trekked down to where we stood. They glanced between Rune, who continued to pace while growling, and me.

Ardley's brow creased as he watched Rune. Gently, he said, "R. Hey man, calm down a little."

Rune whirled around, grabbing Ardley by his shirt. He yanked him close as he snapped, "Calm down? How the hell can I calm down! You saw what happened!" Rune's heated glare turned toward me as he let go of Ardley. "You're Water Fae?"

I fought against the tremble in my limbs as every set of eyes locked onto me. I had barely mustered up the courage to tell Rune the truth, yet now I had to tell *everyone* all at once. Sweat broke out along my brow as I worried about how they'd all react to the news.

Taking a deep breath, I finally answered, "Yes."

He jerked like I'd physically hit him and slowly shook his head. "No. No, you can't be. We tested it."

"We did," I started. "I was still human then. Or rather, I *thought* I was. My powers were still more or less locked away then."

His brow furrowed. "Locked away?"

"Rune," Akira said carefully. "She's telling the truth. Queen Muna sealed her powers."

"Queen Muna?" Rune questioned. "Why would *the* Queen of all Fae do—" Rune froze and stared wide eyed at Akira. "Wait, you knew? You knew she was Water Fae?"

"She told me on your birthday."

"I wanted to tell you," I pleaded to Rune.

Rune's eyes met mine, and despite myself, tears welled in the corners of my eyes.

"I've been trying to tell you. Every time I planned to, though, things … came up."

My cheeks warmed, and I prayed that no one noticed, because now really wasn't the time. Judging by Ardley's subtle grin and small nudge at Rune, I guessed the blush was very noticeable.

Rune was silent for a long moment, and his jaw worked as he tried to fight whatever he was feeling. Finally, he asked, "When did you awaken?"

"The night before our painting picnic. I went back to my dorm to grab your birthday present, and while I was there, Jonah showed up. It was—"

"Jonah showed up?" Rune snapped, concern dripping from his words. "Why didn't you tell me?"

"I was scared, Rune." My voice came out harder than I meant it to, and I wiped at the tears coating my cheeks. "I was so confused and feeling hopeless and *afraid*. Water Fae are your *enemy. I* am your enemy. All of yours." My gaze found each of them only long enough to get my point across. I worried if I looked for too long, I'd see exactly what I'd been dreading in their gazes. "You guys have become such a part of me. I–I think of you as my family, and I was so scared to tell you because I didn't want to lose any of you."

The air became quiet again as my bottled-up fears exploded. I waited for their judgment, their anger, their hatred.

Avana broke away from the group and slowly walked toward me. Her face remained completely blank until she stood right in front of me. Her big, brown eyes searched mine for only seconds before she wrapped her arms around me and pulled me in for a tight embrace.

"*Tiako ianao*," she whispered against my head.

I didn't know what she'd said, but based on the acceptance in her voice and the way she held me as if to promise that everything was okay, I knew it meant something good.

I hugged her back and let the tears fall as I hid my face in her shoulder.

My secret was finally out. The burden of the truth had been lifted, but six new weights had taken its place.

Avana pulled back, but she didn't leave my side. She stood right next to me as I faced the rest of the group.

Bassel was slow to smile, but eventually, he and Carlos walked over and patted my shoulder.

"We're still friends," Bassel started. "Don't worry. While Water Fae and I have our history, I also have a friendship with you. I'll try not to associate the two."

I forced a smile past the small twinge in my heart. It wasn't a jubilant reassurance, but I'd take what I could get. I still didn't know exactly what Bassel had been through, so I refused to hold any reservations he might have against him.

My attention turned back to Ardley and Rune. Ardley focused on his cousin, his brow pinched with concern. He and I were both clearly waiting on Rune.

Rune's eyes zeroed in on me, and despite how hard I tried to decipher his thoughts, they remained a mystery to me. I couldn't read him past my own frantic emotions.

"Go." Rune said, turning to stare straight ahead at some far-off place behind me. He took a deep breath and folded his arms over his chest in a tight grip. "Go inside. Akira will go with you. Stay in our room, and don't leave until I'm back."

I inhaled sharply. He was sending me away. I hadn't even gotten to explain everything, to apologize for hiding it, or to tell him that I still wanted us to be together, despite our situation.

While I wasn't ready to leave things like this, I knew he needed time to process. That, or he planned on losing his shit. Maybe even both. So, while I hated leaving, I knew I must.

I nodded and slowly walked past Rune. Akira followed alongside me and wrapped his arm around my shoulder as though to give me support and comfort. I gave him a half-hearted smile in thanks. Glancing behind me, I stared after Rune as we walked away. He was rooted in place, looking out over the field. His shoulders shook with budding rage, and I knew he was about to explode.

Turning away, I squeezed my eyes shut. I didn't want to see him like that. His anger was overwhelming, but even more devastating was the guilt consuming me. This was all my fault. Everything that we'd worked for was slowly crumbling, because I had ignored his warning to not engage in a game with anyone. My pride had driven us to this point where things now felt broken, and as Akira and I neared the house, another realization dawned on me. My life was still in danger. Not necessarily from my friends, but from Rune's family.

CHAPTER

TWENTY-SEVEN

"WELL, THAT WAS A SHIT show," I grumbled.

Akira and I neared the backyard of the house, but I kept my eyes averted from the home, too afraid to look at it. Not when a potential threat lurked in its halls.

"I mean," Akira said, "the reveal could've gone better, sure, but the reactions were great given everyone's history with Water Fae."

"Speaking of everyone's history," I started cautiously. "What's Bassel's story? Did he lose someone he really cared about to Water Fae, too?"

Akira tilted his head side to side as he slowly said, "He didn't really lose *someone*. Rather, he lost *something*. Do you remember when we first met, and in Bassel's introduction, he said he didn't remember how to speak Arabic?"

I nodded.

"Well, that was a lie. He still knows the language. He still remembers everything from when he lived in Egypt. That was his *home*, and he loved it there. One day a group of Water Fae invaded the small town he lived in, and they took it over. Bassel and the rest of the Land Fae who managed to escape were forced to flee the area. He hasn't been back since, and that kills him. He pretends he doesn't remember life there, because pretending is easier than thinking about it."

Remorse drenched my veins in an ice-cold wave. Water Fae, the group I now led, had hurt far too many people. It made me feel responsible for my friend's pain. Even though I hadn't been the one to take Bassel's home, even though I hadn't even been born yet or known anything about this war, I still felt guilty by association.

"Don't worry," Akira said, placing a hand on my arm. He gave me a reassuring smile. "Bassel doesn't blame you for what other Water Fae did."

That was just one of my many current worries.

I glanced up at the house as though it had ears and would discover my lies. Swallowing hard, I turned to Akira and asked, "What about Myra and the rest of them? Do you think they really believed that Marlow controlled the water, not me?"

"It's hard to say," Akira answered, nibbling his lip. "I think as long as nothing else happens, you'll be fine. Salamander Fae can control that much water if they're skilled enough. Marlow isn't one of those skilled Salamanders, but none of Rune's family knows that. Plus, no one here would ever expect Rune, or really any of us, to actually be associated with a Water Fae. So, I think you should be fine."

At least there was one good thing.

"Why did Myra try to attack Rune? I don't understand."

Akira shook his head, and his eyes slipped closed as he seemed to mull my question. "Trying to understand Myra is like trying to solve a puzzle that's missing half its pieces. It's impossible. One thing is for sure, though. Everything she does, she does for a reason. It may not make sense to us, but every move of hers is calculated. I'm not sure if she was testing him or you or what her motives were, but I do know that her target wasn't really to endanger Rune's life. She needs him, or rather his offspring. She has something bigger in mind with her actions. I just don't know what."

The sentiment was bone-chilling, and the suggestion that she could've been testing me sounded fairly reasonable. If I were Fox Fae like I claimed, I'd use my own fire to stop the flame heading Rune's way. If I were a fake, Rune would get hit, and since Akira was right about Myra needing Rune, that meant her flame probably hadn't been a dangerous one. It could've been like the time Rune had set Bassel's tail on fire but manipulated the flame to keep it from actually being heated.

Regardless, Myra got her answer. I hadn't stopped the flame—at least, not that she knew. It put mine and Rune's whole plan in even more jeopardy, and with three days left in the trip, I wasn't sure how to navigate the remaining days. Maybe we should leave.

I shook my head at the idea. What if we left and, in retaliation, Myra did something to Newt to endanger his life? I didn't think Greshim would be put in such a dire situation since he was her prized son, but I truly feared for Newt. If Rune finally took a real stance against her and her wishes, she wouldn't have a reason to keep Newt around anymore.

We had to stay and see out these final days.

Akira and I carefully weaved our way through the house without running into anyone. Thank God. Even if they believed Marlow had controlled the water, I'd most likely be viewed as a weak, unfit match for Rune since I couldn't even hold my own in a game with Aidan. It would be more ammunition against me.

When Akira and I made it to mine and Rune's room, I hesitated outside the door. Taking a deep breath, I found Akira's eyes, my own flooding with worries. "Is it over? Do you think he hates me now?"

"Bria," Akira whispered as concern pulled his features taut. He grabbed me in a tight hug. "He just needs time. I promise. He doesn't hate you."

Anger. Hurt. Confusion.

I'd seen it all plainly scrawled on Rune's face. I'd deceived him. I'd lied to him. I'd pretended to be something I wasn't, gaining his trust—and even more hurtful—his affection. Now here I was, the truth as barren as a newborn babe.

I was his enemy.

I was what he loathed most in the world.

How could he not hate me?

Needing some time alone, I finally forced myself to retreat into my room. Akira didn't feel comfortable leaving me, so he promised to be next door in the sitting room with the door open. He was prepared to rush to my side at a moment's notice should any lingering Fox Fae decide to make an appearance.

I wasn't sure if that Fox included Rune or not.

I pressed my forehead into the now closed door and tried focusing on that. Wooden. Solid. Not crumbling in a frantic, worried pile of rubble like me.

I couldn't change who I was, nor could I change how Rune had found out about my being Water Fae. I could have regrets and wish for things to have played out differently, but that's all it would be—futile wishing. Rune knew the truth now, which meant all I could do was look for a way to salvage our relationship. We'd come too far, shared too much, cared too deeply for things to end now.

Seeking a way to clear my head and focus on how I'd face Rune, I stumbled to the bathroom. My reflection startled me. I was a mess. My hair was wind tossed and frizzy. My eyes and nose were painted red from crying. My sweater was charred and hanging in tattered pieces around my shoulder where Aidan's fire had singed me. The skin there was still puckered and pink, wrinkling in an ugly and painful burn, having not healed yet.

Letting out a ragged breath, I turned away from my reflection and slipped out of my clothes. The shower called to me, and I happily entered. As soon as the hot water made contact with my skin, all the knots in my body loosened. The ache in my shoulder flared before fading altogether, and I watched in wonder as the pink skin smoothed and returned to a peachy, healthier color.

Under the touch of the water, my skin electrified and buzzed in a blissful rush. A grin lit my lips, and a small sigh escaped me as the water rolled along my arms, stomach, back, and legs. The pleasant vibration that the magical bond stirred in my chest lulled me into a state of contentment, clearing away all doubts and insecurities about what was happening with Rune.

Tilting my head up to watch the clear drops spill out of the showerhead, I let my mind wander back to that moment when I'd controlled the water at the lake. I always felt so alive when harnessing water, as if it were an extension of myself. It was unlike anything I'd felt before, and right now, I wanted that connection. Since no one else was here to spot me, I decided to give into that pull.

Taking a deep breath, I stretched my hand out in front of me with my palm facing up. I cupped my hand slightly, letting the water pool in my grasp, and my eyes traced every drop that trailed down my skin. Focusing all of my attention on the clear, rippling water in my palm, I willed it to move upward.

The water stirred before rising into the air as one long strand. A silent laugh escaped me as my eyes followed the trail of sparkling liquid. It hovered in front of me, spiraling and spinning in a delicate and graceful dance. Where my gaze moved, it followed, and when I willed it to come back to my still outstretched hand, it did so. The hot water splashed back into my palm before trickling through my fingertips toward the tiled floor. My heart skipped a beat when it did, and I wondered if I'd ever get used to this immense power.

Probably not.

"Thank you for helping me protect Rune," I said, knowing the water could understand me in its own way.

Looking around at the streaks trailing down the glass shower, I silently urged the drops of water to still. Without hesitation, everything froze. The steam stopped rising, the drops sliding along the glass door ceased their journey, and the stream spewing from the overhead faucet froze in mid-fall. It took such little concentration to keep it frozen, which only amazed me more.

I released my hold, and the water came rushing back to life. Hot pellets rained down on my skin, and the steam clouded the air and space once more. Smiling, I closed my eyes and relished the tender touch of the water.

As I concentrated, I could feel something more than just lifeless drops. Something warm and moving rapidly with excitement filled me to the brim as the water cascaded over me, and it came from the flow. From the lake behind the house to the water in the pipes, it was humming. Its whispers and desperate voice sang to me, and my bones vibrated as its need to be commanded radiated through my very soul. The water wanted me to call upon it, and it reassured me that it was there for me.

In that moment, it really hit me how powerful I must be. My eyes widened, and my jaw dropped slightly as a slight fear swept through my chest. Immense power surged through me with my fairly new gift, and my hands began to shake. Could I do this? Could I really control and harness this power? There were Water Fae relying on me. What if I couldn't be what they needed? What if my powers overwhelmed me like during my practice with Dallas? Every doubt and insecurity suddenly reared its ugly head, and panic sank its teeth into me.

As my anxiety started to build, the rush of hot water changed. The drops lost their heat and became a fountain of cool kisses. My eyes turned upward into the shower head as the water rained down. It covered my skin, and instead of continuing its path toward the drain, it clung to my body, stitching itself together until I wore a bodysuit made of water. My shoulders relaxed, and my eyes slipped shut as I embraced the cold touch covering my skin. The water soothed me, and its silent whispers told me that I was okay.

I accepted the comfort, and for now, I accepted that my power was within my control. At least for this moment, all was well within this glass shower. As soon as I stepped out, things might not be. I crossed my fingers and sent a silent plea to the water to give me strength in facing Rune, because God knew I needed it.

CHAPTER

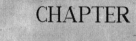

TWENTY-EIGHT

ONLY AFTER THE SHOWER NATURALLY turned cold did I finally get out, and as I dried my hair, I noticed more strands now had blue tips. Even though Rune and the others knew the truth, I still snipped away the color. I didn't like having something I didn't yet understand decorating me so blatantly, especially since there were more than just my friends in this house. The TV played quietly as I finally sat among the comfort of the bed's pillows, but my mind strayed from the show. I couldn't focus on anything with the thought of Rune in the back of my mind.

Glancing out the French doors, I took note of the navy-dusted sky. It was nearly nightfall, and I had no idea where Rune was or what was going through his head. It had been *hours*. Was he so mad that he needed *hours* to calm down? Was he so hurt from the betrayal that he needed *hours* to face me? Or was he not coming back and leaving me for his family to rip apart?

I shook my head at the absurdity of that last thought. That was my worry talking.

I let out a heavy sigh and drew my knees up to my chest. Rune was complicated. He was barely able to admit his feelings when I was "human." How could he possibly accept me now? How could only a short time of loving me replace a century of hating Water Fae?

The answer nearly strangled me.

Because I didn't think it could.

My throat grew unpleasantly tight as I whispered to myself, "Where are you, Rune?"

The knob clicked as the door opened, and I quickly jumped to my feet as a stone-faced Rune walked in. He refused to look at me as he shut the door behind him and locked it. I held my breath, clenching and unclenching my fists, nibbling the corners of my lip, waiting for him to look at me.

Silence stretched between us like an impassable ocean. My rehearsed explanation died on my tongue with the reality of him standing before me. There was so much I wanted—no, *needed*— to say, yet it was as if words were suddenly foreign to me.

I opened my mouth. Then closed it.

I took a deep breath and managed to recall how to at least say, "Rune—"

"Water Fae," Rune interrupted. His shoulders were tense, and his eyes stayed glued to the floor. He kept his arms crossed firmly over his chest as though to shield himself from me, from the deception and hurt I'd caused.

As if staying on the other side of the room wasn't distance enough.

"Water Fae," Rune started again, his voice barely hinting at the anger he held back. "Water Fae are cowards. Water Fae are evil beings. I want all Water Fae dead, regardless of who they are. I said all those things."

My heart hardened into glass with each word, and it shattered into broken fragments on the last.

Rune took a deep breath, and he finally looked up at me. Contempt. Resentment. That's what I expected to find. Instead, his features were turned down under the heavy hand of guilt and anguish.

"I am so, *so* sorry," Rune whispered.

My eyes widened, and the air passing through my lungs stilled. Certain I'd misheard him, I stammered, "Wh-What?"

He took in a shaky breath and ran a hand over his face and through his hair. He finally moved across the room until he stood directly in front of me. Turmoil swarmed his eyes as he said, "Bria, I am *so* sorry. All of those awful things I said ... God, it's no wonder you didn't want to tell me."

I swallowed hard. "I wanted to tell you. I really did. I've been trying, but every time we were alone, I got ... distracted. It's not that I didn't want to tell you. Honest. I was just *scared*."

His brow pinched as he shut his eyes tightly. "I'll never forgive myself for making you feel that way."

Still reeling from Rune's reaction, I slowly asked, "Are you not angry? You don't hate me now?"

His golden eyes slowly opened and locked on mine. "Hate you?" His voice broke on the words, pain gripping his features in a vice-like hold. "Bria, I could never, *ever* hate you. I won't lie. When it first happened, when you first ... controlled the water, I was so shocked, I didn't know what I was feeling. To be honest, I wasn't even sure what I was really *seeing*. I thought I was dreaming. When reality caught up with me, though, and I understood what happened, that you were really Water Fae, I was angry and hurt. I felt lied to and stupid for not knowing."

His jaw worked, then he continued, "But then I realized something as you were trying to explain why you hid it. All of the things I'd said about Water Fae came rushing back until I was left staring at myself. An ugly reflection that said so many horrible things. I realized the only person I had to blame for the secrecy was myself."

I tilted my head back to stare at the ceiling in an effort to keep my tears from spilling over. "How can you be okay with this? How can you be okay with my being Water Fae when they've taken everything from you?"

"Bria, baby, look at me."

I slowly forced my head back down. My eyes found Rune's, and when I saw the emotion I'd been fighting against mirrored in his own eyes, a sob slipped past my quivering lips.

Rune cupped my cheeks and gently drew me closer. "I need you to hear me, okay?"

Not trusting my voice to make coherent words, I simply nodded.

"I love you. That doesn't mean with stipulations. That doesn't mean I love you *only* if you're human. That doesn't mean I love you *only* if you're *not* Water Fae. It means I love you, wholly and fully. I love *you*. The girl who helps random animals in the woods. The girl who loves cinnamon rolls more than life itself. The girl who scrunches her nose when she's engrossed in a painting."

"I don't scrunch—"

"You do," he laughed through his mounting emotion. He beamed down at me and shook his head. "But I'm not finished. Human or not. Water Fae or not. It doesn't matter. You are still Bria, the girl I am desperately in love with. So, you're wrong when you say Water Fae took everything from me because *you're* Water Fae. *You've* given me everything. You *are* my everything."

There was no holding back the tears now. They fell freely, and Rune gently wiped them from my cheeks with his thumbs. So many emotions gripped my chest. Relief. Hope. Elation. Most of all, love. I loved this man with every fiber of my being, and to hear him express so openly and adamantly that he felt the same left me feeling dizzy with joy.

All my worries and insecurities about who and what I was instantly slipped down the drain in my mind. All that remained was my fox.

My love for him.

My desire for him.

My need for him.

Gripping the front of Rune's shirt tightly, I whispered, "What did I ever do to deserve you?"

The corner of his mouth lifted as he crooked his finger beneath my chin and angled my face toward his. "I think I'm the one who should be asking that."

His lips closed over mine in a soft, tender caress, and despite having kissed him numerous times, this one felt different. It felt raw with uncontainable longing. This kiss was slow and deliberate as he parted my lips and coaxed a gasp from me with the flick of his tongue. It was like he wanted me to really feel and taste how much he'd longed for me all this time.

And I was finally ready to show him the same thing.

Pulling away, I guided Rune to the bed and placed my hands on his chest, forcing him onto his back on the mattress. I followed, draping my legs on either side of his hips until the hard mass in his pants pressed right against my soft folds, which were still covered. He grunted as I straddled his need, and an aroused heat lit his eyes.

I traced every curve of his face, took in every flutter of his lashes, and studied each heavy rise and fall of his chest. I could spend hours soaking up his presence. He had become such a vital part of my life, and I was more than ready to share my world and myself with him.

I grabbed for the bottom of my shirt and took my time, pulling it up and over my head. A slight chill kissed my skin as my long hair fell against my bare back, and the shirt slipped from my fingers toward the floor.

Rune's eyes drank me in with a slow, heated prowl, tracing my exposed skin, following the lines of my bra. I bit my lip as I watched him study me, and I couldn't ignore the way it made me ache at my center. His obvious desire for me made me warm and breathless.

When his lust-filled eyes found mine again, he whispered, "Nothing could ever be more beautiful than you."

Beaming at him, I leaned down to press my lips against his, and I instantly melted into him. My ache for him deepened, and my lips parted to welcome him in.

Rune quickly grabbed my hips as our kiss grew hungrier and more desperate. An eager shiver trailed my spine as his fingers roamed up my back and stopped at the clasp of my bra. With a quick tug, the material came loose. His mouth never left mine as his fingers followed the straps' descent down my arms.

My need to pull back and breathe was fighting with my need to keep exploring his mouth. Before either one could win, though, Rune tilted his head to run kisses along my chin and down my throat. My eyes slipped shut, and I bit my lip against the feel of his hot breath tickling my skin in the best way possible. His teeth scraped against my sensitive neck, and his grip around my waist pulled me further into his lips.

I relished the feel of him nibbling at my skin as his lips and tongue sucked gently. One strong arm wrapped around my waist while the other made its way up to my hair. He grabbed a handful of my blonde locks and swept it aside to cascade over one shoulder, exposing more of my neck and collarbone, where he trailed lower and lower.

"I need to feel you," he groaned into my neck as his hands cupped each of my breasts. He squeezed and swiped his thumbs over my puckered tips.

I let out a sharp gasp, and my core tightened with want. "Then touch me more. Take me. Don't stop."

His restraint snapped. He rolled until I was pinned beneath him, my legs still wrapped firmly around his waist. He leaned back on his heels and reached behind him to yank his shirt off, making the muscles of his abdomen tense and ripple with the motion. Rune's undeniable strength and natural power were obvious from every angle.

Not only did his sheer beauty cause my heart to cease beating, but so did the little blue gem resting at the end of the silver chain around his neck. It was yet another reminder of Rune and how much he meant to me. My sweet Fox. The amount of absolute bliss I felt in his arms was indescribable.

I never wanted to lose this.

His hands found their way back to the waistband on my pants and panties, and as soon as I met those tender eyes, everything else disappeared. I was lost to the affection in his gaze and the euphoria in his smile. He slowly pulled the material down each leg before dropping the garments to the floor. His amber orbs remained fixated on mine as he grabbed my left calf, lifting my leg. He finally broke eye contact, and my heart quickened when I realized why.

Rune placed a small kiss on the inside of my ankle. "I think it was when I saw you painting at that class."

I swallowed hard and focused on my words instead of the wet heat pooled in my middle. "What?"

His lips pressed softly to my calf. "When I fell in love with you."

Chest unfurling with warmth, I smiled at him. "Really?"

Another kiss along the side of my knee. "Or maybe it was when I saw you in your Fox Fae disguise for the first time."

Recalling his reaction back then, I gave a small laugh. "You definitely felt *something* then. Although, I assumed you felt it somewhere a bit lower than the heart."

"I definitely felt it there, too," he smirked before placing a kiss on the inside of my thigh.

I inhaled sharply as his touch there shot electricity all the way to my pussy.

"Or maybe it was when you called me out for lying about not missing my dad." His lips branded the skin right by my throbbing need.

All I could do was take a deep breath.

His eyes flicked up to mine from where his lips hovered above my center. "Or maybe it was when you pulled me onto that dance floor."

The tip of his tongue traced the crease of my folds. I moaned before I could stop myself, fisting the blankets beneath me. Electrifyingly sweet pressure built under his masterful tongue. I arched myself further into him as he flicked, circled, and sucked on my clit. Groaning, I tilted my head back against the pillow as I exploded in bursts of pleasure.

"You taste so good," Rune said into my skin.

He sat up and hovered above me, eyes glossed over with lust. With the evidence of my climax still coating his lips, his mouth sought mine in a hungry search. I tasted myself as my lips parted for him, and I plunged my hands into his hair to bring him closer. His hand slipped between us, and I gasped into his mouth when one long finger slowly pushed into me.

"Fuck," Rune groaned against my mouth. His head fell into the crook of my shoulder as he whispered into my ear, "I can't wait to be inside you."

"Then do it," I said, pressing my lips to his earlobe. I barely nibbled and finished, "I want you, Rune."

He lifted enough to find my eyes and shook his head. "Not until I get you ready."

His finger slid in and out of me as our lips connected once more. Soon, another digit joined the first, then another. I felt so full but not nearly full enough, and my rush to have him inside me nearly drove me mad.

"Rune," I panted, with sweat beading my brow. "I'm ready. Please."

He sat back and slowly pulled out his fingers. I quivered under the loss of his touch. I watched as he finally freed himself from the confines of his pants, and my mouth watered at the drop of need gathered on the head of his hard length.

He settled in between my legs once more, and my heart fluttered when he pried my fingers loose from where they clung to the blankets. Our palms pressed together as our fingers slowly intertwined. He lowered them until they were pinned on either side of my head, and he took a deep breath as he pressed our foreheads together. His honey-sweet breath tickled at my cheeks as his body hovered slightly above me. Despite our chests being separated by mere inches, I could feel that the rhythmic beat of his heart matched the wild dancing of my own. We were in perfect sync, and in this moment, the world was ours alone.

"I'm not used to being gentle," Rune said, his voice huskier than normal. "Tell me if I'm hurting you, okay?"

I nodded, which made our noses graze. His lips pressed softly to mine, and my toes curled at the slow caress of the kiss. It was sensual, a slow capture of my tongue on his. At the same time, I felt the tip of his length push against my entrance. My heart pounded madly as he gently pushed in. I squeezed his hands at the slight burning pressure, but within a few seconds, it stopped.

"Are you okay?" he asked, his deep voice strained.

"I'm great," I said, and I bit my lip at how shaky my voice came out.

He took a deep breath. "I'm gonna move now."

Unable to find my voice, I nodded.

His hips moved back, then slowly pushed forward again. I gasped at the sensation of him filling me up, and with each gentle thrust, I became hungrier for more.

He caught my next sigh in a kiss, and heat curled tightly at my center as his movements picked up speed. He groaned in pleasure against my lips and squeezed my hands tighter as he pumped in and out with restrained yet desperate measure.

"Rune," I moaned as my lips parted for him.

"You feel so good," he said, trailing a kiss along my jaw.

That familiar sweet heat throbbed between my legs as Rune positioned himself to rub against my aching core. I threw back my head, unable to contain my cry as the mixture of his thrusts and touch sent me over the edge and spiraling into the euphoric abyss yet again.

Rune grunted as his movements became frenzied and fast. His whole body shuddered, and he joined me in the chasm of satisfied lust.

His hips slowed until he pulled out. I gasped at the sudden emptiness where we'd just been connected, but I didn't feel the loss for long. Rune released my hands to cup my cheeks with reverent fingers, and he leaned down to place a soft kiss on my forehead.

"I love you, Bria," Rune whispered.

I leaned into his touch with a light, joyous smile. "I love you, too. Always."

CHAPTER
TWENTY-NINE

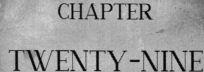

ARE YOU SURE YOU'RE OKAY with this? With me?" I asked.

Rune and I were lying on our sides beneath the blankets, our naked limbs entangled. Rune had cleaned us both after our lovemaking, and now, we rested in bed together. My fingers played with the blue gem of his necklace, and his hand continued its slow trek up and down my arm.

"Do you really need to ask that?" Rune chuckled as he gave me a salacious smirk.

Biting my lip against the threat of turning bright red, I said, "No, I … I guess I'm still trying to process. I psyched myself out, expecting the complete opposite of this." I gestured between our naked bodies.

His hand roamed back up my arm and over my shoulder, up my throat, stopping at my chin. The pad of his thumb brushed the skin below my bottom lip as he pursed his lips and searched my face.

Finally, he said, "It was definitely when you bumped into me at that Italian restaurant."

I quirked a brow. "What?"

"I figured it out. The restaurant. That was when I fell in love with you."

I laughed. "You're still thinking about that?" I shook my head and continued, "There's no way *that* was when you fell in love with me."

"I've always felt something. A certain spark. A certain allure. When I think back now on all our moments together, all I feel is what I feel now. I was done for as soon as that cute, short, doe-eyed girl smacked into me. If only I'd know then that I was staring into the eyes of the girl who would come to be my whole world." He paused to place a kiss on my forehead. "But I know it now. I know that I love you more than I ever thought I was capable of, and that won't change. Ever."

He sounded so confident, sure that his feelings for me were unwavering. And while I desperately wanted that to be the case, I knew the hardest part was yet to come.

He didn't know everything yet, including the worst part of all of this, the part I hadn't even let *myself* dwell on until this very moment.

"Rune, there's one more thing," I said as my eyes searched his. My mouth instantly dried with the weight of my words, but I forced them out in a nearly nonexistent whisper. "I'm the Princess."

He raised a brow, and I could see him questioning what that meant.

"I'm the Water Fae Princess. That means my dad …"

My words hung between us. I saw it the moment realization dawned on him.

His face went ashen, and his eyes widened. He slowly rolled onto his back to stare wide-eyed at the ceiling.

"Your dad killed …"

I lay there frozen, fighting against tears that threatened to break through.

There it was. The hardest part of this entire truth.

My dad had killed Rune's father, the person Rune had seemed to love most in the world.

"I'm so sorry," I whispered. "I don't know the details, but—"

"No." Rune slowly shook his head against his pillow with his eyes transfixed on the ceiling. "No." He quickly sat up and looked down at me. "That can't be right. They didn't have a daughter. They had a—"

"That was a lie," I interjected. I sat up and held the sheet to my bare chest. A wave of my hair fell over my shoulder to shield my face as I kept my eyes trained on the blankets, too afraid to meet his eyes. "The whole story about the King and Queen having a boy was a lie that they spread to keep me safe."

Silence stretched like an endless void. I picked at the gray silk sheets, crumpling them into a wrinkled mess before smoothing them back out with my palm, only to wrinkle them once more. I had no idea how many minutes passed or if, in actuality, it had been only seconds, but with Rune's continuous silence, the pit in my stomach expanded.

Steeling myself for what I might see—loathing, anger, disgust, regret—I dared a peek at Rune. He sat like an immovable statue, his face pressed into his hands as they rested on his bent knees. The muscles in his shoulders were pulled tight in a tense hold.

What to do or say left me. I knew this had to be hard for him. For starters, I'd just told him that the person his kind had been searching for all these years didn't exist. Even worse, he'd literally just slept with the daughter of the man who killed his father.

Finally, Rune's hands slid down his face until he clasped them in front of his mouth. His eyes found mine, and I saw him swallow hard. "So you ... you know your parents now?"

"I know *of* them now. I–I don't know them personally. Dallas said that they're …"

My throat tightened, and I quickly had to look away. I refused to let my heartache take over the moment. This wasn't about me and my deceased parents. This was about Rune and making sure he was okay with the truth. I could deal with my grief later.

I cleared my throat and turned back to him. "Anyway, I don't know the details, but they're no longer here."

Rune's eyes slipped closed, and he hung his head again. Pain inked its way across my chest at the clear struggle he was enduring.

"Rune, I can't tell you how sorry I am. I know how much your father meant to you, and it's been—"

"It's not your fault," Rune said from behind his steepled hands. His eyelids slowly fluttered open to meet mine. "I don't blame you for your father's actions. This is all just …" He took a deep breath.

"A lot," we said at the same time.

The faintest trace of a smile tugged at the corner of his mouth as he reached over to grab my free hand. He gave it a squeeze before tracing a small pattern into my skin with his thumb. "So, Dallas. She was a part of the Water Fae circle you unknowingly ran with."

"She's apparently my personal guard and head of my security team. She's also here in Massachusetts with us."

He raised a brow. "Here?" After a thoughtful pause, he asked, "Was she the friend at the corn maze? The one Yasmine saw?"

I sighed and told him about the bathroom incident, including Imani's slip-up, which Yasmine heard.

"Well, that makes a lot more sense. We'll have to keep an eye on Yasmine to make sure she doesn't piece things together." He shifted on the bed to face me fully. "Can you tell me everything? From the moment you faced Jonah?"

"Are you sure? I know all of this has been a lot for you."

"I'm sure. Nothing's changed. I love you and want to know everything. I want to be there for you in every way I can. You've been dealing with this on your own all this time. That ends now."

Warmth pierced my heart like an arrow striking true. Even after everything he'd learned, he still wanted me. That was far more than what I could've dreamed or deserved. So, after taking a deep breath, I let it all out. I recounted what happened in my fight with Jonah, noting the hardening of Rune's jaw and tightening at the corners of his eyes when I told him of Jonah's attempt to drown me. I explained all I knew about Water Fae and myself, which was far too little, as well as how Dallas and I had been working together on grasping my abilities.

"You've been training?" Rune asked.

"Just a little. I really needed help figuring out my abilities, because they kept getting the best of me. Like that day when things were ... escalating in the bathroom between us. When I said 'no' and put a stop to what we were doing, it was because the water in the sink was reacting to my desire for you, which I couldn't say at the time, since I was still too afraid to tell you the truth then. To be honest, I think I've broken a couple of sinks doing that."

He raised a brow at me. "Forget the sinks. I'm just glad that's what really happened, and it wasn't me being a complete pushy ass."

I smiled. "It definitely wasn't that."

Rune leaned back against the headboard and stared across the room. "So," he paused for a moment, then finished, "You're really the Water Fae Princess, huh?"

"I am."

A smirk appeared. "I can't wait to see how the Water Fae react to their Princess having a Land Fae for a partner."

Biting my lip to fight my hopeful grin, I asked, "Is that what you are? My partner?"

He leaned forward until our faces were inches apart. Our noses lightly grazed, and if either of us tilted our heads even slightly, our lips would touch. His eyes flicked from my mouth back to my gaze. "What do you think?"

"I want to hear you say it," I whispered.

His hand slid up my back, over my bare shoulder, and onto my neck. He pressed his thumb into my jaw to tilt my head up toward his mouth. "I'm yours, Princess. Just as you're mine."

He sealed his words by pressing his lips to mine. I welcomed the kiss and gladly granted his tongue access to tease my own. He urged my face closer while his other hand tugged down the sheet I'd been holding to my chest, letting it pool at my waist. I deepened the kiss as his hand traveled from the sheet to in between my now damp thighs. I gasped against his lips as his finger slipped between my folds and rubbed enticingly against my clit.

I laid back as Rune shifted in between my legs, his hand still making work against my slick heat. He broke our kiss to stare down at me from where I lay hot and breathless against the pillow.

His gaze traced every inch of me as I laid sprawled out before him. He ran his teeth over his bottom lip as he fought against whatever he wanted to say.

"What?" I asked breathlessly.

"Do you have a crown?" he asked, his voice deep and velvety.

I moaned as his finger caressed me in exactly the right spot before forcing the words past my lips. "I don't know. Maybe? Why?"

He leaned into me, and my limbs began to tighten with the building pleasure.

"I want to see you in a crown," he whispered into my ear. "*Just* a crown. And I want to fuck you while you wear it."

I came undone, riding out wave after wave of undeniable

pleasure. Rune angled his hardened length at my entrance and pushed in. His words played on repeat as he pumped into me, and once we were done, I made a mental note to check with Dallas about that crown.

CHAPTER

THIRTY

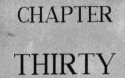

I'D BARELY AWAKENED, FINDING MYSELF wrapped in Rune's strong arms, when a knock came at the door, followed by the measured creak of it opening.

Rune was still sound asleep, so I went rigid with the sudden visitor slipping into our dark room. Instantly on high alert, my heart thudded furiously in my chest. I had no idea who'd just entered or what they wanted.

The door clicked shut, and the faint sound of feet against carpet crept toward us. I willed my naked body to remain as still as possible to feign sleep, but the beating of my heart was so deafening in my ears that I was sure they could hear it, too. Squeezing my eyes shut, I held my breath.

The footfalls stopped directly behind Rune. Before I could even guess at what the visitor wanted came Akira's whisper. "Rune."

Relief washed over me in calming waves. My body rested back into the mattress, and it felt easier to bring air back into my lungs.

None of the monsters belonging to the family had made their way in here to end me as I slept.

It wasn't until I felt this surge of calm hit me that I realized how shaken up Rune's family had me. Despite my attempts at putting on a brave face around them, I'd still been nervous as hell this whole time, and after yesterday, I had lost a lot of my courage. Those creatures were like haunting, ever-present nightmares that brought out nothing but potent fear.

Rune's body moved against me as Akira shook him gently. "Rune. Get your naked ass up."

Gah, I hope he can't see anything!

A groan escaped Rune's lips, and he shifted next to me. With a renewed burst of embarrassment, I kept my eyes shut. I didn't want to meet either of their gazes while in this state.

"What are you doing in here?" Rune asked with sleep laced in his deep, morning voice.

He shifted once more, and gently, the comforter rose higher onto my shoulder. I bit the inside of my cheek to keep from outwardly smiling as Rune covered me and pulled me closer to his chest.

"I came to make sure everyone was still alive in here." There was a pause, and I could practically hear the smile on Akira's face as he said, "I see things went well between the two of you last night."

My cheeks burned bright at his words, so I rolled over to lay on my other side, just in case they could see the blush no doubt consuming my face. Rune's arm fell slack as I shifted, but once I settled, he held me close again.

"Would you leave?" Rune hissed in a whisper. "You're going to wake her up."

Too late!

The room fell quiet again. My ears buzzed with the suffocating silence. There was no way Rune went back to sleep with Akira still standing there, so why weren't they talking? Curiosity begged me to look at them, but glancing over my shoulder to peek would make it pretty damn obvious that I was pretending. My need to survive this embarrassing moment won, so I kept still.

When Akira broke the silence, his voice was farther away as if he were leaning against the wall. His tone was quieter, more serious. "Did you finally tell her? You know, how you *really* feel?"

"I did."

"Good. She deserves a happy ending." Akira's voice grew softer. "And so do you. I'm proud of how far you've come with Water Fae, and I know it's because of her."

I held my breath. I knew I probably shouldn't be listening, but how could I not?

Rune was quiet for some time. Finally, he answered, "She's always been Water Fae. We just didn't know it. Bria is Bria. She was then, and she is now. That hasn't changed, and neither have my feelings for her."

Warmth spread from my chest, making its way throughout my body. I didn't think I'd ever get used to Rune accepting me so fully. The flood of comfort I felt from his words consumed me, and I welcomed the feeling with open arms.

Akira chuckled softly. "I'm glad to hear that. Couldn't have said it better myself. We need to be extra careful while we're here now. Your mom totally suspects that something is up."

"I know," Rune said. "Two more days. That was the agreed-upon schedule between Myra and me. We just need to keep a low profile. I don't want her targeting Newt for breaking our agreement on the timeline, because we both know she will." His voice was low, and a dark certainty shrouded what he'd said. It made chills crawl up the length of my arms, and I had to force myself to not think about the reality behind his sinister words.

"Agreed. I hate that we can't take the twins away. Fae really ought to change their barbaric ways when it comes to parenting."

The space became heavy with the truth of Akira's words. Fae seemed to parent via strict and fierce means. The fact that other Fae didn't find issue with this showed not only how different our worlds were—human and Fae—but also how careful Rune and the rest of us had to be while navigating the remaining days. Taking the twins would just make us and the boys targets as Myra fought—*literally*—to get them back. We'd be on the run, constantly trying to stay out of Myra's crosshairs, and what kind of life would that be for Newt and Greshim? So long as everyone did as they were told, everyone was somewhat safer.

Just emotionally damaged.

"Well," Akira said, his usual brightness back again as his voice retreated in what sounded like the direction of the door. "I guess I'll leave you two lovebirds now. I'm really happy for you, you crazed Fox."

"Akira."

Silence filled the room, and I assumed it was because Akira was waiting for whatever Rune was about to say.

"You deserve a happy ending, too," Rune said. "She's the Princess. Maybe she can find out what happened with Jesiah. You two could find each other again."

From what Akira said, Jesiah was the advisor to my parents. I was sure Dallas would know about him, and if Akira wanted me to find out, I wouldn't hesitate. Except, I didn't think I could give him hope of potentially reuniting with his lover, only to rip it away should Jesiah be gone.

After minutes of silence, Akira said, "We're all next door when you guys get up."

The door creaked open and, seconds later, clicked shut again. My heart twisted at Akira ignoring Rune's offer. Seeing that Akira was too afraid to look for Jesiah meant he probably believed the worst of Jesiah's fate, and it most likely meant Akira wouldn't be able to handle it if that were the case. Just picturing Akira in that state of grief and pain nearly brought tears to my own eyes. It made my throat constrict and my stomach churn. I never wanted Akira to go through that.

Which was why I'd ask Dallas about Jesiah in secret. I'd find out what happened to him, and, only if it was good, would I tell Akira.

With Akira's absence, there were no more prying eyes present, for which I was grateful, but then I became aware of Rune. It was just the two of us again, and I could feel his eyes on me. It sent my stomach soaring on an endless nervous ride, and I debated whether or not to "wake up."

Part of me wondered what sort of things went through his head when he looked at me. Given a glimpse into his honest thoughts, I craved more.

The bed dipped as he settled back down. His arm secured itself around my waist, and he pulled me closer to him. The incredible feel of his warm, smooth skin against mine sent dizzying waves through my head. His touch always had a sweet, intoxicating hold on me. I welcomed it in, fully and happily.

After a few moments of lying there in silence, I decided to stir as if I were waking, rolling over, and taking my time to open my eyes. As soon as our eyes met, his face lit up with a tender glow.

"Good morning," he greeted.

My heart somersaulted as I took note of the affection laced into his voice.

I glanced down, nibbling on my lip. "Good morning."

His strong embrace pulled me all the way to him, and he kissed my forehead. "How did you sleep?"

I leaned into his kiss with a flutter in my chest. "Amazing."

The sweet sound of his laugh filled the space around me. Pulling back to meet my eyes, he tucked a strand of hair behind my ear. "How are you feeling? Are you okay?"

I looked sideways again as I worked to fight against the threat of another blush. "I'm good."

He cocked his head slightly, not bothering to hide his grin. "Good enough to maybe shower with me?"

My laugh escaped before I could hide it. I nodded at him. "Sure. I think I could manage that."

As soon as the words left my mouth, Rune sat up. Pushing the covers aside, he pulled me to him and cradled me in his arms. With one arm in the bend of my knees and one under my back, the entirety of my naked body was easily visible. It took everything in me to keep calm and not think about the fact that Rune was naked, too.

When we made it into the bathroom, Rune set me down on my feet. He suddenly cocked a curious brow and grabbed a strand of my hair, pulling it into both of our views. I already knew what I'd see.

"Did you know your hair is turning blue?" he asked.

Sighing, I turned to the mirror and discovered that there were multiple pieces of my hair with blue tips now, and it was no longer just on the underside of my long locks.

"Yeah," I started. "It began a couple of days ago, seemingly a little at a time. I've been cutting it off to hide it. I'm not exactly sure what it means."

Rune appeared deep in thought as he studied my hair. "I know Water Fae have been known to have blue hair, although it's been forever since anyone has seen one with it. I know *I've* never run into one."

"Great. Just great. With my luck, it probably means something bad."

He chuckled as he turned to switch on the shower. "I think it looks good."

I took the moment to sneak a peek at his exposed skin as he fiddled with the handles. Rune had always been confident about his body, and it was obvious why. He was gorgeous at every angle.

Rune faced me again. Steam started rising over the glass

door, and he held out his hand for me. I happily accepted it and stepped into the shower. Rune followed right behind me, wrapping me in his embrace.

The hot rush of water dripped down my skin as I ran my hands along his broad shoulders, up the back of his neck, and into his velvety hair. Grabbing my hips, he tugged me closer until there was no room left between us. I stood on my tiptoes to press a soft kiss to his lips.

His mouth parted to greet me, and I welcomed his heated kiss. I nibbled gently on his bottom lip and reached for his tongue with my own. The humid water continued raining down as I tugged on his hair, and his palms roamed my bare body, making my skin spark with want. The build-up of my raw, unchecked lust, love, and desperation was slowly making me lose my self-control.

The emotions bubbled up in the pit of my stomach until I felt like I was going to burst. I wanted more of him. I needed more of him.

Suddenly, a stream of water rushed forward from its descent. It morphed into a massive orb, and it shot around us, engulfing our bodies. Rune's eyes went wide as the water rolled away from my skin to completely flood him. He tried stepping away, but the water moved with him, sending bubbles up from his tight mouth.

"Rune!" I yelled.

Panic replaced my sexual desires, and with an intense sense of alarm, the water's current around him went wild. It whirled around him in a dangerous, swift pool. Rune suddenly changed into his Fae form as he clawed around in the water in a desperate attempt to wrench free from its cage.

My hands shook as I fought to calm down. With all the bubbles rising from his mouth, I knew he didn't have much time left.

Taking a deep breath, I reached out to the funnel of rapid moving water. I narrowed my eyes, calling forth all of my focus. Within a few seconds, a pleasantly cool wave washed over me. I felt its comforting movements deep within my body. My limbs began to buzz as my connection to the water solidified.

I could only think one word.

Stop.

Instantly, the water encasing Rune crashed to the bottom of the shower with a wet smack. A desperate gasp escaped Rune's mouth, and he bent forward slightly as he clutched at his throat. My eyes welled with tears as coughs wracked his body. My legs and hands shook, and I collapsed to my knees upon the tiled shower floor. Horrified, I stared down at my quivering hands.

I did that. I hurt Rune.

Tears spilled over the rims of my eyes as I wrapped my arms around myself. Ducking my head in shame, I sobbed. I was at an utter loss. I'd attacked him. Even if it was by accident, I'd used my powers against him. If I hadn't been able to calm my sporadic thoughts enough, he could've *drowned.*

"Rune," I choked. Shaking my head frantically, I tucked my head lower. "I'm so sorry. I didn't–I didn't mean to. I swear. I–I don't know how that happened."

The pain in my chest squeezed tightly at my throat, and tears continued to roll down my cheeks. His erratic breathing had returned to normal, and now, he was quiet. I could feel his eyes on me, but I couldn't bring myself to look at him. I was so embarrassed. Ashamed. Angry with who I was. I'd never wanted to hurt him.

As the torrent of emotions spiraled around inside of me, the water from the shower head beat small drops onto my back. It had calmed, but I still felt uneasy and terrified of its power—of *my* power.

My voice quivered as I started again, "I'm so sorr—"

"Bria."

The sound of his calm, even voice made me jump. I froze and stared wide-eyed at the tiles from where I was crouched. There was no trace of venom or fury in the way he said my name. Instead, it sent a wave of comfort and ease through me.

Swallowing hard, I dug in the pit of my stomach for an ounce of courage. Slowly, I looked up. Through the falling water, I saw Rune, still in Fae form. He sat on his knees in front of me with worry etched into his brow and the tilt of his fox ears.

He reached forward and carefully placed his hands on my arms, avoiding my skin with his claws. Trailing his palms soothingly along my skin, he grasped my hands and stood, bringing me with him. My legs felt like they weren't my own, so I was thankful when Rune didn't let go. He intertwined his fingers with mine and stepped closer, looking down into my searching eyes.

"It's fine. *I'm* fine. It was an accident." His tender eyes searched mine, and he reached up to tuck a strand of wet hair behind my ear. The gesture made a flutter spread in my chest.

"I don't get it," I sighed. "Why did the water attack you? I wasn't in *danger*."

He nibbled his lip as he fought against a playful glimmer trying to light up his eyes. "If I had to take a guess, your desire for me made the water act on its own, similar to what started to happen during one of our previous moments here in the bathroom. The target of your heightened emotions was me, so the water acted on that target, and without guidance or direction, it just engulfed me."

I furrowed my brow and processed that. It made sense. It was like Dallas explained. Until that connection was established between the water and me, it was going to react whenever I did, good or bad.

"I think I'm in need of another lesson with Dallas," I groaned. A brilliant idea occurred to me then, and I beamed up at Rune. "Maybe we could do training today?"

Rune cocked a brow at me. "Do explain."

"I was thinking. You and Dallas are going to have to meet officially sooner or later. What if we all met for another lesson, and we could get those awkward introductions out of the way?"

"Together?"

"Yes, together."

"Together as in the three of us? Gathering in close proximity?"

I folded my arms and rolled my eyes. "That is generally what 'together' means."

He rubbed the back of his neck and stared up at the ceiling as he took a deep breath. "Hanging around Water Fae. Never thought I'd see the day." He found my eyes and reluctantly said, "Okay. We can give it a shot."

Bouncing on my heels, I leaned forward to kiss him, but before my lips could close over his, he reached his hand up between us, pressing his palm to my lips.

Smirking, Rune said, "We should probably avoid anything exciting while in the shower. You know, until you've had that training."

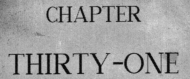

I CAN'T BELIEVE WE'RE DOING this," Ardley said from beside me. "I feel like we're headed into battle right now."

"We're not going into battle. There will be no fighting, I promise," I said.

At least, no physical fighting. Verbal fighting is always a possibility.

Rune and I had joined Akira, Bassel, and the rest of the gang after getting dressed that morning. When we explained that we were going to meet up with Dallas, who was apparently bringing my entire security team, everyone said they wanted to join. It seemed both sides were eager to meet each other. I wasn't sure how to feel about that, but both Dallas and Rune assured me that they'd keep everything civil. Part of me really hoped that this was the first step in having Land Fae and Water Fae get along.

Marlow stayed back at the house where he and the twins were locked in his room. Rune didn't want the boys at the house without one of us there while we had this meeting, and the ever-afraid Marlow had been all too happy to remain at the house where he didn't have to be surrounded by Water Fae.

Everyone except me was in their Fae form as we trekked through the private woods, away from Myra's property, and I couldn't help but notice how Bassel strode a bit taller with his shoulders back or how Rune's eyes seemed to be scanning every tree for signs of *something*. Ardley walked close to Avana, his fingers twitching like he was readying to create fire at a moment's notice. I couldn't blame them for being on edge. A century of war with the very people they were about to face had conditioned them not to trust each other.

I wove my fingers through Rune's and gave his hand a reassuring squeeze.

He looked down at me, and I saw how unsettled and anxious he was about what we were doing. I knew this wasn't going to be easy for him, but I hoped that in the end, it would result in something wonderful.

It had to.

"We're almost there," I told everyone as we neared the area where Dallas and I had trained.

Our group rounded some overgrown bushes, and when we did, we came face to face with a dozen or so people. Dallas stood at the head of the Water Fae with Dax on one side and Rance on the other.

"Woah," I mumbled, not expecting *this* many people.

"Bria," Dallas said with a bright smile. Her eyes briefly flicked to where my hand joined with Rune's before finding my gaze again. "I'm glad you guys made it here okay."

"Why? Were we not supposed to make it here okay?" Bassel asked, baring his liger canines.

I'd never heard Bassel so venomous.

My eyes widened at the suspicion and anger so clearly

embedded in his voice. I knew Bassel's history with Water Fae was long ago, but clearly, the wounds were still raw and bleeding for him.

"She didn't mean it like that," Rance said as he stepped closer to Dallas and placed a supportive dark hand on the small of her back. "We're just … happy that you all came out here. To meet us." Rance looked like he was fighting a smirk as he added, "No need to get defensive, *Kitty*."

"Call me Kitty one more time you piece of sh—"

"Bassel," Avana said calmly, grabbing his arm with an iridescent hand to keep him in place. Her voice dropped for only our group to hear as she said, "Don't. You're better than this. Be calm."

Bassel's jaw ticked, and he opened and closed his clawed fists as he worked to take a deep breath.

"Well, this is off to a great start," Rune mumbled. His gaze scanned the crowd of strangers gathered behind Dallas, and I could practically hear what he was thinking. This looked bad. Over a dozen Water Fae were gathered for what was supposed to be a simple training session with Dallas. It had red flags written all over it.

I squeezed Rune's hand tighter and focused on Dallas. "I thought we were training. Why so many people?"

"Oh, they aren't staying," Dallas explained. "Everyone wanted to meet you officially since your lineage is out in the open now. These are some members of the Royal Guard. A lot of them have been around you your whole life, guarding you from a distance."

"Your Highness," several Fae called at once before dropping to a knee with their heads bowed and a hand pressed to their hearts.

I stared wide eyed and speechless.

"Well, that's one way to greet someone," Ardley said behind me.

"No kidding," Akira whispered back.

Clearing my throat, I forced a smile. "Um, hi … everyone."

"It's an honor to be in your presence like this," an older man said with a bright smile. His gray eyes skimmed over Rune and the others, and his wrinkled smile cracked slightly. "As well as all of your friends."

"Oh, right," I quickly said. "Let me introduce everyone." I went down the line, ending on Rune.

"Yeah, Rune," Dax said with narrowed green eyes. He crossed his arms and raised his chin in contempt. "The *Fox*. We all know him since, you know, he attacked me."

"Dax," Dallas hissed.

Hearing and seeing the haughty attitude of Dax after weeks of being rid of his presence was like stumbling on a piece of garbage that you thought you'd thrown out but hadn't.

My ex and I had a rollercoaster of a relationship, with the most recent exchange ending in his trying to force his affections on me while I'd been battered from a fight with Jonah—the same night of said attack from Rune.

"Believe me," Rune said with a bitter laugh. The gesture put his sharp canines on display, and I imagined his desire to use them was in full swing as he leveled his attention on Dax. "You deserved it. Even so, that was mere child's play compared to the things I'd love to do to you."

"Rune," I chided.

So much hatred burned brightly in his gaze, but as soon as Rune's eyes found mine, the fire settled to a simmer.

"It looks like our Princess took the saying, 'keep your ene-mies close' to a whole new level," Dax deadpanned. "Real great of you, Bria. Sleeping with the enemy. We can tell whose side you're on."

"Dax!" The shouts came from Dallas, Rance, and Imani.

Rune's grip on my hand tightened. "I'm gonna beat the shit out of him."

"Rune," I whispered. "Stop. You know how immature Dax is. Don't let him get to you."

Even if he did deserve a good ass beating.

Maybe even from me.

"Keep your head," Bassel whispered as he moved in closer to us. "Don't let these guys toy with you more than they already have."

"What?" Dax fumed. "We're all thinking it! And it's not just any Land Fae. He's a *Fox.*" Dax turned his narrowed eyes on me. "Fun fact, Bria. It was the son of a powerful Fox Fae family who killed your parents."

In an instant, a tight grip strangled the air from my lungs. "What?"

"I'm gonna burn him alive," Rune said between gritted teeth.

"Leave it alone, R," Ardley whispered.

"Dax, knock it off," Dallas snapped.

"*Everyone* knock it off!" I roared.

My mind scattered in a million different directions. Not only was this a shit show, but Dax's casually tossed-out info was like a punch to the gut when I was already down and struggling to breathe. Now wasn't the time for bombs like that to be dropped, *especially* by Dax.

Taking a deep breath, I tucked away the news to process later and said, "We're all on the same side here. I get it. You guys have hated each other's kind for years, but that ends now. It ends here. Because guess what? We're all strangers here. Dallas doesn't know Rune. Rune doesn't know Rance. Rance doesn't know Akira. No one here can pass judgment on the others, because you don't know them for who they are as individuals. Stop letting your past dictate your present."

Silence fell among everyone gathered. Across the space between our groups, Dallas beamed at me with pride, and slowly, the tension in the air untangled. Things were far from over. There was far too much history between the Fae for them to simply walk away, hand in hand, laughing and skipping through a field of fucking daises. But maybe they'd leave here *thinking* about trying to make it work, about a better future.

"Okay, I think now's an okay time for the majority of us to bid farewell for the time being," Dallas said as she turned to the group of Water Fae guards. "We can do more personal introductions later. Everyone except for Rance, Imani, and Dax, head back to base."

The Water Fae bowed deeply at the waist. They all regarded me much the way they had when greeting me, kneeling and using formal titles, before making a swift exit through the trees.

When only our small groups were left, I released the breath I'd been holding and hung my head. "That was probably a disaster of a first impression."

"You did amazing. You kept your head, not letting anything or *anyone*," Imani said with a pointed look at Dax before continuing, "get to you."

The remaining Water Fae drew closer.

"Also, allow me to formally introduce myself." Imani bowed. "I'm Imani Washington. I'm the head of your Royal Guard, and one of the commanding officers for the Water Fae Army."

Army. The word left a bitter taste in my mouth with all that it implied.

Clearing my throat, I smiled. "It's really good to see you again, Imani. Please stand, though. None of you have to bow like that to me."

Imani slowly straightened, glancing at Dallas. "But—"

Dallas placed a hand on Imani's shoulder as she smiled at me. "Bria, you're their Princess. Their leader. Bowing for royalty is a custom. It shows respect."

I stiffened. "That's not the kind of respect I want—people bowing to me. I don't like that. I don't want anyone bowing or curtsying or anything. Treat me as you would anyone else."

Rance grinned from beside Dallas. "You're our Princess. Treating you like any other person *is* impossible, but we can tone down on that formal crap. No problem."

"Thanks."

"So," Dallas said as she bounced on her feet. "Who's ready to get started on training?"

"If we're actually going to be working together," Dax started, "these guys need to understand who's in charge. You'll be taking orders from me and Bria if we're really going to be on the same side."

I curled my lip at Dax. "And why would they take orders from you?"

"Dax," Dallas hissed in warning.

With a cocky twinkle in his eyes, Dax held his head high while addressing me. "Because I'll soon be King of Water Fae, which makes me second in command. You and I are engaged. I look forward to our future together, *wifey*."

My stomach instantly soured with disgust, and my jaw dropped. "Excuse me?"

"He's dead. I'm gonna kill him," Rune growled.

"Yeah, go ahead," Bassel said with white-knuckled fists.

"I'm not stopping you." Ardley crossed his arms over his chest.

"Engaged?" I gave a humorless laugh. "I'm not sure what gave you that impression, but you and I are far from engaged, Dax."

"We are engaged," Dax retorted. "Before you were even born, your parents decided we'd be married once you were old enough. Your parents, the King and Queen, decided this."

I shot a pointed look at Dallas, who avoided my eye contact. She'd known about this but hadn't told me. I recalled the night we'd had our talk where she'd told me the truth about who I was. She'd mentioned there was more to Dax and his story but said we'd talk about it later. Now I realized *this* was what she meant. Dax and I were *engaged*.

The fact that she'd kept something *this* big from me felt like a fresh cut, and what made the dagger sink deeper in my chest was that she'd done it while knowing my stance on both Dax and Rune.

Was I guilty of withholding pertinent information from my dear friends? Yes. But Dallas was my *best friend*. I hadn't thought she'd ever keep something like this from me, but part of me also felt like I had no right to be hurt by the secret since I'd been harboring my own.

Forcing my hurt gaze away from Dallas, I studied Dax and the arrogant curve of his lips. Suddenly, all of his past behavior made so much more sense. His sudden interest in me, his possessiveness, his insistence on us being a couple. He knew we were practically halfway down the aisle, and he just assumed that included this distorted ownership of me.

Anger twisted my insides in a painful grip, and I finally found my words. "My parents aren't here, Dax. *I* am. *I'm* future Queen, and I can promise you there will be no wedding between us. Consider our engagement off."

Dax's nostrils flared with barely contained rage. Eyes full of loathing flicked to Rune, and he snarled, "Yeah, and you wanna know why your parents aren't here? It's because of *his* kind. Fucking Foxes!"

"We're here to train, right?" Rune asked, his voice dangerously calm. "Watch closely then, Bria."

One second Rune was by my side, and the next, he was directly in front of Dax, smashing his fist into his face. Dax flew back from the force of the impact and rolled across the dirt a good ten feet.

Rune straightened with blood dripping from his unmarred knuckles. "That's called a right hook, but you already knew that. Guess a demonstration wasn't needed. Oops."

Dax leapt to his feet with crimson dripping from his nose and smearing across his lips. "You fucking prick. You're dead!"

Dax launched himself at Rune, who smiled as each fist lit with flames.

"Stop!" I screamed.

Panic skyrocketed through my limbs, and at the same time, a warm tingle spread. As Rune and Dax neared each other with a need for vengeance, I flung an arm out toward each of them. Instantly, water rushed from the creek bed and encased both men in their own watery prisons. I pulled the two far apart within their orbs and set them each with their group before releasing them from the water's hold.

As soon as they were freed, I let go of the breath I'd been holding and braced my hands on my knees.

"That was amazing! You controlled the water perfectly!" Dallas cheered, running over to fling her arms around my neck.

Giving a half-hearted smile, I held onto her arm. "I have no idea how I did that."

"Why the hell are you happy?" Dax fumed from where he got to his feet with a soggy sway. "He just attacked me!"

"You deserved it," Rance said, his jaw hardening. "You have no authority, Dax. Not anymore. Stop acting like you do. If you don't get your shit together and get along, I'll beat your ass *myself.*"

While Rance, Dallas, and Imani dealt with Dax, I rushed back over to Rune where he stood wringing water out of his t-shirt amidst our friends.

"Rune, are you okay?" I asked.

He nodded, and when he met my eyes, I was relieved to find no hint of anger toward me. He grabbed his fox tail and shook the lingering water from the fur. "I'm fine. I just really hate that bastard. I'm sorry. I know you wanted this to be a chance for us to work together and get along. I'm ruining it."

I quickly shook my head. "Dax was being a dick. As usual. Honestly, I'm glad you hit him, because it meant I didn't have to."

"Agreed," Ardley said. "I wish someone would've shut him up sooner."

"Why'd he even get to stay?" Avana asked, peeking at him over my shoulder where the Water Fae were a distance away, still arguing. "He clearly doesn't want to be here."

"Didn't you hear?" Bassel asked sarcastically. "He's 'future King.' Of course he gets to be here."

"I'll actually barf if we keep using Dax and King in the same sentence," Akira said. His body shook with a repulsed tremor, and he quickly wrapped his arms around himself. "Could you imagine *him* leading a whole Kingdom of Fae?"

"I'm trying not to," Rune mumbled as he watched Dax closely. His attention turned back to me, and the corners of his eyes softened. Closing the space between us, he tucked a strand of hair behind my ear. "Are you okay?"

Smiling, I placed my hand over his. "I am now."

"I think we have everything sorted out over here," Dallas announced as she and the others walked back over. "Hopefully, things will go more smoothly now. Ready to continue, Bria?"

I nodded. "Ready."

Rune suddenly grabbed my hand and pulled me back to him. Our bodies pressed firmly against each other, and he shoved his hands into my hair as he pressed our lips together. My thoughts immediately melted into incoherent ramblings as the intensity of his kiss swept through my entire body. His tongue was a delicious beast, seeking to claim mine, and I returned the gesture, just as hungrily.

Rune pulled back only far enough for us to catch our breaths, and he smirked. "Sorry. I wanted to make it clear for him over there that he has no chance."

Clearing my throat, I bit the inside of my lip. "I think he got the message."

"Yep. We all did," Ardley said from beside Rune. "Loud and clear."

Rune released me with a wide grin. "Let the training begin."

Fighting against the embarrassment trying to swarm my cheeks, I turned toward Dallas. Everyone else gathered in a group to make individual introductions, so I decided now was my chance to have a quick talk with my best friend.

As I jogged over, Dallas fidgeted from side to side. When I was close enough that she could whisper, she started, "I'm sorry for not telling you about ... you know."

A burn slid down my throat as I swallowed. "Why didn't you tell me? You know how I feel about Dax. *And* Rune. *Engaged*, Dallas? That's really freaking big stuff."

Her troubled green eyes fell to her shoes, and she toed at the dirt beneath them. "You've had enough thrown your way. I didn't want to add to your list of worries and troubles. It was a shitty move on my part, which I see now. I should've told you."

Even though I knew that Dallas thought she was doing the right thing, the sting of the secret still lingered at the edges of my mind. It made me ask, "Is there anything else I need to know?"

Dallas shook her head. "Nothing like that. Obviously, there's a shit ton of stuff you need to know about being Queen, your powers, Fae, and all of that. But nothing like what you're thinking."

Slowly, I nodded and decided to trust her. "Okay." Taking a deep breath, I stepped back from where Dallas and I had been huddled close together. I nodded to Imani, who left the group of mingling Land and Water Fae to join us. The chatter quieted as everyone's attention turned to Imani, Dallas, and I.

Imani drew water from the creek with a simple gesture, and the orb hovered above her hand. "What all have you learned to do so far?"

"Well," I started as Imani gently passed the ball of water toward me. I quickly held my hands up and slowed it until it swayed in front of me. "I've done a couple of things, mostly by accident. I learned how to make shapes out of the water last time Dallas and I did this."

"Wow," Dax said dryly. Boredom clouded his features as he rolled his eyes. "So impressive. Shapes. Very powerful indeed."

Dallas's eye twitched, and Rance's gaze shot daggers in Dax's direction. With a heavy sigh, Imani quickly pulled a large wave from the creek bed and sent it blasting at Dax. It hit him with such force that his body flew back and smacked hard into a tree trunk. When the deluge cleared, Dax was slumped over on the ground, unmoving.

"Is he unconscious?" Dallas asked with not a bit of concern.

"Looks like it," Imani said as she checked Dax's neck for a pulse.

"Fucking finally!" Dallas cheered. "My God, he's an annoying ass. Do any of you Land Fae want a free kill? Really, by all means. Kill him."

Bassel shrugged and started toward Dax.

Akira quickly placed a hand on his chest and smiled. "She's joking, Bassel."

"I wish I wasn't," Dallas mumbled.

"Now that the nuisance is out of the way," Imani said as she faced me again. "Why don't you give us a demonstration of what you've learned?"

My skin prickled with nerves as I glanced at Rune and the others. While shapes had been easy enough for me to control on command—unlike other times I'd tapped into my powers—I was still nervous to execute the technique with everyone's eyes on me. Feeling slightly overwhelmed by the attention, I turned back to the floating orb hovering above my hands, then back to the expectant faces in front of me. When my gaze found Rune's, he smiled softly and gave me an encouraging nod.

Taking a deep breath, I looked back to the ball of moving water, and slowly, it started to bounce and move around itself, morphing as my mind guided it into its new shape. After only a few seconds, a crystal-clear fox stood in the air before me, and with only a little mental nudging, it leapt, running and darting along invisible ground.

"Whoa," Akira marveled.

Rune's eyes glittered with wonder as he watched the scurrying water fox trot around him before coming back to my outstretched hand. As soon as its four paws landed on my palms, the water expanded before shrinking back into a ball.

"Beautiful," Rance said with a look of awe.

Grinning and toeing the dirt sheepishly, I said, "Thanks, guys. It's not much, but it's something I can at least manage and control."

"Control is going to come slowly," Dallas explained. "The more you use the water, the more you get to know it and vice versa, the easier it will be to govern what it does and when."

"Exactly," Rance said. "I remember when I was first learning to harness my abilities. I constantly tapped into it when I wasn't supposed to. I ruined so much furniture."

"It's the same with us," Rune chimed in, and we all looked at him. He lifted his hand, and a ball of fire erupted above his palm. "Land Fae also have to learn to manage our abilities. If we get overly upset or experience any heightened emotion, our powers can get the better of us. When first learning, that is one of the hardest things to master. Control."

To know that everyone struggled with this, even extremely powerful Fae like Rune and Dallas, made the tightness in my shoulders ease. It made me believe that if they could do it and get to where they were now, I could, too.

"Let's get down to business," Dallas said, clapping her hands together. "The more you practice, the better grip you'll get on your abilities."

Dallas, Imani, and I walked over to the stream, which was roughly ten feet away from the group. As we neared it, I pulled

Dallas aside. Leaning in close to her, I whispered, "Any news on the *rat*?"

Knowing I was referring to the investigation into who hired Jonah, Dallas shook her head. "Nothing of substance. Alibies are still being checked. Dax said he's managed to rule out some, but not all yet."

Disappointed that the person who wanted me dead was still a mystery, I forced myself to focus on Imani. She explained how to take water shapes a step further, and while I listened, I glanced over to find Rance now standing beside Rune. The two shook hands, although I noticed the tension in both of their shoulders. At least they were making an effort.

Imani pulled up another large wave from the stream, and it twirled above us. Her hands moved, pushed and pulled, urging the water to change shape until a tree stood brilliantly before me. And I mean a *tree*. Every groove in the bark, every individual vein running through the leaves, every bug scurrying across the piece of nature. Every minute detail was in the water.

"Well, that's gonna be hard," I mumbled.

"You have an artist's eye," Dallas said encouragingly. "Just see it in your mind. Every feature, every facet. Guide the water through those details. Show the water what it looks like in your mind."

"I'll try," I said as Imani gently guided the tree back into the creekbed, where it disappeared with the current.

"So," Rance started, his voice drifting over to where I stood. I glanced sideways while urging the water forward and saw him addressing Rune. "Out of curiosity, what's your last name?"

"You're doing great," Imani said, watching the tall wall of water start to shift itself into the shape of a tree.

"It's Sinclair," Rune answered.

My grip on the water snapped, and the wave fell back to the stream with a loud crack.

"That was a good start," Dallas said, placing a hand on my shoulder.

"Yeah. Just keep trying. You can do it," Imani cheered.

Working to catch my breath, I peeked over Imani's shoulder at Rune. His eyes only briefly found mine before meeting Rance's again as Rance worked to make small talk.

I didn't understand. That was such an innocent question, yet Rune had lied. His last name was Beckett, or at least, that's what I'd always believed. Yet no one—not Ardley, Akira, Bassel, any of them—contradicted Rune's answer. It made me wonder if perhaps *I'd* been given a fake last name, but that still posed the question of why.

"You okay?" Dallas asked.

Quickly turning back to her, I forced a smile. "Yeah, sorry. I'm good. Let's try again."

I readied my stance, bringing my arms back in front of me to guide the water up and out of the stream. As we spent the next hour working on my abilities, I couldn't help but keep going back to Rune's answer. After having completely cleared the air between us about any and all secrets, it was disturbing to hear Rune lie. I vowed to find out what he was hiding.

CHAPTER

THIRTY-TWO

W E'D JUST RETURNED TO THE house and made it up to everyone's respective rooms when I finally got a moment alone with Rune. Shutting our door behind me, I found Rune staring at me from where he stood by the bed. It was almost like he knew my questions were coming.

"What's your last name?" I asked, getting straight to the cause of my current headache.

He ducked his head and rubbed at the back of his neck. "So, you did hear that." He glanced up from beneath his lashes. "It's Beckett."

My brow pinched with my obvious confusion. "Why'd you tell Rance it was Sinclair?"

"My family is a well-known one, and I knew if I told him my real last name, it would only bring up the history between my family and

Water Fae. We'd already had a rough start to the meeting, so I didn't want to blow it up all over again."

His explanation reminded me of Dax's declaration. The son of a powerful Fox Fae family had killed my parents. Rune was powerful, and he belonged to a well-known Fox Fae family. That wasn't necessarily the same as a *powerful* family, but still, the idea briefly flickered through my head of *what if*. What if Rune … I shoved away the idea, because it was too absurd to even consider. There was no way Rune killed my parents.

Slowly, I nodded. "Okay. That … makes sense. What sort of—"

Sudden loud knocks came at the door, followed by two voices calling, "Big brother!"

Rune sighed and went to answer.

As soon as it opened, Newt and Greshim crossed their arms. "Where were you all day?"

"Sorry, boys," Rune said. "We all had some stuff to do today."

The twins shared a look, and Greshim whispered, "Grown-up stuff." Looking back at Rune, he asked, "Are you all back now? Can we hang out with you?"

"Sure," Rune said with a soft smile. He reached down to ruffle each of his brothers' heads.

Newt inched closer to me and asked, "D-Did you have a g-good d-day?"

I smiled. "I did. What about you?"

"We had fun," Greshim said, scratching at his fox ear, which twitched in response. "We stayed with Marlow in his room, but then Mother needed us for our studies and training."

Rune and I quickly shared a panicked look until Newt said, "*Papá* didn't let us th-though. He had M-M-Marlow take us out for ice cream in town instead."

I raised a surprised brow at the news.

Rune shared my shock as he asked, "And Mother let this happen?"

"Well," Greshim said as he looked like he was weighing Rune's question. "She wasn't happy. I think she and *Papá* got into a fight about it when Marlow left with us."

"We haven't seen her or *Papá* since," Newt added.

I glanced at Rune to gauge what he made of all of this, because I was reeling. I knew Alvaro was protective of the boys, yet he still let Myra do as she pleased with them. She used them against him just like she did with Rune.

To hear that Alvaro was willing to truly intervene and fight Myra on whatever she'd been planning most likely meant it had been something severe. I feared it was getting dangerous for the boys, and I wished that Alvaro would take them away from all of this, especially if he was pushed to the point of getting involved now.

Anger boiled inside me, and I gritted my teeth to keep from outright slandering the boys' mom in front of them. I couldn't help but note that Myra attempted whatever her devious plan was *after* the fiasco yesterday. Myra was reminding us who held the power in this situation—steps out of line, spectacles like yesterday—were a deviation from her plan and would not go unpunished.

The twins needed to get away from this hellhole, and while I couldn't give them that, I could at least give them a distraction.

"How about we all go hang out in Akira and Bassel's room?" I offered. "I think everyone's gonna be over there."

Newt's eyes brightened, and he nodded his head quickly. "Okay!"

The four of us made our way next door where everyone else had already gathered on the couches, all in their Fae forms. I was the only one not, but since it was just our group in here, I didn't see the harm in not wearing my disguise.

"Here comes trouble," Ardley joked when he saw the twins.

"We aren't trouble," Greshim pouted and ran over to punch Ardley in the arm.

"Ouch!" Ardley yelled as he clutched his arm and feigned pain. "You got me. I'm done for."

"You are an actual dork," Akira mumbled from where he was stretched out on the couch with his wings tucked behind him, flipping through TV channels with a bored frown.

"I'm hungry," Marlow said. He lay on the carpet on his back, staring upside down at the TV.

"I think the cooks were making homemade pizza. I can go grab some and bring it up here," Ardley offered.

He received a unanimous "yes" in response.

"I have a movie we can all watch," Rune said. "Let me go grab it from our room."

"Be careful," Marlow said as he stared wide eyed at the TV.

Shaking his head, Rune sighed. He opened the door and said, "I'm just going next door, Marlow. I'll be fine."

The salamander skin on Marlow's arms glistened gold. His blank eyes were transfixed on nothing as he mumbled, "You never know. Foxes are here. Foxes are scary. Foxes could get you."

Bassel walked over from his place at the mini bar in the back of the room to kick Marlow's foot. The frail boy jumped at the sudden touch, and his glassy eyes flicked toward Bassel.

"Dude," Bassel started. "Calm down. Those are silly stories you were told when you were little. Not all Foxes are scary."

Marlow swallowed hard and glanced at the twins. They flashed him toothy smiles, and he seemed to waver. Meeting Bassel's eyes again, he said, "Myra is scary."

Greshim slid off the couch and walked over to Marlow. Grabbing his hand, Greshim said, "Mother is scary. But you don't have to worry. I'll try to protect you."

"What a lovely Prince Charming you are, Greshim," Akira laughed. "Just like your older brother." Akira's brow furrowed in thought, and he pursed his lips. Tapping a finger against his mouth, the wheels seemed to turn in his head. "Actually, I take that back. You are much cooler."

Greshim sat up taller and pushed out his chest proudly.

We laughed, and at the same time, the door clicked as Rune came back in. Quirking his brow, he asked, "What are we all laughing at?"

"*Nandemonai.*" Akira shrugged. "We were most definitely *not* talking about you."

Greshim and Newt giggled, looking up at their brother. Rune smiled at the two of them, who passed a silent message between each other.

The smell of greasy, hot pepperoni pizza suddenly filled the room as Ardley appeared with the food. Everyone grabbed slices before returning to their places. Rune produced his movie— the horror movie I'd gotten him for his birthday. Greshim and Newt promised they were brave enough to watch it with us, so the nine of us lounged on the plush couches, enjoying the simplicity of pizza, friends, and good films.

In such a short amount of time, everyone in this room had come to be like family to me. These moments were precious, and the thought of losing any of them, even my newer friends like Ardley, caused a crack to form right down my chest.

It had been so long since I had truly felt at home with people other than Dallas. Spending my whole life not knowing my real family or where I came from had always left me feeling like something was missing. I was thankful for Greg and Wendy who took me in, but I never felt like I was truly *home* with my "family." When Dallas and I became best friends, that sort of void tucked away in my chest started to fill. She was always there for me, and I knew she would be by my side through everything. She was my family.

But now, my family had grown.

And it had all started with Rune.

What happened at the club those few months ago—nearly getting robbed and murdered—was a horrible experience and memory. That fear and desperation I felt was something I would never wish on anyone. Even so, I wouldn't be where I was now, feeling what I was at that moment, if it hadn't been for that night. I had found a family. Akira, Bassel, Marlow, Avana, Ardley, the twins.

Rune.

Glancing sideways, I drank in the sight of Rune. He sat back on the couch on the other side of Greshim. He was in the middle of talking to Akira, so his gaze was far from my own. His broad chest rose and fell with every breath, every laugh. The corners of his eyes were creased at the sides as he chuckled about something, and the sound of his deep, honey-sweet laughter made my heart flutter on the wings of birds taking flight. This was the man I loved. Even the parts about him that weren't human were now endearing to me. The subtle twitch of his white fox ear, the canines that glistened in the light, and the flick of his fluffy tail draped next to him. I had come to love it all because they were a part of *him*.

His laugh melted into the air as he met my gaze. I held my breath under his stare, and a tender warmth flooded his eyes as he smiled at me. If we were alone, I would've wrapped myself in his embrace and basked in all the bliss I felt. As it was, I returned the gesture with a smile.

We'd be alone soon enough.

Once the movie ended, Rune stood and reached for the empty pizza tray. "I'll run this back to the kitchen. Anyone need anything?"

Everyone declined as Rune made his way to the door.

I quickly got up and trailed after him. "I'll come with you."

Rune looked back at me, and concern pricked at the lines on his forehead. "Are you sure? We may run into people."

"I'm sure. If I keep hiding away, it will probably look suspicious. I need to at least act like I'm not scared."

"*Are* you scared?"

I held my head higher. "No."

Smirking, he grabbed my hand with his free one, and together, we made our way downstairs. As soon as we made it to the grand staircase, Myra rounded the bottom banister. Her eyes immediately narrowed when she saw us descending the steps. "Rune. We missed you at dinner," she said.

We stopped walking once we were face to face with Myra.

Rune's voice was devoid of remorse as he responded, "We had dinner with our friends."

"How ..." Myra paused as her eyes found me, "convenient."

I tilted my chin up a hair, refusing to let her get to me.

"If you'll excuse us," Rune said, capturing his mother's attention once more. "We were in the middle of something."

We turned to make our exit. When our backs were to Myra, her unusually bright voice followed us. "By the way, I was in my study just now, and I noticed a person hiding among the trees by the lake. It was a Water Fae, no doubt. I know it's been some time since you've had your taste of blood, Rune. Why don't you go take care of her for me? Bring back her head so I can add it to my collection. She had *lovely* red hair."

My blood ran cold, and it took everything in me not to react.

Rune pulled me along as he tossed over his shoulder, "Yeah, I'll handle it."

We weaved through the hallways, but they practically blended together. I couldn't seem to take in a full breath, and my heart beat wildly in my chest.

As soon as we entered the vacant kitchen, Rune tossed the tray on the counter and whipped around to face me. He quickly cupped my cheeks as my breaths came out fast and hard.

"Bria, baby, calm down," Rune whispered.

"Dallas," I panted in between gasps. White starbursts started dancing across my vision as my head grew fuzzier. The room spun around me, and I fought to catch the breath that seemed to be running away from me. "Dallas."

Water suddenly erupted out of the sink across the room. It gushed from the silver faucet and barreled toward us. The water bled onto my skin, and I could feel its calming touch soothing me, but my panic kept it from fully taking root.

"Fuck," Rune hissed under his breath. He quickly pulled me into a tight hug, which encased his arms and chest in the growing ball of water. "I'm here. I'm right here, Bria. Breathe."

It took every ounce of strength inside of me to focus on Rune's words. I repeated each one in my head, and I tried to inhale and exhale to the beat of his heart pounding within his chest. Between the current of the water and Rune's strong embrace, I was able to rein in my alarm enough to get my breathing back under control. Once I could feel air moving through my lungs again, I silently ordered the water back to the sink. It followed my command, slipping down the drain, and eventually, only small drops fell from the faucet in a slow pit-pat.

Rune didn't let go of me. He held me firmly to him as he said, "Dallas is okay. Let's go call her. You need to hear that she's okay."

I tried to nod, but I had no idea if I managed to move or not.

Dallas.

She'd been spotted.

By *Myra*.

Myra wanted to … hang Dallas's head. She wanted to add it to that sick wall in her office. The mere idea had my dinner trying to climb back up my throat. Dallas was in danger. All of the Water Fae were, and I was the reason they were here. Their lives were endangered because of me. If something happened to them …

"Bria."

I looked up at the sudden sound of Rune's voice, and when I did, I was shocked to see we were in our room. Water dripped from his damp arms and the front of his shirt due to the episode in the kitchen, and I briefly wondered if we'd made a puddle throughout the house.

Rune held my phone out to me. "Call Dallas."

I nodded slowly and took the phone with quivering fingers. I dialed her number and held my breath as the phone rang—a noise that seemed to last years.

"Gummy worm?"

The tension in my chest cracked wide open at the sound of her voice, and I fell to my knees as tears spilled over my eyes.

"Bria? What's wrong? I'm coming with—"

"No, no. Stay," I said, wiping at tears. "I'm fine. I was just worried about you and everyone else."

I told her what Myra had said, and she groaned. "Shit. I thought I was out of their sight range. I was trying to get close enough to confirm the identities of those in the house. We haven't been able to I.D. anyone other than the group you came with, Yasmine Cashing, and Aidan Lovehue."

"Well, don't worry about identifying anyone. Stay back from the house. Please. I can't even think about what would happen if you were caught."

"As you wish, Princess."

Letting out a breathy laugh, I rolled my eyes. "Don't call me that."

"Yeah, yeah. No formal shit. Blah, blah, blah."

Taking a deep breath, I smiled into the mouthpiece. "I love you, Dallas."

"I love you too, my little strudel doodle."

"Much better."

We hung up, and relief settled deep within my bones. Everything was fine. She was fine, the group was fine. We only had two days left of this trip, so as long as they stayed back from the property as I'd instructed, there shouldn't be any more issues. They'd stayed hidden with only one slip up for this long. They could avoid being spotted for two more days.

"Are you okay?" Rune asked as he squatted in front of me.

"Yes. Thank you. Sorry about your kitchen sink and for freaking out. I just—"

"You have nothing to apologize for. I get it. You were worried about your friend. I'm just glad everyone is safe and away from the house."

"Me too. Hopefully, they stay away for the remainder of the trip. What are you going to do about Myra? She's expecting you to bring back …"

Rune shrugged. "I'll tell her I didn't see anyone when I went looking."

I slowly nodded, though my mind was already moving on to new worries. It hadn't truly hit me until right then that my being here put me and my whole Water Fae team at risk. As Princess, my life was tied to so many others. Dallas, Rance, Imani, *everyone*. My safety and their safety were linked. From now on, I had to think about more than just my own well-being as I traversed the world. That realization had the weight of a thousand lives falling onto my shoulders, and it took every ounce of strength to not let myself crumble beneath the load.

After a moment of silence, Rune asked, "Do you want to do something? Just the two of us?"

Sensing that Rune was looking for a distraction for me, I met his eyes and processed his words. Quirking a brow, I glanced at the bed. "Just us two?"

Chuckling, he grabbed my hands and helped me to my feet. "Not what I had in mind. At least, not right now. I was referring to something else."

"Oh." I tried to not sound disappointed, but judging by his smirk, I failed. Clearing my throat, I asked, "What did you have in mind?"

"I thought we could go to my room."

Confused, I looked around the bedroom. "I know I spaced out for a minute, but I'm pretty sure this *is* our room."

"I said *my* room. As in, my old bedroom from when I lived here."

Curiosity and sudden excitement had me nodding with wide eyes. "Yes. *Yes!*"

I followed him out of the room and realized we were just going down the hall. We came to the same door I'd seen Rune enter on our very first day here.

"I never let anyone into this room." Rune looked back at me and continued, "I keep the room locked and off limits from everyone. It's … sacred, I guess. It's a tomb, really, of the past. My past."

My heart clenched tightly, and I waited with bated breath as he slipped a key into the lock and turned. Swallowing hard, I clasped my hands in front of me as he held the door open.

Shelves lined one expanse of the wall, and books filled each of the ebony planks. The small ones contained poetry, short stories, fables, and plays. Thick tomes held works of art, reciting lost stories from eons ago or handwritten accounts in foreign languages, as well as books on architecture. The dust coating their crinkled, yellow pages was like a blanket, keeping them preserved for when their master came home.

Trinkets littered the floor and small tables throughout the room. Blueprints with elaborate sketches of buildings, envelopes with foreign stamps that looked like they held letters, and a vase of preserved flowers. Everything seemed so personal, so fragile, so bittersweet. But nothing tugged at me the way one side of the room did.

As I turned toward the one bare wall, my chest grew tight. The dark blue paint had cracked in places over the years, and cobwebs took residence in the corners. The naked expanse of plaster would have felt out of place in the room full of treasures if it hadn't held one thing. I took slow, measured steps as the threat of tears built. Tacked in the center of the wall was a picture frame.

Behind the glass of the frame was a picture of Rune when he was small. He sat on the shoulder of a large man, and his frail arms reached down to squeeze the man's neck. Rune's face lit up as if he squealed in delight. The man held him with one arm reached high, and the other wrapped tightly around the woman he held close. The man was laughing as he looked up at Rune, and the woman's wide smile lit her rosy cheeks as she pressed into the man's side. Her small hand reached up toward little Rune, and she laughed at her two boys.

My mouth quivered as a tear slipped down my cheek. It was a photo of him and his parents. Of a happy, loving family. Balgair, Rune's father, must have been a great man. I wished I could've met him, seen what he was like and what Myra was like before he had died. I wanted Rune to have more than a picture to hold onto.

I wanted Rune to have his mother and father back.

A small, sad chuckle broke Rune's lips as he turned me to face him. Cupping my cheeks, he tilted my head back to look at him. He put on a brave front, but the pain behind his eyes peeked through. "Why are you crying?"

Squeezing my eyes shut, I shook my head. "I hate being Water Fae. I don't want to be one of the people who took everything from you."

If only there wasn't a stupid war between the two races. If only Balgair hadn't fought the Water Fae King, my *dad*. I didn't want to be connected to the beings who stole Rune's smile. The Fae who stole *everything*. Myra's ability to love. Rune's father. Even my own parents were lost to this feud. Maybe if my mom and dad had been human, we'd still be together right now. I'd have a family of flesh and blood. But I didn't, and it was all because of this idiotic hatred.

Why do I have to be one of them?

Rune was quiet as he pulled me into his arms, burying my wet cheeks against his chest. Resting his chin atop my head, he said, "Human. Water Fae. It doesn't matter. You're still you, no matter what race you belong to. Don't hate yourself just because of what you are. I love you, every part of you. Even the Water Fae part. I didn't bring you in here to make you feel bad about what or who you are."

Rune pulled back enough to gaze down at me, and he tucked a strand of hair behind my ear, letting his fingers brush softly across my skin.

The huskiness of his voice dropped to a hushed whisper as he finished, "I brought you here because this room has everything important to me in it. I've never shared so much of myself or my treasures with anyone before, but I've also never loved anyone the way I do you. Water Fae or not Bria, *you* are my most precious treasure."

My throat tightened, and my chest grew warm with fresh emotions. Hearing the raw truth of Rune's feelings sent my own flooding forward, bursting past every bit of wall I'd ever built. My heart belonged to this man.

"I love you," he whispered, inching his lips toward mine.

Sniffling, I smiled against his mouth. "I love you so much, you damn Fox."

CHAPTER
THIRTY-THREE

After a long session of sensual, slow kisses, Rune and I lounged back on his queen-size bed. The mattress sank beneath our weight in an inviting, fluffy embrace. He showed me his extensive personal library, flipping through both old, crinkled paper as well as new, glossy pages. My eagerness visibly bubbled over when he pulled out blueprints and sketches of buildings he'd created.

"Wow," I gasped as I carefully spread the prints over the bed. My eyes traced every line, every precise decision etched onto the paper. Passing my gaze from these proofs to a photo of the final product was mesmerizing.

"This building is used for a small, privately owned business. They specialize in interior decorating, so they wanted a clean, and as they put it, 'unique' building. Typical square glass windowpanes seemed a bit boring, so I went with an angled glass tower with obtuse panes."

"It's stunning," I said breathlessly.

His lips turned up in a warm grin. Meeting my eyes, he said, "Thank you. I'm really proud of my work."

He folded me into his arms, pulling me back against his broad chest. I settled in his hold with a content smile as he set all the papers aside on the floor. The air moved through my lungs with ease, and I snuggled deeper into his arms. This was all I wanted; sweet moments with just the two of us where things felt safe and normal. I craved more moments like this with him, and for the first time, I really felt like that was a possibility.

Shifting, I glanced over my shoulder to find those golden eyes. They were bright, blazing embers, burning sweetly into mine.

It made me slightly curious. One of my first experiences with those eyes was the day I'd saved him as a fox. It had been so long since then, and I realized that I hadn't seen him as a *fox* in a while. Growing even more curious, I realized I'd never seen my fox while knowing it was Rune. The knowledge of who he was gave my fox a whole new feeling.

Turning to face him, I pursed my lips and fingered the blue pendant hanging around his neck. "Can you turn into a fox whenever you want?"

Laughing, he quirked a teasing brow. "Of course. Like my human and Fae form, I can manifest as a fox at any time."

Jumping up to crouch on my knees, I leaned in close with excited eyes. "Can you do it now? I want to see."

A playful glimmer lit his face, but he quickly masked it with a dismissive shrug. "I don't know." His words were slow and feigning uncertainty. He stretched his arms above his head and gave an overdramatic yawn. "I'm pretty tired. Maybe if I had some sort of motivation?"

Giggling, I slowly ran my finger under his bottom lip. "How about you show me your fox form, and I *might* give you a kiss afterward."

A heated smirk pulled at his lips. "Fair enough."

I settled at the foot of the bed to give him space. Watching him with hungry eyes, he slowly tugged his shirt over his head, the hard muscles of his stomach and chest flexing as he did. The long, silky strands of his white hair became slightly disheveled, making my fingers itch to run through them. Everything about him was stunning, and I didn't think it could get any better.

Then he shrugged off his pants and boxers.

My cheeks flushed at the sight, but despite myself, I couldn't tear my eyes away from his perfect, naked form. I wanted to devour every inch of his bare skin, and my hands begged to reach out to him. I suppressed the urge as I waited for his transformation.

After shedding all his clothing, his body contoured until he was crouched on all fours. His body shrunk and shifted with loud snaps, making me grit my teeth. The popping of bones and snapping of flesh finally stopped as lush, black fur with white tips covered his new form. Within seconds, a Silver Fox sat in his place.

I swallowed hard as a new set of emotions flooded me. Seeing this little animal in front of me again after so long had my heart thundering. I had spent weeks obsessing over what it would be like to meet and see him, and now that he was here, I didn't know whether to cry, laugh, or remain still.

His round eyes stared up at me, waiting for my response. Grinning from ear to ear, I held out my hands for him. His paws padded across the bed as he made his way over to me, and I could barely sit still, the excitement making me fidget. I knew this was Rune, not your everyday fox, but seeing him like *this* was all I could really focus on at the moment.

Rune's paws brushed against my folded legs. A giddy laugh slipped past my lips as I ran my hands gently through his coat. The fur was silky as it glided through my fingers, and his tail gave a contented flick.

My finger hooked behind his ear, scratching tenderly. He leaned into the gesture and closed his eyes against the massage. I bit my lip to fight off the threat of another laugh and shook my head at him. The blue gem of the necklace twinkled in the light, and I found myself beaming at him.

Overcome with nostalgia, I said, "Who would've thought that the fox I saved that day would end up being the man I fell in love with?"

His eyes bore into mine with a fierce desire. I kept my eyes locked on his as his body morphed and shifted. Bones regrew into place with cracks, and black fur gave way to golden flesh. The transformation looked and sounded painful, but Rune didn't even bat an eye. He kept his focus on me until he rested on his knees in front of me, naked and human.

I stared up at him, holding my breath. He was so close, the heat from his nude body radiating off him. The fire buried deep in his eyes didn't help my aching desire to reach out and touch him.

Running the back of his hand softly against my cheek, he asked, "Do you regret it? Do you regret saving me?"

I shook my head. "Not even a little." He tucked my blonde strands behind my ear as I asked, "Do you regret saving *me?*"

"Never." He paused and reached next to us to grab his black boxers. He slipped them back on as he seemed to be weighing what to say next. After he resettled on the bed, he slowly continued, "Sometimes I regret dragging you into this mess, forcing you to put up with all the drama and chaos. I regret making our beginning a deal instead of something wonderful that you deserved. I regret not opening up about how I really felt toward you sooner. I planned on giving it a real shot after we talked that day in the field. I was ready to try, but as we headed here, as we got closer to my mother, I locked up again."

Surprised, I asked, "What about getting closer to your mom had you freeze up?"

"The realization that I could turn into her." His eyes—now clouded with desolation—fell to the bed. "It's true that I was afraid of reverting back to the angry asshole version of myself, but it was more than that. I've been so afraid to fall in love, because I saw what happened to my mother when she did. She loved my dad fiercely, so when she lost him, she became ..." Rune fell quiet, and his eyes squeezed shut. Turmoil strained his features, and even though he couldn't find the words, I knew what he meant.

Myra was a monster. A true, living monster.

He took a deep breath and barreled on. "I was afraid I'd end up like her. If I fell in love, whether it be with a Fae or a human, I was afraid of that day when I'd lose them. I was afraid of losing my mind, my very soul, along with them, until I was left hollow. Unable to feel anything for anyone. Including my own flesh and blood."

My heart fractured with the admission, and I realized just how hard it must've been for Rune to finally give in to what he felt. I also realized the true depths of Myra's brokenness. She was merely a husk of a person, a ghost wandering life lost. Seeing your own mother become that would no doubt deter you from following down that same path. So, what did he do? He had closed up. He had hid himself away from anything that could've pulled him in that direction, guarding his heart as though it were made of fragile glass.

"What made you finally open up about how you felt?" I asked, leaning in close as I ran my finger along his brow and down his jaw.

"A few things. Keeping my feelings in check became harder when I saw the way you were with my brothers. Every time you made them laugh or welcomed them with open arms, it got harder *not* to fall even deeper for you. Then we started fooling around, and while I had gone into that thinking it would be no big deal since that's what I've always done—sex with no feelings tied to it—it was definitely *not* like that with you. But the biggest thing that encouraged me to open up was—" He took a moment, the silence gathering, until finally, he glanced over my shoulder at the wall behind me and finished, "My dad."

I froze and let his answer seep into me. I turned around enough to see the photo of his dad hanging proudly on the wall. "Your dad?" I glanced back at him as he nodded.

His eyes never once left the photo. "He loved, and he did so just as vehemently as my mother. Instead of focusing on my mother's version of love, I focused on his. Some thought he was weak for loving my mother. For loving me. Now I realize it made him stronger."

Rune found my eyes again and finished, "When I thought about how happy my dad was, despite all the dark shit happening with our kind, I understood that my feelings weren't something to be afraid of. Sure, my mother's love got distorted after he died, but that didn't mean *my* story had to end that way. I know my dad wouldn't want this for her. Things out of our control may happen throughout our lives, but I know now that it will be worth it. Being with you wholly and fully will be worth anything thrown our way. Just like it was worth it for him. So, I decided to love the way he did, not the way Myra did."

I smiled warmly and moved to sit directly beside him so that the photo of him, his dad, and Myra faced us. I leaned my head against his shoulder and slid my hand into his. "Can you tell me about him? I'd love to know more about your dad."

"My dad—" he started in a slow whisper. He swallowed hard before continuing, "Was *everything* to me."

I squeezed Rune's hand as a sign that I was here. He was safe. Talking about this was okay.

"My dad liked books." Rune glanced at his full bookshelf and gave a slight chuckle. "I guess that's something I learned from him. He loved to read every chance he got. I can remember so many nights when I'd sneak out of bed to go to his library where I'd always find him reading by the fireplace, a book in one hand and my mother's fingers in the other. They'd laugh when they saw me trying to sneak in, but they let me sit with them anyway. Mother would hold me while my dad read us a story."

My throat tightened with a bittersweet pang. It was such a beautiful tale. And a heartbreaking one. It was a memory full of warmth, love, family, and fun. But also painful, raw, and aching, because that's all it was for him now. A memory.

"He sounds amazing," I whispered.

I felt him nod slowly. He fell quiet, and I held onto his hand while rubbing a soft trail up and down his arm with the other. It wasn't much, but it was a comfort I could provide in that moment.

"I hate those damn books."

I looked up from where my cheek still rested against his shoulder at the sound of anger in Rune's whisper. Rune stared at the photo with tears pooling in his eyes.

"After he died, I'd go into his library where the fireplace sat cold and empty, where my mother refused to set foot, and where those damn books sat on the shelves, untouched. I'd find his favorite ones and flip through them, catching his scent on the pages. At least I had that. I shut the room and locked it, trying to preserve the smell. But while the books stayed, his smell didn't. Why? Why did those books get to stay but he didn't?"

My heart broke as the tears finally slid down Rune's cheeks. I wiped them away as they fell and pulled him close. I couldn't erase his pain, no matter how much I wished to. I couldn't go back in time and stop my dad from taking his. All I could do was be there for Rune in that moment, to hold him, kiss him, and be the rock he needed right then. And, maybe, as future Queen of Water Fae, I could finally put an end to the war, once and for all, so that no other child had to lose a parent like he did.

Or like I did.

"There are no words that can take away the hurt," I started as I gently combed my fingers through his hair. "Your dad shouldn't have been dealt the ending he was. But maybe he knew that since he was gone, you needed a new kind of love in your life. Maybe he saw how you were hurting from wherever he is now, and so he sent double the love for you to have in his place. He isn't here anymore, but because of that, you have Newt and Greshim."

It wasn't the same. I knew that, but I also knew that those boys were two of the most important things in Rune's life. Even though it didn't make losing his dad better, I was sure having the twins made dealing with the pain *easier*.

He sat up straight and looked at me with an unreadable emotion buried in his eyes. The tears had mostly cleared, and as his gaze searched mine, a tender light flooded them. He reached forward to press a soft kiss to my forehead. "Thank you. You're right. I like that—to think my dad played a part in getting Newt and Greshim here. But maybe he also saw you." His thumb brushed lovingly across my cheek. "Maybe he saw you and knew that what I really needed in my life was someone who could *see* me and help fill a void I've had for so long, so he sent you to me."

Tears rolled out of the corners of my eyes, and my lip quivered. "Then I guess I should say, 'thanks, Balgair.'" I looked back at his photo. "Thank you for letting me find Rune."

Rune gave a small laugh and faced his dad's picture, too. "Thanks, Dad. Thank you for sending me Bria."

I WAS CAREFUL NOT TO wake Rune the next morning as I slipped out from under the covers and tiptoed out of his room, making sure to lock the door from the inside as I left since I wanted to ensure that Rune's special room remained hidden from all other eyes. It was still early, and while I had longed to stay wrapped in arms that seemed to hold promises of forever, I also wanted to take the rare opportunity of alone time to sneak back to my room and draw. The artist in me was famished and only drawing would satisfy her.

A quiet stillness hung over the house as I made my way down the hall, so I assumed everyone was still asleep. Not wanting anyone to stir, I moved as quietly as I could along the carpeted floors. My fingers reached out for the knob to my room just as an eerie voice called out my name from behind me.

I instantly froze, my blood running cold. Swallowing hard, I turned to face Myra, who stood at the end of the hall in her Fae form. She smiled at me, but the look didn't quite reach her eyes. There was nothing but venom beyond those upturned lips.

"Yes?" I asked, meeting her gaze. It took everything inside me to keep my voice even. I refused to let the woman see how much she unnerved me.

Crooking a clawed finger, she beckoned me forward. "Would you come with me? I'd like to have a word with you."

A shiver ran up my spine as her golden eyes bore into mine. I knew I should refuse. I didn't need to go anywhere with her alone again. It was too risky. But so was refusing. Telling her no would be like admitting defeat. It would seem like yet another red flag, proving what she probably already suspected: that I was hiding something.

Taking a deep breath, I feigned as much of a smile as I could. "Sure."

Her grin widened, making her fangs glisten. She turned and walked down the hall with me trailing slowly after her. That one look told me everything. I had walked right into something I'd soon regret. Whatever battle was soon to commence, she had just won, and I had basically handed her the victory.

My stomach was in knots the entire time I trudged behind her, because I wasn't sure what she wanted or had planned. Was this going to be another talk where she essentially told me I wasn't good enough, so I needed to hit the road? Or did she have something more nefarious up her sleeve? Something in my gut told me this was bad, so I quickly pulled out my phone and shot Dallas a text while Myra's back was to me.

Gummy Worm - stand by

Myra led me down the two flights of stairs, around the corner at the bottom, and out the back doors of the house. Her flowing black gown seemed fitting for this dire moment. I mean, why else would she want to have our discussion out *here*? She probably didn't want to make a mess in her house as she tried to murder me.

Myra came to a standstill in the middle of the back yard. The early morning sky was overcast, which only added to the dark and ominous meeting. With the house on her right and the lake on her left, she faced me with a wicked smile, and seeing that expression rattled me all the way to my core. I had never seen Myra smile more than I had in these five minutes, and not knowing the reason made dread prickle along my skin.

"Did you have a nice night?" she asked.

My eyes never left hers as I stood my ground. "I did."

She smirked, folding her hands in front of her. "I'm sure you did. I do find it rather odd that you aren't in your Fae form. It's much more comfortable than our human one, as you know. Why don't you shift into your Fae form?"

I sucked in a sharp breath as panic settled in my bones, because Avana's illusion wasn't in place. My stomach twisted as I fought for an excuse as to why I couldn't switch forms.

Giving a nonchalant shrug, I said, "I don't mind my human form. It's actually—"

"Shift." Her mouth stretched into a thin line, and her cold command sucked all the argument from my lungs.

Her sharp eyes cut into me, and I swallowed hard. My feet were rooted to the spot, and my mouth seemed to dry and fill with sand, rendering me unable to utter a sound. There was nothing I could do. No argument I could make, no place to hide, and no chance of me miraculously shifting into a Fox Fae.

I was caught in her trap.

"Well?" she asked, raising a single brow at me.

Shaking my head, I whispered, "I can't."

"I know," she laughed. The sound of it made my skin crawl and itch. It was eerie, like the sound of nightmares.

She began to walk a slow circle around me. "How dumb do you think I am? I knew there was something off about you the minute I saw you. Your guise was well put together, but it was evident from your mannerisms that you weren't Fae. You're human."

She came to an abrupt stop directly in front of me. Her amusement had hardened as she glared at me with a raging heat buried in her eyes. Her mouth curled as she spat, "Or at least that's what I thought. You're not human at all, though. You're Water Fae."

My throat tightened as the world began to sway. Trying to hold back my mounting apprehension, I started, "No, I'm—"

"And I don't think you're just any Water Fae, either." She pursed her lips as her narrowed eyes scanned me from head to toe. "I knew there was something familiar about you, and it was never flashes of Blayze and Seraphina Bowen as you'd tried to have me believe. No, it was someone else I'd seen in you. And when I realized who, well, everything made sense."

I held my breath as the words fell from her lips. My palms grew sweaty, and ice prickled along my skin. Even as I prepared myself for Myra's next words, they still struck me like a painful blade sinking into my gut.

"You're the Water Fae Princess."

CHAPTER
THIRTY-FOUR

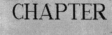

VOMIT FOUGHT ITS WAY UP my throat, and I took a deep breath to keep it down. My brain screamed to deny, deny, *deny*. Myra was smart and sneaky, and while she had me figured out, I couldn't hand over that kind of admission. I had to sway her somehow, to make her believe she was mistaken. There was no way she had actually solved everything.

Swallowing hard, I said, "You're wrong. The Water Fae King and Queen had a son, not a daughter."

"Yes, an excellent strategy," she laughed darkly. Pressing her fingers to her temples, she turned and began to pace. "Spread a rumor that your only child—the heir to your kind—is a boy to throw us off your scent. No wonder we could never find a *Prince*. You were a *Princess* all along."

Myra's laughter grew into a cynical and bitter cackle as she doubled over. My hands began to shake by my side, and everything inside me begged me to move, to run. I took a small step backward before her head snapped up in my direction. I froze under the daggers of her eyes, and she sneered at me.

"You," she spat. "*You*! Your family took everything from me! You took my Balgair!"

Her voice broke on his name, and tears flooded her eyes. For a moment, I actually wanted to reach out to comfort her. She looked so fragile and broken, displaying more emotion than I'd ever seen from her. Her heart had been shattered, and the only thing still holding it together was her bitter resentment for Water Fae.

"Myra," I whispered, reaching toward her.

Her eyes became thin slits, and a deep guttural growl rose from her lips. Malice suddenly engulfed all other emotion within her gaze until all that remained was dark loathing. "You will pay. I will make you pay for what all your people have done."

Her clawed hands erupted in flames, and she roared as she swung the orbs right at me. I rolled to the side as streams of fire barreled in my direction, but I wasn't fast enough. A small flame brushed against my ankle, and I gritted my teeth as my flesh bubbled and burned.

Myra twirled her hand above her head, sending fire flying from her fingers until it circled us in a hot, flickering wall of flames. I stumbled to my feet and fought to ignore the searing heat at my ankle. Flames licked the space around us as her odious glare found me once more.

I took a deep breath and tried to reason with Myra. "I'm not your enemy. I'm—"

She was quick. In the blink of an eye, Myra stood in front of me, snapping out her arm, gripping me tightly around the throat. My words died on my tongue, and the air trying to move through my lungs got stuck beneath her palm. I fought against her grip, yanking and pulling at her hand, but even with my own Fae strength, she remained immovable.

"You," Myra started, leaning in close to spit in my face. Her sharp claws dug into my skin with a biting sting as her grip tightened, and drops of warm liquid suddenly dripped down my neck.

I was vaguely aware that it was blood, but I couldn't seem to focus on that. I was too busy opening my mouth in a desperate, futile attempt to suck in air.

"You aren't my enemy?" Myra started again. "You are the embodiment of all I hate. You are the personification of all that is wrong in this world."

She flung me back, dragging her nails across my throat as she did.

I sucked in a large breath and clutched at my throbbing, bleeding neck. Searing heat immediately flared beneath my fingertips, and I bit back a strangled sob when I felt the seeping gashes.

I looked at Myra with trembling limbs, and bile rose up my throat. She sneered at me as she ate the chunks of my skin from her finger nails and licked the blood dripping down her wrist. I swayed on my feet, both from shock and from lack of oxygen. I at least had enough clarity to notice that all-too-familiar buzz starting up in my limbs. The water called to me, wanting to come to my aid, but I held it back. I believed there had to be *something*, some way to reason with Myra.

I thought wrong.

Myra's cynical smile chilled my body all the way to my bones. Her narrowed eyes never left me as she cackled, "I'm going to enjoy killing you. Your screams as I rip your life from your lungs will be my ultimate lullaby."

Her eyes glowed with contempt as she raised her arm high, and flames took shape in her palm once more. I realized that there was no salvaging this or getting through to her. She was determined to kill me, and my entire body buzzed as the water from the lake begged me to call upon it.

But, at the last second, I hesitated.

Hurting people, regardless of the circumstance, was something I didn't enjoy doing. I'd learned that when I fought Jonah. I hadn't felt like myself when using my powers against him. I'd felt like a monster, and I didn't want to be a monster.

Sensing my hesitation, Myra swung down her arm, her flames barreling right at me. There was no time to react. Moving through time as though it were nonexistent, the flames erupted along my skin. As soon as the fire painted my body though, it was suddenly gone. There was no burning. No searing of my flesh. Nothing.

Not understanding what happened, I looked at Myra. Her icy eyes were locked on something past me. I snapped my head in that direction as the ring of fire ensnaring us burned away. My knees buckled when I looked past the smoke toward *him*. Rune raced across the yard in my direction, flames lit in his clawed hands. Akira, Ardley, and the rest of my friends were right behind him.

As soon as Rune was within arm's reach, he grabbed me and wrapped me tightly in his secure embrace. He shoved his hand into my hair and pressed my face into the crook of his shoulder as he held me close. My breath came out on a choke as I bit back a sob. Relief flooded my body from head to toe as though I'd had a bucket of water dumped over me.

He pulled back to look me over, and his face went ashen when he saw the blood oozing from the gashes in my neck. Then all at once, he changed. I *felt* it the moment he changed. The air thickened with heat, and smoke slowly billowed up from the ground where he stood. His eyes darkened, and a low, deep growl tore from his throat as he turned his deadly eyes on Myra.

This was no longer Rune standing in front of me. This was a Fox Fae thirsty for blood, regardless of the prey. Even if it was his own mother.

Sensing what was coming, I quickly cupped his cheeks. "Rune, don't."

His feral eyes never left Myra, and I nearly tripped as he took a step toward her.

"Rune," I pleaded, yanking his head close to mine until he had to look at me. "That's your mother. *Don't*. It's your mom, Rune. Don't do this."

His chest rose and fell with heavy breaths, but I refused to let up until, slowly, I saw *my* Rune coming back to the surface.

"Did you know?" Myra snapped. Her voice was cold and probing, and when I glanced at her, I found her narrowed eyes trained on her son.

Rune didn't let go of me, nor did he face her. He kept his eyes locked on mine as the beast within him continued to settle.

"Did you know she's Water Fae?" Myra demanded, her tone no longer imploring but accusatory and furious.

"I did," Rune answered without hesitation. Again, his eyes stayed trained on mine.

"How could you?" Myra bellowed.

I couldn't help the small jump that shook my body when she screamed, and I didn't miss the way Rune's jaw hardened. Something feral flashed across his eyes once more, but he quickly stomped it out and finally looked at his mother. "I love her."

Throwing back her head in a humorless laugh, she howled, "My, my. A traitor for a son. All of you! Traitors." She glared at our friends surrounding us. Meeting Rune's ferocity with her own, she hissed, "You're a failure of a Fox Fae. You're a failure of a son."

Flames erupted around Myra in a whirlwind of flickering rage. Her usually perfect hair flew wildly around her livid face, and her claws curled as fire ignited them.

Rune took a readied stance beside me, and our friends followed suit on either side of us.

"Stay ready," Ardley mumbled from next to Rune. "She's going to use fire to win. She knows she's outmatched if she enters close combat."

"I know," Rune commented darkly.

Everyone was preparing for a fight, and Myra seemed all too eager to grant that request as her wail filled the skies and her wicked fire arched toward us.

In the next moment, Akira rushed forward on a beat of his black wings, and his eyes sharpened to a deadly black. He flung his arms out wide, sending a gush of wind toward the fire. The two elements met in a hot explosion. Stray flames rolled away as the wall of fire that had been heading right for us extinguished in a smoky trail.

"Don't get in my way," Myra screamed at Akira. She raised a fisted flame before hurtling it at him.

He quickly flapped his wings, darting out of the way at the last second. The fire towered high and licked at the ground as it tried to spread along the blades of grass.

My stomach rose up into my throat as the heat licked at my skin, but just as Rune waved his hands over the flames to extinguish them, water from the lake rose high above us, then plummeted down like a shield between us and Myra.

Gray smoke billowed into the air, and everyone hesitated a moment, casting their attention to me. Water dripped from our chins and hair, and our clothes clung to our now-soaked bodies.

Rune looked at me in silent question, but I shook my head. *That wasn't me.*

"Bria!"

Dallas raced toward us from across the lawn, her fiery red hair whipping in the passing wind. She was flanked on either side by Rance, Imani, and Dax. The rest of the team was right behind them, running in our direction.

"Dallas!" My heart soared with relief to see her and everyone else.

Dallas's face scrunched up in a livid scowl as her hands lifted and swept sideways in front of her. At the same time, water from the lake rose up into the sky, and as she clenched her fists, it instantly morphed into dozens of ice daggers. Her arms swung downward, and the shards of dangerous ice headed directly for Myra.

Rune flung his arms wide, a burst of fire rushing through the air to meet the ice in a smoky explosion. Small flakes of ash and drops of water slowly fell upon our skin as Dallas and the rest of them made it to us.

Myra kept her glare trained on us, even as the Water Fae came up behind her.

"Why'd you do that, Rune?" Dallas snapped, although her attention never left Myra's back.

"You were going to kill her," Rune said in between gritted teeth.

"That was the point!"

A low growl emitted from Rune's chest. "Don't touch my mother, *Water Fae*. She's not yours to deal with."

"She just tried to kill our Princess," one of the Water Fae soldiers yelled. "Whose side are you on, *Fox*?"

Myra's cynical laugh suddenly rang through the air, and my skin crawled. We all zeroed in on her, watching as she doubled over with a cackle.

"Theory confirmed," she roared, glaring at me through her smile. "What a small, small world. I knew you looked familiar. You might as well be the spitting image of Alesta."

My heart clenched painfully, hearing my mother's name come out of Myra's mouth.

"Not only has my worthless son brought home a Water Fae," she continued. "He brought home their *Princess*, daughter to the man who killed my Balgair."

Dallas and the others took in a harsh breath. Her eyes sharpened as she whispered, "Balgair? That means—" Her narrowed gaze flicked to Rune, and her petite face morphed into something dark. The water next to us began beating against the shore in a fitful rage as Dallas screamed at Rune. "You're the son of Balgair. *You* killed our King and Queen!"

Every beat of my heart, every ounce of air in my lungs, every thought racing inside my head stopped. Everything stopped. My parents. Rune.

No.

No.

It couldn't be true.

"That's not true," I whispered, shaking my head.

"Bria," Rune pleaded. "I—"

Myra let out another howl. "Water Fae truly are brainless. Rune didn't kill them."

"Mother!" Rune shouted in warning.

She ignored him. Smiling wickedly, her eyes met mine. "It was me."

"You?" Dallas gasped. "No. It was the *son* of Balgair who killed them."

"A rumor started by said son," Myra snickered.

The Water Fae behind Myra began to shake with their fists clenched tightly at their sides. Their hate-filled eyes bore into Myra with the intensity of a thousand suns.

I was still trying to process who truly killed my parents when Dallas let out an angered cry. I looked at her just in time to see her rush at Myra. Water swept up from the lake toward her outstretched hand, elongating in her palm as a sword of ice.

Dallas wielded the blade, ready to strike Myra, who stood perfectly still with a smirk on her face.

My voice got stuck in my throat, watching in horror as my best friend prepared to fight a woman who clearly believed she was about to win.

Rune suddenly ran toward the two as Dallas's blade sliced through the air. Flames erupted around Rune's body, creating a barrier against the ice sword as it swiped at Rune.

Dallas became visibly outraged with Rune now standing between her and her prey.

Scoffing, Dallas roared, "Fine! You want to protect that woman, the enemy to our people? Then I guess you aren't really on our side after all!"

I sucked in a sharp breath as panic flooded my veins.

Dallas launched herself at Rune. She had the point of her sword aimed at his heart, and although I knew somewhere in the back of my head that Rune could defend himself, I couldn't stand there and watch.

I had to protect him, and since there were no more secrets to hold me back, I stopped fighting against the whispers of the water. I beckoned them in, and the buzzing in the back of my mind reached a crescendo, sounding like the crashing of waves.

An itch ran along the inside of my skin, leading to a vibration in my fingertips. Sensing my intentions, the water from the lake moved with the flick of my hand. Rushing forward at an alarming speed, the blue wave engulfed Dallas and lifted her off the ground. Her eyes went wide from within the flickering ball of water, and small bubbles drifted up as she tried to speak to me from inside her prison.

Concentrating, I pried the ice sword from her grip, and the water inside did the rest. Shattering the blade, the small crystals dissolved into the rest of the water, leaving Dallas flailing around inside. All eyes were on me as my outstretched arms slowly lowered Dallas back to the ground where she collapsed in a watery puddle.

Dallas's coughs rang out as I walked forward to stand in front of Rune. Facing my friend, I stared down at her. "Enough."

SYLVER MICHAELA

She gazed at me, still coughing on her hands and knees. "H-How can you defend him? He, *they*, are your enemy, the killers of our kind. Of your parents!"

"No. They're not my enemies. They're my *friends*."

Rance helped Dallas to her feet, and all the Water Fae stared at me with bewildered eyes. Myra took measured steps away. Her eyes, still filled with unmatched venom, scanned both groups like she was waiting and deciding her next move.

I couldn't focus on her right now. I had to get through to Dallas and the others. Maybe even get through to Myra. I was the Water Fae's "Princess" as they said, yet here I was, taking the side of someone else. But that was the thing. I didn't want to pick a side. I didn't want to choose between my friends. I didn't want to choose between two worlds that called out to me in their own way.

So, I wouldn't.

Taking a deep breath, I started, "Are you not tired? Are you all," I swept my gaze around everyone here before continuing, "not tired? Can you even remember the *real* reason you started fighting, or has it now just become an act of vengeance for lost loved ones?"

Silence answered me.

"Look, I know there is a century's worth of tension between Land and Water Fae. Countless Fae had their lives robbed of them, and people you love suffered unimaginable pain. You've lost many to gruesome deaths. So have I. My parents …"

I swallowed hard. "I don't want any more kids to lose their parents the way I did, the way Rune did. I don't want anyone else to lose their husband or wife the way Myra did." I glanced at her then, and I was met with a surprisingly blank—yet somehow calculating—stare.

I pushed on. "No more. No more loss, no more death, no more fighting."

Squaring my shoulders back, I met the eyes of the Water Fae. "I'm your Princess, you say? Then here is my first order to you. Stop your war with Land Fae. I can't speak for Land Fae, but I can and *will* speak for us. I want peace. I want this idiotic war to stop. So, the first step will start with us. *Stop* fighting."

"Stop fighting?" Dax roared. "They'll slaughter us all if we don't fight. Just because you want peace doesn't mean peace will actually come. Land Fae will *never* agree to it."

"Then I'll talk with them," I said. "I'll speak to whomever I must to ensure this ends."

"I'll help you." Rune now stood beside me, and his gaze was firm as it searched mine. "The Land Fae King is a difficult creature to deal with, but I'll help you. It's going to be hard to put everything behind us, to forgive all that's been done, but a fresh start without so much hate sounds *really* nice."

"I'll stand beside you too, Bria!" Akira smiled. He walked over to where we stood, linking his hand with mine. Giving it a small squeeze, he said, "I'm ready to be done fighting."

Ardley and Avana exchanged a look before they joined us with Bassel and Carlos trailing them. Myra continued to watch us all. Her gaze studied each person as they fell in line beside me.

Ardley clapped a hand on Rune's back. "To hell with fighting! To be honest, I personally never got the point of this bullshit."

Marlow watched us with large, round eyes. He fidgeted and looked at the ground. His voice was barely audible as he asked, "May I join you as well?"

We all smiled.

Nodding, I said, "Of course."

His glossy eyes met mine. Grinning, he bounced over to us. "We will join you, too!"

Greshim raced forward from wherever he was behind us. I hadn't even noticed that he was there, and when I glanced over my shoulder, I realized *everyone* was out on the lawn. Rune's grandparents and family stood close by, inching their way closer to Myra, who now watched us with an amused smirk. Even Aidan and Yasmine stared from the sidelines, but instead of looking amused, they seemed utterly baffled.

Newt followed behind Greshim until they stood in front of me. Newt beamed up at me, pushing his glasses back into place from where they had slipped down his nose.

Looking back at Dallas, I said, "We can do this. We can stop the fighting. I know it won't be easy. We *all* know that, but we're still willing to try if it means helping all Fae. I'm sure there are more out there who want this war to be over."

Dallas held my gaze, and I waited. While she had accepted Rune and my friends for the most part—clearly not fully judging by this exchange—asking her to accept peace with Land Fae would be a lot. But I knew she could do it. This was the girl who wrote letters to law enforcement agencies, encouraging them to look further into missing persons' cases. This was the girl who gave her last dollars to strangers on the street.

She would do the right thing.

Finally, she kneeled, going down on one knee in front of me. "As you command, Princess. I will follow you on your journey toward peace."

The group of Water Fae behind her exchanged hesitant looks before following suit. Dax was slower to kneel, but he, too, bowed his head. In unison, they shouted, "As you command, Your Highness!"

A scoff sounded from near me. Turning, I found Rune's grandmother, Lilith. Her narrowed eyes bore into me, and I realized the only reason she and the other Fox Fae weren't charging us right now was because Myra had her arms held out, keeping everyone back. Which only unnerved me, because why would she do that?

"You think you can bring peace?" Lilith asked. "You think people will actually listen to you? You're wasting your time. Land Fae will never agree."

I swallowed hard. The truth of her words felt heavy on my shoulders, but I couldn't let her see that. I had to stay strong and believe in my new mission.

Myra held up a hand to silence her mother. She tilted her head higher as she regarded me coldly. "How diverting. It will truly be a delight to watch you lead the downfall of your people. As much as I want to split your stomach down the middle and see your innards stain my lawn, I won't. I'm a predator, and what do predators do best? We *wait*. We wait until it's the right time to strike, and while I could easily steal your next breath, I will wait. Let us see the end of those vile creatures under *your* leadership. You and I aren't finished. We'll meet again, I'm sure. Only it will be at your grave, your blood dripping from my lips, and your life snuffed out by my hands."

CHAPTER

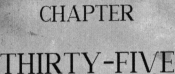

THIRTY-FIVE

MYRA WALKED AWAY. *WALKED AWAY!* It was a huge gut punch for so many reasons. For one, she was willing to walk away from the very people she loathed, because she truly believed I'd destroy them anyway. The rest of her party obviously agreed with her, because not one Fox Fae advanced on me or any of the Water Fae present.

I hoped they were wrong.

Even more disheartening were her parting words. They felt final, heavy, and dire—not a mere threat, but a promise. She wanted to draw out my death and make it as brutal and messy as possible. The knowledge made my breath get stuck in my lungs and my body to grow rigid with chills.

Everyone had a grim reaper, and I'd just stared into the eyes of mine.

Rune's family trailed after Myra, throwing furious glares in our direction. Aidan and

Yasmine were slow to follow, and I noticed their expressions were far less clear than the rest. The last to leave was Alvaro. The man surveyed his sons standing proudly next to me before he shared an indiscernible look with Rune and walked away. Rune, Dallas, and everyone else watched in stunned silence, and I wasn't sure if it was because they were all shocked that the Fox Fae were actually leaving or if it was because of Myra's threat.

I was struck silent from both.

The anger being cast toward us by the retreating party made a new worry settle in my gut. As if I didn't have enough already.

How could the twins face their mother after choosing us over her?

"Bria."

I stiffened at the sound of Dallas's voice. I turned in her direction to find her eyes pleading with me.

"Are you sure this is what you want?" Her gaze flicked to Rune for a brief moment before finding me again. "Are you sure you want to go down this path?"

"I'm sure," I said without hesitation. "To me, this is the only path. Fae need a fresh start and a chance to reconcile. There needs to be peace for *everyone's* sake."

She took a deep breath. "It won't be easy. You'll have a lot of people against you." She paused. "But I'll be here with you. I'll do whatever I can to help."

"So will we," Akira said with pride lighting up his black Raven eyes.

"Reconciliation is long overdue," Avana said. "It will finally put an end to an era of violence, grief, and hatred, and replace it with one of regrowth, healing, and unity."

"Gorgeous girl has it right," Imani said, not even batting an eye when Avana looked at her with surprise. "This could be what both sides have needed for a long time."

"Maybe it will let people return to old homes, too," Carlos said with a knowing smile as he nudged Bassel.

"We could do a lot of good things, *if* we pull it off," Bassel said.

And that was the real question. How to pull this off. From what I knew, Water Fae were scattered throughout the world in hiding, and I had no idea how I was supposed to reach them or spread the news of this impending battle for peace. Even more than that, I wasn't sure how to get in contact with the Land Fae King.

"So how do I do this?" I asked, passing a glance around the group. "Where should I start?"

"*We* start by getting you back to the Water Fae Kingdom," Dallas said.

The use of the word *we* made the air move a bit easier through my lungs. It was a reminder that I wasn't in this alone. I didn't have to figure it out by myself, because I had a family here on my side to guide me through this blinding darkness.

"You'll start training to be a Queen and learn the ropes of what that entails," Rance said. "We'll make the official announcement that you've returned, call Water Fae back home, crown you, and all of the formal stuff."

"Which will make communicating with the Land Fae King far easier," Imani added. "Becoming Queen will add the necessary weight you'll need to discuss peace realistically."

My mind raced to follow everything they said. As it did, one glaring truth hit me *hard*.

"So," I started slowly. "I won't be returning to school, or–or be going to Italy?"

"Bria," Rune said softly.

I looked up at him to find concern buried in his eyes.

"You can still—"

"Are you shitting me?" Dax snapped. "Stop being selfish, Bria. You're asking everyone here—every fucking Fae out there—to accept this pursual of peace and to let go of how we've been living all this time. Yet you're concerned about *school*? About your stupid *art career*? You have an entire *Kingdom* counting on you, waiting for you, and looking up to you. I think your schooling and childish desires are of little importance right now."

"Dax, oh my God!" Dallas shouted. "If you—"

"No," I said, silencing Dallas. My eyes held Dax's fuming glare, and I swallowed hard. "He's right."

"Thank you," Dax said as he threw up his hands. "Finally, someone sees it."

For once, Dax *was* right, and I *hated* having to admit that. But it was selfish of me to still want to go to school or to take that trip to Italy. There was so much to do now that I knew who I was and what had to be done to create a better world for Fae. Going back to school. Working to become a painter. Those things…

Those things had died the same day my human self did.

"I need to focus on learning what it means to be Queen and on creating peace," I said. "That's it. That's all that matters."

Rune's fingers grazed mine, and slowly, they intertwined. He squeezed, and I focused on that instead of the sharp pain filling my chest.

Dallas seemed to weigh my words for a beat, then said, "I guess we should get out of here then. It's a long drive back to campus. The sooner we can pack and get to the Kingdom, the better."

"Okay. Let me get my stuff," I said.

Dallas nodded and gestured back behind her. "We'll park the SUVs down the road, that way. Are you okay to be here alone?"

"I'm sorry," Ardley said sarcastically as he looked around at Rune, Akira, and the rest of the group. "Are we invisible or something?"

"She's not alone," Rune said, standing up straighter. "We're with her."

Dallas's eyes narrowed a fraction. It was so miniscule, I wasn't sure if others caught it, but I knew her. She wasn't happy leaving me here with Rune and the others after the intense confrontation that had taken place. A lot of anger and hurt had been thrown around at each other during the fight, which most likely sent everyone back a few steps on their journey toward trusting each other.

Dallas took a deep breath. "Fine. Watch out for her and make sure she gets to us. Fifteen minutes. If she's not to the SUVs in fifteen minutes, we're busting into the house."

"Dallas," I snapped.

When her eyes found mine, her features softened in apology.

"I'll be fine," I insisted. "I'll be there soon. Give me time and *trust* them."

She clenched and unclenched her fists, tapping her foot, as she fought to agree. Finally, she reluctantly said, "Okay. Okay, fine. Take your time. We'll wait at the cars."

Smiling, I said, "Thank you."

The Water Fae made their retreat, and our group slowly trickled back up the yard for the house.

"Akira," Rune said. "I don't want Bria walking through the house with everyone in there. Will you fly her up to our balcony?"

Akira grinned, unfurling his wings, which had folded against his back at some point. "Of course."

Akira closed the space between us.

Wrapping my arms around his neck, I held on tightly, and he did the same around my waist. As soon as my feet left the ground, my arms tightened their hold, which made him chuckle.

"Don't worry. I've got you," Akira reassured me.

The air rushed along my skin the higher we went, and before I knew it, my feet were planted firmly on the balcony. Looking up at Akira, I smiled. "Thanks."

He gave a dismissive wave. "No problem." He bit the inside of his cheek before daring to ask, "How are you holding up?"

Swallowing hard, I glanced away from him. "It–It's a lot to take in. I'm honestly kind of overwhelmed. There's so much I need to do, and I just don't want to do it *wrong*."

That last word came out strangled. I was anxious about messing up and making things worse. I mean, hell, I didn't even know what I was getting into. Yet here I was, declaring that I'd bring peace between Land and Water Fae. Part of me thought doing so was naive and stupid. Who was *I* to do those things?

I was just an orphan from Tennessee who wanted to paint, binge junk food with her best friend, and sleep beside Rune every night.

"We'll be here for you. You aren't alone in this," Akira said, squeezing my hand.

I smiled but didn't quite feel it. My mind was too raw and too chaotic right now.

The bedroom door clicked as Rune came in and shut the door behind him. He and Akira shared a nod before Akira waved at me and left the way we'd come.

I turned to face Rune, and his jaw worked as he approached me. His eyes weren't on mine, but rather, they were trained on my neck. With the attention there, it hit me that my throat no longer hurt, and when Rune's fingers swept over the skin of my neck, no pain followed.

"Your healing is getting quicker," Rune commented, his voice quiet.

I swallowed hard and searched his distant gaze. A thousand worries, questions, and concerns darted around my head—more than I could process at the moment, but the burden in Rune's eyes took precedence.

"Rune," I whispered, wrapping my hand around his, which was still coasting along my throat.

"I thought—" Rune started. He stopped, closed his eyes, and started again. "I thought she would change. I was hopeful that one day, she'd get better. That she'd go back to being the mother I remember. It was always a wish I kept tucked away, though one I rarely vocalized, because I was afraid saying it aloud would somehow jinx it. But I truly believed that one day she'd learn how to love again. Love *me* again. I thought coming here this week and giving her what she wanted might trigger something inside her. I thought that seeing me in love might remind her what it means to feel."

He paused to take a deep breath. "It finally hit me down there that she'll never change. The woman who raised me, who would make silly faces when I was upset, who would sing songs without a care in the world, is gone. She's never coming back. My mother died the same day my dad did."

I bit back a sob and reached up to cup Rune's cheeks. It all made so much more sense now. This week wasn't just about getting Myra off his back about marriage and kids. It was far more complicated than that. He did *all* of this to earn her love. And that broke me. No one should have to earn their mother's love. No one should have to try so hard for their mother's approval, yet he did, because *he* loved *her*. He wanted his mom back to her old self, and I couldn't blame him for that. If anything, I wanted the same thing—my parents back.

Forcing back my tears, I whispered, "I'm so sorry, Rune."

It wasn't much. It wasn't anything really, but the four words were all I had to offer. I couldn't change Myra. I couldn't go back in time and stop my dad from killing Balgair. But I could be here in this moment and act as a rock for Rune to lean on.

Rune grabbed each of my hands, and he gently placed a kiss in each palm. He finally met my eyes again, and the anguish from his confession simmered in his gaze. "I'm sorry that she hurt you. I should've been there to stop her or—"

"Don't. Don't you *dare* put any blame on yourself. Myra chose her actions, not you. Let's just be glad you were there when it mattered most."

Reluctantly, he nodded. I could tell he wasn't happy with that, but I was thankful when he dropped it. He picked up my suitcase, placing it on the bed. Glancing at me, he asked, "Bria, are you okay? I know what happened out there wasn't easy."

I gave a humorless laugh, going into the bathroom to gather my toiletries. "That's an understatement. I feel like my already messed-up world just got turned over on its head. It's just," I paused, coming to stand next to him. "I'm not even sure how to put everything I'm feeling into words."

"Well, I need you to know that stuff my mother said at the end ... That will never, *ever* happen. She won't touch you. I promise."

I swallowed hard. "I'm trying not to think about what she said."

"Good. Don't, because it won't happen." He paused, and after gauging my avoidance of the topic, he moved on. "I also want you to know that I really do support you. We all do. Trying to create peace ... it'll be a huge task but a good one. I think everyone's been holding on to the past for so long, focusing solely on their anger and pain, that we haven't tried to move forward. You're doing the right thing."

"I hope so." I glanced up at him. "Can I ask you something?"

"Of course." He turned toward me, my suitcase forgotten.

"Dallas said that you killed the King and Queen," I paused, swallowing the lump in my throat. "My parents. But Myra said she did. What actually happened?"

Rune took a deep breath, his brow furrowing. Sitting on the edge of the bed, he ran a hand through his hair. "The night you told me who you were, I wanted to be sick. Because while you felt bad for being the daughter of the man who killed *my* father, I'm the son of the woman who killed *your* parents. I was still trying to grapple with the news of who you were, so trying to also come up with a way to tell you the rest became difficult. It's been making me sick that you didn't know, but I wasn't sure how to tell you yet.

"My mother killed them. After finding out that the Water Fae King murdered my dad, she went on a rampage. She eventually found where they were hiding in a log cabin in some mountains. She killed them there. I was afraid that word would spread that the wife of Balgair had murdered them, so I started a rumor that the *son* of Balgair did it. Any Water Fae looking for revenge would come to me instead of her."

My next inhale *hurt*. Not because Rune's mother killed them or because Rune hadn't told me as soon as he realized the truth. It was because I now *knew*. I knew what had happened to my parents. I knew where they were in their last moments, who had taken them from me, and if I tried hard enough, I could picture the way Myra had probably ended their lives. Knowing what happened hurt far worse than anything I'd conjured up in my mind, because this was real. The truth of their last moments made the reality blaringly clear.

Dallas had already told me that my parents were gone. I had come to terms with that and accepted that I'd never get to see them. Yet my heart—my stupid, *stupid* heart—had still held onto this small sliver of light that, just maybe, Dallas was wrong. Maybe they weren't actually dead, and it was all some huge plan to keep them safe. Maybe they'd be waiting for me when I took the crown, or maybe they'd pop up from the shadows where they'd always secretly been hiding.

That fragment of hope crumbled into mere ash that scattered into nothingness. With Rune's words, it was finally real. There was no more room for hope. There was no more room for my heart to hold onto silly dreams or fantasies.

They were gone.

They were really gone.

Rune dropped his head into his hands. "Myra is a monster. She's a heartless creature, but she's still my mother. I had just lost one parent. I didn't want to lose another. Spreading the lie that it was me who killed them was my way of protecting her. Though I'm no longer sure if I should've."

The bed sank beneath me as I sat next to him. My chest felt heavy with the weight of his confession and grief.

Meeting my gaze, his eyes pinched with remorse. "I'm so sorry."

"This war has caused a lot of pain, huh?"

"On both sides."

Reaching for his hand again, I threaded our fingers together. "Then let's make sure it ends so that no one else has to lose their parents like we did. Let's make sure no one has to hurt like this again."

His gaze held mine for another beat. He leaned in, tenderly pressing a kiss to my temple. Smiling down at me, he said, "I never thought I'd see the day when I actually wanted to get along with Water Fae. Now here I am, in love with the Princess." He let out a small laugh. "Let's do it. Let's make a world where loving each other is okay."

As we gathered my belongings, Rune tried hard to keep my spirits up. He could tell I was a nervous and frazzled mess, so he told me funny stories from when he and Ardley were younger or moments he'd shared with the twins. By the time we were done packing, my sides hurt from laughing, which felt nice after the extremely shitty morning.

But then there was nothing left to pack, and it was time to face my new reality.

Rune led me out onto the balcony, my suitcase in one hand and my hand in the other. He gave me a reassuring squeeze. "Everything will be okay. We'll meet you guys back in Tennessee, and then we'll figure all of this out together."

Rune and the others had some loose ends to tie up here before heading back. This was where we'd separate, but it wouldn't be for long. Our futures were tied together by far too much now.

A sudden flap of wings snapped my attention to the edge of the balcony where Akira hovered again. Grinning at us, he reached out a hand to me as he landed. "Your chariot, milady."

Breaking into a wide smile, I took his outstretched hand. "Why thank you, good sir."

"I'll meet you guys down there." Rune backed up into the room. "You know, via the less terrifying means of transportation. The stairs."

"Rude!" Akira gasped. "I'll have you know I am a *very* safe flyer."

"Right," Rune laughed, jogging across the bedroom to the door with my bags in tow.

Turning back to Akira, I wrapped my arms tightly around his neck. He hugged me close and leapt into the air. My stomach dropped at the speed of our descension, but, thankfully, my feet were back on the ground in seconds.

"I think that was even scarier than going up," I said breathlessly. "Are you guys going to be okay here? You know, in the same house as a bunch of Fae you just sided against?"

"Are you kidding? Your life got uprooted and you're worried about *us*? We'll be fine. They can't do anything to us when we're together. Plus, we're all leaving today, too. No point in sticking around, making nice with them when the fox's out of the bag."

"Good idea."

Footsteps headed in our direction as Rune made his way across the yard, my suitcase still in hand, and the rest of our friends followed him.

"Did you pass any raging family members on your way out?" Akira asked.

Rune smirked. "Of course. Do I care? Not a bit." He met my eyes. "Ready?"

"Almost," I said before taking a moment to hug all my friends and the twins.

Saying goodbye sucked, but I knew I'd see them all again soon. We were a team now. This was just the beginning of our journey, and I was confident that with everyone here, we could make a better, beautiful world.

Rune and I watched everyone retreat back to the mansion for a moment before making our way to the desolate road in front of the house. Dallas and the others were supposedly parked half a mile away so as not to be near their *enemy*.

We were going to have to work on their trust of Land Fae.

"Are you sure you guys don't want to drive back with us?" I asked Rune, throwing him a nervous glance.

Rune placed a reassuring kiss on the top of my head. "We'll be fine. We can take care of ourselves. We'll meet back up later. I promise. I just need to sort some things out."

I pushed out my lip in a pout, hating the idea of leaving him and the rest of our friends here with a household of murderous Fae. Though I also knew Rune was right. He could handle himself.

"You know," Rune started, grabbing my hand. "What you said back there about wanting to finish school and go to Italy … it *does* matter. And those are things you can still have and do."

I looked up at him, trying not to latch onto his words. "Who knows when or if I can have those things. It's better to not think about them. Not when so many people are counting on me."

"I know this is still new, and yes, the beginning is going to be full of struggle and challenges, but you're still an individual, Bria. You're still allowed to want things. You're still your own person."

I swallowed hard and looked down at the rough asphalt. "I'm not so sure."

He stopped and grabbed me, forcing me to meet his intense gaze. "All of this crap aside, do you still want to be a painter?"

"Of course, but—"

"Then you're going to be a painter, which starts with Italy. You're going to Italy one day. I'll take you there myself. It may not be by spring. It may not even be by next year. But you'll go. I promise."

I took a deep breath and swallowed the ache building in my chest. Forcing a smile, I said, "Let's focus on ending the war between our kinds. We can dream another day."

Rune stayed quiet as I pulled him along again, for which I was thankful. I wasn't as convinced as he was that I'd get the chance to do the things I wanted. I didn't regret accepting my new role, but I hurt for the one that was being left behind. From the sound of it, I'd be consumed by training and learning how to be Water Fae, how to be a Queen, and how to bring resolution to the century's long war. Then I'd have to actually *do* those things, and if I managed to complete the task—bringing peace—my job wouldn't be done. I'd have to maintain that civility, and I'd possibly still have to be present to continue leading and guiding Water Fae. So, while I desperately wanted to believe that I could still be a painter someday, my gut told me that was no longer in the cards for me, which meant it was best to move on and not dwell on the dream that couldn't be.

We'd walked far enough along the road that I could now see a group of cars. Dallas's red hair stood out, even from this distance, and I could tell she was looking our way.

Turning back to Rune, I tried to put on a brave face. "Okay. I'll be fine from here. You should probably get back to the house in case all hell breaks loose."

He glanced over my shoulder to the waiting party before meeting my eyes once more. He held my gaze for a few endless beats. I knew what he was thinking, because I was, too. We'd been together every day for months, so separating was going to feel strange, like when you forgot something important at home and kept going to grab for it, only to find it's not there.

Getting onto my tiptoes, I pressed my lips to his. His strong arms circled my lower back as he pulled me against him. We kissed as though we were starved for air, and the other was our oxygen.

His hand slid into my hair, tugging me closer despite there being no room between us. My hands gripped the back of his neck as his tongue swept past my lips. I wanted to melt into him, feel his heart beat in tandem with my own, and feel his skin on mine.

We pulled back slightly, our foreheads pressed together. My breathing came out ragged as I closed my eyes to soak up this moment with him. Gently brushing my fingers across his lips, I memorized the smooth touch of his mouth and focused on the beating of his racing heart as it pounded against my chest. I inhaled deeply, getting drunk on his scent.

"If you need anything, just call, okay?"

I nodded. "I will. I'll see you soon."

Stepping back from him, my chest constricted. He smiled at me, but I saw worry and hesitation buried in those eyes. He was no doubt afraid to let me go with them, but I knew I'd be okay. With time, I had faith everyone would see the other could be trusted.

With one final hug and kiss, I went to walk away. His hand tightened around mine, and when I turned back to him, he looked at me as if I were the only thing in the world that mattered. "I love you, Bria."

My heart leapt into my throat, and my eyes filled with tears. I didn't think I'd ever get used to him saying that or ever grow tired of hearing it.

Smiling, I gave him one more soft, gentle kiss. "I love you, too."

With that final goodbye, I made my way toward Dallas and the others. The long stretch of road felt more like a swaying bridge that was seconds from collapsing rather than solid ground. I was walking away from my old life to start a whole new one, blind.

Dallas smiled as she watched me approach. "Ready to go?"

Hell no.

"Ready," I forced myself to say.

"You're in the middle SUV with me, Rance, Imani, and Dax."

Great. I got to be stuck in a car with Dax for the 17-hour drive back to Tennessee. *Yippee.*

After climbing into the sleek, black SUV, I made my way to the third row seating where Dallas joined me. Dax rode shotgun while Rance drove, and Imani rode in the middle seat.

We headed out onto the road, and that's when everything caught up to me. The stress of the week, the chaos of the past two days, and the burden of my new role. I laid my head back against the seat, and within moments, I was drifting off to a world full of no stress, no chaos, and no burdens. Filled only with paint, cinnamon rolls, laughter, and Rune.

CHAPTER

THIRTY-SIX

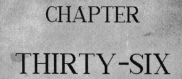

N OT TRUE," RANCE SHOUTED.

"So true!" Dax argued.

Blinking, I sat up, rubbing the sleep from my eyes. Familiar buildings passed by, and I realized we were almost back to campus. The storefronts on main street brought a small sense of comfort. I was back home, safe and sound.

Rance groaned, clutching his forehead with one hand while the other remained poised on the steering wheel. The car swerved slightly, and I swallowed hard.

I was *almost* back home, safe and sound.

"Are you that much of an idiot?" Rance sighed.

Dax glared at him. "You're obviously the moron. I don't understand your logic at all."

Glancing at Dallas, I found her watching them with a very bored, if not annoyed, frown. They must've been arguing for a while. She noticed me awake and turned to smile. "Hey."

"Hey." Leaning closer, I whispered, "What are they arguing about? I feel like a fight is about to break out."

She faced the front again, glaring at them. "Oh, nothing important. Those idiots are just—"

"Wrong," Rance bellowed. "It's *your* logic that's warped. In what world is a Reese's better than a Butterfinger? Reese's are *way* too sweet."

I blinked, then glanced back at Dallas, who waved a hand at them as if to say, *there you have it.*

"They are *not* too sweet," Dax countered, leaning in toward Rance. "And what about that crap in Butterfingers that sticks to your teeth when you eat it? Who enjoys that?"

"Me. Duh. That gives you a treat to have later."

"You're disgusting," Dax spat.

Rance glanced in the rearview mirror and spotted me watching them. Instantly, he brightened. "Princess! You're awake. Perfect. Tell Dax that Butterfingers are better than Reese's."

Smiling sheepishly, I said, "Actually, I prefer fruity candies. You know, like Skittles or Starbursts. Chocolate isn't really my thing."

Rance and Dax both stared at me for a moment, and the car went deadly quiet. Dallas stifled a laugh next to me.

Rance cleared his throat and focused on the road again. "Reese's are nice occasionally."

"Yeah. Butterfingers are cool sometimes." Dax nodded, turning back around in his seat.

Imani angled her head to look at me. "You're already solving conflicts, Princess. First day on the job, and you're doing great! By the way, two things: one, is Avana single, and two, is she into women?"

I cocked a brow at her. "She's Land Fae, you know."

Imani shrugged and flashed me a wide smile. "I'm practicing my peace-making skills."

I laughed and made a mental note to let Avana know she had made an impression. The front of the car erupted into chatter as Rance and Dax discussed the latest episode of some show they were watching. Imani shook her head and joined in their discussion every now and then. Dallas lay back in her seat, smiling at me before closing her eyes.

The atmosphere in the car felt warm and normal, as if this were an ordinary day. To anyone else, we would look like a group of best friends out for a drive. I honestly wished that were the case. Instead, it was a Princess being escorted home by her guards.

Huh.

Princess.

That still felt strange.

Not long after, we reached campus. The looming brick building I'd come to consider home greeted me. I was finally able to release the strangled breath I hadn't even known I'd been holding. It felt good to be back at the place that was the start of my new life. This place was the beginning of my story with Rune and the world of Fae. Seeing it now with that lens was bittersweet.

Once parked, Dallas and I climbed out of the SUV. The other cars with the rest of the Water Fae team had kept driving, parking at different locations on campus. Even though the campus was relatively empty since it was still fall break, they wanted to watch the area to ensure I remained safe.

"So," Dallas started, reluctantly handing me my suitcase.

She had tried to carry it, but I refused to let anyone do that. I could carry my own freaking stuff.

"You probably won't need a lot from here," Dallas continued as we made our way into the silent dorms. "Your textbooks, school supplies, a lot of your clothes. It can pretty much all stay. The stuff that you'll need from now on will be at the palace."

We reached our room, and I turned to face her with my hand on the doorknob. "I don't want the stuff at the palace. I want *my* stuff. I want *my* bedding, *my* books, *my* clothes, *my* art supplies."

I took a deep breath and closed my eyes. I was letting everything get to me. I thought after sleeping it off in the car, I'd feel levelheaded and ready. Knowing that my life was no longer just mine was hard to stomach. Everything was changing so quickly.

"I'm sorry," I whispered, shaking my head. "I didn't mean to snap like that."

Dallas placed her hand on my back. "This is a lot, huh?"

I nodded, leaning my head against the door. "What if I can't do this, Dallas? What if I can't be who you guys need? What if I really *do* lead everyone to their demise?"

"Bria," Dallas said softly as she pulled me tightly into her arms. "Don't think that way. It's new and scary right now, but you can do this. You're an absolutely amazing fucking person, and I know you are going to be the greatest Queen Water Fae have ever seen."

"How do you know?"

She pulled back, and when she did, her mouth was curved in an encouraging grin. "Because I know you. I know the kind of heart you have. I know how courageous you are. I know how fierce, loyal, and determined you can be. *That's* what makes a good Queen. You *will* be an amazing leader."

Tears threatened to make an escape, but I sniffled them back. While it would take time for me to truly believe in myself, Dallas's words made a spark of hope flicker in my chest. She made me *want* to believe I was capable of doing this, and I guessed that was the first step. Wanting to succeed. Wanting to become the leader Dallas believed me to be.

"Thanks, Dallas," I said as I squeezed her one more time.

"Don't thank me for telling the truth. Now then," she said, placing her hands on her hips. "Are you ready to pack up your things? We can bring as much as you want."

"It's fine. If you say I'll have plenty of clothes and whatnot at the palace, I—I can use that stuff. My things can stay here until I come back."

I left the last part hanging in the air, waiting to see if she'd confirm or deny that I'd be coming back. Instead of doing either, she just followed me into our room.

The space was as it had been the night Dallas and I came clean about who I was, who she was, and the truth about my origins. Her bed was unmade, and mine was rumpled from where we'd lounged on top of it. Dirty clothes were piled in the hamper. Forgotten school assignments littered our desks. Unfinished paintings leaned against the foot of my bed. It was all the same. The only things different in the room were Dallas and me.

We stayed mostly quiet as we gathered some of my things. I grabbed my favorite clothes, my fluffy pink blanket, my sketchbooks, paints, and my unfinished fox painting.

As I stuffed some underwear in my duffle bag, I wracked my brain for something to talk about to distract me from what was happening. Finally, I asked, "Have you learned anything about who was working with Jonah?"

Dallas sat on the bed next to my open bag. "I still haven't had time to look into it personally since I've been watching over you and performing those duties. When I last checked with Dax, he was still waiting for confirmation on a lead."

I snorted sarcastically. "Well, isn't that kind of Dax. I still can't believe he offered to help with something that doesn't benefit him."

She laughed. "Tell me about it. He never wants to do work or be helpful, probably because he assumed he shouldn't have to as the 'future King.' Maybe he was trying to win brownie points with you. You know, defending his 'wifey' from the big bad guy who tried to have her killed." She pointed a slender finger at her mouth and gagged.

"He's definitely *not* future King or my to-be husband." I rolled my eyes and tossed a pair of pajamas in my bag. "Maybe the real reason he was invested was because he faced off with Jonah personally."

"I wish I could've been a fly on the wall for that. Dax said he did a major number on Jonah, which I would've loved to see."

I laughed and cocked a brow at Dallas. "He hardly did a number on him. It was actually pretty anticlimactic. As soon as Dax showed up, Jonah basically tucked his tail and ran. There wasn't really any fighting."

Dallas's face creased as she processed my words. "Really?"

I nodded and thought back to that night. "Yeah. They said a few choice words, and then Jonah—I don't know—gave up, I guess?"

Dallas was quiet as she stared at me. The pinch of her brow and sudden frown made my curiosity spike.

"What?" I asked. "What are you thinking?"

She slowly shook her head and looked across the room. I could practically see the gears spinning in her head. "It can't be," she mumbled.

"Can't be what? What's happening?"

She remained silent and unmoving for a few endless seconds until, finally, she turned to me again. "That night Jonah first attacked you, why were you out there? Why were you in the woods that late at night alone?"

"I was out there because—" I paused and held her increasingly frantic gaze. My mind immediately started to assemble the pieces as I finished, "Because Dax asked me to meet him."

"And the night your powers awoke, you said you *weren't* the one who killed Jonah, right?"

"Right. He seemed like he was about to tell me who hired him, and that's when someone beheaded him. There was no weapon from what I saw. It was almost like an invisible blade or something cut right through him."

"A water blade," Dallas whispered, hanging her head.

"A what?"

"A water blade. It's something we can do. We create a thin disc of water that can slice through almost anything, including bone, if you're good enough. Water blades are Dax's specialty." Dallas tipped her head back as she groaned at the ceiling. "The night your powers awakened, Dax had been at the hideout with a lot of us. At one point, he had gotten a text, and after that, he left for a bit. He said it was because another guard messaged him about an issue at the border, which I confirmed with that guard. Now I'm having doubts."

My stomach pitched forward with the threat of nausea. I collapsed onto the bed and clutched my head. "Holy shit. *Holy shit!* Do you really think it was Dax? Why would Dax want me killed? What could he gain from that?"

Dallas shook her head and clenched her fists tightly. "I'm not sure, but I plan on finding out. Are you okay to finish packing alone? I need to make some calls. I'll just be right outside."

I nodded quickly, and Dallas shot up from the bed and left the room in a hurry. As soon as she was gone, I rolled onto my back and stared up at the ceiling with thoughts that seemed to be on a rampage.

Dax. My high school crush. My first boyfriend. My supposed fiancé. Could he really have been working with Jonah all this time? The mere thought of him watching and hoping for my death made bile climb my throat with a fresh wave of disgust. I knew we didn't necessarily get along or even like each other these days, but to try to have me killed? It was far too much to process, especially since it didn't make sense. If Dax wanted to be King, that could only be done by marrying me, and I was pretty sure marrying my corpse wouldn't suffice. He needed me alive, so why plot to kill me?

I grabbed my pillow and screamed into the material. I screamed out all of my worries, my questions, my fears, and my frustrations.

Did it eliminate all those issues? No.

But did it make me feel better? A little.

With that, I got back up and finished packing my things. Turning to the wall by my bed, I found Rune's painting, which still hung proudly. Thinking back on that night filled me with both a sense of delight and melancholy. He'd taken me on a surprise fake date, and I'd had more fun that evening than I thought I could given our attitudes toward each other back then. It was an easier time when the world felt far simpler and things made more sense. But I'd still been unsure of who I was, and Rune and I had still held boundaries we refused to cross. So, while life felt easier back then, I wouldn't change where I was now.

I carefully removed the painting from its place on the wall and added it to my box of art supplies for my new home.

"Please tell me you're not actually bringing that with you."

I whipped around to find Dallas frowning at Rune's painting. She'd just come back into the room, phone still in hand.

I glanced at the canvas. "Of course I am."

She rolled her eyes and mumbled, "You're too nice."

Ignoring her comment, I asked, "So what happened? Did you find out if it was Dax?"

"I was verifying everyone's whereabouts for the night your powers awakened. The only one unaccounted for was Dax. I've called for a meeting with everyone under the pretense that we're discussing the strategy for getting you to the palace, but really, we'll be arresting Dax for treason."

I swallowed hard. The words "arrest" and "treason" echoed in my head. They were heavy words with grave meanings, and I felt the room spinning under the weight of Dax's actions. Dax, the guy I'd spent my teen years crushing on, the guy I'd *just* spent a 17 hour car ride with. This was real. Dax was really behind what happened to me, and he was going to face dire consequences.

"You can wait here if you want," Dallas suggested. "I'm sure going to watch this confrontation is the last thing you want."

Did I want to go? Dax would no doubt put up a fight. I wasn't fond of conflict or watching violence.

Despite this, I found myself saying, "I want to go."

Dallas's eyes widened in surprise. "You don't have to. Really. Everything will be—"

"I want to go. If Dax was really behind this, I want to know why. I want answers."

Slowly, she smiled at me, pride filling her green eyes. "Okay then. Let's go bust a traitor."

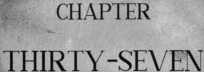

CHAPTER

THIRTY-SEVEN

DALLAS AND I MADE OUR way to the meeting spot, and to make the traitor sweat, I decided at the last minute to change the gathering location. Instead of meeting at the team's hideout, we'd be getting together at my creek.

I watched everyone as they filed into the clearing, standing in a half-circle around Dallas and me. Dax followed Rance and Imani into the group as they arrived last, just like Dallas and I had wanted. We had Rance and Imani wait an extra few minutes so that the dozen or so gathered eyes would be on their party. In other words, all eyes would be on Dax.

Dax's eyes tightened a fraction as he joined everyone, and while others made brief small talk amongst themselves, Dax remained uncharacteristically quiet, his eyes continuously glancing at where I stood.

The very spot in which Jonah had died.

"I'm glad everyone made it," Dallas started.

The group hushed as attention turned to us, but the only gaze I could seem to hone in on was my would-be killer. The man who'd been feeding me lies.

Lies about believing we were meant to be.

Lies about being on my side as part of this team.

Lies.

"This is our first meeting with our Princess, your future Queen, present," Dallas continued. "I believe she'd like to lead this meeting today."

The anger and betrayal simmering in my gut fueled me with a certain kind of confidence. Even with all eyes on me, I found myself steady, focused, and sure as I raised my head higher and started forward.

"Hello everyone. It's wonderful to finally have this moment where we can gather openly as a group, although, I do wish it were under better circumstances."

A few passed confused glances between each other. Dax's brow furrowed as he studied my slow prowl forward. Rance and Imani inched back minutely on either side of Dax, preparing for what they knew was coming.

Forcing a smile, I passed a look over the gathered party. "Do you know where you are right now?"

"This is the creek you often frequented," a bright-eyed girl said from within the circle.

I nodded. "That's right. Forgive me. I don't think I know your name, yet."

"It's Mingxia, Your—" she started to bow but quickly stopped. Her freckled cheeks grew crimson as she said, "Sorry. I forgot. No formal stuff."

Smiling, I waved it off. "No need to apologize." I casually moved closer again and made a point of looking at everyone. "Mingxia is right. This is the creek where I often came. But that's not all. This," I gestured to the space around us, "is where my powers awakened when a Bat Fae tried to kill me."

I paused to let my words sink in. Some seemed shocked, others angry as they looked at the space in disgust. Dax remained stoic.

Which only pissed me off more.

"And I'm afraid," I continued, walking with my hands clasped behind my back. "That the Bat Fae wasn't working alone. He'd been hired to take me out." I came to a stop a few feet in front of Dax. "By one of you."

A chorus of gasps rang throughout the group.

"Your Highness, we'd never!"

"You are our beloved Princess. We are loyal to you."

"Ask us anything! We have nothing to hide!"

"Silence!" Dallas snapped.

The space fell quiet again, and I let the stillness spread, stretching time as I stared at Dax, whose fingers twitched by his sides. His nostrils flared slightly, and his jaw clenched as he held my gaze.

Finally, I asked, "Dax, where were you the night of the attack?"

He huffed in defiance and crossed his arms over his chest. "I was at the hideout. You can ask almost anyone here. They were with me. Maybe you should be asking fucking Marcus where *he* was. He wasn't at the hideout."

"Excuse me?" A tall, broad-shouldered guy stepped forward to glare at Dax, and I assumed this was Marcus. "I was on scouting duty! I was posted at the rear entrance of campus, which has a security camera. You can check it, Dallas. I was there the entire time."

"We know, Marcus," Dallas said from directly behind me. "We already verified your exact whereabouts. We've confirmed *everyone's* whereabouts for the entirety of that night. Everyone except you, Dax."

"You were at the hideout. Until—," Imani started, turning her doubtful eyes on Dax.

"Until you got that text," Dallas finished. "You know, the one that had you needing to leave. What was it again? Something about checking out a threat at the Water Fae border?" Dallas probed, suspicion dripping from her voice.

"Yeah," Dax said calmly. "Samantha informed me there was a threat, so I went to make sure everything was secure. You can check with her. She was with me the whole time."

"We did check with her," Dallas said. "In her initial questioning, she claimed you were there, but when re-questioned, it wasn't long before she broke down and admitted that you weren't actually there."

"So, again, we can't confirm your whereabouts after that text," Rance said. "We know you weren't at the border."

"Where were you?" Imani questioned.

Dax's chest rose and fell with heavy breaths, and his gaze darted between me and Dallas.

Plastering on a wide smile, I said, "I know where you were. And you know where you were. And *Jonah* knew where you were. You were right here, watching as Jonah tried to drown me, watching as I got my powers, watching as Jonah nearly gave you up. So, you silenced him."

Dax reacted. A ball of water darted past my head from the creek, and shrank in his hands until it was a flat, sharp blade. It was only a beat before he hurtled that disk right at me.

Instinct took over. I put up my hands to block the attack. As soon as the blade reached my palms, it melted into liquid that stretched along my hands like gloves. Meeting Dax's wide eyes, I threw my hands back down to my sides, and the water shot off my skin, sinking into the grass on either side of me as shards of ice.

The entire encounter felt endless but took mere seconds. Once everyone processed what they'd witnessed, they moved. Imani and Rance rushed forward to grab Dax by both arms, and Dax thrashed around, screaming as he tried to escape their grips. Everyone moved in close, some hovering around me while raising their hands up preparation for an attack, while others closed on Dax where Rance and Imani had shoved him to his knees, cuffing his hands in large metal shackles.

"Get off me!" Dax roared. "I'm King! I. Am. *King*! Let me go!"

I squatted in front of Dax, and he whipped his head around to glare at me as he took quick, heavy breaths.

"Why?" I whispered. "Why did you do it?"

He let out a humorless laugh. "If you think I'm going to answer to *you*, you're a fucking idiot. You aren't my Queen. You're a fake. You're a *disgrace*, and I look forward to the day when you *rot* under the mound of your failures."

I swallowed the burn his words created. They cut into me, reopening each of my insecurities. I couldn't give into those feelings, especially not with the very one uttering them in front of me. It took everything inside me to keep my face even, giving away none of the fear his verbal attack evoked.

"Then I guess *you'll* rot," I said evenly. "In prison. Get him out of here."

I stood and watched as Rance and Imani yanked Dax to his feet. The pair led him away, but that didn't stop his sickening laugh as he called over his shoulder, "All hail the mother fucking Queen!"

CHAPTER

THIRTY-EIGHT

I PULLED INTO THE FAMILIAR driveway and took a moment to drink in the one-story brick home. So many days I'd spent here with my Land Fae friends. So many memories within those walls. I didn't know when or if I'd get to see the house again, but the knowledge didn't hurt, because it wasn't the house I needed.

It was the man standing on the front porch.

As soon as I was out of the car, I ran for Rune. His eyes pinched with worry after taking in the look plastered on my face, and he opened his arms as I reached him. I leapt into his hold, wrapping my legs around his waist and arms around his neck. He took me into his strong embrace as I crushed our lips together in a hungry kiss. He groaned in need as I swept my tongue past his lips, and my hands skimmed up the back of his neck and into his hair.

Pulling back only enough to take a breath, I asked, "Who all is home?"

"Just me."

I nodded, relieved for once to find that the gang wasn't present. As much as I loved everyone, I wanted—*needed*—the comfort that only Rune could provide.

"Take me to bed," I whispered against his lips.

He sucked in a sharp breath before turning and carrying me into the house. He kissed me with an all new urgency that I felt in every fiber of my being. I reached down to pull off my top, letting it land where gravity guided it as Rune carried me through the living room.

He peppered kisses along my throat and said, "God, I can't get enough of you."

I gripped the back of his head, holding him close to me. "I need your body on mine."

Rune nudged open his cracked bedroom door, and as soon as we were inside the familiar blue and black toned room, I slipped out of his hold and pressed my hands firmly against his chest. I pushed him up against the door, making it slam behind him, and not even a beat later, my mouth was on his. He gripped my waist tightly as the hard mass in his pants pressed against me.

Rune pulled back a fraction to look at me, but his hands never left me. They trailed up my bare back to the clasp of my bra. "As much as I love what's happening, I feel like something's wrong. Are you okay? What happened?"

I hadn't told Rune about Dax and that horrific meeting yet since it was still fresh on my mind—not even an hour had passed. As soon as I'd seen Rune's text that he was back home, I'd driven straight here, needing to see him, feel his touch, and hear his deep voice. I needed his comfort, his support, and his affection, because without it, I was sure to lose myself to the demons of inferiority.

I shimmied out of my bra as Rune guided the straps down my arms, and once his hands were free of the material, I grabbed them and walked us backward for his bed. Turning, I placed my palms on his chest and pushed him to sit on the edge.

Standing between his legs, I stared down into his golden eyes. "I want to be good."

Smirking, he flicked the bead of my nipple with the tip of his tongue. "I don't think that's a problem."

Inhaling sharply against the jolt of pleasure, I took a deep breath and reached down to tug off his shirt. "I don't mean in that department. Although, I *do* want to be good at that, too."

"Then what do you want to be good at, Princess?" he asked, tilting his head up to look at me as he pulled me closer, the heat from his bare chest warming my skin.

"That," I said.

Rune slipped his hands into the waistband of my pants and underwear, pulling both down the flare of my hips.

I stepped out of the garments and placed my knees on either side of his body until I straddled him, completely bare and aching at my center. When my wet middle nestled against the hard mass in his sweatpants, I bit my lip and took a deep breath to continue talking. "Princess. Queen. I want to be a good leader."

Rune's palms coasted over my skin, climbing from my thighs to my stomach, settling on my breasts. "You will be. What's making you feel this way? Did someone say something?"

I forced a smile and gave a nonchalant shrug. "Maybe."

Rune's eyes were unwavering as they held mine, and he seemed to be searching my face for something. All of a sudden, Rune rolled to the side, pinning me beneath him. He leaned down and placed soft kisses on each of my closed eyes. "These eyes. They see people. Not the façade people put on the exterior, but you see who those people are at their core. You see past the lies, past the defenses, past the mistakes. You see the good in people."

Rune leaned down to place another slow, sensual kiss to my lips and whispered, "These lips utter truth, kindness, and forgiveness, even for those undeserving of such gifts. You speak with a need to spread love and happiness, whereas so many others can't wait to spit profanities and hatred."

He slid down my body until he was able to place a kiss in the center of my chest. "This heart, this soul, is full of so much warmth. Compassion. Bravery. Resilience. Love. Bria, I don't know who placed this doubt in your mind, but there is not a single person out there more fit to be a leader than you. Anyone would be lucky to have the right to call you their Queen."

Tears pricked at the corners of my eyes. My entire being clung to his words, latching on like a bee to nectar. It amazed me to hear how he saw me, to hear how much Rune believed in me. His words washed away the bleeding gashes from Dax's hateful words, and in that moment, I felt myself fall in love with Rune all over again.

I sat up and cupped his cheeks. My mouth closed over his, and I kissed him deeply, trying to show him how much I cherished him. I rested my forehead against his and whispered, "I love you, Rune. So, *so* much."

His palm smoothed back my hair and found its place on the back of my neck. "You're my light, Bria. You're my breath, my heartbeat, my dream. You're my *Queen*. Let me worship you the way you deserve."

He pushed me back to lie against the mattress, and my heart quickened its pace as he lowered his mouth to hover where my legs spread. His hot breath against my sensitive middle made me quiver, and goosebumps broke out along my arms. I held my breath, waiting for the first feel of his tongue, and I nearly screamed out in bliss when it finally licked across my budded nerves. His tongue was relentless in coaxing my climax, and I gripped Rune's hair tightly as he flicked, circled, rubbed, and loved me without pause.

"Rune," I cried, on the edge of something dangerously hot and overwhelming. "Ahh, Rune! Please. Don't stop."

The ache grew, and my hips moved to match the way his tongue swiped up and down against my clit. His finger pushed inside me, thrusting back and forth to the same beat as his wicked mouth. The delicious sensations sent me spiraling, and I let out a loud groan of ecstasy as I spilled myself into his mouth, staining his lips with the taste of me.

He sat up straight, licking the shine from his lips, before smiling down at me. "I could drink from you all day."

Breathless and still hungry for more, I grabbed for the hem of his sweatpants and yanked them down. He tossed them aside until his long, thick length was freed. It was my turn to push him onto his back, and his hungry eyes watched my every move like a predator watching its prey. I hovered above him with my knees hugging his hips on either side, and I gripped his shaft, holding it to my entrance before I slowly sank down.

I welcomed the pressure as his cock filled me up, and Rune's head tilted back as he let out a small gasp. The still-sensitive bud in between my legs throbbed at the sound, and I found myself rising up only to sink back down to hear it again. My own groan danced with his as I placed my hands on his firm chest, using his hard body to guide my hips up and down on his shaft.

It was good.

Too good.

"Am I doing it right?" I gasped as I rode him slowly.

"God, yes," Rune said in a husky voice. His eyes were glazed over with lust as he reached up to pinch my nipples between his fingers, tweaking them as I continued to move my hips in a rhythm that seemed to let Rune touch me in delicious places. "Fuck! Oh, fuck. You're so good, Bria."

I moaned as my middle ached with need while Rune's length pushed inside me. His fingers rubbed my peaked nipples, sending a shock of hunger straight between my legs. Needing to feel more, yearning for the ache to be soothed, I slipped my hand down his chest and in between my thighs. I bit my lip and flung my head back as I found the bundle of nerves and rubbed my finger over the heat to the same beat of my riding his cock.

"That's it," Rune gasped, watching my hand and my bucking hips. "Play with it. Ride me. Tell me how it feels."

"It feels," I gasped. "It feels … ah … good."

"Cum for me. Cum with me, Bria."

He met the movement of my hips with his own thrusts until, finally, we both groaned as our climax swept over our bodies. His hot release spilled into me, and I trembled through the shock waves of my own orgasm. Absolutely spent, I fell forward, lying on top of him as I tried to get my breathing back under control. Rune wrapped his arms around me, holding me to him, and I felt him place a small kiss on the top of my head.

I was tired. I was warm. I was at peace.

I fell asleep, lying atop my love, smiling, with all my worries momentarily forgotten.

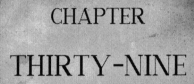

CHAPTER

THIRTY-NINE

SOMETHING WARM BRUSHED THROUGH MY hair, tucking it behind my ear.

"Bria," came a whisper.

I knew that voice as well as my own. Forcing myself to wake up, I fluttered my eyelids open. Rune smiled down at me from where he sat on the edge of the bed. He'd covered me with warm blankets at some point, and despite myself, I snuggled deeper into the comforter.

Chuckling, Rune said, "You may want to get up. We have company."

Groaning, I waved my hand at him. "Five more minutes."

"That's what I told them. Twenty minutes ago." He flashed me a cheeky grin.

With a sigh, I sat up. Rune handed me my clothes, and after I tied, dressed, and smoothed my hair, I left Rune's room to see who the heck these "visitors" were and why they'd interrupted my nap.

As soon as I made my way into the living room, two voices squealed, followed by pounding footsteps as Newt and Greshim rushed toward me. Instantly perking up, I held my arms open for the twins to fall into.

"Oh, my goodness," I said as I looked at each of them. "What are you two doing here?"

"We left when Brother did," Greshim explained as he bounced on his heels.

I realized this must've been why Rune needed to stay back to handle some things. He'd meant getting the twins to safety where they couldn't be used as pawns in Myra's manipulative game.

"Myra let them leave? Or did you take them? Aren't you worried she'll come after us now?" I raised an unsure brow at Rune.

"They didn't come alone," came a deep voice from across the room.

I whipped my head around to find the source of the voice, and my stomach dropped when I saw the space was far from empty. Not only were Akira, Bassel, and Marlow back home, but Avana, Carlos, and Ardley were here, too. Even more to my surprise were Dallas, Rance, and Imani. The most shocking of all though was the source of the voice.

"A-Alvaro," I said, quickly rising to my feet. I swallowed hard, unsure of what his presence meant.

"Bianca," Alvaro nodded his head in greeting.

"It's Bria," I mumbled.

He knew my name. I *knew* he knew my name, so why couldn't he ever freaking use it?

"Apologies," Alvaro said with a tight-lipped smile. "The boys wanted to tag along with their brother and help in your pursuit of creating peace between Land Fae and Water Fae. I came to ensure they're kept safe."

"*Papá's* on our side," Greshim added.

"Correction. I'm on the side that I think is better for my sons, and right now, that seems to be here."

Oddly, I found that to be almost a compliment.

I offered a smile. "Thank you. We're glad you're here. Speaking of here …" I looked at Dallas, Rance, and Imani, who sat together on the couch. "What are you guys doing here?"

"Waiting on you, of course," Dallas said. "Everything is set and ready to go for our return to the Kingdom. Well, everything except you, so Akira invited us to come hang out while we waited for you to wake up. We figured it was a good opportunity to get to know each other better since we're all working together now."

I looked past Dallas to Rance and Imani. "What about Dax?"

"Marcus and his team took over," Rance answered.

"He's being escorted to his prison cell as we speak," Imani added.

"They filled us in on what happened," Rune said, his jaw clenching. "About Dax being the one who hired Jonah and what happened today." There was no missing the edge to his voice, nor the murderous light filling his eyes.

I ducked my head, trying to avoid the stares. "At least now we know. Even if his motive is still unclear."

"Don't worry," Dallas said with a mischievous smirk. "You'll have plenty of time to question that lying son of a—"

"Dallas," I snapped, reaching forward to muffle the twins' ears and hug them to me. I glared at her.

"Oops," Dallas nibbled her lip. "Sorry. Well, if you're ready now, I think it's finally time to return to the palace."

I looked around at all the people gathered and gave a teasing laugh. "You keep saying palace and Kingdom, but we're not *actually* going to a palace, right? I mean, where would you hide a whole Kingdom from humans?"

"Has no one explained this to her?" Ardley asked incredulously.

"Explained what?" I questioned.

"There's been a lot for her to learn," Dallas said with a deep sigh. "I didn't want to overwhelm her."

"The palace isn't in the human world," Rune said. "It's in the Fae realm."

My head was starting to hurt. "You lost me."

"Right now, we're in the human world. It's where a lot of Fae have lived for centuries, because of the safety here. It's harder to get away with war here, so Fae are less inclined to attack in this world, though some still do. Plus, it's pretty convenient. There's a realm of magic connected to this one, which contains our real home."

I nodded, pretending that this made total sense even though I was completely lost. "And how do we get there?"

"There are gateways all over the world that Fae can access. Depending on where you want to arrive within the realm, that determines which gateway you use."

"And the gate we need to go through is—" Dallas stopped and glanced around at everyone gathered in the living room. With a sigh, her eyes found mine again. "Well, it's supposed to be secret, but I guess we're all on the same team now, which makes everyone here privy to the information. The gate we'll be going through that leads to the Water Fae Kingdom is located at a nearby lake."

"Finally," Ardley yelled and clapped his hands before rubbing them together. "I now have the secret location to the gate and can go slaughter all the Water Fae!"

Everyone turned to look at Ardley, who passed around his

wide grin. When he realized no one was smiling, his face went serious.

"That was a joke," he explained. "Bad timing? Yeah, I guess that was bad timing."

"Anyway," Dallas started, drawing out the word. "Everything's set and ready for us to go."

"All of us, right?" I asked as I looked at the large party in the living room.

"All of us," Rune answered, weaving his fingers with mine.

THE DRIVE TO THE LAKE was a good hour, but it felt far shorter—like we got there *too* fast, leaving behind the world I'd always belonged to and known. As soon as I stepped out of the car, I was no longer Bria, the girl who watched way too many movies with her friends, the girl who dreamt of canvas and paint, the girl who longed for a simple life. I was Bria, the future Queen of Water Fae, leader of many, pursuer of peace. But even if a lot was changing, some things were certain.

I had a family. Akira, Bassel, Avana, everyone.

I had my best friend by my side.

I had Rune.

And all of that was enough to help my feet trudge along the lake's edge until we reached a pair of trees whose limbs were tangled in such a way that it made a towering, natural arch.

Our large party stopped in front of it, and Dallas looked back at me with an excited bounce. "Here it is."

I searched for something strange or magical but came up short. All I could see were the trees lining the lake. "I don't see anything."

Chuckling, Imani said, "It's not open yet. To open the gate, you have to place your hand on it. We thought you should do the honors since it's your first time entering the realm."

I swallowed hard and stared at the open air between the kissing trees. "How will I know when I'm touching it if I can't see it?"

"Trust me," Rune said with an encouraging squeeze to my hand. "You'll know."

Taking a deep breath, I stood before the archway, and the closer I got, the tinglier my body felt. When I was directly in front of the open air, I slowly lifted my hand until I was met with a slight resistance that fizzled beneath my fingertips. A hole in the air began to open around my hand, melting away at the edges to reveal more and more of a world beyond our own.

My jaw dropped as the scene materialized, and my heart ceased its rhythm, stilled by the realm before me.

"You did it," Rune said proudly as he placed his hand on the small of my back.

"She sure did," Dallas said, beaming at me. She moved to stand directly beside me, staring into the open gate. "This is it. You're home. Welcome to Ambrolia."

ACKNOWLEDGMENTS

There are so many people I want to thank.

Firstly, thank you to my AMAZING editors. Ariel and Nicole with Ad Astra Editorial are an absolute gift, and I am beyond thankful I got to work with these two lovely ladies. They really make me feel confident in my stories, and I always know that my story is a better version of itself after they've worked their magic.

I want to thank all my beta readers who gave great feedback on this one. Alexia, Anais, Cherilyn, Jals, and Kia. You guys are the best. Thank you for loving and helping me with the early version of this story. Y'all helped me shape it into the great book it is today.

Thank you to my cover designer, Emily Wittig, as well as my formatter, Enchanted Ink Publishing. You guys nailed it again with this one, just like I knew you would.

Thank you to my sister for your support, encouragement, and hype through this book. I know you will love it even more now than that initial read through.

Thank you to my husband for being by my side through the long nights, tiring writing sessions, and sob fests where I complained about how I suck.

Last but not least, thank you to all of my fur babies. To my ponies, my donkeys, my goats, my pigs, my dogs, and my chickens. Y'all always make me feel better with your plentiful hugs and cuddles when imposter syndrome creeps in.

SYLVER MICHAELA

is an avid book reader, coffee drinker, true crime junkie, and animal lover. She is also a huge fan of K-Pop, Korean dramas, and East Asian culture. Nothing compares to a lazy day where she can binge Korean Period Romance dramas, or curl up with a romantasy book from a fellow Indie Author. When she isn't hard at work on her next romance book, she can be found on her farm, reading amongst the donkeys, ponies, and goats.

HTTPS://SYLVERMICHAELA.WIXSITE. COM/MAGICALPRINCESS.COM

INSTAGRAM: @THE_SYLVER_MICHAELA

Made in the USA
Columbia, SC
09 November 2024

46085528R00238